Magnolia City

Magnolia City

DUNCAN W. ALDERSON

KENSINGTON BOOKS
www.kensingtonbooks.com

KENSINGTON BOOKS are published by

Kensington Publishing Corp.
119 West 40th Street
New York, NY 10018

All Kensington titles, imprints, and distributed lines are available at special quantity discounts for bulk purchases for sales promotion, premiums, fund-raising, educational, or institutional use.

Special book excerpts or customized printings can also be created to fit specific needs. For details, write or phone the office of the Kensington Special Sales Manager: Kensington Publishing Corp., 119 West 40th Street, New York, NY 10018. Attn. Special Sales Department. Phone: 1-800-221-2647.

ISBN-13: 978-0-7582-9275-9
ISBN-10: 0-7582-9275-9
First Kensington Trade Paperback Printing: April 2014

eISBN-13: 978-0-7582-9276-6
eISBN-10: 0-7582-9276-7
First Kensington Electronic Edition: April 2014

10 9 8 7 6 5 4 3 2 1

Printed in the United States of America

Dedicated to
Isabel Lark,
my fabulous wife and best friend

ACKNOWLEDGMENTS

I am deeply indebted to all those who helped me spin this tale: to my writing coaches from The Humber School for Writers—Austin Clarke, Nino Ricci, and especially Sarah Sheard, who coaxed me to tell Hetty's story; to Melody Lawrence for her encouragement and insightful editing services; to my visionary agent, Carolyn Jenks, who believed in me as a writer; to my editor at Kensington Books, John Scognamiglio, who added the last masterful strokes; and, most of all, to my talented students at The Rabbit Hill Writers' Studio who allowed me to workshop my novel even though I was the director. In my research, I am obliged to all the folks at the East Texas Oil Museum—especially the director, Joe White, who told me the story of the turtle crossing the road, and to my man, Robbie Rogers, whose knowledge of the technicalities of drilling oil wells was essential to this book; to the helpful reference librarians in the Texas Room of the Houston Metropolitan Research Center; to my resourceful team of researchers—Crystal Ragsdale in San Antonio, Diane Tofte Kropp and Jeanette Piecznski in Houston; to my mestiza consultant and Spanish translator, Celeste Guzman Mendoza; and to Marguerite Johnston for introducing me to my own hometown in her classic work, *Houston, The Unknown City,* from Texas A&M University Press.

For permission to quote material, I am grateful to the following: Penfield Books for passages from *Mexican Proverbs* by Arturo Medina; *Texas Monthly* magazine for details about tequila and barbacoa; to Anne Dingus and Bob Bowman for colorful Texas colloquialisms; to Kathryn Dobie for material on tequileros from *Horsebackers of the Brush Country,* by Maude T. Gilliland; to the *Kilgore News Herald* for material from articles about the oil boom of 1931; to Thomas H. Kreneck for slogans about Houston; and to Arhoolie Records for a transcription of "Corrido de los Bootleggers," from the album *Corridos & Tragedias de la Frontera.*

Chapter 1

She couldn't get a good look at his face, and it was driving her crazy.

Esther Allen was glad she'd chosen the peacock mask. It allowed her to stand atop the grand staircase of the Warwick Hotel and peer at the stranger secretly through a mist of feather ends. Yellow silks and red satins fluttered by her; a lace petticoat flashed over a high-button shoe. She could smell camellias mingling with car fumes, followed by streaks of perfume as women rushed by her into the lobby. Some of the hands she'd just shaken in the receiving line were cold and clammy, others fat and sweaty. She tried to recognize eyes behind the masks, a timbre of voice. Except for the new fellow down there in the leather jacket, everyone was wrapped in fantasy to attend tonight's masquerade ball, the Nineteenth Annual No-Tsu-Oh Carnival of 1928. Her eyes kept flicking to him parking his car under the porte cochere—although *parking* didn't really describe what she was seeing. It was more like a plane landing on water as the speedster came flowing to a stop, wearing its chrome like jewelry.

It was without doubt the most beautiful car she'd ever seen. Top thrown back, all cream and whitewall tires, fenders gliding up and down, the spare bolted on its side like a shield. She had to know what kind of man would drive a car like that, but when she looked through the crowd, the brim of his hat was snapped down on one side so all she could see of his face was the linear thrust of his jaw. Mentally, she sketched in the features hidden there.

"Hetty? *Hetty!*" Esther's date, Lamar Rusk, caught her attention with the nickname all her friends used. Hetty dipped her feathered mask in his direction as he bounded up the stairs, shaking the bells on his court jester's hood.

"Do you mind?" said Hetty's sister, Charlotte, trying to keep up with Lamar as she clung to his elbow. Hetty turned her head to look at them directly—the mask cut off her peripheral vision. Having just stepped off her flower float from the parade, Charlotte was attempting to ascend the grand staircase with the kind of hauteur appropriate for the one Houston debutante destined to be crowned Cotton Queen later in the evening. *We're getting too old to share the same boyfriend,* Hetty thought, locking arms with Lamar and steering him toward the solarium so they could sit in the wicker chairs and have a smoke. But Charlotte hitched them back toward the top of the reception line, where their parents waited. *It's starting,* Hetty thought—little trickles of irritation beginning to erode her party spirits—*the usual push-pull I always feel with my sister.* She slipped a glance back at the driveway, but the car was gone and the driver had disappeared into the crowd.

When she stood before their father, Hetty had an absurd urge to curtsy. He took up the space of two men, one hand holding a scepter, the other gripping his sword. Conscious of his descent from Augustus Chapman Allen, one of Houston's founders, Kirby Allen—or Kirb, as everyone called him—had draped himself in the robes of state worn by Edward VII at his coronation. A grand cape of ermine and crimson plunged from his shoulders; chains and coronets swept a silver light across his chest. That same light was in his gray eyes as he greeted his daughters with his usual aloofness. Hetty kissed him on the cheek above the full beard he'd tacked on with spirit gum to resemble his idol.

"Have you been smoking?" he growled into her ear.

"Of course!" Hetty laughed and turned her lips away from his. *Somebody needs to tell him about the world war,* she thought. *He's still living in 1913, when only prostitutes smoked.* Moving on to take her mother's hand, she realized that it wouldn't be his wife. Nella Ardra Allen had adorned herself in harem pants and jeweled slippers straight out of the Ballet Russe, but Hetty scoffed. *Mamá may parade around as a Belle Epoque bohemian—but I know it's only a pose.* A smile played over Nella's delicate white face as she reached for Hetty's sister and said, "Congratulations, darling." She drew back and gazed at Charlotte for a long moment, eyes unfathomable. "You have no idea what a triumph this is." Hetty waited for someone to comment on the tasteful silhouette of her silver kimono, but was quickly upstaged by Jessie Carter, who was in line just behind her.

As Lamar drew the sisters toward the ballroom, Lockett Welch latched onto the three of them. She was their neighbor, inhabiting the suite across the hall from their own spacious apartment on one of the residential floors of the Warwick. She was dressed in high Gothic, her sleeves sweeping the ground, her crowned hat broad as a cake plate and hung with veils that danced as she bobbed her head about, talking incessantly.

"Congressman Welch!" Lockett shouted at her husband. "Here are Nella's daughters. And they're *both* with Lamar Rusk." Her veils trembled at the thought.

"Don't surprise me at'all," he said, waving a fat palm toward Lamar. "How's the joker tonight?"

"Ready to frolic," Lamar said, kicking up a leg sheathed in green and yellow striped hose.

Hetty was swallowed up in veils as Lockett leaned over to kiss her on the cheek. "Don't feel bad, Esther. Princesses have more fun than queens. And look at you, darlin' Char, you clever thing. What a blue blood! Snatching that little ol' tiara away from simply *everybody* in Houston!" *HEWStun*. She continued chattering as they walked away.

Once through the great bronze doors, the revelers drifted in spangled clusters through the hotel lobby and into the candlelit ballroom. Hetty lingered by a potted palm, telling the other two to go in without her. Charlotte flounced off in her wide hoop skirt, Lamar dancing a jig around her. Hetty hung about the lobby hoping to spot the strange man again. She fell into a sofa and slipped her mask off. Out of her beaded evening bag, she pulled a pack of her favorite cigarettes, Lucky Strikes, and lit one, tugging on her turban. She thought her costume was so much more sophisticated than her sister's, who'd been allowed to spend a fortune on petticoats and flounces because she was to be enthroned on giant petals in the parade. Hetty had scrounged her outfit from her mother's closet: a Paul Poiret kimono-styled silver lamé gown that draped so beautifully and dragged a little on the ground. She loved that period before the war, when women had unlaced their corsets to cultivate an air of seduction and danger. Hetty had an ancient memory of her mother wearing this very same dress, glissading into their twilit bedroom as she often did before going out for the evening. She hovered over Hetty like a silvery shade in the floor-length lamé. Sometimes Hetty only dreamed she was there, and sometimes she really was. She appeared for an instant and was gone, leaving behind her a haunting musk of Nuit de Chine.

Hetty sank a little deeper into the sofa when she saw the stranger step up to the check-in desk. He nodded and reached for his billfold. The hat still eclipsed his face, but now Hetty could see that he was wearing, of all things, the gear of an oilman: boots laced up under riding breeches and a leather jacket. Was it only a costume or was this the man she'd been waiting to meet? As soon as he turned toward the elevators, she withdrew behind her mask.

When Hetty entered the great hall, revelers were parading about to waltz music, showing off their costumes. She joined them. The ballroom wore a disguise, too. They could have been anywhere but on the prairies of Texas—a hall of mirrors in France, a palazzo in Venice during *carnevale*. Dark green leaves gleamed in the candlelit shadows all around. Bushes like no one had ever seen in a cotton field offered up bolls made of white roses.

Hetty walked among tables clustered subtly by class: closest to the dance floor, place cards for the old cotton barons of Courtlandt Place circled by a tier for the nouveau riche of oil. She ended up on the sidelines near her parents' table, earmarked for the officers of the Citizen's Bank of South Texas. She laid her mask down and lit another Lucky, moving out of the shadows so she'd be under a chandelier. Across the room, she caught a glimpse of the stranger with the congressman's son, Glen Jr. She sent out some smoke signals, but he didn't notice her. Three young ladies huddled in the middle of the dance floor did. Winifred Neuhaus came tripping over first, a slender boyish blonde in a satin tux and top hat. She was followed closely by a pair of amber eyes smiling behind a white silk mask.

"Hey, Doris Verne." Hetty grinned back. "How's my favorite person?"

"Jealous, honey child," Doris said, lifting the white mask to her forehead. "As usual, you've upstaged us all. Look at you!"

"Just something I found in Mom's closet."

"Did you know you have charcoal all over your eyes?" asked Winifred.

"It's kohl."

The last to glide their way was Lockett's daughter Belinda Welch, cool and decorous in a towering powdered wig. Winifred slid a pack of Luckies out of her mannish tux jacket and passed them around. The three girls lit up, their smoke blazing in the light of the chandelier. They blew out as much as they could, knowing it would irritate their parents, taking long sensuous drags out of red, puckered lips. Winifred floated smoke rings above their heads. Hetty soon noticed her father frowning at her from across the room. She struck the pose of the Statue of Liberty, holding her cigarette as the torch. The other three girls followed, their four arms raised in smoldering sisterhood. Nobody was going to tell them they couldn't smoke in public anymore. Not in 1928. This was war.

"Lucky girls!" they all chanted together before lowering their arms.

"Liberty's still our lady, isn't she, girls?" Winifred asked.

"Only till we find someone better," Hetty said. "She was a gift from the French." Winifred was referring to their search for a local seraph who could hold them rapt with uncanny magic. It had started when they were classmates at the Kinkaid School and found out that Athens, Texas, had been named for the Greek goddess of wisdom.

"And whadda WE have?" Hetty had scribbled in a note to

Winifred. "Hugh's town?" The four of them always sat Indian-style, one behind the other, so it was easier to pass notes. "Why weren't we born in a place called Aurora?" Doris Verne had added to the scrap of paper. "Or Juno?" Belinda had responded. "Too Greco-Roman!" Hetty had replied when the note returned to her. "I want a goddess for MY time and place." Winifred had giggled and written back: "Good luck with THAT in Harris County! Only Jesus saves here."

Belinda twirled with her cigarette in the air. "You could do worse. At least Liberty gives us freedom."

"I don't know how you expect to dance in that skirt, Bel," Hetty said, "since nobody can get within four feet of you."

"You think I want to dance with these college freshmen?" she said, putting on her usual air of bored contempt.

"Says you," piped in Winifred.

"I just want to get canned as soon as possible," Belinda said, sweeping them with her ice-blue eyes. "Who's got some hooch?"

"Probably just the college freshmen," Hetty said, dropping her smoking butt into a spittoon. "But that new fellow with your brother—he looks older."

"The choice one? Forget it, Hetty. I've already got my sights on him."

When the band struck up a fox-trot, they started arguing about who would ask him to dance. Lockett Welch sashayed into their group, tripping over her endless medieval sleeves. "Be quiet, y'all. You can't dance with that gate crasher sitting at the Rice Institute table . . . ?" She raised her voice a tad at the end, turning the statement into a question and looking from one to the other for a response.

"Was there something you wanted to tell us, Mother?" Belinda asked.

"I'm just so put out with your brother for inviting this person into our festivities. Anyone can see he doesn't belong here."

"Oh? Aren't they old friends?" Hetty asked.

"Hardly. He showed up at my door one day completely unannounced, saying he was new in town. It was the most awkward moment I've experienced in years!"

"But he did have a letter of introduction," Belinda said.

"From someone I didn't even know—his mother Arleen."

"But Dad knew his father."

"Vaguely. They were in the Senate together."

"Ah, a senator's son," Hetty said.

"He doesn't act like a senator's son, I must say," Lockett declared. "The first thing he did was take Glen on a bear hunt in the Big Thicket—why, that's somewhere in *East Texas!*" Her veils quaked as she spit the words out.

"Mother, he's not a Thicketeer."

"He's not? What did *you* hear?" Lockett said, her eyebrows raised like question marks.

"Glen told me his father was in mining in Montana and made a fortune . . ." Belinda said.

"Mining? Fortune?" Lockett's ears perked up.

"And he moved here to wildcat . . ."

"Wildcat?" Winifred chuckled. "He's only about twenty years too late."

"At any rate, I beg you to remember he's a gate crasher," Lockett admonished them. "I want to go on record that I did *not* invite him to this party," she said, herding her daughter toward the congressman's table.

As she was pulled away, Belinda made a face and said, "He's mine."

Doris Verne Hargraves murmured to Hetty, their heads tipped together, "Look—he sat down with Melba and Butch and those kids. The ones who put on petting parties."

"I'm moving in," Hetty said and sauntered over to the buffet. She grabbed a cup of punch and sipped it while eyeing the cluster of hunters and their friends, all in a huddle. They had the noisiest table in the room. The stranger openly handed a bottle around. They all laughed. Hetty felt drawn irresistibly in their direction and started to drift that way, but was cut off by her father. He brushed past her, followed by two waiters. She paused to see what they would do. Kirb rounded the Rice table and, tossing his heavy cape aside, confiscated the bottle from a girl about to take a swig. One of the waiters tapped the man from Montana on the shoulder and motioned for him to leave. Instantly, the table grew quiet. Words shot back and forth. As the waiters reached to lift him out of his seat, he stood on his own and brushed their hands away. Heads turned from all over the ballroom. The music played on.

Everyone watched as the stranger—with a defiant swagger—was escorted down one side of the dance floor. Hetty veered over to get a better view. His face wasn't quite as suave as she'd pictured—a first rough cut at handsome. His black hair was worn sheik-style, parted down the middle and slicked back, the firm jaw clean-shaven.

Kirb tried to block her view of the interloper, but she was able to crane her neck to see his eyes. Crystalline blue, in spite of his black hair. The color you see when light strikes a prism. He locked eyes with her. *Finally, he's noticed me,* Hetty thought. She was about to pursue him when her mother materialized at her arm.

"Esther, dear, stop staring at that man. You know what I've always told you girls: The eye is a sex organ. You're being wanton and don't realize it." Nella spoke smoothly as she entwined her arm in Hetty's and gracefully escorted her back toward the dance floor. She smelled of whiskey and roses.

"Why are they throwing that fellow out? Everybody's drinking—including you, Mother."

"He doesn't look like he belongs here, anyway."

"And we do? If they knew the truth about us, they'd probably throw us out, too."

"Shhh!" Nella's eyes darted about, but her mouth wore a gracious smile as she murmured, "How would anyone find those things out?"

"Don't worry, Mamá, I may be wanton, but I'm not stupid. I won't reveal your little secret."

Nella's fingers caught Hetty's arm in a vise. "Ah, here's Lamar. I think he's wanting to fox-trot with you."

Hetty was passed from one arm to another. Lamar led her onto the dance floor jingling, her kimono ashimmer in the pale light as it trailed behind her.

* * *

After dinner, the waltzes raised the pitch of the party a few notches, leaving the floor littered with limp bows, red sequins, and trampled black masks. Hetty skirted the dessert table, where the dancers, out of breath and hungry, lined up for slices of triple chocolate cake. They were all waiting for their parents to leave so they could bring on a jazz band and dance the toddle and the black bottom. Char had her clutches into Lamar, determined to dance more numbers with him than her sister. Hetty reached for a plate and toyed with a piece of cake as she watched the two of them flirting over by the bandstand. *I'm not going to fight with her. I don't want to do anything to spoil our fun tonight. If Lamar wants to dance with me, he'll have to ask.* She let a forkful of semisweet icing melt across her tongue. Triple chocolate cake was her favorite Warwick dessert, a little short of divine. One of the best things about living in a hotel was being able to order room service until midnight. Hetty often did, even though they had their Mexican maid to cook her chilies and moles for them.

Dear Lina, Hetty thought, *she's the only member of our family who's not down here.* Hetty pictured her sitting alone in the kitchen upstairs with no light on, drinking and muttering to herself in Spanish. She'd worked so hard today getting all the ruffles on Charlotte's crinolines starched and pressed. Hetty slipped between two chattering dancers, exchanged her half-eaten piece of cake for a fresh one, and pushed through the swinging door into the kitchen. Several faces with coppery skin stared at her as she passed, but Hetty didn't feel out of place: She liked haunting the hallways of the Warwick, finding shortcuts and back ways that no one else knew about. A hallway was more than just an empty space to Hetty: It was a place to be alone, an escape from her parents, and a bridge to the world. Now it was taking her to her beloved little Lina, alone in the dark. She took the service elevator up to the eighth floor, being careful not to get the hem of her kimono caught in the heavy doors as they slid shut.

From the dim hall where trash was kept and deliveries made, she came into a passage that led from the kitchen of the Allen suite into a servant's quarters the size of Nella's closet. Only a bare bulb burned in the pantry. Hetty stepped into the kitchen and flicked on the light. There was Lina exactly as she'd pictured: crumpled over the breakfast table with a Carta Blanca sweating in a circle of foam. She was so short she looked like a child curled up in the chair. Pots dripping with sugar and gelatin still stood on the stove top.

"I brought you a piece of cake." She slid the plate next to the beer.

"¡M'ija!" Lina always addressed her with the familiar Spanish term for *daughter*. She lifted her head and smiled wanly at Hetty, her eyes swimming with intoxication and exhaustion. "You always think of your little Lina." Her skin was the color of cinnamon.

"You shouldn't be sitting here in the dark. Come down with me and take a peek, kiddo. The ballroom looks so swanky."

"Lina would not be welcome. She knows her place." Ever since being rescued years ago from the jute mills in *El Arenal,* the sand pits of East Houston, Lina was terrified of ending up back there. She was guarded around everyone but Hetty. "You go. You dance. Lina is happy when her Esther is happy."

"I'd love to dance with Lamar, but Char's monopolizing him. We were supposed to take turns."

Lina scowled and hissed, "Miss Charlotte! Don't tell her Lina says—but you should be queen, *m'ija*. Let me look at you." Lina stood and motioned for Hetty to turn around. "I remember when your mother wore that dress."

"So do I."

She looked Hetty up and down and nodded. "*Si,* you are queen."

Hetty laughed.

"¡Es verdad! Tu es la reina." Lina threw her arms open. Her head only came breast high as Hetty bent down to hug her. She made little cooing sounds as she swayed gently back and forth. Hetty's earliest memories were of being rocked in those wiry brown arms, and she still liked it today. Only Lina understood the ache she carried inside; only Lina could soothe it.

Then she pulled back and assumed her scolding tone: "Don't you let Miss Charlotte get the best of you. You go back down and you grab Mister Señor Rusk and you dance with him. *¡Andale!*"

"All right, I will."

* * *

As soon as Hetty entered the ballroom, Belinda sidled up to her and murmured, "He sent for you."

"Who?"

"Mac. The fellow they kicked out."

"Oh, really?" Hetty said, trying to sound indifferent but wanting to know more. "That's his name, Mac?"

"Garret MacBride. He's got a room. And he's got the goods. I'm so glad somebody does." She was referring to a practice that went on at a lot of their dances: One of the young men would hire a hotel room where couples could meet secretly and share bootleg they knew was safe. "I tried to nab him, but he only wants you. What did you do to him, girl—pet in a dark corner? Anyway, it's room two twelve. That's where I'm spending the rest of the evening," Belinda chirped as she drifted away.

Hetty wanted to follow, but the band started playing her favorite song, "Charmaine." In a falsetto voice, the singer crooned the words that always made her want to glide across the dance floor in an easy rhythm: "I wonder why you keep me waiting, Charmaine, my Charmaine . . ." This would be a test for Lamar: He knew it was her favorite song, even calling her Charmaine when he was feeling amorous. If he didn't dance this number with her, that was it. Hetty waited while one couple after another drifted out into the twilight of candles. Then she heard a jingle and felt a tap on her shoulder. She turned. He was there, smiling his crooked smile at her and holding out his hand.

"You better not forget."

"Be nice to me. I'm the one who asked them to sing it."

"You did?"

"Of course. Just for you, kiddo."

Hetty felt a new lilt come into her legs as they danced. *Slow, slow, quick, quick.* Lamar pitched his voice high to sing along: "I'm waiting, my Charmaine, for you."

It's the other way around, she thought as they opened up into a promenade. *I'm waiting for you to decide between Char and me.*

After that, Lamar wouldn't leave her alone. They danced until Hetty's feet throbbed with delight, then he kissed her right there in front of everyone. This inspired a wolf whistle or two. She drew her lips away and murmured, "How come you always manage to get me into trouble, my little Lam?"

"Into fun, you mean." He had that glint in his eye that meant he was plotting something. "Come upstairs with me."

She glanced around to see if her parents were watching. "Stop it, Buster! You know that could spoil my whole night."

"Not if you're with me." He pulled her off the dance floor and into the shadows. Pretending to head to the restrooms, they dodged Charlotte and scrambled up two flights of stairs.

As Lamar tugged her down the hall, she could hear raucous laughter from a room up ahead. A rat's tail of smoke floated out of the open door. They lingered on the threshold, noticing the highballs tinkling in everybody's hands. The crowd was laughing at Belinda, who was trying to lounge back on the bed in her wide pannier skirt. It kept springing up to reveal layers of lacy petticoats underneath. Hetty spotted him at the room's desk mixing drinks. *Mac.* She wanted to meet him in the worst way but couldn't let on to Lamar. She watched as he handed a drink to an underclassman, then moved his restive eyes over the room. They lingered at the open window, as if searching out the next bright spot along Main. The Twentieth-Century Jitters. He had them, too. Like he never slept, just kept moving through the night. Hetty itched to follow.

Then he glanced over and spotted the two of them, his blue eyes reeling them in. Lamar leaped into the room, his bells jingling. Everyone applauded at his entrance. He turned and gestured for her to follow. Hetty lifted her silver kimono sleeves, relishing the peril and delight she always felt in Lamar's wake. She was about to step across the threshold when someone grabbed one of the sleeves and pulled her away from the doorway.

"Don't you dare go in there," Charlotte sniped at her.

"Why not?" Hetty jerked her arm away. "Lamar brought me up here."

"He's older than us. And a man! We're not allowed, and you know it."

"How's Mother going to know? Unless you tell her."

"This is just like you, Het, spoiling my special night!"

Hetty fastened her eyes on her sister, who glowered back. "And this is just like you, being such a stickler for rules. Don't make me fight with you, Char, *please*." With a toss of her head, she stepped through the forbidden door and ambled toward the desk, trying not to look too eager. The inkwell had been shoved aside to make room for bottles of Canadian Club, Gilbey's, Johnnie Walker, and Four Aces. Lamar had already been served and was entertaining the crowd with Shakespearean riddles.

"My messenger found you," Garret said.

"Yes—it seems I've been summoned."

He picked up an empty glass. She hesitated, not wanting to acquire whiskey breath before the coronation ceremony. "You're not one of those girls who drinks ice water, are you?"

"That's not it. I'm here with my date, Lamar. Lamar *Rusk*."

"Who's paying absolutely no attention to you."

This remark left Hetty speechless. She tried to fight back the blush she could feel steaming into her cheeks. "It's not that," she quipped back. "I shouldn't even be talking to you till we're introduced."

"Says who?"

"A few centuries of Southern society. I guess you don't have rules like that up on the frontier."

"Southern? I thought we were in the Great Southwest."

"You're wrong, mister. Would they call us the Magnolia City if we were Western? You want cowboys, go to Fort Worth." She pointed to the bottle of Gilbey's gin and asked him what part of Montana he was from.

"I was born on the Continental Divide."

She laughed and turned on the fast line of gab she'd practiced for such occasions. "Congratulations on finding No-Tsu-Oh, kiddo. Not bad for an old bear hunter."

"What *is* No-Tsu-Oh?"

"Oh, if you have to be told, you're not in the know. It's the cotton carnival—the high point of Houston's season. It goes on for six days. Tonight's only the climax."

"Well, at least I didn't miss the climax."

"And that's the most important part!" She exchanged a knowing glance with him. "My sister's queen this year, you know."

Without warning, he reached over and traced the outline of her face with his forefinger. "*You* should be queen."

"That's funny. Someone else just told me that." She shrugged his finger away. "But don't feel sorry for me. I am a member of the court—a princess."

"What table are you sitting at?"

"Citizen's Bank of South Texas."

He nodded, impressed. "One of the oil banks. How do you rate?"

"My father's president. He's the one who threw you out."

"Oh, yeah. King Eddie! And you are . . . ?"

"Nnamreh. Princess Nnamreh. Consort to Queen Nottoc XIX. But my name's Hetty if that's what you're trying to find out." She gave him a teasing glance. "And yours is Mac."

Flashbulbs went off in Garret's eyes. "How'd you know that?"

"You made yourself rather notorious downstairs."

He chuckled, his eyes gleaming. "I think the cotton carnival could use a little excitement before it conks out completely."

"You may be right. But No-Tsu-Oh will never die."

"Why not?"

"It's a place."

"And where is this place?"

She looked around. "Well, at the moment, you're in it. Need I say more?"

Hetty's fast line of gab worked. When she sat down with Lamar on the sofa, Garret turned the bartending over to Butch and joined them. She introduced the two men, and they talked oil across her for a few minutes. The cushions were so soft, she was wedged between their bodies and became aware of how different they smelled: Lamar with his usual scent of sandalwood cologne, Garret emanating the musk of leather and Stacomb hair cream. A couple of Lamar's college friends came over and interrupted, so Garret engaged her in a tête-à-tête. She was grateful they were sitting down.

She didn't know whether it was the gin or the look in his eyes that made her knees feel like melting candles.

"I love your car, by the way," she told him. "What kind is it?"

"An Auburn. Want to go for a ride sometime?"

"Why not?" She laughed, hoping Lamar wouldn't hear her.

But her laugh wasn't lost in the general hubbub. It ricocheted through a silence that had crept over the room. She looked up. Nella had planted herself in the doorway, surveying the scene icily. Drinks were set down, and cigarettes snubbed out. Hetty rolled her eyes at Garret and stood to leave.

Nella grappled onto her arm and pushed her down the hallway. "You know what this means, young lady."

"I'm confined to my room again?"

"For the rest of the weekend."

Oh, well, there's still tonight, Hetty told herself.

"And don't think you're staying for the rest of the party tonight. As soon as your sister's coronation is over, it's upstairs."

A bitter taste stained Hetty's mouth. *Ratted out again! Char did this on purpose so I'd miss the carnival's jazz finale—my favorite!* She was about to protest, when the court jester sprang to her rescue. "Who was the ninny who nabbed Princess Nnamreh?" Lamar said to Nella.

She shot him a frown over her shoulder.

" 'Not I,' said the queen. 'I was dancing with the king,' " Lamar continued. "So what ninny nabbed Nnamreh?"

Nella turned to Lamar and chuckled in spite of herself.

" 'I'm afraid it was I,' said the court jester. 'To amuse her with ninniness. Forgive me, your highness.' " He kissed Nella's hand.

Nella pretended to be annoyed, but Hetty could see the smile playing about her lips. "Back to court with you both."

Monday morning, Hetty and Charlotte walked a few paces behind their mother as she swept through the long lobby of the Warwick Hotel. Nella's departures were nothing short of theater. She descended through the various levels of the lobby as if stepping off the dais of a throne. The staff all greeted her by name as she passed the massive columns of black walnut. Next, she would cross the Saxony carpets of the solarium, where white wicker divans flickered in the shade of potted palms. Never one to open a door by herself, she waited at the main entrance until an attendant rushed over so she could step out and stand at the curving balconies of the terrace to see who might be disembarking from a chauffeured brougham. Finally, the descent down the staircase to the palatial porte cochere, where her own Packard town car waited at the top of a circular drive.

Hetty was back in favor after patiently serving a penance watched over by Lina. Lamar's riddles hadn't been sufficient to charm Nella out of her disapproval. Hetty had tried to remain cheerful during her confinement, but she simply wasn't the type to sit around and do nothing. The very walls of the hotel had vibrated with dance music and, at one point, she'd looked out her window and seen revelers far below on the sidewalk, drifting into the park.

Now, as she followed her mother and sister out into the porte cochere, Hetty looked up from under a hat that buried her face to the brow. Light streaked the white ceiling: The tropic sun of South Texas blazed off a cream-colored sports car dripping with chrome. Behind the flashing windshield, raked at a forty-five-degree angle, she spotted Garret, his face cool under a Panama hat, his eyes secretive behind sun shades.

Joy irradiated Hetty at seeing him again, but she didn't let it show on her face. She bowed like the lady she'd been raised to be: a faint smile on her lips, a gentle inclination of her head. Garret leaped out without opening the door and tipped his hat in their direction.

The door of their black Packard town car swiveled open and her father's young Negro driver, Henry Picktown Waller, waited for them to step in.

Garret strode over. "Good morning, Mrs. Allen. I'd like to take this opportunity to present my card—Garret MacBride, ma'am." He held out an ivory envelope. "My mother Arleen introduced me to the Welches, ma'am."

Nella's gloved hands shrank into fists, then one of them fluttered open. "Well . . . if Lockett received you, I suppose . . ."

Hetty walked down the driveway and circled Garret's car, her fingertips sliding over the highly polished wax. She purred. The lines of the car flowed like warm cream in the mid-morning light. Garret came over.

"Aren't you afraid King Eddie will kick you out again?" she asked.

"I'll take my chances. I've been parked out here for two mornings now."

"Not looking for *me?* Aren't you sweet."

"Just stubborn. Ready for the spin you were promised?"

Hetty jumped in and perched atop the back of the seat, posing as the dedicated hedonist like her idol Joan Crawford in *Our Modern Maidens.* She squealed with delight and longed to feel the cool spring air flowing over her as they drove. "Let's go," she told Garret, sliding down into the passenger seat.

Garret jumped in beside her, revved the engine, and edged past the Packard. "I'm riding with Mr. MacBride," Hetty shouted, not giving Nella a chance to say no. They set out into the clear morning, in tandem, the Auburn leading the way. It had a luxurious leather bench, and Hetty had to squeeze rather close to Garret and move her long legs to one side so he could shift the gears. She said a prayer of thankfulness that she'd remembered to rouge her knees.

She brushed her hat off and whispered to Garret, "Can you ditch my mom?"

"Now don't get me into trouble. I'm trying to get into her good graces." He blipped the throttle. "But I could if I wanted to. When you open'er up, she'll do eighty easy." He tapped the dashboard, where a signed plaque certified that the car had been driven 100.2 miles per hour before shipment. He passed a couple of Model Ts along the wide boulevard of Main Street, sailing by the staring faces with that exotic hood ornament leading the way, a naked woman with wings flying before them.

"What brings a Northwesterner like you to the sultry subtropics?" Hetty spoke into the wind.

"Need you ask? Same thing that's bringing thousands here. One magic little word."

"Rhymes with royal?"

"How'd you know?"

"That's all my father talks about."

"My dad was in copper," he told her. "But mining's dead. Along with you and your cotton carnival. Yeah—we're living in a new golden age, only it's black gold this time. Why—look what happened at Spooltop."

"Spindletop," she laughed. "I'll have to educate you about our history."

Hetty could see he would need a guide to the local customs. But how could she possibly convey to an outsider what the time before the war meant to Texans? The tales from that era—tales that she grew up hearing—had grown so tall they dwelt on a plane only a little south of Mount Olympus. Her mother had spun them out like fairy stories, glimmering and strange. Once upon a time, she'd been told as a child, in the flat coastal land near the sea, there was something called a salt dome. Hetty had pictured a white mound like a pyramid with the blue Gulf in the distance. This salt dome hid fabulous treasure. From its depths, a black geyser shot into the sky. Spindletop erupted with one hundred thousand barrels of oil a day and took ten days to bring under control, wasting $90 million worth of petroleum. There was so much richness spewing from the earth, those early Texans squandered it.

Nella had painted these wildcatters as bigger than life, like Johnny Appleseed or Paul Bunyan. They could hear oil flowing underground, she said. They learned how to drill through solid rock. They could tame the heart of the earth itself, bending the elements to their will. And, as a result of these superhuman powers, they grew hugely and suddenly rich.

"Only in America," her father the banker used to say, "can a man own the mineral rights to the land. In other countries, these belong to the king."

And so the risk takers had made their fortunes before the World War, then migrated to Houston to live like royalty. They built their mansions behind the palatial gates of Courtlandt Place, where magnolia grandiflora trees unfolded huge, glistening leaves over lush Saint Augustine lawns. They ran their empires from skyscrapers that looked like temples: the Esperson Building, the Splendora Tower, the Humble Oil Headquarters. They didn't have names; they had initials. Or titles like "Chief" Rusk, Lamar's father, founder of Splendora Oil. He'd been Chief so long, nobody remembered what his real name was.

"Spindletop?" Hetty glanced at Garret's profile and sighed. "That was so long ago."

"I don't care. Another oil boom's coming soon."

Hetty couldn't believe what she was hearing. "Do you really believe that, kiddo?"

"I hope to tell you!"

"I'd like to believe it, but my dad keeps telling me all the booms are over."

"He's wrong!" he shouted over the revving of his motor as he outraced the long black car in their wake. "Land on that hill in Beaumont jumped overnight from ten dollars an acre to *one million dollars an acre?* It'll happen again—why, did you know the other day Ford built nine thousand new Model As in one day? They all need gas!"

"You seem to be up on all the latest figures, kiddo," Hetty said.

"Got to be." He tore through the traffic lights at Polk and Dallas, then brushed her legs as he shifted gears to cruise more slowly along the busy stretch of Main.

Hetty looked behind them. Her mother was nowhere to be seen. She whipped her hair off her face and peeked at Garret out of the corner of her eye. "But hey—I notice you don't drive a Model A."

He smiled back. No, the speedster was his style—gliding like a yacht past the flivvers puttering through the currents of downtown traffic.

"Pull over here at Everitt-Buelow." Garret grazed the curb, and Hetty stepped out onto the sidewalk. "What's the little door in the side of your car for?"

"Golf clubs. I'd be glad to demonstrate." He asked her where the best greens were.

"Here comes my mother," Hetty said as the Packard pulled up behind them. She twisted her hat on so Nella wouldn't notice how intently she was peering into the blue eyes that had emerged from behind Garret's shades. She had to see this man again. "I like to go strolling in the park in the afternoons."

"What time?"

"I don't know. Before dinner. I'll be in the sunken garden tomorrow."

"It's a date," Garret said a little too loudly before he drove away.

In a moment, she heard Nella at her side chiding, "You didn't make a date with that man, did you?"

"Oh, Mother! He gave me a ride in his car, that's all."

The new hat styles were so handy for avoiding eye contact.

They made their way toward the entrance of the shop, where they were greeted by Everitt-Buelow's ubiquitous floorwalker, Ellison: "Mrs. Allen, Miss Allen, Miss Allen." The institution of the floorwalker was one of the amenities of life for Old Houstonians. All the fashionable shops had one, a distinguished white gentleman whose job was to make shoppers feel coddled. Hetty just found his presence intrusive. *As if I can't carry my own bags out to the car!* When Ellison opened the door for her on cue, she hesitated.

"Coming, dear?" Nella asked.

"I think I'll walk over to the bank first. I'll find you."

"I thought we were going after lunch—together!" Charlotte said.

"I want to talk to Dad."

"About what?"

"Mamá!" Hetty strode away.

As she walked over to Travis Street, it wasn't hard to spot her destination. Last year, a mirage had materialized in the sky above Houston. Up there in the clouds, thirty-two stories high, a round Greek temple floated in the haze. Twelve ionic columns held it up, at the top of the soaring new Esperson Building. The skyscraper was so tall—taller than anything else in Texas—that a red beacon flashed at night atop a giant bronze tripod at its zenith so planes wouldn't crash into it. Hetty crossed Travis and stood on the sidewalk at the base of the massive building, tipping her head back far enough so she could see past the brim of her cloche. The struts of the building shot straight up, broken only by encrustations of Italian Renaissance carvings. Even though it gave her vertigo, she loved this view. It reassured her that the modern age had finally arrived in Houston. The city now had a center, a place where the flat prairie could rise up and touch the heavens. "It's our axis mundi," Nella liked to say, "our new cathedral." She steadied herself on a lamppost, then joined the stream of people flowing through the Travis Street entrance.

Hetty headed for the banking quarters, glad her father's bank had been one of the first tenants of the building. Just walking through the lobby made her feel flush. Everywhere she looked, there was some flourish, some elegant inlay—"four million dollars of Esperson oil money!" her father liked to boast with a kingly wave of his hand—lavished on every last detail.

Once inside the banking quarters, Hetty walked up to a teller cage and dropped her handbag on the marble counter. She pulled out her black leather passbook. CITIZEN'S BANK OF SOUTH TEXAS flashed at her in embossed gold letters. She opened it. Inside, *Esther Allen* was written in elegant calligraphy beside the words "In account with." This had been given to her by Kirby after her coming out, along with a stipend of thirty dollars a month. All she had to do was present this at one of the tellers and she could withdraw as much as she needed for spending money each week. "Don't want a daughter of mine doing without," he told her and Charlotte.

"Five dollars, please."

"Of course, Miss Allen." The teller entered the amount under the withdrawals column, balanced the account, swatted it with a rubber stamp, and scribbled his initials. Fawning over her, he handed the passbook back with five crisp new dollar bills tucked inside. She gloried in the whole ritual, the gold letters, the name *Allen* written in swirls of calligraphy that swept her right back to her iconic ancestors, John Kirby and Augustus Chapman Allen. Across the banking floor, she could see her father enthroned at his desk beside the stainless steel vault.

Hetty made her way to the back of the tellers' cages and waved at the coin boy, Lonnie. He opened the gate and admitted her into the inner sanctum of the banking floor.

"I'd like to see my father," she told him.

"Yes, ma'am." They dodged a cart of ledgers rolling by on wheels as he led her up to Kirby's wide walnut desk. She sat down and looked across at her father, knowing better than to try and kiss him in front of the staff. He'd brush her off with a whispered *"Decorum!"* Barking an order at a teller in the vault, he pivoted around, far too stout for the desk chair that groaned underneath him.

"Princess!" He flashed her a quick smile, then shouted, "Lonnie, how many bags of coins have you rolled this morning?"

"Four, sir."

"I would have had six done by now. Speed it up!"

"Yes, sir!" Lonnie scrambled back to his station.

"He can't keep up with you, Dad. You were the best coin boy ever."

"I set records that have never been broken!"

"And you never let anyone forget it."

"Never."

A bookkeeper drew his attention away for a moment. Hetty glanced around at the bustle. Although Kirb had a private office in back, he rarely used it. She always found him out here, manning this command post in the war of affluence. His ears seemed to crave the dissonant music of money changing hands, the clacking of adding machines, the tinkle of coins in the Brandt manual cashier, the snap of bills being counted. On his desk sat his Edison stock ticker with the ticker tape streaming down to the floor and curling in a pile. Next to that, two pictures in gilded frames: the famous one of King Edward in his ceremonial robes and Kirb's wedding portrait, with Nella as the perfect Gibson Girl.

"By the way, Dad," Hetty said once he turned back to her. "I was telling a friend how Mr. Esperson got his start."

Kirb squinted at her. "Why this sudden interest in oil? You usually act bored when I talk about it."

"I guess your little girl's growing up."

"About time. Well . . . tell your friend, the first thing he's got to do is get himself a lease in an oil field. Esperson had one right up on Moonshine Hill in Humble. That was the easy part. Then he had to talk a banker into loaning him money."

"You?"

Kirb shook his head. "Union National."

"So it's just that easy? ABC?"

Kirb's paunch shook with a deep belly laugh. "Easy? He drilled one dry hole after another. Four or five as I remember."

"And they kept giving him money?"

Kirb shrugged.

"Why?"

"They loaned on a man's character back in those days." Then her father crooned his favorite words: "Before the war." A new light came into his gray eyes as he gazed over her head into the far reaches of his memory. Kirb nursed an unwavering nostalgia for the lost years of his youth, not a golden age in his mind but a silver one, polished and genteel, an Edwardian order untarnished by the hot breath of modernism. "That was before *your* generation, of course."

"Oh, we're just finishing the job your generation started."

"No, no, you can't blame this on us. We knew the rules."

"Rules?" Hetty waited while he stared her down. "For instance . . . ?"

"For instance, not bringing liquor into the cotton carnival."

"Well, thank God you were there to restore order promptly, Dad. Civilization can continue."

"But then your mother finds you in a hotel room with that fellow?"

"Well, not alone."

"Don't split hairs with me, Esther. You know it's not allowed. All your mother and I are trying to do is maintain some decorum. For your own good."

"I know. I'm sorry, Dad. I guess I'm like Lonnie. I can't keep up with you."

Kirb chuckled. "You might be surprised. I got into my share of mischief when I was at Rice. But I knew how to keep up appearances. Your generation goes too far."

"Let's just say we have a different idea of how far too far is."

"Be careful, Esther. That's all I ask. Remember, you're an Allen. People are watching."

"It's a deal, Dad. Now . . . how about I make it up to you?"

Kirb's eyebrows lifted in expectation.

"What if I found you the next Mr. Esperson?"

He laughed derisively. "These boys today?" Leaning back in his desk chair, Kirb unbuttoned his suit coat and snapped his striped suspenders. "I haven't met a young man in years I'd bet on."

"Well, Dad, maybe you will."

Maybe you already have, she thought.

The next afternoon, Hetty planned her strategy for sneaking out to meet Garret. She peered down the hallway outside her room and saw at a slant Nella's *postigos,* ancient colonial doors from Mexico with little barred windows too high up to peer through. *That means she's home,* Hetty thought. If Nella left the apartment, the *postigo* doors were locked; only she and Kirby carried a key. No one saw what was behind those doors, not even her best friend Lockett. As far as Hetty knew, Lockett had never been that far down the hallway.

Hetty strolled into the kitchen and came back into the drawing room carrying a glass of water. Nella sat in her black-enameled armchair cutting the golden twine off a package wrapped in fine linen rag.

"Oh, Aunt Cora," Hetty said, recognizing the carton. Every few months, Nella's only sister would ship her four bottles of a mysterious liquor without any label on it, nestled in raffia.

"Yes, it came in today's post."

Hetty strolled back into the shadows where she could only see her mother's hands, light glinting off the bottles as Nella raised them from the box. She immediately opened one. Hetty breathed a sigh of relief. When these packages arrived from San Antonio, Nella would sit here for a day or two sipping out of a snifter, getting quietly drunk. She held her liquor well—most people wouldn't notice any difference, but Hetty would. Her mother started going adrift, staring off into space and humming to herself old ballads in minor keys. Scraps of golden twine would litter the floor. Kirb would join her when he got home from the bank. Dinner would be late. Then it would all be over until the next bottle was opened. Hetty smiled, edging her door closed as she heard the first splash trickling into a nearby snifter.

An hour later, Hetty threw on a long strand of pearls, grabbed her shoulder bag, and walked through the drawing room to the front door. From the armchair, Nella looked at her out of lidded eyes. "Where are you going?"

"For a fag."

"Don't let your father catch you. He'll be home soon."

"He knows I smoke, Mamá!"

Once she escaped onto the esplanade that stretched out before the hotel, Hetty exhaled fully. This was her favorite spot in all of Houston, where the two great boulevards of the city flowed together like destinies meeting. Main Street surged up from the heart of downtown and collided with Montrose Boulevard, which slanted in at an angle to form a wedge of land Houstonians liked to call the Cradle of Culture. Here rose the Corinthian columns of the art museum, the walled mansions of Shadyside, the triumphant arch upon which Sam Houston mounted his magnificent bronze horse. Everything came together in a huge traffic circle that rotated around a sunken garden. Hetty liked to stand down there, alone at the axis, watching the carousel of cars swirl by from all directions. Only a few honked their horns, but everyone saw her.

She descended the steps and strolled among the sago palms and formal rows of flowers, watching for a creamy sports car to appear. She lit one Lucky. Then another. She glanced toward the museum, its deep blue shadows reminding her of the show of modern French art held there in January. When she'd glimpsed her first Fauve painting, it was as if a film had been peeled off her eyes. *Les Fauves:* the wild beasts! such deconstruction! such streaks of color! "I want to live with this kind of intensity," she'd told Winifred, as they browsed among the burning canvases. Doris Verne and Belinda had trailed behind, each girl choosing a favorite quote about modern art from the wall copy accompanying the exhibit.

HETTY: We live in a rainbow of chaos.—Cézanne
WINIFRED: I am an artist . . . I am here to live out loud.—Zola
BELINDA: With an apple I will astonish Paris.—Cézanne
DORIS VERNE: I shut my eyes in order to see.—Gauguin

Hetty ground her butt under her heel, smiling at the memory. More cars wheeled by. She was about to give up waiting when a long burgundy brougham entered the traffic circle and started revolving. The driver wore a Panama like the one Garret had on yesterday. Hetty dashed across Main and walked up the center of the esplanade that led into Hermann Park. The car stayed on her tail and finally pulled up to the curb.

"Excuse me, madam, could you direct me to a place called No-*Tsu*-Oh?"

When she recognized the voice, she almost smiled, but caught herself and kept on walking. "You're pronouncing it wrong. The accent is on the first syllable."

Garret shifted into first, following her at low speed. "Sorry. *NOTE*-Su-Oh. Can you get there from here?"

"Not really." She looked at him, almost tripping over a crack in the sidewalk. "So is this what you do? You're a chauffeur?"

He laughed. "Would madam like to be driven somewhere?"

"I'm on my way to the lagoon, actually."

He slammed the brakes on and was outside the car, doffing his hat and opening the door. "Allow me, *please.*"

Hetty shuffled her feet. Praying that no one was spying on her, she stepped into the sedan and felt the door shut with finality behind her. Inside, the cab was all fragrant leather and polished wood, complete with a Tiffany panel lamp. Garret taxied onto the green at the far end of the lagoon, parking the car and throwing his door open to catch the evening air. Light tinkled on the water like fingers across piano keys, and long strings of tree shadows were pulled across the grass, humming with darkness.

"There oughta be a little panther piss in here," he said, climbing in and reaching into a side pocket on the door. "Don't worry, it's safe," he said, pouring into crystal glasses from a silver flask. "Canadian."

Hetty glanced around again to be sure no one was watching, then reached out. They clinked glasses, and he proposed a toast. "Here's to clandestine meetings in the back of a brougham. May we soon move on to bigger and better things."

"Oh, I don't know. You could go on giving me rides in your cars for quite some time. You seem to have so many."

"It's a weakness of mine. I love automobiles." He pointed out some of the luxury features of this particular model. "But the ride's more fun if there's a destination at the end. Like the roof at the Rice Hotel for dinner and dancing—say, on a Saturday night?"

"Pour me some more of that panther piss," she said, her face going hot. "I think I've just been asked out by a strange man from Montana." She couldn't look at him.

"You have," he said, opening the flask, reaching for her drink, and topping it up. "And the stranger hopes you'll accept because you look more beautiful than ever when you're blushing."

He held out her glass. She kept her eyes down as she reached for the drink and started taking bigger sips than she'd intended to. Her nose caught a whiff of men's cologne, a curl of lime. She could feel him watching her. By inches, she let her gaze unravel, first to the rich leather upholstery, then to the wide pleats on his trousers that led to an alligator belt that led to crisp white sleeves rolled up over tanned muscular forearms. Then she met his eyes. He was watching her in the shadows of the compartment without smiling or blinking, his blue eyes liquid and entrancing under black lashes any woman would butcher babies for.

Nella's right, she thought. *The eye is a sex organ.* She looked away, her fingers fidgeting with her necklace.

"I like your pearls."

"They're okay," she said, letting them fall. "What I really want is a double strand from the floor of the Sea of Japan."

"Fine. I'll get you some."

"You'll have to strike oil first, mister!" She stretched out, crossed her legs luxuriously so that her skirt came sliding up over her rouged knees. The leather seats were so soft and fragrant, she wanted to rub her cheek against them. Through the windshield she watched the golden sun slowly being engulfed in a stand of blue pines, like a lantern being dipped into water. "I'm afraid I can't go out with you yet—not legally, anyway."

"So I'm to call on your family first?"

"You got it, buster. I shouldn't even be here today."

"That's what I like. A girl who takes chances."

"I can't tell you how many times I've been housebound. And my sister never is."

"That doesn't seem fair."

"Fair? Ha! She's the one who tattles on me. Which is why Dad likes her better. They're in cahoots, I think."

"Traitor!" Garret pronounced, making Hetty laugh. He poured them a fresh slug. "I wouldn't let anyone stand in my way. Even my sister. I believe in risk. It's what keeps me going."

"Then you'll like it here. As my father's always saying"—she lowered her voice as much as she could—"Houston's a young man's town."

"So if Houston's a young man's town, what's No-Tsu-Oh?"

"That's only for Old Houstonians."

"Are we there now?"

"Yes."

"So it includes the park as well as the hotel?"

"Sometimes."

He eyed her suspiciously.

"Here—you have to see it in writing." Out of her shoulder bag came some linen stationery and a tortoiseshell pen. She unscrewed the cap, printed the word *NO-TSU-OH* in letters big enough for him to decipher in the pale light, and flashed the paper in front of his face.

He read it, then shrugged.

She continued to hold the name in front of him. "Spell it backward, silly."

Garret chuckled after a moment and looked a little sheepish.

"It's the opposite of what people expect, you see." She folded the stationery back into her bag.

"Is your family a part of this inside-out old Houston?"

"Of course, I'm an Allen."

"Am I supposed to know what that means?"

"The Allen brothers were the founders of the city. John Kirby and Augustus Chapman Allen."

"Daughter of the founders—wow!"

"Great—" Hetty stopped. She had started to say great-granddaughter, but realized she was sounding boastful. It wasn't the pedigree that she cared about anyway; what stirred her blood was the kind of entrepreneurial daring the Allen brothers had shown in founding a city on this godforsaken prairie, flat as an ironing board and hot as the iron in high summer. Kirb made sure she had some starch in her as a girl. If her mother recited legends, her father spouted slogans.

"Houston started as a real estate deal!" he would roar at Char and her. "Remember that!"

"It's a rainbow town, part reality, part mirage!"

"Your forefathers built cities! Remember that!"

Hetty told Garret the whole story of the founding of Houston, how the Allen brothers took a city that didn't even exist and made it the first state capital. She quoted some of the slogans. As she talked, she looked across the lagoon at the statue of Sam Houston on his triumphant arch, leader of the Texas Revolution, barely visible in the dusk, pointing into the distance with his forefinger.

The light began to ebb around them, pulled away by the retreating sun. A tide of darkness rose and washed into the car. Neither of them spoke for a few moments, knowing she had to go soon.

"I think I came to the right town," Garret said.

"I think you did," she answered, and tried to find the whites of his eyes in the night.

Chapter 2

Saturday afternoon, the matinee crowd streamed out of the new Loew's Theater onto glistening sidewalks. Hetty and Charlotte snapped open their umbrellas and headed up Main Street without talking. Hetty's yellow slicker fell off one shoulder and, over her head, she twirled a paper parasol decorated with a dragon. She'd bought it last year at the Pagoda Shop even though the salesclerk had insisted, "No good for rain." Hetty's eyes were as glazed as the streets, she was so under the spell of the moving picture they'd just seen: *A Woman of Affairs* with Greta Garbo and John Gilbert. She hoped Charlotte wouldn't say anything to spoil her mood.

They waded through the gutters at the corner of Main and Texas Avenue. Cold water flooded Hetty's unbuckled galoshes. She shivered, thinking of the look in Garbo's eyes. She learned so much from studying her face—how to give a man a sidelong glance that made your intentions clear. That's what the movies were for as far as she was concerned: lessons in love. Where else was she going to find out about these things (other than the marriage manuals Winifred liked to read out loud to shock everyone)? *I must go back to see this movie again, at least three times,* she told herself. *I must.*

They stood under the wrought iron veranda of the Rice Hotel and waited for Henry Picktown Waller to fetch them.

"Pick better get here soon," Charlotte said. "Look at those clouds."

Hetty's gaze was drawn up. Strung on wires over the intersection, huge letters made of electric lights spelled out the name of the stage for vaudeville and melodrama: **MAJESTIC THEATER**. She thought how well that word—in all caps!—described the city, *her* city. There really was something MAJESTIC about Houston—the rainbow town she'd told Garret about earlier in the week. The fact that it existed at all was a marvel. When her forefathers had disembarked at Allen's Landing just a few blocks from here, they'd envisioned a great acropolis on the shores of Buffalo Bayou. And now Hetty could look down the street and see the buildings they'd dreamed of, disappearing into the mist. They'd longed for greatness, the Allen brothers, and their descendants had been driven to do the impossible ever since.

Houstonians had taken the snake-infested bayou and dredged it out for thirty or forty whole miles, all the way to Galveston Bay, creating the Ship Channel and a "port" many miles inland. Hetty chuckled whenever she thought of the Japanese who'd come to her father for loans to buy land, immigrating here because the Gulf marshes were so perfect for rice farming. They could look up now from their flooded paddies south of the city and hear fog horns echoing, see huge ocean liners floating in the distance like mirages over the flat land.

Yes, there was something surreal about her city, leaving Hetty preordained to a belief in miracles. She was a Houstonian head to toe, growing up on these sandy grasslands, eyes turned to the sea. As a girl, her hair had been combed by bay breezes that came whistling through sedge and sea oats, her skin kissed by a supple beauty bred only in this kind of moist subtropical clime. Her childhood wasn't subject to the laws of nature: She played in the shade of trees that never lost their leaves, heard birdsong at Christmas, and had yet to see snow on the ground. Wildly converging climates waged an endless war in the heavens above her head: Warm tropical rains could be routed instantly by a Blue Norther dropping the temperature fifty degrees in one day.

"The earth and sky don't meet properly here," Nella used to say.

And Hetty knew she was right. Mystery and whimsy came and went like fog over Hetty's homeland. Birds out of legend alighted on their waters: great egrets, roseate spoonbills, the elegant white ibis. Hers was a vast delta of migration and magic, prone to flood waters in the fall but, in early spring, flickering with the shadows of land birds—millions of them descending at dawn from their nocturnal passage over six hundred miles of open sea. "They navigate by the stars," her father told her. Vast wheeling flocks of flycatchers, swallows, and blue-winged warblers would ripple overhead like pollen scattering on the wind. Hetty longed to take wing with them in their journey northward. Once in Hermann Park, she'd sat spellbound as hundreds of ruby-throated hummingbirds had darted by her, funneled back into the Central Flyway from Mexico and Panama.

Houston was a hub for more than birds, Hetty knew. Kirb called it "the city where seventeen railroads meet the sea." She couldn't imagine being anywhere else at the moment. The ambitious, the unemployed, and the hungry all flocked here to find work. Freighters choked the Ship Channel, oil clogged the pipelines, and the avenues roared with commerce. Everything swarmed and teemed in the great tropic heat. Even more so in the rain, she thought as she looked up Main. This was Hetty's favorite time to be downtown, when the streets gleamed like fingernail polish with the red taillights of Model As whizzing by.

Two trolleys clanged along the tracks in the middle of the street before an endless black town car, glistening with raindrops and wax, came cresting up to the curb.

"Finally!" Charlotte said.

Henry Picktown Waller emerged, leaping over the trickling gutter to open the back door. Charlotte ducked in, pulling her wet black umbrella behind her, but Hetty climbed in the front so she could sit beside Henry Picktown and tease him if necessary. "We're pals, Pick and I," she told people. Her mother, Lockett, and Charlotte all thought this was highly inappropriate, which made Hetty want to do it all the more. She had a proprietary interest in Pick, as she'd been the one who'd discovered him and talked Kirb into hiring him.

When he got into the car and slammed the door, Hetty pulled four crinkling bags out of the pocket of her rain slicker. "Look what I found at the movies—buttercream candies! I got some for your brother and sisters. There're bears for Addie, dolls for little Ollie, lions for Lewis, and pigs for Minnie because she *is* one. Can we stop by?"

Pick made a face. "Miss Charlotte ain't going to want to."

"Want to what?" came the voice from the backseat.

"Stop by the Wallers on the way home," Hetty said.

"You're not taking me to Settegast!"

"You can stay in the car!"

"I hope to tell you I'll stay in the car. And you'd better lock the doors."

Pick turned left at Texas Avenue and headed east toward the Ward. Hetty cracked her window and let the scent of rain flow into the car. She could hear Charlotte sniffling in the backseat. "I don't understand this morbid curiosity you have with slums, sis," she said.

"Char, Pick lives there."

"You should move, Picktown. Really."

Hetty shot her a dirty look.

Charlotte huffed with resentment. "It's not regular. Ever since you worked at that clinic, you've got a complex. Savior of Dark Town or something evangelical."

"My complexes are none of your business."

"Says you! Pick, did you know my sister was treating coloreds with syphilis? We found that out after. And to think, I was sharing a bathroom with you!"

Henry Picktown Waller gripped the steering wheel with both hands when they hit the puddles of Dowling. He exchanged a wry smile with Hetty while Charlotte went on muttering in the backseat. As they rumbled over the railroad tracks, Hetty felt again the shudder of horror the Dowling Street Medical Clinic had brought up in her. She would never admit this to her sister, of course. She had maintained her usual confident stance, the stance that had gotten her into the clinic in the first place.

The debutantes of last year had been gathered around the table at the Blue Bird Circle, nibbling on shrimp salad. In Houston society, blue bloods and Blue Birds were practically synonymous: All were expected to serve the community out of a Southern gentlewoman's inbred sense of noblesse oblige. The president of the Birds had passed out sheets listing their charities and the various duties the girls could sign up for: planting azaleas for the Garden Club, throwing boat parties aboard Camille Pillot's yacht, or sewing hems on cup towels. The Blue Bird cup towels were quite popular, they were told; restaurants bought them by the dozens. Hetty had scanned the list, but her finger kept being drawn back to a name under the list of charities.

When called upon, Hetty said, "I want to work at the Dowling Street Medical Clinic."

Hetty's request caused the kind of furor among the Blue Birds that she'd hoped for. The committee was appalled, Charlotte was mortified, and Nella was furious. But Hetty had her way. In good conscience, none of them could deny Hetty her wish. She became the first white girl in history to volunteer at the Dowling Street Medical Clinic. Weekdays, it was housed in the small auditorium of the Recreation Center in Emancipation Park. She imagined a single gold trumpet announcing her arrival the first day. She was percolating with importance as she took the steps two at a time—drunk on insurrection. The black physician in charge, Dr. Jarvis—a kindly but harried man—seemed dubious that any white girl would be able to stick it out there for long. "This is going to be worse than you reckoned," he told her.

Hetty had taken a deep breath and, shimmering with idealism, said, "I'm prepared."

But she wasn't. She'd never seen patients in the final stages of syphilis. Dr. Jarvis wouldn't let her dress the skin rashes because he said they were contagious. But he did teach her how to identify the ulcers and how to administer the mercury treatment. Having gotten herself into this just to shock her mother, she now had to carry through with her dare. How pleased Nella would have been to know that she, Esther Ardra Allen, quavered when she went into that auditorium where the stench alone had caused her to pause at the threshold before she could bring herself to enter the room. She assisted Dr. Jarvis in draining the lungs of tuberculars and helped him fit braces to polio victims. They gave out remedies for hookworm, influenza, and pneumonia. Hetty often had to steel herself to keep from vomiting. She smoked a lot of cigarettes. She pilfered her mother's liquor. She made it through.

"If I hadn't worked at the clinic, I wouldn't have met Pick," she reminded her sister in the backseat. The car swerved onto Garrow Street, bringing the odors of the Ward through Hetty's open window. "You *do* know that's how I met Pick," she taunted her. "His poor mother—"

"I don't want to know what went on in that clinic. Just roll up your window—do you mind?"

Pellagra was rampant in the Ward due to malnutrition and chronic diarrhea. Dr. Jarvis had asked Hetty to help with a desperate case: a woman with the blackest skin she'd ever seen who brought her family in every couple of weeks with the "summer complaint" as she called it—Velma Waller and her four children: Addie, Ollie, Minnie, and Lewis. There was an older brother but no father, Dr. Jarvis told Hetty. They were all so skinny their clothes hung on them like scarecrows, and their mouths were full of canker sores. When Hetty asked why the children had diarrhea so often, the doctor had said, "The water's gone bad."

"You mean their well's polluted? Why?"

"You ever been to Settegast, ma'am?"

She shook her head.

"You wanna go?" he chuckled.

And she had. In his rattling, smoking Model T, the doctor had driven her one afternoon up to the Ward that grew like a fungus along the eastern edge of the city. *Settegast.* In her crowd, the name was never mentioned, or if it was, only with a lowered voice. Now she saw why. As they drove along the dirt streets, Hetty looked out the window and saw rows of two-room shacks crowded together along muddy ditches. She looked for a street sign or an address, but could see none. Only rickety porches, rocking chairs, morning glory vines. The tin roofs were all rusty. Something rank haunted the air—old garbage perhaps, or rancid grease. Men in white undershirts sat on the stoops while out in the dusty streets, children played a game of tag the doctor identified as Chickamy, Chickamy, Crany, Crow.

They stopped by the house of the Waller family, although how the doctor ever found it Hetty couldn't imagine. First, he took her to the shed that served as a kitchen and pumped up some water. She cupped her hands under the spout. It smelled vaguely of sulfur. "I don't suggest you drink it."

She glimpsed an outhouse in the back and heard the buzz of flies.

"Rats outnumber folks here three to one," the doctor had said.

But you never see the rats, Hetty thought as the Packard turned onto North Innis Street. Rain pelted through the window. She rolled it up and glanced over at Pick. He was looking so handsome in his chauffeur's rig, beaming as he pulled up in front of his house. He always drove the long black Packard into his own neighborhood with such pride, eager for his people to see how far he'd come up in the world. He kept the car buffed like a piece of fine jewelry—onyx perhaps, like his own black black skin—and displayed a natural charm and courtesy to all his passengers. As Hetty stepped out to go visit Pick's family, she heard two things: her sister clicking the locks on the back doors and the rain drumming on tin roofs all up and down the street.

When Velma Waller heard that Hetty was there, she rushed in from the kitchen shed, wiping her hands on her apron. Hetty studied her face. *Not as gaunt.* She asked her to call the children into the living room and have them line up on the braided cotton rug: Lewis in his overalls first, then Addie with her black shiny hair in finger coils, Minnie—barefoot and bold as ever—and finally, little Ollie with a pink bow tied in each one of her nappy braids. Hetty drew the four crinkling bags out of her slicker pocket.

"What you got for us, ma'am?" Minnie asked.

Pick patted his brash sister on the head. "Shush now."

"It's all right, Pick—buttercream candies!"

Minnie thrust her palm out, but Hetty wanted to feed them the first candy so she could have a good look inside their mouths. "Open up!" she ordered.

An hour later, Hetty trailed Charlotte into the foyer of their suite at the Warwick Hotel. Shrugging their rain slickers onto the marble floor for Lina to hang up, they checked their makeup in the round mirror with the pink tint that was so flattering to a woman's complexion. Nella had hung it there, of course. She loved tinted mirrors and had scattered them all over the apartment in various hues and shapes: blue trapezoids, immense rose-colored circles.

Hetty's knitted cloche rippled so close around her eyes that she had to tip her head back a smidgen in order to see clearly. But she didn't mind holding her chin so high: The hat's scruffy charm fitted nicely into her image of herself as a *bohemian de luxe*. She could pull off the look because she had her mother's gypsy eyes. Charlotte, on the other hand, was Kirb's daughter all the way: Even in the pink glass, her eyes had the metallic glaze that identified an Allen. *Was that why he was so soft on her?* Hetty wondered.

A clock chimed five times, followed by the sound of ice cubes colliding against crystal. The two sisters stood at the threshold of the apartment, as if in the wings of a theater: Nella sat center stage in a pool of light, the room around her receding into its cool mirrored depths. Hetty could smell cigar smoke but couldn't make out her father in the shadows. He was probably off in the study, taking his Saturday afternoon nap on the big leather sofa.

Their suite was not like the other apartments in the Warwick, most of which were still choked with Edwardian artifice. No, Nella lived in rooms the color of eggplants or emeralds, preferring the drama of the darker shades. This palette had been chosen, Hetty remembered, after her mother's edifying trips to Paris after the war when she'd come back reading Le Corbusier and preaching Purism. The resultant *mise en scène* was svelte and self-consciously sophisticated. Nella meshed with it perfectly as she awaited their entrance into the drawing room, ensconced in a highly modern armchair. "Chairs are architecture, sofas are bourgeois," she was fond of quoting from the master. Stacks of oversized art books crowded the black-enameled coffee table. Charlotte rushed in to kiss her mother on the cheek, chattering about Loew's Theater and its elaborate Egyptian decor. "During the stage show, the lights change color in time to the music. This week, they've got twenty-five banjoes all playing at once—"

"Twenty-five?" Nella made eyes at Hetty. Then she glanced over at an immense bouquet sitting on the ebony sideboard. Her black bobbed hair flashed in the lamplight, as streamlined as her furniture. Charlotte had her back to the flowers.

"It's called Banjomania. Mamá, you'd love it."

Hetty could see that the flowers were her favorites, tulips and anemones. Two ivory cards were nestled among the blossoms, one clearly bearing the crest of the Rusk family. *So that's why Nella keeps eyeing me,* Hetty realized. *Lamar has sent flowers.*

"You really should go to the matinee with us sometime. There's more to life, after all, than playing mah-jongg in the women's lounge."

Charlotte still hadn't spotted the flowers. Nella grabbed both her hands, while flicking her eyes from Hetty to the bouquet, from the bouquet back to Hetty. She was wearing one black pearl on the little finger of her left hand and one white pearl on the little finger of her right hand. "You know I love you, don't you?" she said to Charlotte.

"Yes, Mamá—what's wrong?"

"Something happened today that we've been waiting for . . . a long time."

Hetty entered the room and followed the trajectory of Nella's gaze. She had to see whose name was on the two cards. She plucked them out of the red and violet blossoms: *Charmaine* was scrawled across one; the other was a formal invitation bearing the Rusk crest that was addressed to *Miss Esther Ardra Allen, Warwick Hotel.* She opened the smaller envelope first:

> *If I could catch the green lantern of the firefly, I could see to write you a letter.*
> *Love, Lamar*

She set the card back down on top of the envelope and opened the invitation:

It would give us so much pleasure
to have you dine with us Saturday a fortnight—

She slapped that down, too, and headed for a divan buried under heaps of silk cushions. She burrowed into them and held one close to her breast like a shield.

Charlotte had finally seen the bouquet. She extracted her fingers out of her mother's and dashed over to the sideboard. She picked up the smaller card first and laughed. "Isn't that sweet? Amy Lowell. Lamar's such a dear." Then she spotted the envelope. Hetty hugged the cushion closer.

"Charmaine?" Charlotte looked at her mother, then at Hetty. Panic was starting to smolder in her eyes. She read the invitation, saw whom it was addressed to, then scanned the entire drawing room for the equivalent number of yellow roses, *her* favorites. "Did you put mine in my room?"

Nella took a sip of her Johnnie Walker but didn't say anything. Hetty couldn't stop the victorious smile that spread across her face. A few beats thudded by. Charlotte's panic flamed into searing knowledge. "He chose *her!*" She looked at Hetty with hatred scorching her eyes. Her face crumpled into tears, and she fled the room, fanning the pleats on her georgette dress. Sobs ricocheted down the hallway.

Nella followed, leaving Hetty alone on the divan to meditate upon this momentous event. She dug deeper into the silk cushions and curled up among them. She would have to accept the dinner invitation from the Rusks, of course. It would be rude not to, plus she would incur her mother's deepest wrath if she didn't. Nella had groomed her daughters carefully to become the well-bred wives of No-Tsu-Oh's finest sons. Bloodlines were important in Texas, Hetty knew, whether you were talking about your cattle or your kinfolk. All her girlfriends were looking for men with the right pedigree, and Lamar had one of the best.

Hetty simply couldn't be bothered with such matters. What was important to her at the moment was that the Waller children had completely recovered from their pellagra thanks to the food Pick could now afford and the clean water he carted in by the gallon. When she told them to open their mouths wide for buttercream candy today, she hadn't spotted a single canker sore. She considered that a personal victory, something much more essential than fighting with your sister over a beau. On the other hand, she was as fascinated as every Houstonian by the Rusk clan and their illustrious lives. Gaining entrée into the inner sanctum of that family would certainly have its advantages. And she *was* fond of Lamar and was sure she could grow to love him. If only she hadn't met Garret! They were like two tuning forks, humming with the same dreams.

There was commotion down the hall. Lina had been called in from the kitchen to make a cup of hot chocolate. Nella came back rubbing her temples and collapsed into an armchair. Her peach fingernails flickered as she downed the rest of her scotch. She was sitting before the centerpiece of the room, her prize find from Paris: a spectacular three-panel metal screen by Edgar Brandt depicting Diana on the hunt, a stylized deer leaping behind her.

"You mustn't rub this in your sister's face," she said.

"Why would you even think that?"

"I mean it, Esther. When Lamar comes to pick you up for dates, you must meet him down in the lobby."

Hetty waited for a word of congratulations.

"Meanwhile, I'll see that Picktown carries an acceptance over to the Rusks promptly. We've got two weeks. That's plenty of time to find you a new dinner gown. In fact, you'll need a whole new wardrobe. If this isn't an occasion for shopping, I don't know what is."

"How did you know it was for dinner?"

"I peeked at the cards, of course. Well . . . how could I resist, Esther? This is the day your father and I have been waiting for!"

Hetty studied her mother's face, rapt in lamplight.

"What makes you think I'm hunting for a husband? Diana may be your goddess, but I'm not sure she's mine."

Nella shot her an alarmed look. "You can't turn down an invitation like this. It could be our entrée back into Courtlandt Place."

"I know," she sighed. Hetty felt a twinge of resentment that her decision would be freighted with so much Allen family history. The Courtlandt Place cutting was one of those private matters locked up in her father's study. She knew Kirb kept the letter somewhere, stained now by whiskey. He occasionally pulled it out and read it to them when he'd had too much to drink. The trustees of the Courtlandt Association had signed it, names that were legendary among Old Houstonians: Carter, Taylor, Dorrance, Neville, Judge Autry, and of course, Chief Rusk himself, Lamar's father. In polite language, they had turned down Kirb's application to build a house there after he'd become President of the Citizen's Bank of South Texas. "We regret to inform you," the letter had begun. And *Regret* with a capital *R* had haunted her father for years after that. Regret that he wouldn't come home to formal dinners behind the balustrades of a beaux-arts mansion; regret that his daughters wouldn't ride their own ponies and celebrate their birthdays with dancing parties for dozens of their special friends from down the block. Banished from those lamplit boulevards behind the gates, the entire Allen family, Kirby and Nella and Esther and Charlotte, had been pushed into social exile: a suite at the Warwick Hotel all the way out on Hermann Park.

Nella poured more Johnnie Walker over ice cubes. Hetty could hear them cracking in the silence. After a while, she said, "I'll make a deal with you, Mamá. I'll go out with Lamar if you'll let me go out with Garret."

"If you spoil your chances with Lamar over some ne'er-do-well from Montana, I'll kill you!"

"Mac is hardly a ne'er-do-well."

"Mac?"

Hetty played with a silver tassel.

"When did you become so familiar with him, young lady?"

"That's what everyone calls him."

"So he *is* a friend."

"I like him, Mother. I want to see him again. Is that so horrible?"

"I can't give my permission."

"Why not?"

"I don't know enough about him. And neither do you."

"I know all I need to know. Please, Mamá."

Nella shook her head.

"Then you're going to have a hard time explaining to the Rusks why I've turned down their invitation."

"You wouldn't dare."

"Watch me." Hetty marched over and slid the invitation off the sideboard, heading toward her room to pen a refusal.

Nella glared at her as she passed. "Oh, all right!" she barked. "Invite Mr. MacBride to call. And I hope you come to your senses, you silly girl. Now go in and comfort your sister. She's heartbroken."

Hetty hovered in the door to Charlotte's bedroom, holding the invitation behind her back. Whiffs of hot chocolate floated in the air. Two bleary eyes glared at her from a mound of eyelet lace on the four-poster bed.

"Can I come in?"

"No! I'll never speak to you again. Go away!"

Hetty retrieved the tulips and anemones off the sideboard and lugged them into her own room, kicking the door shut with her foot. She slid the heavy vase onto her dresser, in front of the mirror. To let in more light, she parted her black and orange draperies bearing the Chinese emblem of happiness. She turned around and appraised Lamar's gift. It was grandiose, like everything he did. A giant spray of purple anemones and dipping red tulips that towered over all her other possessions. Hetty's room was still stacked high with the quaint splendors of the Pagoda Shop in downtown Houston, leftovers from her obsession with chinoiserie as a girl. There were carved soapstone boxes poised atop antique tables, elephant bookends huddled together before an ornate Chinese screen, and lots of crystallized ginger in smart little brocade boxes. Nella hated the clutter and thought the draperies were in especially bad taste, but Hetty had hung them there as a kind of talisman against despair. She never really believed happiness would be hers.

Not in the spontaneous way it came to her sister. She glanced back at the Chinese calligraphy rippling on the gaudy orange silk now incandescent with sunlight—taunting her with its double meaning of "blessed." Even though she'd awakened to these black brushstrokes of luck every morning, they had failed to work their charm. She noticed for the first time how much the letter resembled a dagger, its downward stroke a razor-sharp blade. "Yeah," she sniggered to herself. "That's what fortune has done to me—stabbed me!" Hetty's hand moved to her breast. She had never talked to anyone, not even Lina, about the burr lodged there, but it was a constant irritant: *My father prefers my sister.* He never said so, of course, but showed it in so many ways. Fathers don't realize how they reveal themselves. Long before children start to talk, Hetty knew, there's another language they learn from the way people act. She remembered how Kirby had doted on Charlotte every time he gazed on her pale baby's skin and her gray eyes. The radiant smiles that would light his face. This was *his* daughter . . . Charlotte Baldwin Allen, named for the wife of his famous ancestor Augustus Chapman Allen. Charlotte Baldwin had been married to one of the largest landholders in the Texas Republic, the founder of the city, her house built on a prime spot along Main Street. There was gravity to the name and lineage, the blessings of good birth—whereas Hetty had been named after her mother's remote relatives in San Antonio . . . Esther Ardra.

Some of Hetty's earliest memories were of Kirby rocking colicky Charlotte to sleep, letting her nap on the big leather sofa in his study, which Hetty was not even allowed to sit on. "She's only a baby," Hetty was told, which didn't make her feel any better. Then, when Charlotte was a little older, there were the covert trips to the bank, the outings to Ligget's Drugstore for chocolate shakes. Charlotte realized early on how many points she could score with her sister by bragging about the special privileges granted to Kirby's favorite daughter. At Christmas, there would be way too many presents under the tree for Charlotte, excused because she was younger, while Hetty got gifts more appropriate for her age.

It wasn't conscious, of course. Doing things for Hetty somehow slipped Kirby's mind, until he remembered himself and apologized.

But it was too late; the damage was done. When Hetty complained that she never got to go to the bank, he would take her along, then ignore her while he conducted business. She would sit there in a creaking office chair with the Edison stock ticker to keep her company. It would click into life periodically, tapping out its esoteric messages, one symbol per second. Hetty would watch the tape jerk out of the ticker and unspool across the desk. She wanted to cut it off, learn to read what it said, and wear the ribbon in her hair. She could never tell what the ticker symbols meant, but knew they had something to do with the value of stocks. She began to think of it as a time machine, tap, tap, tapping out messages from her past, telling her why her stock was down, spelling out vital secrets if only she could decipher them. She always imagined the hand that was tapping out the message on the keys at the other end and wondered whose it was.

Hetty shook her head to rout out the tapping and sat down at her desk. She reached for the tortoiseshell pen her father had given her last Christmas—typical of the kind of "practical" gifts she always got. She filled it with midnight blue ink and slid out a few sheets of her linen rag stationery with the deep blue monogram. She smiled when she saw the letters EAA. Finally things had turned her way. A man had actually favored Esther Ardra over Charlotte Baldwin. Lamar had chosen *her.* The subtle odor of tulips and anemones wafted across the room. She let the fragrance fill her with a deep delight. Orange light fell across her desk. Happiness was finally within reach. But then she remembered Charlotte's swollen eyes and wondered—how can it be perfect happiness when it's at someone else's expense?

By dinnertime, Hetty had written an acceptance to Rachel Rusk and a thank-you card to Lamar for the flowers. The gamey taste of glue slid over her tongue as she licked the linen envelopes and sealed them. She left both on the silver tray in the foyer for Pick to hand deliver, then went down to the solarium for a smoke. When she returned to her room, she found a letter that had been slipped under her door. It read:

CAB

Dear Hetty,

From now on, I will only communicate with you through the written word. Please do not attempt to talk to me at any time. I have nothing to say to you.

What have you done to bewitch Lamar? I can't imagine—well, yes, I can, knowing you. I can't imagine why Lamar would choose you over me, unless you are squandering the only thing a woman has that she can give her husband upon marriage. If you've done that, I can't forgive you. You've not only debased yourself, but our whole sex. Don't you know that Lamar won't ever respect you if you give away the pearl of great price? You'll only earn his contempt. But I wouldn't put it past you—I've seen how you behave at petting parties—I've seen how far you're willing to go with boys and with what sangfroid you're willing to do it.

You'll never know how much you've hurt your little sister, how deeply you've wounded my heart with your ways. And then to rub salt into my wounds by preferring Garret to Lamar. Yes, Mamá told me of the horrid bargain you made with her. How could you steal my boyfriend away from me when you don't even want him? You are the wickedest sister anyone could ever have. I hate you.

Love, Char

Hetty filled her pen with more midnight blue ink and answered it immediately:

EAA

Dear Char,

Why do you always think the worst of me? Your judgments are so harsh—I feel like I'm being scolded by a schoolmarm. Why would you blame me because Lamar chose me over you? How is that my fault? Between you and Mother, I can hardly breathe. I've done nothing to bewitch Lamar, other than being my usual wild and wicked self. Can I help it if boys like that? You should try it sometime.

As far as choosing Garret over Lamar, I haven't done that yet. I'll have to date both men for a while, of course, so I can decide which one I want to spend my life with. It's not an easy decision. So much depends on it, I have to take my time and really be sure. I don't want to hurt either one of them. And I don't want to hurt you, either. I never did. Forgive me if I have, but if you knew what was in my heart, you wouldn't feel this way.

Love, Hetty

PS: Don't worry, I won't try to talk to you. Mother says I'm to have Lamar meet me in the lobby so you won't have to lay eyes on him. And could I have my vermilion lipstick back?

Hetty folded the letter into one of her monogrammed envelopes and threaded it under Charlotte's door, which had been kept shut all day. She stood there in the dim hallway listening for any response from inside. There was none. She started to knock on the door, then hesitated. Even though she'd agreed in the letter not to talk to Charlotte, she longed to slip into the room and curl up among the eyelet laces for a tête-à-tête. She remembered what it had been like being sisters before things had gone so sour between them. A Spanish song rose up in her memory, one that Lina sang to them. *Cielito lindo, dame un abrazo*. "Pretty little darling, give me a hug." Lina would sing it over and over—*cielito lindo, cielito lindo*—and they would dance together holding hands, then break apart and run over one at a time to embrace her. They liked dancing in the sunlight that seemed to stream endlessly through the nursery window in the old Allen manse when they still lived downtown. They'd been true playmates for each other back in those days, skipping between their giant Victorian dollhouse and their Humpty Dumpty Circus Tent, racing their Spinaway Coasters up and down the hallways laughing. The hallways seemed endless . . . and so did their childhood.

But it wasn't, they soon found out. Flood season hit one fall, and it was all over. Day after day, the nursery window ran with rain. Hetty was sent off to grade one at the Kinkaid School, and Nella packed her bags and started traveling. In a house gone cold, thundering with a mother's desertion, Hetty was left alone with Kirby and Charlotte pitted against her. What followed had forced her to adopt her best friend, Doris Verne Hargraves, as a sister substitute. It all started with the spiders—*but I can't think about that now,* Hetty realized as she raised her hand again to knock. Her knuckles grazed the wood and stopped. The letter had ended: *I hate you. Love, Char*—so which would it be this time? Love or hate? She never knew and decided she didn't want to spoil the perfect happiness she felt inside. She turned and tiptoed back into her own room, easing the door closed on the empty hallway. Communicating through the written word was just fine with her.

Hetty waited in the foyer for Garret's knock, doing a final once-over in the rosy glass of the great round mirror. The alabaster clock had just chimed six the next Friday night, and she wanted to be sure she had pulled together a sufficiently vampy look. Her evening wrap of feathers floated up like a mist around her face, which had the necessary pallor slashed by oxblood red lips. Silver beads glinted on her head, making her look like Joan of Arc in chain mail. *These aren't hats,* she thought. *They're helmets.* She tried to keep a little nonchalance in her walk as she answered a light tap at the entrance. She threw the doors open to reveal him standing there, looking sharp in a navy club blazer and oxford bags. He tossed her a gift.

"What's that?"

"Something you wanted."

She jiggled it. "Hmmmm. Sounds interesting. Thanks, kiddo. Let me give you a tour before you have to run the gauntlet."

The lights were low. It was the cocktail hour, which Nella celebrated nightly with appetizers and candlelight. They ended up in the kitchen, where Lina was putting the final touches on the hors d'oeuvre. The rich aroma of pâté and truffle oil made Hetty's mouth water.

Garret sniffed the air. "Do you eat this rich every night?"

Hetty rolled her eyes. "My dad likes living beyond his means." She showed Garret the white marble bath and her own room hung with chinoiserie. As they stepped back into the hall, she pointed at a door that was shut and whispered, "That's Char's room."

Garret peeked into Kirby's dark library, walked farther down the hall to the *postigos*. "What's behind these?" He shook the heavy wooden doors.

"My mother's secret room."

"Is that where you keep your idiot brother?"

Hetty just laughed.

"Excuse the grape juice," Hetty said to Garret. They were sitting in the drawing room with Nella, waiting for Kirby to arrive home from the bank. Lina hovered at the sideboard plating the appetizers.

"I've told my daughters they can drink once they're twenty-one or married, whichever comes first," Nella said.

"Yes, ma'am," Garret said.

"Why don't I open this lovely gift Garret brought me?" Hetty clawed nervously at the wrapping. Out of a blue velvet box emerged the longest strand of pearls she'd ever seen. "How swanky!"

"They're from the Sea of Japan."

Hetty looped them over her head. They hung down to her knees. *Well, that settles it,* she thought. *He's no chauffeur.* She doubled them up. "Aren't they beautiful, Lina?"

"¡Bella!"

"*Bella* they are," Nella cut in. "But I'm afraid you can't accept them, dear."

"Why not?"

"She told me she's always wanted some pearls from the floor of the Sea of Japan," Garret said.

"I'm sure she does. That's where the best pearls come from. But a lady can't accept jewels from a man until she's engaged to him."

"But—why not?" Hetty asked.

"It implies an obligation she can't fulfill. I'm afraid you'll have to return them."

Hetty uncoiled the pearls and threaded them reluctantly back into their velvet box. She handed it to Garret. "Mother has spoken."

Garret held the box limply and said, "Sorry—I didn't know."

No one responded. Hetty felt her cheeks flaming as the silence stretched on, broken only by the tinkle of ice cubes. Lina excused herself to the kitchen. Hetty glanced at her mother. A triumphant smile played over Nella's lips as she sipped her highball and witnessed Garret's embarrassment. *This was just the sort of social blunder she was hoping for,* Hetty realized. *She's going to let him sit here and writhe, the bitch.* "Aren't we going to be late for dinner?" she asked Garret after a moment. She grabbed his hand and started pulling him toward the door when Kirb barged into the foyer. "Sorry I'm late. We had trouble batching up the bank. A teller out seven dollars and three cents. A goddamned three cents!" He planted himself in front of the doors, six foot three, two hundred and forty-six pounds, the candles casting a monstrous shadow on the ceiling. He towered over Garret as he pumped his hand. "Mighty pleased, sir, mighty pleased," he croaked.

"I think I owe you an apology, Mr. Allen. For my blunder at the cotton carnival."

"You'll learn our rules soon enough." Kirb wielded a Citizen's Bank cash envelope. "Here's another one," he said, unbuttoning Garret's blazer and dropping the parcel into his vest pocket. "No pay-and-pet for my daughters. That should cover Esther's dinner."

"Dad! Let us by, please."

Hetty's irritation at her family soon evaporated into the open air over the Auburn as they glided along the esplanades of Main and arrived at the Rice Hotel. Twilight was dyeing the sky a deep blue, and streetlamps were warming up the flickering shadows all along the ornate wrought iron veranda. Garret tossed the keys to a colored attendant and came around to open the door for Hetty. A satin slipper stepped down to the sidewalk, and all the lights ran to the snowy feathers that frosted her shoulders. White, too, was the lobby they walked through, cool and immense, faced with Italian marble and lit by the sparkling wheels of crystal chandeliers. The elevator girl took them to the eighteenth level, where they ascended the wide steps to a dance floor that unfolded under the stars. As the maître d' escorted them through the glamorous maze, Hetty felt a little airborne, as if she'd already had a glass or two of champagne, when in fact she'd only had a few strong whiffs of Garret's lime-rich cologne. They wove between cages full of twittering canaries and widely spaced tables flowing with skirts of white linen. Hetty spotted a couple of Blue Birds and some oilmen with their wives. After pulling out Hetty's chair, the maître d' struck a match to three candles of different heights, protected from the night winds by hurricane lamps.

They lit up and toyed with menus, settling on prime rib. They passed Garret's flask under the table, laughed about Nella's grape juice, and gazed at each other's faces through a golden haze of candlelight. They discussed the future. And the past. She asked why Garret had left Montana.

"There's no future there," he told her. "Over two hundred banks have failed."

"Two hundred banks! Whatever for? The rest of the country is flourishing."

"Years of drought and plague busted the homestead boom."

"You don't seem like the Old Testament type."

"Nope. Not me. I came to the Promised Land."

"You mean the young man's town?"

He laughed and lowered his voice to imitate her father: "Mighty pleased, mighty pleased."

"I'm sorry about the pearls."

"That's all right. I wouldn't want you to be obligated to me."

"Oh yes, you would."

"It's true. I admit it. I had my heart set on paying and petting." A cigarette danced in Garret's fingers. "So you want to go on dating me?" he asked, as he lit it.

"I hope to tell you!"

"Even though Mom and Dad don't approve?"

"I try to tell my mother nobody cares about that stuff anymore. It's not modern. When I get stuck on the right guy, I'll know it."

He smiled at her, a long sweet smile. "Are you feeling the least bit gluey tonight?"

She looked away and raised one bare shoulder out of her evening wrap. "Yes, now that you mention it, a little sticky."

"Think we could get glued together on the dance floor?"

"I think we could," she answered and let the feathers fall in a whispering cascade to her chair as she rose.

Their prime rib grew cold as they moved among the other couples, dancing number after number, letting it loose for the shimmy and pulling up tight for the slow dancing, when Hetty felt as though she were being ushered through low-lying clouds as she laid her cheek on Garret's chest and looked up to see the faintest glimmer of stars spinning by as they turned.

She'd always prided herself on being a little cynical when it came to romance and was amazed at being smitten by the very feelings she found so silly in love songs. Like the one being played by the band right now about whispering. She wanted to step up to the mike and sing. As if reading her thoughts, which happened a lot when she was with Garret—they were so in sync, he started crooning the lyrics into her ear, slipping his warm breath up under the beads of her cloche. *He's getting through my armor,* she thought and tried vainly to resist.

> *Whispering while you cuddle near me,* he sang softly.
> *Whispering so no one can hear me*
> *Each little whisper seems to cheer me . . .*
> *Whispering that I love you.*

And then they sang the words together, moving in a lazy foxtrot.

Finally they feasted on rare roast beef dripping blood into cold mashed potatoes and finished off with cherry cheesecake, another Rice specialty. When the waiter brought the check, Garret pulled out the envelope Kirb had given him and placed it on the table. They both looked at it. Hetty shrugged. "Just use it."

The hour grew late. Garret bundled her into her velvet wrap and brought her over to the very edge of the rooftop, where they stood at the wrought iron railing and followed spoke after spoke of lights radiating out into the flat dark land. The cupola of the Esperson Building, illuminated, floated above them. They were at the center, leaning close together. He brushed his cheek against the feathers that surrounded her face, until he was nuzzling in her neck and turning her face up gently to kiss her. His lips grazed hers once or twice, then stopped and opened a bit until she could feel the warmth and wetness of his mouth, urgent and tobacco-scented. She liked men who smoked. She glanced back, making sure neither of the Blue Birds was watching, then unbuttoned his blazer and snaked her arms around him, wanting to unbutton his shirt to find the source of that deeper, richer smell. She held on, being kissed, stirring her legs restively under the slinky dress, aroused. Maybe next time she *would* let Garret pay.

"Tell me what's behind those doors," he breathed into her ear.

"Not yet," she whispered back.

On the way home, she grew quiet. She was already thinking about the dinner she would attend the following evening at the Rusk mansion. How different it would be from tonight. Lamar would know things Garret didn't. He was from an old Texas family, after all. He would know to bring her flowers, not jewels, on their first date. He would know how to present her properly to his family. It would happen in the largest residence in all of Courtlandt Place: Splendora—Chief Rusk's immense antebellum estate with its sprawling gardens, greenhouses, and tennis courts. There would be no question of who would pay. They and dozens of other guests would simply share in the largesse of the Rusk oil fortune, spread out in baronial style throughout three or four grand reception rooms.

Lamar would escort Hetty across a wide veranda in the shadow of towering white columns right off a Greek temple. A Confederate flag would hang next to Old Glory. Under the blazing light of chandeliers, Chief Rusk would look at Hetty the way he looked at his prize heifers on the Splendora ranch: Was she good for breeding? How many Rusk grandsons could she bear? Rachel Rusk would be her usual charming but dotty self, making Hetty feel like the guest of honor even though the circular dining tables would be crammed with an intimidating crowd of Courtlandt Place neighbors. Hetty would have to sit at the head table next to some socialite like Etta Garrow or Jessie Carter and endure her scrutiny. All through the evening, both Rachel and Chief would smile at her approvingly and would drop subtle hints that she was worthy to marry their only begotten son.

She would drink a lot of really good champagne but still wouldn't be able to douse the doubt smoldering at the back of her mind: Would Lamar still want her when he found out what was behind the *postigos?*

Would Garret?

Would any man?

Chapter 3

Hetty had underestimated the difficulty of dating two men at the same time. She'd seen it merely as a matter of logistics, making sure they didn't show up in the Warwick lobby on the same night, avoiding the least mention of one to the other, storing each in different compartments of her mind. She trusted in the Darwinism of desire: The one most suited to be her mate would eventually prevail through the rituals of courting. As the female in her season, all Hetty had to do was wait for a sign, a scent, a flash of bright plumage, and she would know. *He's the one.* She couldn't let tribal customs cloud her judgment, doing her best to ignore the drumbeats of gossip her dating life was stirring up in the distance. "You should hear what the old ladies are saying about you," Wini reported with glee. "I won't repeat the monikers . . . unless you want me to." Hetty declined the offer. She'd expected to be misunderstood. What she hadn't counted on was the inconstancy of her emotions. Biology wasn't everything. The human heart had four chambers, after all, each one spacious enough to house her passion for the right kind of man.

Adding to her confusion was the frenzied pace of life in the city that spring. Thanks to businessman Jesse Jones, Houston had won the bid over San Francisco to host the Democratic National Convention in June. As April's wet nights melted into the humid, radiant mornings of May, it seemed the whole town was under construction. A vast coliseum was being erected that would seat twenty-five thousand cheering, sweating delegates. Contractors were throwing up hotels to house the expected one hundred thousand visitors, outfitting penthouses with palm courts and terraces elegant enough to entertain the most distinguished guests. Streets were closed, traffic a tangle. The ground often shook under Hetty's feet when she was downtown shopping. Overhead, prop planes buzzed by heading to the new municipal airport.

Within the secluded niches of No Tsu-Oh, all was in a flurry. Word got out that only *six* women would be invited to play hostess at the Hospitality House. Nella was determined to be one of them.

"I'm just so glad I was never interested in politics," Hetty overheard her mother telling Lockett one afternoon. "Now I can declare myself a Democrat without feeling hypocritical."

"I think we should all strive to be bipartisan at a moment like this," Lockett answered, then murmured something in a confidential tone.

Hetty sat at the dining room table eating the ham sandwich Lina had made her for lunch. She looked into the drawing room. She could just make out the profiles of the two women huddled together in the art moderne armchairs. Nella fanned herself with one of the black lace fans that were scattered around the apartment. Lockett's normally raucous tones had been hushed in order to convey insider information she'd gleaned from her husband, the congressman. There were to be lots of parties, she was telling Nella, but only two were significant: The first was the opening Sunday brunch at the Cupola Club, at which Mrs. Woodrow Wilson would be in attendance. "That's the one we have to go to. There's going to be another breakfast for her on the Roof at the Rice, but anyone can go to that by paying a dollar and a half."

"How democratic," Nella said.

"Exactly. Which is why we want to be at the other one. But"—Lockett leaned forward, panting—"wait till you hear what's happening later in the week!" She went on to describe the second party, at which attendance would be mandatory for Old Houstonians of any note: a private reception Saturday night at Bayou Bend in River Oaks. Hetty could hear her mother moan in the other room. She knew she'd been itching for an invitation for years now, ever since the estate became one of those magnetic centers to which the denizens of No-Tsu-Oh were drawn. Bayou Bend: the fabled pink mansion, home of Houston's most celebrated hostess, Ima Hogg. Not only was Ima heir to the Hogg oil fortune, she was a connoisseur of the finest taste, an urbane world traveler and founder of the Houston Symphony. To stand on her terrace and be served a Bayou Bender by her butler, Lucious Broadnax, was to arrive at the pinnacle of social eminence in the city.

"The congressman tells me all the bigwigs will be there," Lockett said, "the Roosevelts, Will Rogers, H. L. Mencken. Ima's using it as an occasion to unveil her new Diana Garden."

Nella's fan beat at the air. "Sounds like an event we can't miss—"

"Y'all forget, there're going to be a hundred thousand people in town that week. Invitations will be scarce as hen's teeth."

"Whatever can we do?" Ice cubes tinkled as Nella poured Lockett some more iced tea. Hetty slid her chair back and stood up, wondering what it would be like to shake Will Rogers's hand. She turned and smiled at him in the blue trapezoid mirror over the sideboard. Then she licked her fingers and formed two perfect black spit curls on her cheeks.

After their date, Lamar kisses her good night in the lobby of the Warwick Hotel. He never comes up to the apartment because of Char. Hetty takes the elevator to the eighth floor and steps out into a jungle. She wonders when they installed a terrarium in the hallways. She wanders through the damp air and catches the scent of freshly turned black soil. Large leaves have the color of limes and drip with moisture. She parts them and looks up to see luminous pink flowers scaling the walls of the hotel. They glow with an inner light that strikes Hetty as dangerous, a lure for insects and small birds. She glimpses Garret through the foliage. Fear stabs her. Did she make a mistake and invite both men on the same night? He beckons to her. She follows him to a hill where an exotic woman is singing. Somewhere there is a piano. Hetty can't understand the lyrics but loves the throaty timbre of her voice. She has the eyes of a lizard. They look into Hetty's, and she becomes aroused in her sleep. Then, the long lime-colored dress of the woman, slit high up her thigh, opens and reveals that she is a mermaid. But her bottom half isn't a fish. It's a snake. She hovers there on the hill, coiling and uncoiling. Her singing turns into a rhythmic hissing, and all the leaves begin to undulate to her beat. Hetty tries to step behind Garret, but he isn't there. Then blue light breaks through the trees, and Hetty awakens in the dawn.

She sat up in bed. She knew she'd had another one of those dreams . . . visions that gave her enigmatic glimpses of days to come. This had happened to her since she was a girl, but she had never mentioned the dreams to anyone. They were forbidden. She never foresaw trivia but always something fateful, a turning point, a closure or beginning. The night before Garret appeared at No-Tsu-Oh, she had dreamed of his car. She had seen the Auburn moving through her mind as if lit by sparklers. That was why she'd been so intrigued when she first saw him. Hetty rolled over in bed, her pillows smelling like last night's perfume. She pushed the covers back and swung her bare feet off the mattress, then pulled them back up. She scanned the floor to be sure nothing was creeping by before running down the dim hall to the bath.

On Sunday, Hetty sat at brunch in the gardens of Splendora. Antique wicker chairs were shaded by the tangled vines of wisteria. The heavy fragrance was lulling her to sleep next to Lamar. Chief Rusk was slurping his second Bloody Mary while his wife Rachel asked Hetty for her indulgence. "When I invited y'all for brunch, I had no idea my entire staff would take the day off." She'd done her best to cobble up some omelets.

"Where's Tuggie?" Hetty asked. Tuggie was the much-feared boss of the Rusk household, a stout no-nonsense cook who always dressed in starched white cottons and had a sassy word for anyone who tried to cross her. Visiting Splendora as children, Hetty and Charlotte had often eavesdropped on her drilling the other servants with military efficiency. They had found it amusing. "Prods 'em like cattle," Chief Rusk was fond of boasting. The Rusk family could not have functioned without their treasured Tuggie, and they knew it, allowing her to accompany them when they traveled to cooler climes in the summer.

"Oh, Tuggie goes to Pilgrim Branch Baptist Church every Sunday," Rachel said. "Big doings. You should see the hats she wears."

"I'd like to whip somebody real good." Chief Rusk downed the last of his Bloody Mary. "The whole string of 'em gone."

Lamar came out of his slouch on the sofa beside Hetty. "It *is* Sunday, Dad. A day of rest."

"I hope to Jesus Tuggie took some of 'em to church," Rachel said. "They all need religion." Rachel Rusk always looked as if she smelled an unpleasant odor, her immaculate blond hair marcelled into perfect waves. She was never seen without the armor of eye shadow, mascara, and rouge.

"It's like this, son—I keep my liquor locked up or those dingy bastards drink it."

"Finding help is my biggest headache," Rachel said wearily. "And we pay good wages!"

"Too good!" barked Chief. "Those niggers—"

"Baby, watch your language!"

"That's not something I do."

"How well I know. Y'all better not use that word in Tuggie's hearing."

"She uses it more than I do."

"Yeah, well, she can. You can't. It's not polite."

"Polite! Those niggers go rotten working here. We're Splendora's niggers. We work for the Chief. We're fancy. I'll show 'em polite. Why have staff if you have to prod 'em every goddamn minute? Like to drive poor Tuggie crazy." He ranted on. Hetty tried to think of a way to change the subject. She scanned the tennis courts, then caught a flash of light from a dormer window in the gabled roof.

She waited for Chief to catch his breath. "Is the attic still a playroom?" she asked.

"I haven't moved a thing," Rachel said. "I'm saving it for my grandchildren—if a certain young man of my acquaintance ever decides to produce an heir."

"You should never pressure a man around heir production," Lamar said. "It's a good way to make him impotent."

His father knuckled him in the arm. "I better not hear about you being impotent, son."

"Let's go up there, Lam," Hetty said.

"Y'all don't!" Rachel drawled. "It hasn't been cleaned in ages."

"I don't care. C'mon." She reached for Lamar's hand and tugged him out of his nest of cushions and down the colonnade. He led her through the cavernous kitchen spangled with copper pots. They took the spiral staircase that the servants used, creaking as they climbed to the top. The door rattled when Lamar pushed it open—the long attic stretched before them, the upper half of its walls slanting in with the ceiling. Sunlight spilled through the dormer windows, glinting on sudden motes that floated up as they walked. This had been Hetty's heaven as a child, a room in the sky devoted wholly to play. It was all still here: the yellow-striped wallpaper with the blue sailboats, the wide window seats. They passed marionettes hanging on their floppy strings, the rack of dress-up costumes, and the shelf of tall illustrated books.

At the top of the room stood the puppet theater, with players on sticks that you moved through grooves in the stage floor. Hetty flicked on the cabinet light that lit the stage, and it flashed across the face of a clown leaning to one side. Lamar closed the red velvet curtains. The pulley squeaked, and a smell of must rose up that entered Hetty's lungs and left a pang in her heart.

Automatically, they sat at one of the tables where a Chinese checkers board had been abandoned mid-game. The chairs were too small for them now. Lamar made a move to continue the game. "Oh no, I'm not playing checkers with you," Hetty said.

"Why not?"

"Because you used to cheat. You would change the rules in the middle of the game so you could win."

Lamar watched her across the table, his skew-jawed smile fading. The desolate look drifted into his eyes, the one he only showed her, the one that allowed Hetty to forgive him his trickery. "Who's the one that's cheating now?"

Hetty smiled at him meekly. "I can't help it that I met Garret."

"But you don't have to date him." He toyed with the checkerboard, jumped two of her marbles, and took them. "Do you know how that makes me feel?"

He looked so wounded, all Hetty could do was touch his hand and whisper, "I'm sorry. How can I make it up to you, dear Lam?"

"We've been invited to the reception at Bayou Bend during the convention. My folks said I could bring a date. I'll take you if you promise to stop dating Garret."

Hetty held his gaze for a moment, then looked away. In the dim corner behind him, she spotted Lamar's panpipes fanned out in the shape of a bird's tail. Their notes rose in her memory like returning swallows, twittering as Lamar led her and Char around the room in a dance, so seductive. His offers were always like that, too good to refuse but too easy to reject. The piper who plays for a price, inviting you to places you've always wanted to go but couldn't afford without him. He was giving her a wing into the splendor of Bayou Bend and knew she wouldn't be able to refuse. It was the party everyone wanted to go to, the only place to alight on that Saturday evening in June. But was it worth giving up Garret for? She didn't know yet.

"I'll make you a deal, Lam. Ima's party will be my deadline. I'll choose between you and Garret before that night."

"All right, kiddo. And you know," he said, standing up and shoving his hands into his pockets, "I should invite Mac over for a game of tennis, or something."

Hetty's chair scraped the floor as she stood up. "Don't you dare."

"Why not? He's part of our set now, isn't he?"

Hetty tried to read Lamar's eyes to see if he were plotting something or merely being kind. She was never sure with him. "Go ahead," she said. "He won't come."

But Hetty was wrong. Garret accepted Lamar's challenge, and the tennis match was set for the second Saturday in June. As the date approached, it became clear to her that the invitation was anything but a signal of Southern hospitality. The two men had sensed each other's presence in her life for weeks and had sniffed the other's cologne in the curves of her ear. Now they were hankering to meet face-to-face, to joust it out with the lobs and lunges of the court.

The light broke entirely too bright on the day of the game with hardly a cloud in the broad Texas sky to smudge edges a little. By noon, the sun had entirely inundated the courts at the Rusk mansion. Even under the arbor, it leaked through the wisteria vines and began to corrode the shade. Hetty could feel a headache pounding at the back of her eyes. She'd been so nervous this morning, she'd forgotten her sunglasses.

Once the match started, there was no sound but the tinkle of ice cubes in tall sweating glasses and the distant thud of tennis balls volleying back and forth. The men gathered in grim silence around the court to see who would take the lead. Glen Jr. kept score while Todd Eldridge tossed out fresh tennis balls when needed. The girls avoided the sun as much as possible. Winifred and Belinda stretched out on matching wicker chaises piled with pillows. Doris Verne had her legs drawn up on a wicker love seat deep in the shade. Two Carter girls and Diana Dorrance sat around one of the circular wrought iron tables. Hetty pulled the big brim of her straw hat closer to her face.

Winifred soon got bored with the game and started reading out loud from a heavy tome propped in her lap. Actually, she wasn't reading; she was translating a sex manual that hadn't been published in English. Hetty listened halfheartedly to her halting rendition, amused as always by the various roles Wini adopted for herself: sex expert, German translator, interpreter of European customs. She had been to Berlin with her family. She had witnessed cabarets and things that would be unthinkable in Houston, Texas. She cut her hair like a man and wore tailored golf slacks. She claimed to have read every marriage manual published since the war. Quoting Margaret Sanger on the importance of birth control, she had made herself rather notorious in the sheltered circles of No-Tsu-Oh. Winifred Ilse Neuhaus always had a group of giggling, blushing girls clustered around her over in some secluded corner as she lectured them on the facts of life. She explained what would happen on their wedding night. She told them bluntly what they had to do to keep a man happy. "But don't be a doormat," Wini counseled. "Demand your equal rights. Keep your maiden name when you marry. Join the League of Women Voters!"

"It should be the boys hearing this." Belinda laughed as Wini read how a skillful husband worked to get his wife sexually aroused. *It's like coaxing a flower to open,* Hetty thought.

The language became so explicit that Doris Verne covered her ears and said, "Honey child—stop!"

This, of course, egged Wini on all the more. She gave them the highlights of a section meant to teach the husband how to kiss amorously, then ended with a German phrase that she drew out suggestively before translating, "Or, in English, 'the genital kiss'!"

The two Carter girls erupted in shrieks while Diana Dorrance shot Wini a dirty look.

"Is that what it really says?" Belinda glared at the book.

"I swear. *Der genitale Kuß,*" Wini read.

"Your husband's supposed to kiss you down there?" Doris Verne asked. "Ohhh my god."

Diana Dorrance made a face at Doris Verne, but Hetty didn't share their disgust. She was glad to learn that something she'd wondered about actually had a name.

"You may stop reading now, thank you, ma'am," Doris Verne said.

"What?" Wini assumed a quizzical look. "It's the best way for him to get you lubricated."

The Carter girls shrieked again and collapsed in each other's arms, laughing. Glen Jr. shushed them, unable to concentrate on score keeping. Hetty turned her attention to the game again. Lamar had apparently just taken the first set. "Lamar!" Glen Jr. shouted out, and they all applauded politely. Garret rallied with some swift volleys close to the net and managed to win the second. As they moved into the third game out of five, Hetty could hardly stand to watch. The tennis court became a battleground upon which Lamar was determined to defend his honor and superiority. Tapping years of training, he unleashed a bombardment of ace serves that sent Garret lunging for the ball time after time and missing it. He was all over the court, sweating, while Lamar hardly moved from his command post behind the baseline.

At the break between the third and fourth set, Garret came up to her table to guzzle some iced tea. As he stripped his wet shirt off and wiped the sweat from his face, Hetty poured him a glass. He threw his head back to drink it, the Adam's apple in his thick neck bobbing up and down as he swallowed. She let her eyes fall like fingers over his naked skin, so tanned and smooth that nothing stopped her as she glided over the round swelling of his chest, stopping for a moment to brush the brown nipples, like perfect little pebbles. *He'd make a good swimmer,* she thought. He had the kind of muscles that skim through water, long and lean. Hairless, too. Except in the armpit he flashed when he raised his drink. She found that thick tuft of black shocking in a way that entranced her, a wild fragrant herb in a manly garden usually hidden from view. She wondered if a wife was expected to give genital kisses to her husband, too. When he finished drinking, he slammed the glass down. "That bastard is beating me."

She stood up and enveloped his head in her hat brim. She whispered in his ear, "Losing this match doesn't mean losing me—relax." She could smell the musky health of his sweat.

The two men swaggered back to the court. Hetty watched as Lamar, looking a little wan in the bright sunlight, served his smooth, high opening pass, then caught her breath as Garret leaped into the air to slam it into the court with a savage overhead.

The contest wasn't helping her sort out her feelings about the two men at all. Lamar blazed with such confidence she felt herself pulled into orbit behind his comet's tail of victory. If he invited her for a celebratory cruise around the bay tonight, she knew she would accept in spite of herself. She loved the luxury of the Rusk yacht, the freedom of the launch. On the other hand, she found Garret's desperation touching. If he lost, she couldn't leave him in limbo by himself. She would want to spend the evening assuring him that it didn't matter.

During most of the fourth set, she hid behind her hat brim. She tried to distract herself by listening to what Wini was reading out loud again over the objections of Diana and Doris Verne, how a modern woman might return the genital kiss.

I knew it! I want to do that to Garret! Hetty thought, amid the uproar this latest erotic tidbit created among the girls. They all seemed to be talking at once, shouting their objections to the whole idea. "No, no, no! Oh, no, oh, no!" Diana Dorrance spoke out the loudest: "You'd never get me to kiss a boy down there, kiddo, unh-unh."

"No, ma'am," Doris Verne agreed.

"But you girls say you want equal opportunities," Wini said. "Well, here's your chance!" She read again about how today's woman has earned the right to take a more active role in every aspect of lovemaking and not just be the toy of an amorous man. Wini looked up and cast them a coy glance. "Just think of it as our sexual suffrage, girls."

Belinda admitted that she liked that idea, and Hetty was going to agree with her, when a commotion from the tennis court drew her back to the game. The men were chanting Lamar's name. He only had to take one more set to be the champion. Every groan and cheer made Hetty wince. She listened to the thud of balls back and forth, but couldn't watch. The contest dragged on and on, making Hetty's headache worse. She felt faint in the sticky heat. Then she saw Winifred jump up from the lounge screaming, the sex book falling to the floor. *Lamar had won.*

She looked out at the court, blinded by the high sun and the nakedness of Garret's defeat. He didn't have Lamar's polish; he didn't know how to finesse things with a little humor, a worldly reference or two. He paced on his side of the net, his abdomen rising and falling rapidly, keeping his head down as Glen and Todd circled Lamar, whooping.

Tuggie sent the kitchen staff out with silver trays bearing cut glass pitchers of her famous iced tea. Everyone gathered at the wrought iron tables under the arbor and toasted the winner. Only Garret remained on the other side of the netting that curtained the court. Hetty wanted to go to him, walk hand in hand away through the spreading sago palms. Then Lamar remembered his manners and beckoned him over with a glass of iced tea. He tugged his white shirt back on and ambled their way.

Lamar shook his hand, then handed him the drink. "I guess you don't get a lot of chances to play tennis living over there in the Heights."

"You live in the Heights?" Belinda asked.

Garret nodded.

"I don't believe I've ever met anyone who lives in the Heights," said Diana Dorrance.

Garret sipped his tea. "I'm not home that much."

"So you live in your car?"

"Cars," Garret said.

"You know, kiddo, that Auburn of yours, that's not a real sports car."

"Yes, it is."

"Not really. Now you take my Bearcat—that's a real sports car. Eight cylinders, real powerful—clean as a whistle."

Hetty didn't think Garret's cheeks could get any redder, but they did. "Look here, *kiddo,* that's not the only car I own, you know. I drive it because Hetty likes it. She said it's the most beautiful car she's ever seen. Didn't you say that, honey?"

"Well . . . yes, I did."

"You did? More beautiful than my Bearcat?"

"I just like the tail on it—but why are you boys arguing over cars?" she said to cut the tension. "Don't you think that's a little silly?"

"You're right, Het," Lamar said. "Let's talk about something serious. How about THE DEMOCRATIC NATIONAL CONVENTION."

"Hear, hear," shouted Todd.

"What parties are y'all going to?" Lamar asked. One by one, the girls listed the events they planned to attend. Then the turn came around to Lamar. Hetty felt on edge again; she hadn't told Garret about Lamar's invitation. "I have an important announcement to make. Miss Esther Allen has agreed to accompany me to Ima Hogg's reception at Bayou Bend Saturday night."

The girls all shrilled in envy, except for Belinda who pouted on the chaise. "I hate you."

Garret threw Hetty a sullen glance. She felt a stab of anger at Lamar for putting her in such a bind. She didn't want to sully his triumph on the tennis court by branding him a liar in front of all their friends, but resented any man who trespassed on her freedom. She'd have to find a way to convince Garret of the truth later. For now, she was noncommittal. "I've always wanted to go to Bayou Bend," was all she'd say.

"Mac?" Lamar said. "What are your plans?"

"It all sounds kind of boring to me. I've got a better idea. This coming Friday I'll take all of you to something really democratic—a Black and Tan."

"A Black and Tan?" Lamar said. "I'm afraid none of us know what that is, kiddo."

"That's where white people visit a club for coloreds." Mac's offer was met with a shocked silence. "For the jazz. Anybody game?"

"I wouldn't think of taking a white girl to a place like that. But I wouldn't think of driving an Auburn, either. I guess that's the difference between me and you, Mac."

"I guess. Any of you kids change your mind, meet me at the Warwick Friday at eight p.m." He brushed by the hanging wisteria and left. Hetty could see him waiting for her on the other side of the clipped hedges. She pulled Lamar aside.

"I've never seen you like this."

"Maybe now you'll realize how serious I am." His face darted under her hat brim, and he kissed her with his tongue, knowing Garret was watching. "Stay with me tonight," he urged, hugging her close. She threw her head back and tried to decide which man to follow. She glanced up and caught a glimpse of the dormer windows in the attic staring out with their vacant eyes. For a moment, she thought she saw a face reflected there, the face of a young girl with her left eye red and swollen. *Then she remembered.* She had seen Lamar like this once before. When they were children. Lamar had been cheating as usual at Chinese checkers one Saturday, rewriting the rules so he could win. She usually forgave him his cheating but didn't feel like giving in that time. He'd reached for his blue steel barrel gun with the cork bullets. It had come with a shooting gallery where black crows were the targets. He loaded it and began firing the corks at her until one hit her in the eye and left it bruised. That had sent her stumbling down the stairs screaming for Tuggie, who'd put ice on it.

She pulled away from his embrace. "Not tonight," she heard herself saying.

The following Monday afternoon, Hetty was picking out the right dress to wear to the Black and Tan when Lina appeared in her doorway. "Your mother would like to talk to you, *m'ija*."

"Uh-oh," Hetty said and followed her out into the drawing room where she could smell afternoon tea brewing. It was Mah-jongg Monday. Lockett Welch was ensconced in an armchair chattering away with Nella. Lina slunk into the kitchen.

"Yes, Mamá?"

"Would you like a cup of Darjeeling—and you haven't said hello to Lockett."

"Hey there, Lockett. How was mah-jongg? Did Mamá beat the pearls off you as usual?"

"Don't be rude, dear," Nella came back at her. "The truth is, Lockett was so full of startling revelations today, I could hardly concentrate on my tiles."

"How else can I steal tiles from you?" Lockett dropped another cube of sugar into her tea. "Nella Ardra Allen—the mah-jongg queen of the South. But I confess, the Welch grapevine was buzzing a bit more than usual this afternoon." She pivoted her broad hips until she was perched on the edge of her chair, eyes locked on Hetty. Mounds of handkerchief-pointed flounces made up her dress, with a huge velvet bow riding on her left hip.

"Did you want a cup, Esther? You never answered me," Nella asked.

"Sure." Hetty settled into her favorite spot on the divan and tucked her skirt under her. Several sounds filled the silence that followed: the trickle of hot Darjeeling tea being poured, the tinkle of a silver spoon against a thin china cup, Lockett clearing her throat several times to make an announcement. Nella brought the steaming tea over and set it down on a Macassar ebony side table.

Lockett was watching Hetty intently. "First of all, I'm here to inform you that my daughter will not be accompanying you young people to the jazz club on Dowling Street Friday night."

"That's all right. I'll give her a full report."

"I just found out about the plan at the tournament today," Nella said. "I was so shocked, I almost forgot to shout 'pung' when picking up discarded tiles."

"I'll be perfectly safe, Mamá," Hetty said. "I used to volunteer there, if you remember."

"How could I forget?"

"But you never went there at night," Lockett jumped in. "You girls shouldn't be listening to that jungle music. Why, in its original form it—"

"Was used for voodoo ceremonies—I know," Hetty said.

"It causes nervous hysteria and makes you lose control."

"Oh, Lockett! Self-control is out of date. Haven't you read Freud?"

"This is a serious matter, Esther. I'll tell you the same thing I've told Belinda a million times—gin and jazz have ruined more than one girl, so beware," she said, wagging a finger at her.

Hetty used the teacup to cover her amused smile. "Anything else? I was in the middle of something."

"How many of your friends are going Friday?" Nella asked.

"It looks like it's just going to be Mac and me."

"I thought a group was going."

"Everyone else is afraid to. So Garret's taking me. We have a date."

Lockett slurped audibly at her tea before setting it down with a rattle. She clutched her breast and looked at Nella with large, sad eyes. "Nella, dear, I am so sorry! I feel so responsible for this. But at least I'm doing my part to untangle things."

"Untangle?" Hetty asked.

"Why, yes! I'd describe it as a tangle. A terrible tangle. And to think I began it all by receiving this person. Thank God I devised a way to allay my guilt—"

"I knew you'd find a way, Lockett," Hetty said.

"I sicced Congressman Welch on the trail immediately—and it didn't take him long to pick up the scent."

"Really?" Hetty asked cautiously.

Lockett gazed up at the ceiling and batted her eyelashes. "The first thing I have to say is that we traced the MacBride family to their origins. They're from—well, of all places, from Butte. A hellish place! Full of immigrants who came to work the copper mines. Drinking, gambling—*whoring!*"

"Oh, dear," Hetty laughed. "Houses of ill repute."

"We're not talking about houses, my dear," Lockett said. "We're talking about cribs the girls lease by the night. A dark, unholy place. They say the city is so thick with fumes that streetlights have to be turned on in the middle of the day—in the middle of the day, my dear!"

"What's all this got to do with Garret?"

"I was getting to that!" She sat forward in her chair. "His father was Termite MacBride."

"That was his name? Termite?"

"Yes. One can only imagine why."

"And—?"

"Don't you see, Esther?" Lockett said. "MacBride? They're shanty Irish!"

"They were immigrants!" Hetty protested. "Garret's father was a senator."

"But he didn't finish out his term."

"He didn't?"

"No. Congressman Welch remembers the name MacBride. He left in the middle of the session for some strange reason. The congressman can't remember why. I won't rest until I find out, of course. I just know what this is liable to be."

She had edged so far forward in her chair, Hetty was afraid she'd fall out. Her eyes burned into Hetty's like sunlight through a magnifying glass. "What's that, Lockett?"

"A scandal!" she hissed.

"Don't be silly," Hetty said in a dismissive voice to cover the anger that was boiling up inside.

"I just thought you should know what I found out." Lockett gulped down some tea, looking a little wounded. "I'll never forgive myself for introducing this person to Houston society. If only I'd known!"

After a few minutes of strained chitchat, she stood up. "Well, I must be off, dears. Thanks for the cup," she said, flouncing toward the foyer with her handkerchief points bobbing. "Good-bye, Esther. I'd be leery going to a Negro club with a shanty Irish if I were you. You know he's liable to drink." To Nella, she said, sweeping open the front door, "I can't believe you're allowing it, my dear."

"I'm not," Nella said, and closed the door firmly behind her.

Hetty was fuming when Nella came back into the drawing room. "How dare you discuss my private life with a bunch of Edwardian dowagers in the women's lounge."

"And how dare you plan a trip to Dowling Street without my permission. I don't appreciate finding out about it at a mah-jongg game, let me tell you. I felt so ashamed, I didn't know what to say."

"I'm old enough to make my own decisions!" Hetty said, standing up.

"Perhaps." Nella edged up to her daughter. "But I can't approve this Dowling Street plan. I'll not have my daughters slumming in the Ward. Do you understand me?"

Hetty glared at her. "Yes."

"Do I have your solemn promise?"

"I can't give you that," Hetty muttered and made for her room.

Nella came around the divan and snapped at her. "You'd better, young lady. If you set foot in that neighborhood, you can kiss your Garret good-bye."

Silence. Hetty looked at her mother aghast. They had been warned by Kirby since childhood that emotion was out of place in the drawing room. They were used to polite murmurs, discreet laughter, and a mild command or two. But not this. Not Nella in a rage. Hetty found it frightening. "Don't you dare threaten me, Mamá. I won't stand here and let you make a dartboard out of me.

You know what you can do? You can just stew in your own juice! See if I care. See!" she cried, fleeing the room.

Hetty broke the news to Garret in the elevator on the way down to the lobby. She was surprised when he wasn't angry.

"It's simple. We won't go. That was only going to be your initiation. The truth is, Dowling Street's for tourists. You want to hear the real Houston blues, baby, you gotta go to the source. West Dallas Avenue."

Hetty looked at him wide-eyed. Dowling was not that unfamiliar to her after her stint at the clinic, but West Dallas lay across town in the shadowed backyard of the city, where a wrong left could take an unsuspecting driver right down into the dark, foggy streets by the bayou. *"West Dallas!"* she said, following him through the lobby. "Is it safe?"

"We'll probably be the only white people there. Of course, if you're afraid . . ."

Hetty fell into the seat of the Auburn and moaned. It was the kind of dare she loved, something really offbeat and a little dangerous. She could just hear Belinda squealing with envy when she told her about it on Monday morning. Hetty Allen, the first girl in her set to hear the *real* Houston blues. It was irresistible. Then another voice crept into her thoughts: deeper, commanding, "set foot in that neighborhood—kiss your Garret good-bye." Hetty knew in her heart what *that* neighborhood meant: every shantytown she could think of that blistered the map of metropolitan Houston. Nella had given her a clear choice. But what she hadn't counted on was Garret's cleverness. He was offering Hetty an out: She could plead not guilty on a technicality by avoiding the street expressly forbidden: Dowling. She hugged Garret's arm and bent close to whisper in his ear, "That's what I love about you, honey. You're in the know. Let's do it!"

She kept snuggling up to him and nibbling on his ear as he sped all the way north on Montrose to Lincoln. When he finally wheeled the bright blond convertible onto the muddy tracks of West Dallas Avenue, its freshly polished chrome picked up and sparkled with all the colored lights from the saloons and clubs they passed. He nosed the car into a spot just past a blaze of lime and pink neon that twisted itself into the name "Andy Boy's."

The club inside was dark and noisy and, since it was Friday night, already jammed with a crowd that looked pretty dingy to Hetty and was busy rocking to the riffs of a combo on the glittering stage. They wedged themselves between two other tables and ordered tonics to spike with gin from a hidden flask. Shadows of the male singer crisscrossed their table as they listened.

In a gravelly croon that chased the saxophone but barely kept up, he was singing about a black snake in his bed. Garret pointed a cigarette her way, and they both lit up. No matter how unruffled she always tried to appear, she had an annoying habit of blushing at moments when she was caught off guard. She thought about the lyrics she'd just heard and felt heat rising up into her cheeks. Her forehead started to flame. She glanced quickly from side to side. Why didn't she have on something dark and smoky like the other women in the room? Instead, she'd chosen to wear her white net over silver lamé, the one that was spangled with paillettes and pearls. She was not only the lightest woman there, but had a brunette's incredibly pale white skin that flowed together as one with the slinky dress and made her fairly glow in the rosy beams radiating off the stage.

He topped off her drink and signaled for her to take a sip. She downed half of it in one gulp, gagged on the raw gin, and soon felt better as the blood in her veins ran warm. When the band swiveled into faster and faster tempos, she found she couldn't fight the music but simply had to surrender to it in order to save her nerves. It was the kind of hot stuff you couldn't stand in the path of for long. The drummer drove them unmercifully, topping off the beat with a constant *clickety-clack* sound that left the brass free to wander, the clarinet whistling in and out way over the top of it all. Finally, they all slowed down together, and the great wheels of music rolling off the stage churned almost to a stop, with only the clarinet player still climbing and circling in a flight all his own, higher and higher, on and on, till the pianist shouted at him, "Chase it—that's what I call fried chicken!" and the voice of the audience rose up in one great cheer.

Garret worked his chair through the writhing mass till he was sitting close to Hetty. He put his arm around her shoulder and shouted into her ear: "This is real Texas boogie-woogie you're hearing. They call it the Santa Fe sound 'cause these guys work a circuit on the railway going West." Hetty nodded, noticing again how the rhythms they struck sounded so much like train wheels turning on an iron track. She couldn't keep her feet still.

Later, when everybody had had too much to drink and things were getting mellow, they brought on a singer named Brown Sugar and a suave pianist to back her up. She had a sultry look and the perfect voice for blues, rich and deep. Hetty loved her dusky, honey-colored skin and the lime satin dress that dropped off her shoulders and shimmered as she sang. Her big brown eyes with heavy lids straight off a lizard reminded Hetty of something. Then she remembered her dream. The singer looked down at them after one of her songs and she said, "Hey, Mac," then gave a throaty chuckle and added, "Ain't no bayous going to run dry tonight, y'all." This brought some whistles from the back of the room and a wave from Garret where he sat near the stage.

Hetty was drunk enough that when Sugar went on to sing things like "Empty Bed Blues" or "Bayou Run Dry," she didn't even blush, though the singer was looking right into Garret's eyes as she crooned:

My bayou's run dry since my baby been out,
My bayou's run dry since my baby been out,
My man he better come and end this lovin' drought.

Instead, Hetty ended up sitting in Garret's lap, hanging on his neck and telling him, over and over, that she was ready to go park somewhere. Lockett was right. This music did make you lose control. Or was it the gin?

Hetty felt slightly dizzy as Garret swerved the Auburn into the circular drive of the Warwick. She was half asleep and had no idea what time it was. She just knew it was late, *very* late. She could only hope that Nella wouldn't still be awake to witness how ossified she was. Garret tried to park the speedster under the porte cochere, but it was already choked with Kirb's long Packard town car. She wondered what it was doing here in the middle of the night.

He steadied her as they stumbled through the lobby and caught the elevator to the eighth floor. Its upward surge flooded her head with guilty thoughts from the evening. They had ended up parked beside the lagoon as they usually did. "Let's get hot," Garret had said as he steered into a dark spot and pulled out his silver flask. Ever since the tennis game, they'd gotten into some pretty heavy petting, although, like most of her girlfriends, she drew the line at intercourse. She'd gone a little further each time, letting his hands into secret places, pulling his tie off one time, unbuttoning his shirt to smell his heat the next. Now she was hooked: She always wanted him to take his shirt off completely and was even at the point of unbuckling his belt and letting her fingers slide over the tempting rise of his buttocks. Usually, she let Mac take the lead, only stopping him if he tried to go too far. But tonight, Wini's words had echoed in her mind, how a modern woman might return the genital kiss. Hetty sat up and worked his Oxford bags down, pulling his boxers back. She'd bent over him and held his cock in her hand, then kissed the head of it. She was fascinated with how spongy and smooth it was, with the musk that rose off it and how it began to swell and stiffen between her fingers. She wished it weren't so dark: She'd wanted him to see her brazen red lips closing over the head of his cock, adoring it.

When they reached suite 810, she started fumbling in her evening bag for keys until Garret pointed out that one of the double doors was cracked. Her heart sank. She crept into the foyer and, despite the haziness hanging over her mind, noticed several things at once: Garret's face reflected in the pink mirror, his sleepy blue eyes peering into the suite timidly, Nella looming in the doorway in a flowing silk kimono, two dark figures standing guard behind her.

"No more petting parties for you, young lady," she announced immediately. "You're under house arrest for two weeks."

It took Hetty a moment to register what she meant. "House arrest?" she asked groggily. "For two weeks?"

"Yes. Until the party at Bayou Bend. I'll let you go to that with Lamar."

"But why?"

"I told you Dowling was off limits. This is the last straw."

"But we didn't go to Dowling Street. I kept my promise."

"No, you went to West Dallas—that's even worse."

"Why?"

"For God's sake, Esther, wake up. It's the red-light district."

Hetty caught her breath and glanced over at Garret. "You didn't tell me that, honey."

"Of course he didn't," a gruff voice shot out from the drawing room. The two dark figures rustled ominously. One of them materialized as her father's stern face, his gray eyes regarding Garret with chilling hauteur. "That's how men like this take advantage of girls like you."

Kirb came past Nella and clutched Hetty's arm so tightly she whimpered. He pulled her away from Garret and stepped between them, massive. "Now, I'll have to ask you to leave my home, sir. You are not welcome here."

"Leave Mac alone, Daddy. Just leave him alone. It's not his fault. Even if I'd known, I still would've gone. Besides—how'd you know where we were?" She glared at her mother. "Are you spying on me again?"

"Spying?" Nella spat out a bitter laugh. "That was hardly necessary. You were a bit conspicuous, my dear, being the only white girl there. We have a witness."

She moved aside, and Hetty peered into the murk of the drawing room. The other person stepped forward into the light, but his face remained as dark as ever under the cream-colored brim of his straw hat.

It was Pick, his eyes never rising above the level of her feet. "I'm sorry, ma'am," he said.

Then Hetty noticed Charlotte lounging on the sofa, witnessing her humiliation. "It's not fair!" she cried. "You're all ganging up on me." She turned to hug Garret good night, but her father was still blocking the way, forcing him out into the hall. She craned her neck to search out his gaze. He was looking at her with such a burn of longing that her own eyes went hot in return, steaming with tears. Then the door slammed between them. She could feel him right outside, his heat radiating through the walls.

"Don't leave me, honey," she shouted. "Don't leave me here."

Chapter 4

Voices woke Hetty out of haunted dreams. She heard footsteps padding down the hall. For minutes, she refused to open her eyes. Then she sensed light. She looked over sleepily and saw morning sunlight already streaking across her orange and black draperies, giving her room an eerie glow. She stretched and rolled over to check the bank calendar she'd pinned to the wall months ago under a teakwood lantern. The last four days had been circled to chalk up what Nella liked to call her "moon." She'd taught her daughters to track their monthly cycles like astronomers, though it was hardly necessary in Hetty's case. Her ebb and flow came like clockwork and never slowed her down. But more important than that were the big red Xs across the days. Nine days of house arrest down, five more to go.

Today was Monday, June 25, the calendar said—the first day of the Democratic National Convention. Hetty had itched all weekend for this morning to dawn, knowing that her mother and sister would finally vacate the apartment for a few hours so she could telephone Garret. She hadn't talked to him since she'd managed to sneak behind the telephone screen late one night. Hetty slipped out of bed and opened her door, then crawled back under the sheet and pretended to be asleep. She listened to the sounds out in the hall, the scurrying, the shouting, Lina's mutterings in Spanish as she passed back and forth with blouses to iron or shoes to polish. A whiff of lavender floated into Hetty's room. During her solitary confinement, she had been humming the words of an old song that Lina used to sing as she worked: *"Nunca me harás llorar."* "You'll never make me cry." *"Nunca, nunca, nunca."* "Never, never, never," Hetty had chanted in her mind to help her hide her misery.

It seemed to take her mother and sister forever to get ready. Hetty grew drowsy but didn't think she could sleep anymore, especially with the sun kindling such bright orange embers in her curtains. She could only melt a little in the haze, like stepping down many stairs into an unlighted house.

And then she was cold. There was a wind rattling and ceilings so high they seemed to disappear into the night sky. She wondered why she wasn't in the hotel anymore. This was the inglenook that was built in at the bottom of the stairs next to the fireplace, but it frightened her because the fire had gone out and the whole house was drafty and cold. She began to tremble because no one came to kindle the fire, and the house was a thicket full of tangled furniture and frightening curios.

Then her dreams became memory. She remembered why the fire had gone out. She remembered the fog horns that kept thundering, like the deepest note on a organ, as an ocean liner passed like a great wall sliding through the Port of Houston, heading abroad. And her mother was at the top of that wall, waving down to Hetty, who stood so small on the dock beside Lina and who couldn't wave back because she had to hold Char's hand, and Char was crying because her mother was leaving them again and wouldn't be back for months. But Hetty couldn't cry—*Nunca me harás llorar*—because she was two years older and had to be sure Char didn't fall off the dock into the water. Kirby said it was her duty to look after her younger sister.

At night the two of them would huddle in the inglenook and remember when their mother was home and would make them a fire before bedtime and tell them old legends by the light of the crackling flames. Nobody knows the peril of a house without a mother; only the children know. Hetty would lie there trembling in the dark, listening to the sounds of the house: Lina haunting the hallways singing a sad song in Spanish about the husband who'd left her years before, Lina's door closing, the creaking of the steps when her father finally went to bed, Char's breathing falling into sleep. She would curl up amid the smells of old fires long burned out. She couldn't sleep until she'd managed to push the cold shudder out of her heart by singing Lina's words softly, over and over, to herself—*nunca me harás llorar.*

And then there were the spiders. Even though Lina swept away cobwebs daily, there were too many corners she couldn't reach with her brooms. Because Kirby thought spiders were beneficial, he refused to have the old house fumigated. They were everywhere—daddy longlegs hiding under toys, little black jumping spiders on the windowsills, yellow orb weavers on the potted palms. Charlotte, especially, was terrified of them because of stories she'd heard at school: Spiders drink from your mouth at night, brown recluses hide in your clothing, wolf spiders travel in packs. After a spider sighting, she once sat in a chair with her legs drawn up and refused to walk across the floor for hours. It got so bad Lina took them to the library on McKinney Street to check out books about arachnids. They learned that their father was right: Most spiders were harmless and helped humans by eating bugs. There was only one they had to avoid: the shiny black widow with the deadly red hourglass on her abdomen. She was so venomous she would eat her own husband after mating with him. They read about all kinds of exotic specimens: peacock spiders, assassins, even spiderlings who turned and ate their mother after being hatched.

In spite of all Lina's efforts, Charlotte never overcame her arachnophobia. Worse than that, she began to spin a web of her own as she grew up, becoming a tattletale to catch her older sister in a tangle of transgressions. This gave her a lot of power for an eight-year-old. She worked hard to maintain her status as Kirby's little darling. She memorized all the rules out of *The Child's Book of Etiquette* he had given them as girls, always making sure to brush her hair and don a freshly pressed smock by the time he got home from the bank. She never raised her voice in the drawing room, rose when guests entered, and always fulfilled her father's requests with an adoring smile. Hetty, on the other hand, simply couldn't be bothered with all these silly Edwardian rules. Her hair was always a snarl, she hurtled down the stairs two at a time, screamed with delight, and collected spiders in a old drawer out of a dresser. If she didn't agree with an adult, she said so, and expressed her opinion freely. She was constantly breaking the rules, and Charlotte took note. At dinner every night, she would delight her father with a song she had learned at school, the A plus she had gotten in spelling, and the rules that her sister had broken that day. Lina tried to brush this off as just being Hetty's high spirits, but Kirby often ended up frowning across the table at her.

Charlotte's list of privileges grew, while Hetty was put under house arrest time after time. They argued bitterly when Kirby wasn't around, and Hetty started withdrawing and spending more time with Doris Verne. Their roles became reversed: Hetty had stepped in as surrogate mother when Nella was away, but now Charlotte had transfigured herself into the scolding parent. Like those spiders Lina had told them about in Mediterranean countries—the heartless Stegodyphus hatchlings that ate their own mothers—Charlotte had turned on her sibling and begun to devour her. Hetty remembered a lithograph from Nella's book on Odilon Redon where he drew a spider with spindly legs and a human head. Yes, that's where this rattling wind was blowing, that's where her dreams had taken her, into a whispering house of memories haunted by spiders. And all of them had Charlotte's face.

When the telephone rang, it was like thunder in a glass sky. It brought her with a white jolt back to the hotel, pulling her out of bed. She dashed into the living room and dove behind the telephone screen, catching the call in the middle of the fourth ring.

"Hello," she exhaled into the phone.

"Are they gone?" Garret asked.

Hetty looked around the dim drawing room. All was silent. She didn't even hear Lina in the kitchen. "It looks like it. Honey, I miss you like crazy."

"We're getting married."

Hetty held the receiver away from her ear for a moment while she caught her breath. "We are?"

"Don't you want to?"

"Could you ask me after I've had a cup of coffee?"

"I'm serious. You probably can't tell, but I am down on one knee. Will you marry me, Esther Ardra Allen? I'm in love with you."

The marble floors were cold under her bare feet. They sent a shiver that traveled all the way up her spine. It was the first time he'd actually spoken those words. "I'm in love with you too, Garret MacBride." Her lungs expanded their capacity three times as she spoke.

"Is that a yes?"

"My folks would never let me marry you."

"Maybe if they knew my intentions were honorable, they would. I'm calling your father at the bank."

"All right, see what he says and call me back. I need a minute to think about this."

"It's what's behind the *postigos,* isn't it?"

"Yes. I can't agree to marry you until you've gone into that room."

"It won't matter. I love you."

"Wait until you see what it is."

"I'm calling your dad."

Hetty went into her room and nestled her chilled feet in a pair of embroidered Chinese slippers, then sat back down behind the telephone screen and waited. Her toes no longer touched the marble floor, yet she couldn't stop shivering.

It wasn't long before Hetty heard the front doors bang open and saw Lina staggering through them lugging a box that she could hardly get her short arms around. She sat it down with a thud on the floor of the foyer and glanced in at Hetty half-hidden behind the telephone screen. "*¡Ay! Tanta agitación*. Lina, bring this. Lina, take that. *Ándale, ándale*—we're going to be late. *¡Éso es el colmo!*"

"You can relax now."

Lina came into the drawing room and sat down breathless on an ottoman. Her black eyes narrowed in suspicion. "Why are you sitting by the *teléfono?*"

"You have to let me talk to Mac."

"Sí, pero no," she said, shaking her head.

Just then a *braaang!* sounded out. They looked at the black phone, then at each other. Lina jumped up as Hetty reached out. *"No, m'ija, por favor."*

Hetty's hand hung in midair. Another *braaang*. "Garret asked me to marry him."

Lina gawked at her, speechless. A third *braaang* rattled in the air. When she caught her breath again, she cried, "Answer it!"

Hetty lifted the receiver and said, "Yes."

"He hung up on me."

"Damn him!"

"I didn't even get a chance to ask. We're going to have to run off."

Hetty started shivering again. "Run off!"

"It's the only way. They'll never let me marry you."

The shivers turned into goose bumps all along her arms. The idea of stuffing her clothes into a steamer trunk and just walking out of her mother's marble prison made her tingle all over. Suddenly, her body ached for Garret. For his smell. She couldn't bear it another minute. But then she thought of the *postigos* down the hall, their black bars locking things in—and out. "Not till you come over here."

"When can I do that?"

Hetty looked at Lina. "I want to show him Mother's room."

Lina shrugged.

"I know you have a key."

She shook her head again. *"¡M'ija, por favor!"*

"Let me talk to her. I'll call you back." She dropped the receiver onto the base and studied the figure on the footstool. Lina was sitting there with her hands clasped tightly, her eyes downcast, a sad mask of torn loyalty stretched tightly across her brown face. Hetty knew that she was putting her dear little Lina into an unbearable bind, but couldn't stop herself. The memory of Garret's old kisses made her mouth move. "Linita, surely you understand. I can't marry him until he knows the truth."

"If the Señor Mr. MacBride truly loves you, it should not matter."

"That's what he says, but he hasn't seen what's on the walls in there."

Then the phone rang again. Lina stepped over and answered it. She kept nodding her head and saying *"sí"* over and over in a solemn tone, then ended the conversation by saying, "Yes, Mr. Allen, *se lo prometo.*" She hung up and stood looking down at Hetty gravely.

"You must not talk to the Señor Mr. MacBride, and he must not come here. It is forbidden by your father."

"But you don't understand—"

"*¡Silencio!* Do you want your Linita to lose her job? To end up back in the jute mills? You heard me—he made me swear." She placed her hand over her heart. "Do not make Lina break her word."

Hetty pleaded with her, but she only threw up her arms, then cried in Spanish, "For stupid words, deaf ears," and refused to discuss it further.

Her father must have tipped Lamar off, too, because three dozen red roses were delivered to the suite after supper. When Hetty tossed the lids back, she found blue velvet bags tied around each bouquet by a white satin ribbon. The note in the first box read: "Please slip this on if you find me 'engaging.' " Inside the pouch, Hetty found an engagement ring studded with the largest diamond she'd ever seen.

"It should come with a warning," she told her parents, who were hovering over her shoulder. "Do not observe with the naked eye."

In the second box, the note read: "Don't keep me waiting another minute, my Charmaine." The reference to their special song made her smile. That pouch gaped open with the weight of a Chanel watch, its face surrounded with two perfect little circles of high-carat stones. Over a hundred diamonds, Hetty estimated, holding it up.

"I think someone's in love with you," Kirb chuckled.

The third box contained her invitation to Ima Hogg's reception at Bayou Bend, along with the message: "Give me your answer Saturday night in the Diana Garden." When Hetty untied the bag attached to those stems, a little silver quiver fell with a tinkle onto the dining room table, filled with miniature golden arrows. This made Hetty's head swim. She picked up one of the tiny arrows, letting it pierce her heart in spite of herself. *I am yours, my little Lam!* "I wonder where he found that on the spur of the moment?" she said, heaping the treasures together in a pile so she could skirt the table and watch them flash with light and color as she moved.

Nella stood across the table and beamed at her daughter. Her eyes twinkled with sparks from the hoard down below. "Now these jewels you may keep, since you're practically engaged."

"Practically," Hetty said, trying on the watch. It looked smashing on her wrist. She resisted picking up the ring, knowing she'd be undone forever.

Kirb came over and stood beside his daughter. "Now that's what I like to see," he said, finishing off his brandy and smacking his lips. "An old-fashioned courtship."

Later, Lina helped Hetty move the three bouquets into her room. She wanted one beside her bed, one on her dresser where the roses would be reflected in her mirror, and one on the Chinese table, where she kept her brocade boxes of crystallized ginger. Using the white ribbons, Hetty hung the gifts among the blossoms because the diamonds looked so resplendent against the crimson petals. Gentle aromas began to pervade the room.

She sighed. "Lamar's campaign of jewels and roses. How can I resist it?"

Lina scowled at her. "We have saying . . ." she muttered. Just as Lina always carried a dust cloth in her apron pocket, so she always had a Mexican proverb she could pull out and apply to the big important questions of life. Tonight's was: *Amor con amor se paga:* "Love has to be paid with love."

"You're so wise, Lina," Hetty said, taking her hands and kissing her on the forehead.

"Not wise enough, sometimes," she answered, and Hetty felt something cold being dropped into her palm. She ran her fingers over a metal object. It was the big iron key to the *postigos*.

* * *

As soon as Charlotte and Nella were finished in the bathroom the next morning, Hetty drew herself a hot bath and soaked for a long time in the steamy air. She wanted to wash the dark side of her moon away and scrub the smell of bitterness off her skin. Once she felt clean enough, she attacked her closet to find the right dress to wear—something that would make her look available but not eager, enticing but not whorish. She chose a vine of deep purple and blue flowers with long sleeves. She slipped it on over purple silk stockings and lit her face with a little silver eye shadow and vermilion lipstick. The woman gazing back at her through the roses she had placed in front of her mirror looked cool and radiant, ready to face a man wanting her to elope.

She heard his footsteps first, echoing down the long hall outside Lina's room. The door was right there. She could slip into it, lock it behind her, and never see him again. This was the moment. Her feet wanted to run, but then she saw him and was smitten all over again. He looked even better than she remembered, dressed in his usual wildcatter's rig—the tall sexy boots, the rugged leather jacket, a snap of a hat. She could see herself on the arm of such a man, walking out of the hotel in front of everyone.

He didn't come right up to her but stopped a couple of feet away. Neither said anything. Under the brim of his Panama, his blue eyes found hers and filled with the cold color of his loneliness. She wanted to go to him with every fiber of her being but held back, not sure how he would react to what she was about to reveal.

Then she was in his arms. He took off his hat and buried his face in her neck, almost lifting her off her feet by the strength of his embrace. Once Hetty smelled him, she couldn't hold back any longer. It was always the smell that got her, that forbidden spice of male musk. She hugged him back, opened her mouth to his tongue. His kisses were deep and urgent, as if he were trying to make up for all the petting he'd missed in the last week.

After a few moments, she forced herself to pull away and whisper—"Quiet!"—as she opened the back door of the apartment and pushed him through.

* * *

On the way to the *postigos,* Hetty stopped in her room to get the big iron key. Garret spotted the roses and the jewels draped among the petals. She warned him not to read the three cards, but he couldn't resist. *He might as well see it all,* she thought, *so he knows what I'm giving up for him.*

Then they made their way down the hall, past her father's secluded study and the master bedroom, to the portal of Nella's quarters. Hetty inserted the key and turned it. With a click, one of the heavy colonial doors shuddered open. As she pushed it back, the ancient iron hinges groaned, revealing Nella's secret room. Hetty led Garret in and let him look around. It wasn't like the rest of the apartment at all. The walls here bore the color of sun-drenched marigolds or fiery red chilies. Mayan crosses stood atop a Mexican *armario,* whose crudely carved cedar had weathered to the color of old leather. Quarter-moon chairs sat at a hacienda table where Nella worked at her embroideries.

At one end of the room rose the altar, the very fount, of Nella's practiced femininity: a *bureau de dame* in black lacquered wood with little ivory compartments stepped like an Aztec pyramid down the back. A drawer had been left partway open, and geometrical jewelry spilled out, flashing enameled facets: triangles of onyx and amazonite, sunbursts of sapphire, coral, and gold.

At the other end of the room sat a four-spindle church pew; above it hung painted masks of goats or devils. There was an altar table, some candles. The most noticeable things on the walls, though, were not the brightly painted masks but a series of black-and-white photographs of an old plaza town in Mexico and its dark-skinned inhabitants. Some were family portraits taken in formal parlors. Others were shots of old men telling stories at sunset on the massive stone benches in the plaza. One was a wedding picture: A dusky bride wore a shawl as a headdress, cinched in her hair with a Spanish comb. Her husband was blond and fair. He looked out of place amid all the bronze faces, stiff and frowning. These family photos were surrounded by strange close-ups of grave markers and gargoyles and spirals carved on the lintels of old stone houses.

Hetty noticed Garret studying a lace fan that had been framed and labeled: *Guerrero, sin recurso.* Then he looked at her, puzzled. "I don't understand. Who are all these Mexicans?"

"My ancestors. That bride is my grandmother, Liliana Ardra Herrera de Beckman. Her husband was a German from the Hill Country."

Garret looked at the picture, then back at Hetty, trying to understand.

"I'm mestiza, Garret."

"Mes—what?"

"Mestiza. Mixed blood. My mother always said the word came from a costume they used to wear in Yucatan that was half white, half black. That's what my grandmother was like—half Spanish, half Indian, born where the light meets the dark. The town you see there in the pictures—Guerrero, along the border. Her people were stonecutters."

Garret seemed speechless. He looked at the photographs, then back at Hetty's face. It was as if he didn't recognize her anymore. His eyes grew puzzled. She could feel the knots drawing tighter in her stomach, the lump welling in her throat.

"You're *Mexican?*"

Hetty nodded. She was afraid if she said anything, the tears would start to flow. She sank into one of the quarter-moon chairs, steeling herself for the moment Garret would walk away.

He stammered for a response. "I'm—I'm—" He wouldn't look at her.

"You don't have to say anything." Hetty's voice quivered. "Just leave, please." She lowered her eyes to the striped wool rugs on the floor. She didn't want to watch him walking out, leaving her alone with those ghostly gray faces staring at her from the black-and-white photographs.

"I don't want to leave. I just want to look at you with new eyes." *Scornful eyes,* she thought. He came and stood over her, placed his hand on her head. "So that's where your black hair comes from, your dark eyes . . ." Hetty felt his fingers tightening on her scalp, imagined him tugging her by the hair, insulting her in subtle ways. *Now he'll feel free to make love to me, do what he wants, take the kind of liberties he wouldn't dare take before. He'll see me as fallen,* she thought. *When one of our children is born with darker skin, he'll blame me. The sin of my color.*

"I've always loved your black hair. Now I know why."

"I'm sorry I didn't tell you sooner. I should have."

"It wouldn't have mattered, you silly girl." He cupped her chin in his hand and lifted her eyes to his. "I don't care if your grandmother was an Eskimo. It's you I love, Hetty. Not your family."

"Don't lie to me, Garret. You were shocked. I could tell."

"It's just a surprise, that's all." He knelt down in front of her. "But I couldn't really care less. Hell, I'm Black Irish myself. My mother always said we were descended from Spanish sailors. Who knows? What difference does it make?"

"I can see you're not from Texas. It makes a difference here. That's why we've kept it such a secret. Nella is terrified her society friends will find out and shun her."

"Who wants friends like that?"

Hetty resisted when he tried to hug her. So much anguish and love was dammed up in her throat, almost choking her, yet she was afraid to let it out. *Nunca me harás llorar.* "I was worried you were going to walk out on me," she cried. "That you would hate me."

"Never, never," he said, and tried to hug her again.

"You really mean that?"

"With all my heart."

He sounded so sincere, she decided she *could* let him see her weep, after all. She always felt safe with Garret, which was why she loved him so much. She couldn't carry this cramp in her heart forever. She let her head fall to his chest. She let her feelings come flooding out, staining the leather of his jacket with the bitter juices of rejection and fear. She couldn't believe he was staying with her. She wrapped her arms around him and held on tight, sobbing.

After a few minutes, she lifted her head and wiped her eyes with the flared sleeve of her dress. "So you really don't care?"

"No. In fact, I'm relieved. I have a secret, too."

"You do?"

Garret pulled a quarter-moon chair out from under the table and sat down. He looked at her sheepishly. "I run a little rum on the side." He watched for her reaction. "But it's only to raise money for my wildcatting ventures. I don't plan to do it much longer."

Hetty's tears turned into laughter. "I love it. The greaser and the legger. Aren't we a couple of wild beasts? So modern!"

"So you'll still go away with me?"

Hetty paused for only a moment. Garret's confession might have given her pause yesterday, but at this moment she was swept up in such a rapture of deliverance, she didn't care. This was the kind of intensity she wanted in her life! "Of course I will," she said, sitting on his lap and kissing him so hard their teeth scraped together.

"Let's leave now," he said, urgent and aroused.

"Are you crazy, kiddo? I need time to pack."

They had to wait three days for their marriage license to come through, three endless days of hellish indecision for Hetty. She spent the long hours packing for her honeymoon, hiding the two suitcases deep in her closet. She was so afraid her mother would discover them or that Charlotte would notice toiletries missing from the bathroom. Hetty couldn't eat and woke up in a cold sweat at night. "We live in a rainbow of chaos" became more than a quote from Cezanne. It was suddenly her future. She stopped by the bank and made a withdrawal out of her passbook. Ten dollars. She was reluctant to take everything out, worried that the teller might tip off her father. Every time she uncapped her tortoiseshell pen to write Lamar, the midnight blue ink would dry on the tip as she sat there staring at an ecru note card. What if she came to regret the words? Only Garret's voice on the telephone could comfort her and convince her that she was doing the right thing.

Finally, the eve of her elopement arrived. Hetty stayed in her room during dinner, sending a message with Lina that she wasn't feeling well. She feared she wouldn't be able to look her parents in the eye through the maze of tall white candles and crystal wineglasses.

Later, she grew hungry and decided to investigate leftovers in the kitchen. She got out of bed, sheathed her feet in Chinese silk, and cracked the door a little. All looked dark and quiet in the hall. But when she tiptoed into the drawing room, she discovered her mother hidden behind the great Diana screen, drinking in a circle of light. It was almost as if Nella were waiting to ambush her. *Damn mothers and their intuition!*

"Lina tells me you're not well."

"I just finished my moon."

"Get lots of rest. Tomorrow is your big night."

"*Yo sé,* Mamá."

"Have you decided what you're going to tell Lamar?"

"Sí."

Hetty pulled her kimono tighter and let the silence stretch out uncomfortably. Her mother eyed her suspiciously from a haze of light.

"Esther, have I ever told you the fable of the fox and the coyote?"

"I don't think so."

"I'm sure I did when you were a child. It was one of your grandmother's favorites. I think it's time you heard it again. Sit down for a minute."

Hetty didn't want to do anything to make her mother wary, so she crawled in among the silk cushions on the sofa. Nella finished her drink, fished ice cubes out of a bucket, and poured in more scotch. But Hetty knew she wouldn't drink much of it. She had seen this happen many times before. Nella would get so involved in the imaginative process of acting out her story that the cubes would melt down like candles on an altar. And indeed, in Nella's expressive hands, the retelling of one of these ancient tales did reach the level of cherished rite, as it had with her mother before her, who'd brought the tradition with her from across the Rio Grande.

"This is how it goes. The fox and the coyote were enemies, constantly dodging each other under the light of the full moon. One night, the thirsty fox stole up to the edge of a *laguna* in which *la luna* was reflected. As she was about to drink, she spotted another face mirrored on the surface. It was the ugly gray coyote, teeth bared, poised to eat her. Now La Zorra was a great beauty, her slanted brown eyes and auburn fur glistening in the pale light. She turned her delicate snout up and asked: '*Tío,* what do you see in the pond?'

"He looked down and spotted the moon. 'I see a large round flan, *chica,*' he growled, 'swimming in a bowl of caramel.'

" 'I *adore* flan!' said the fox, preening. 'Will you fetch it for us, *Tío?* We can share it and then you can eat me after.'

"The coyote, none too wise, thought for a moment and said, 'How shall I do that?'

" 'By diving into the delicious caramel and grabbing it with your strong teeth, of course.' At that, the coyote threw himself into the water, and the flan melted into a million pieces. He pulled himself out, chilled to the bone, howling '*¡Yi-yi!*' and chasing the fox through the prickly pear with fury in his eyes."

Nella recited all the ways the cunning fox got the best of the thickheaded coyote, tricking him with firecrackers, scorpions, and thorns. For her final revenge, La Zorra waited until the church bells had rung midnight and led him, in bright moonlight, through the town plaza and into the Municipal Palace. He followed her bushy tail into the *sala de baile,* relishing the thought of devouring her. But the coyote was awed by the splendor of the ballroom, the ornate musicians' gallery above, the red silk on the walls, and, above all, the gleaming mirrors. He had never seen a mirror and was bewitched.

"Everywhere he looked, coyotes looked back at him," Nella said, "doing the same thing he was doing. But then he saw another pack behind them, a pack of foxes snickering at him. La Zorra stood on her hind legs in the middle of the great room, holding her belly with laughter. When he remembered how he'd been fooled by her, he took chunks of fallen plaster and broke all the mirrors, but that didn't stop the laughter. He could still see bits of fox faces leering back at him, like a cubist painting, so he leaped into one of the broken mirrors to attack La Zorra and was cut to pieces by the shards of glass."

Nella paused and seemed surprised to notice that her drink was watered down. "And that was how *Tío* Coyote came to his end. . . ."

Hetty watched her mother, puzzled. "That's all?" she asked. "Could you explain that to me in plain Spanish?"

"Fables can't be explained, darling. That's why they're fables."

"So who am I? The fox or the coyote?"

"I'd say that's up to you."

"*Ay, madre.* I don't understand you—you speak in parables."

"Sometimes, Esther, it's the only way. *El que sabe, sabe.*"

He who knows, knows.

Hetty awoke out of restless sleep to lie frightened in bed, watching for the first pale light of day to appear at her window. When it came, sudden, blue, she forced herself to get up and dress in utter silence, afraid even to breathe too loud lest she wake up another member of the family. After making her bed, she placed on it the three pouches of jewels in a row along with the letter she'd finally penned to Lamar.

With a suitcase in each hand, she tiptoed to the front door and was just about to open it, when she turned and was startled by something moving. She let her breath out. It was only her own image turning to look at itself in the foyer's round pink mirror. In this gloom it looked mauve, her face pale as a winter moon about to set, her eyes two haunted black stars. She could see the fear that darkened them, knowing that if she crossed this threshold to be married to Garret MacBride she might never be welcome to return. She would miss the ball tonight at Ima's pink palace, break the heart of the prince, and be banished forever from the kingdom of No-Tsu-Oh. But somehow, she didn't care. She wasn't going to let Nella and her fables intimidate her. *El que sabe, sabe,* indeed. She knew exactly what she wanted. She flung the door back and let the warm lights of the hotel hallway pull her out into the day.

Later that morning, she and Garret stood together in a deserted courtroom of the old City Hall on Travis Street, listening to the justice of the peace read from a black book in his hands. Hetty wasn't expecting much—she assumed that a civil ceremony would be brief and impersonal, allowing her to remain detached. But what she hadn't counted on was that the current justice, William Ward Kinkaid, was a kind greathearted man, bearded and blessed with one of those deep sweet Texan voices that can melt any woman's reserve.

"We have come together here today," he read, "in the sight o' God, to witness the joinin' o' two hearts."

He went on to ignore the book and talk to them like a father would about the commitment they were making. He spoke to Garret, reminding him of his duty to protect and provide for his new wife, then he turned to Hetty and out of his mouth came words that took on radiant new meaning: "Hetty, as Garret's wife, you must share your life completely, lettin' the joys o' each be the joys o' both, and the sorrows o' each the sorrows o' both."

When Justice Kinkaid intoned the next part—"Into this holy union these two souls come now to be joined"—his voice resounded with such vibrancy that she yearned deeply for the moment to become holy, become truly holy. She looked to the side and saw only rows of empty benches and pale, vacuous light that filtered down so unfeelingly from the drab windows. *No one knows I'm getting married,* she thought. *There's no one here to celebrate with us*. Her own mother and sister wouldn't even know that she had left the house until they went into her room and found her bed made up, tidy but vacant, scarred with a guilty letter to Lamar. Most girls are given away by their fathers. Suddenly, she wanted hers there, passing her on to the man she loved. She longed for Kirb's blessing, knowing she had lost it forever. *How can I get it back?*

When the justice asked her if she took Garret as her lawfully wedded husband, loving and respecting him and being faithful to him as long as they both should live, the courtroom around her seemed so vast and empty that her own voice felt far too small to fill it as she uttered a shattered "I do." And when he said the final words, "By the authority vested in me by the laws o' the state of Texas, I now pronounce y'all man and wife," she couldn't even kiss Garret but could only hold on to him tightly, hiding her face and bawling, trying to draw enough warmth out of his body to fill all of the four hollow chambers in her heart.

Chapter 5

Hetty remained tearful all through lunch with her new husband. "Maybe chaos wasn't such a good idea, after all," she sniffled, pulling a lace hankie out of her purse. She couldn't lift herself out of the dumps until, two hours later, they crossed the long Galveston Island Causeway. There's nothing like a bridge, she realized, to transport one into a new state of mind. As they rose higher and higher, she looked through the window and saw nothing but bay water underneath, washing them away from land and all connections. She breathed in deeply and smelled the ocean up ahead, splashing its salty scent far inland. When they finally hit the island and sped by the lush oleanders, she felt the sea winds blowing away her old life and its restrictions, leaving her buoyant and free. Billboards welcomed them to the Playground of the South—by map only an hour or so from Houston but in attitude and atmosphere a continent away.

They drove down the seawall boulevard and up to the portals of the Galvez Hotel, lifting its white tropical spires high over the beach. Down below, flags flapped on the gaudy bathhouses and palm leaves fanned in the breeze while the endless surf surged across the sand under the white wings of seagulls lifting.

As Hetty stepped out of the Auburn and walked under the great white archways of the Galvez, she felt light-headed and leaned against Garret's shoulder. She still couldn't believe she was a bride—not until they checked into the bridal suite and the bellboy referred to her as "Mrs. MacBride." That made it official, along with the toile wallpaper, the gigantic bed, and the long gauzy drapes rippling like waterfalls at the tall windows opened across the front of the hotel. They stood in front of them as soon as they were alone, kissing amid the whispering silks.

Before they could sample room service, Hetty knew she had to call home. Her finger trembled slightly as she dialed the operator to place the call. She noticed that her nails needed doing. She lit a Lucky Strike to calm her nerves.

Nella answered the phone herself.

"Mamá, it's your daughter."

"Tu ni eres mi hija. ¡Puta! Has perdido el privilegio. Jamás quiero hablar contigo. ¡Imbécil! Nunca me vuelvas a llamar."

Hetty heard a thud, then the dial tone. She set the receiver down. "Uh-oh. She's really mad. She's cursing in Spanish."

"What did she say?"

"She called me a name I won't translate and said that I wasn't her daughter anymore. She told me never to call back."

"Wait five minutes and do just that."

While Garret called down for a pot of coffee and some chocolate cake, Hetty watched the hands of the clock on the bedside table inch forward as she tortured her cigarette.

"Do you think it's been long enough?"

Garret handed her the receiver. Hetty lit another Lucky and placed the call.

"Yes."

"Don't hang up on me, Mamá."

"Are you *embarazada?*"

"No! Why would you even think that? Garret's been a perfect gentleman."

"Because that's the first thing anybody thinks when a girl runs away. Don't you know that? *¡Estúpida! ¡Tonta! ¡Imbécil! Ay,* as usual you're only thinking of yourself, not the shame you've brought on our family. *¡Qué vergüenza!*"

"You left me no choice, Mamá."

"Choice? You dare to talk to me about choice? *¡Eres una sin vergüenza!* This was not my choice. Not this, *m'ija.* Never this. To abandon your family, your friends. To bring disgrace on the Allen name."

"How's Dad taking it?"

"How do you think? He locked himself in his study and won't come out."

"Send him a bottle of whiskey from me."

"No, *m'ija,* not that easy. He'll never forgive you. Have you so little respect for marriage? And for Lamar?"

"I left him a letter."

"Yes, he's here, *pobrecito.*"

"He's there? Let me speak to him."

"You've hurt him enough—*tienes la sangre bien fría*. Your poor sister is comforting him. *¡Qué barbaridad!*"

"Oh, don't be such a flat tire, Mamá," Hetty said, the Lucky dangling from her lips. "I haven't committed murder. I only got married."

"*Ay,* but you have committed murder. You are dead to me and to this family. *¡Muerta!*"

Nella's voice was like a bell tolling a dirge, rattling Hetty's composure. She hung up. When she snuffed her butt in the hotel ashtray, her hands shook. Garret took them in his and tried to console her. When the room service cart came clattering in, he made her eat some cake along with a cup of black coffee loaded with sugar. They talked it through until Hetty calmed down enough to paint her nails so they could dry before dinner in the crisp Gulf breeze.

Hetty spent the afternoon unpacking and hanging up her dresses, fending off her new husband's advances till she was in a more romantic mood. When the light changed colors, he called her to the windows. She looked out at the ocean turning purple. He said he knew what would cheer her up and pointed to a long pier that snaked out over the Gulf of Mexico. Its pagodalike roof rose high against the sunset sky, the waters underneath shimmering with

Japanese lanterns being lit in the twilight—the Balinese Room casino, where the roulette wheels whirled until dawn.

They made their way down the long pier, past two guards who nodded and smiled. Finally they came up to a ponderous door with a small window in the middle. Garret knocked. After a long pause, the little window opened and he gave his name. There was a grunt of recognition. They entered breathlessly into a dimly lit windowless room, initiates into pleasures that were rare and forbidden back on the mainland.

Garret purchased a hundred dollars' worth of chips and signaled the attendant to start them on their round of cocktails, mixed with liquor smuggled onto shore and unloaded right below their feet. "The tables?" Garret murmured into her ear. "They're hollow underneath." In case of a raid, the tops were turned over, and the chips, the dice, the smoking ashtrays, and the tumblers filled with bootleg cocktails all went sliding off the tabletops and fell directly downward into the waters.

Hetty drank along with Garret as he gambled, kissed him when he won, groaned with him when he lost, and felt herself getting drunker by the minute. *Nella was so Edwardian!* she thought as she lit a cigarette. This was just the sort of fun she'd known she could have with a man like Garret. She felt safe with him, even in a wild place like this.

After a while she became bored. She kept glancing over at the more glamorous roulette wheels where even Shebas like herself were having fun playing the odds. Garret had been winning regularly placing pass line bets and big eights, but he hadn't made any of the spectacular free-odds wagers he often bragged about. She nudged him. "You're not taking any chances."

"Oh? Then wish me luck." He turned and gave her a French kiss she felt all the way to her feet. He bet half his chips on the line laying odds of two to one.

Hetty was thrilled. She hugged his arm and whispered in his ear, "Good luck, darling."

The dice cup rattled like a snake about to strike as the shooter shook it a couple of times and made a toss. The whole table watched in silence as the dice bounced off the back wall and landed on the green felt. One of them turned up a five. The other slid under a curling dollar bill near Hetty, its skyward face hidden. The dealer motioned for her to uncover it.

"Carefully," he whispered.

Everyone stared at her hand as she gingerly lifted the dollar bill away without tipping the die. Thank God she'd done her nails that afternoon! She was admiring the way her pink polish glimmered against the green baize of the table when suddenly everyone around her was cheering. She hadn't even noticed what she'd revealed: five more spots. The shooter had made his point. Garret let out a great yelp and pulled her to him. "Do you realize this will pay for that damn bridal suite?"

They dined on raw oysters overlooking the waters. The dance floor was crowned by palms with coconuts wired for electric light. Couples swayed in a fox-trot to "One Sweet Letter from You," played by the traveling swing rhythms of the Kensington Hall Orchestra.

Hetty pulled Garret up for the next Charleston. She wore long dangling earrings, and her shimmering satin dress had a draped girdle finished with a cascade of large loops that kicked and jiggled along with her flying heels. About halfway through the following number, the band swung into a waltz rendition of the wedding march. Hetty noticed everyone leaving the dance floor as a bright spotlight blinded her. She frowned at Garret.

"I can't help it, Hetty. They know me around here."

Hetty felt a blush rising with a fury into her cheeks. A man whistled loudly. In the crowd just off the dance floor, his face came into clear focus—a sharp jaw undercutting dark, dangerous eyes.

"It's your wedding night, Mac," he shouted hoarsely.

"Mac, Mac, Mac." He started a chant and was joined by other men ganging around him. They all had the same sinister swagger, rude and well-groomed.

The saxophone careened around her ears and the drinks set her head to spinning in the noise of the crowd. It suddenly hit her what she'd done that day—she'd *eloped*. Run away. Her mother's words echoed with a hollow sound through the caves of her mind: *To abandon your family, your friends—have you so little respect?* She lost her breath for a moment; her knees started to give. She inhaled deeply and felt a wave of clammy air wash across the room, smelling of damp, salty things like mollusks and moon snails. Garret caught Hetty in his arms and slipped out of the room with her as the bartender pulled a fish through the hole in the floor and displayed it, smiling, for all to see.

They walked away from the night-lights and followed the surf along in silence, into the deserted darkness.

She peeled off her silk stockings and shoes to wade in the water. She wanted to lose herself in it, to slide deep into the brine and leave her dress billowing on the surface like a silken jellyfish. She started humming the wedding march.

He stripped off his shoes and socks, too, rolled up his pinstriped pants, and waded out to her.

She turned her face up to his. He ran his hands along her bare arms. He kissed her as a new wave swirled in around their feet, releasing into the air its underwater scent of sargassum and clams.

She looked down.

"God, was I blushing!"

"It's okay, kiddo. It's the first night of your honeymoon."

"How come so many people know you in there?"

"My partner and I do a lot of business here."

"People were shouting your name—*strangers.* Those—men . . ."

Garret shrugged. Her cheeks still felt hot when she thought about it. She laid one on his chest, cool from the dank Galveston air. The alcohol was wearing off, and her mood sagged. She closed her eyes and let him hold her for a few moments. When she opened them again, she saw a curl of a crescent moon tingling the sea with light.

"Galveston a little too racy for you? Want to leave? Baby want to go home, coochie-coo?" He tickled her chin and made her chuckle.

"Not on your life, Mr. MacBride." A new wave hit them. The bubbles felt like champagne on her feet.

* * *

Lights still played up and down the shore, music drifted in with the sound of the surf, a banjo strummed far off somewhere, a strain of jazz slanted off the water like the tawdry light of electric bulbs strung up along Murdoch's Pleasure Pier.

When they entered their suite, the lights were off and only the Gulf winds and the pale reflections of the sea washed into the room. Garret laid her softly into the bed and gently peeled her dress down and off. It billowed in the breeze as he lifted it up. That was what Hetty remembered most of all about that night—the scent and flow of those Galveston winds that drifted through the dark room, laden with sea scents and cool moisture and the lost chords of dim, echoed music.

After he'd undressed, there was the perfect counterpoint of temperatures in their vigil, the cool winds flowing over them through the open Gulf windows and, close to her, the pervading tropical warmth of his body. She'd never been completely naked with him before, had never been able to wrap her arms and legs around the full stretch of his skin.

As she did so, she trembled.

She had lived through this moment so often in fantasy that she didn't imagine it would hold any surprises. But it did. There were things Wini hadn't told her.

As he slowly ran his hand down her opening thighs, she felt herself being aroused in subtly threatening ways, all deep and undreamed of. They exchanged genital kisses, and she lingered over his hard cock, taking it deep into her mouth, letting him push her head down on it with his big hands. Then, he took over, ripping the controls right out of her hands. She handed them over to him easily, even eagerly. She was prey willingly trapped, at the same time frightened and enthralled. When he entered her, she groaned with the pain of being pierced slowly by his thrusts, but the pain soon mingled with a mounting pleasure. She clung to him and buried her face in his neck as he penetrated her deeper and deeper. He pulled her legs up as far as they would go and pinned her under him. Welling out of her throat came sounds she'd never heard herself making.

Yes, she was seeing it all now: Sex wasn't just petting with all your clothes off. There was more to it than that. She had to tell Wini. Here you were dealing with lock and key finality, with realms of authority and jurisdiction—ownership even. She was getting her most secret wish right then and there: to be ravished, really and truly ravished, not just toyed with. But in order for this to happen, she had to become submissive, completely and totally submissive. The bed rocked like the waves out in the ocean. She heard them break on the beach down below. *Obey,* they thundered.

From then on, it was an open course through the rest of their honeymooning week in the Queen City of the South. They slept in every morning, dubbing their room the MacBridal Suite. There was a host of cinemas to see: Garbo in *The Divine Woman; Ladies of the Mob,* starring Clara Bow; the spectacular melodrama *Noah's Ark,* with Ronald Colman. There were a dozen places for dancing: You could go slumming at the Tokio, downtown to the speakeasy Roseland, or back to the beach for balls at the Crystal Palace on the sands. Garret took her shopping, drove her along Post Office Street to see the brothels, then for a freshwater swim at the Crystal Palace. Balconies surrounded the pool on all sides leading up to the roof, filled with spectators admiring the girls below in their newly daring one-piece bathing costumes.

Garret swung on the rings in his black tank top, then did something that surprised her. He climbed the ladder to the high dive and stood there dripping wet in front of the fully dressed spectators. He did a push-off so high Hetty thought the board was going to crack, then sprang way up into the air where, to her surprise, he floated for a few breathless moments in the most beautiful swan dive she'd ever seen. It was elegant, weightless, Olympic. People pointed. He sliced into the water without a ripple, then bobbed up gasping right in front of her.

"Where did you learn to dive like that?" she asked him after the applause died down.

"In Missoula. At the university. My folks sent me."

She gaped at him as if he were a stranger. "Your folks . . . ?"

He wiped water off his face. "Arleen. And Termite."

"Termite? That's kind of an unusual name for a senator, isn't it?"

"That was his nickname." Mac rolled into the swaying water.

"And your mother? Arleen?"

After a few moments, he floated in front of Hetty, blowing water out of his mouth. "Talk to me, Mac!"

"She still lives in Butte," he sputtered.

"So were you on the diving team?"

"For a year."

"Why did you quit? You could have gone to the Olympics!"

"That's not a story for our honeymoon," he said, and sank beneath the water.

Hetty simmered with unsatisfied lust. For two days, Garret had been daring her to swim to the sandbar beyond the other bathers. He promised her a wild time out there in the Gulf, but she was afraid of sharks and the purple Portuguese men-of-war she'd seen washed up on the beach like deflated balloons. He kept reassuring her with his confident laughter, arousing her with lotions and massage. As the shadows grew, so did the itch in her loins. She decided it was now or never.

"I'm ready," she announced. Garret leaped out of his beach chair and drew her toward the water. As they passed the lifeguard stand, he pointed up to the sky and shouted back at them, "The seagulls are circling. Bad weather's coming." She could hardly hear his voice in the whiffle of the wind.

"Com'on," Garret urged, pulling her in deeper. She caught her breath and plunged into a breaking wave.

The sandbar was not as far out as she'd feared. It was shallow enough for Garret to stand with his shoulders out of the water and lift her up onto his thighs. She hoped the lifeguard could still make out their tiny heads bobbing in the distance.

They were out beyond the point where the waves crest and break; here there was just the gentle roll of the water, rocking them softly in its shifting back and forth—an incessant, almost erotic roll and return all around them. She clung to him there, her body rocking against his flesh, riding him astride, frantic with desire as he slipped her bathing suit up and off and started exploring her labia with his fingers.

She looked beyond him to the beach and to the spires of the Galvez Hotel and to the sky beyond, where blue rain clouds gathered as the hot haze of the day rose higher and higher to focus the light through a prism of pastels. As Hetty watched, a radiant pink spanned out from the setting sun to spangle the clouds and the enormous wingspans of laughing gulls that wheeled in a giant spiral above them. *Finally!* she exalted. *My life is like a Fauve painting.*

Amid the revel of their caws, Hetty heard her own voice rising again with those uncontrollable sounds seeking release, the release she'd longed for all week. She looked at Garret for some sign, some direction. He knew exactly what to do. He touched her in all the right places, over and over, faster and faster until he brought her peaking with his fingers alone. Her hips moved of their own accord, unleashing the wild beast inside. Like a wave that begins unnoticed out at sea and rushes toward the land, rolling forward and building up its speed until it comes with a sudden sliding thrust sideways, she felt herself break for the first time in her life with orgasm.

She clung to him out of breath, all her doubts dissolving, bound to her man by a silver cord of pleasure and gratitude.

Even after the sun set that night, it was too hot to be indoors, so Garret pulled off Stewart Road and headed for a brightly lit billboard that read: *Greyhound Races at Texas's Only Turf.* He nosed the speedster slowly through the crowd gathering around the grandstand, Hetty sitting up on the back of the seat like a celebrity, hoping to cool off in the salty Gulf breeze. She noticed the headlights of a black car following them. They parked where they weren't supposed to, found a spot at the rail, placed reckless bets, and cheered as the sleek animals flashed by. In the lulls, music floated down on the sultry evening air from a dance floor atop the grandstand, where a band called the Merrymakers never missed a beat.

They emerged an hour later, poorer and drunker, to find two

black cars stacked as bookends to the Auburn. They were parked so close Garret couldn't budge an inch. He lit a Camel, cursed, and blasted the horn several times. One by one, almost unseen, men begin slipping into the cars without saying anything until they could make out several dark heads huddled in the seats. Only one of them looked their way. Hetty recognized the razor chin and cagey eyes of the fellow who'd embarrassed her the first night at the Balinese Room. He seemed to be their leader; at least he'd taken the wheel of the front car and was the one who'd led them in that rude chant the other night. *"Mac, Mac, Mac,"* they'd jeered over and over, making her blush all the more. The lights of the two black cars came on, and they edged out. The rear car hugged Garret's bumper, while the front one blocked his every move to try and pass or turn off Steward Road. He was grimly silent.

Hetty felt panic swoop through her like bats in the humid night. "Weren't these the fellows at the Balinese Room? Who are they?"

"Rose's Night Riders."

"Rose?"

"Poppa Rose. Rosario Maceo. He and his brother, Sam, own the Balinese Room. Don't worry—he's a friend of mine."

"You're friends with the Maceos?" She'd heard the name before, of course. The closest thing Texas had to a Mafia was the Maceo family, Sicilians who ran the rackets that made Galveston such a romantic destination. "Are we in trouble here, honey?"

"I don't think so. Just stay calm." He tried to reassure her, but fear quivered in his voice and leaped into Hetty's mind like a grass fire jumping a ravine. *A little too much chaos, thank you!* The numbers on the street signs began to climb way past the area she was familiar with, the convoy passing 49th Street, 53rd, 57th, until there were no more street signs and they were outside the city limits, plunging down a dark empty road.

Then—tall, abrupt—stucco posts loomed out of a lush garden. Cars passed through massive wrought iron gates and pulled up under the portico of a graceful white Spanish villa. Hetty blinked two or three times to clear her vision. There were acres of oleanders and, in the moment before the car lights flicked off, bananas hanging low under broad green leaves.

Everyone got out, the men from the other two cars swarming around them silently, efficiently. Garret held her arm as they were ushered inside and the man with the eyes she didn't like introduced himself to her: "My name's Silvio. Rose sent me. You're his guests." Arches led in all directions, and the other men melted into them like vapors.

When Hetty realized they weren't going to be hurt, she relaxed a little and let Garret lead her on a tour conducted by Silvio—amazed by what she saw. Her fear melted into awe. She thought they had discovered all the best spots in Galveston, but Garret hadn't told her about this one, and it was by far the best. There were people everywhere, and a classy crowd, too, which surprised her considering the desolate location. When they came to the threshold of the dining room, Hetty knew she'd had way too much to drink.

"Dining and dancing for five hundred," Silvio said. "*The* five hundred."

They stood for a moment while Hetty gaped. The hall seemed endless. Multitudes of well-heeled diners feasted at tables circling an immense polished dance floor, lit by the soft glow of crystal chandeliers with tiny multicolored lights. She could hear a band somewhere and watched, wide-eyed, as waiters passed them hoisting trays of cocktails and flutes bubbling and dripping with champagne.

"But . . . where do all these people come from?"

Silvio exchanged smiles with Garret. "Nothing like this in Kansas, honey. You notice it's air cooled." He unfolded a hand with a flourish, and Hetty realized for the first time that she was no longer sweating. The air all around them felt like it was being fanned out of an icebox. She shot him a puzzled glance. He just laughed. "Welcome to the Free State of Galveston."

They came up to a table near the stage that must have had a dozen chairs upholstered in bold zebra stripes. They were occupied by four or five immaculately dressed men, each of whom had a Mediterranean beauty at his arm, women with clear olive skins and the kind of tangled, dark manes of luxuriant hair Hetty hadn't seen on women since she was a child. No one acknowledged them until Silvio bent down and mumbled something into the ear of the swarthy man at the head of the table. He rose to greet them, suntanned, smiling, everything tailored to a T except for the nostrils that swelled out of proportion to everything else.

"Hey, Mac, Mac!" he beamed. "I'm glad Silvio found you. So this is the new bride."

"Honey, meet Sam Maceo."

Hetty took his proffered hand and smiled, not knowing what to say. The usual "Nice to meet you" would have felt naive in this setting, so instead she asked, "And which one's Poppa Rose?"

Silvio raised his voice. "Rosario, say hello." And a man down the table with the same bulbous nose but more gray in his hair waved at her. The women didn't look up.

Sam Maceo draped an arm around her shoulders as if they were old friends. The snout was right in her face, and he was chuckling. His skin looked very greasy. "I'll bet you like roulette wheels, don't you, hon?"

She tried to lean her head away from him a little. "Did my husband tell you that? I'm annoyed with him for not bringing me here sooner."

"Mac's been a very bad boy," he muttered and pulled her a little closer. "But Uncle Sam's going to make it up to you, sweetheart. I'm going to let Silvio take you into the back room and set you up at the wheel as my personal guest. On the house. What do you say?"

"Oh boy." She laughed, turning her face from him. "But isn't Mac coming, too?"

He patted her on the back as he pulled his hand away. "Mac's going to stay here with me, sweetheart. We need to talk."

Hetty looked at her husband, who just shrugged and said, "You know me. I like craps."

Then a scrawny man was escorted to the table and introduced to her as Prairie Dog. He kept glancing around the room through greasy horn-rim glasses and had to be asked twice to sit down in one of the chairs. Garret seemed to know him. Hetty wanted to take his glasses off and clean them.

The back room was a lot quieter, with gamers intent on their bets. Silvio found Hetty a spot with a stool and an ashtray at one corner of the double-ended table. He got the croupier to issue her a rack crammed with yellow chips and brought her the first of many glasses of the best champagne she'd ever tasted. Then he left her to amuse herself for an hour or more at the game she found so entrancing, hypnotized by the *clickety-clack* of the little white ball spinning round and round the whirl of black and red.

Later, Hetty hunted through the whole club for Garret. She found him outside the front entrance, pacing around the car smoking.

"Ready?" he said curtly.

Coming out of the air-cooled club, the warm air made her reel. She could hear the ocean churning out there in the darkness. She hugged her husband around the waist. "Oh, honey," she said dreamily, "don't you want to dance with your little wife?"

"Let's just get out of here."

She hiccupped. "Can we come back here, honey? Pleeeease!"

"We're not members" was his only answer.

Mid-morning, Hetty woke to the sound of drops pelting against the windows. Thin sticks of lightning ripped open the belly of the clouds and a piñata of rain poured down. She could smell the sweetness of ozone in the air. She groped for Garret, but he wasn't beside her. She glanced around the room. He was standing at the windows, smoking and not noticing that the windowsills were getting wet. She pulled on a robe and went over to close the windows, glancing up at his face. He looked tired. She couldn't face the discussion she knew they were going to have until she'd fortified herself with some caffeine. She ordered breakfast from room service and got dressed. When the trolley came rolling in, she tipped the bellboy and went straight for the coffee, pouring a cup for both her and Garret.

"Look, honey, I've got to make a run tonight," he said, coming over. "I'll only be gone a couple of hours."

Hetty buttered a slice of toast and spread strawberry jam on it. She held it in front of her face, ready to take a bite. "My, this has been a short honeymoon."

"I'm sorry. I know the timing's bad, but I can't help it. I'll make it up to you. We'll go downstairs. I'll order you the best dinner they have—six courses. I'll leave when you start the soup and be back by the time you finish dessert and coffee. I'll stash a bottle of Mumm in the room—you won't even miss me."

Hetty's head still throbbed in spite of the coffee. "Uh-uh. No more champagne."

The phone rang. Garret strode over to the bedside table and snatched up the handset. "Yeah," he barked into the mouthpiece. "I don't care, Odell. I'm going. Prairie Dog and me are going out together. You know, the buddy system." There was a long pause. Hetty chewed on her toast. Strawberry seeds got caught in her teeth. "Don't worry. Dog will cover me." The handset rattled as he dropped it into its cradle.

"Who was that?"

"My partner, Odell."

"Odell?"

"Odell Weems. I told you I had a partner."

"If he's your partner, why isn't he coming with you?"

"I told you—it's just business. Stay out of it."

She dropped the limp remains of her toast. "I'm not staying out of it."

"Yes, you are."

"No, I'm not." They glared at each other in silence. Thunder grumbled overhead. Hetty couldn't believe he was clamming up like this after the closeness they'd shared the last few days and after the scare they'd been through last night. She didn't know what he was hiding, but she found his evasive answers exasperating.

"Baby, what I do is illegal."

Hetty just laughed. "Oh, please. Don't be such a flat tire. Nobody believes in these liquor laws but Baptists. Com'on, Mac. You've turned me into a woman—now treat me like one."

Garret gave her a sidelong look and sighed. "Okay. Two schooners are coming in tonight from British Honduras with a shit load of hooch. I've got to take the boat out."

"Out where?"

"Where do you think, Hetty? The three-mile line."

"In the Gulf?"

"Well, of course. They're not going to deliver the stuff to my hotel room. They have to stay out in International Waters. I need to do this, honey. This is how I make my living," he said. Then he thought better of it and added, "At the moment. The less you know, the better."

The dismissive tone in his voice made Hetty go white-hot inside. "You're right. I'm just your little debutante wife who shouldn't fill her pretty head with all these nasty details. Why don't I just go back to Houston until you finish your business and then maybe we can resume our marriage. Better yet, maybe we *won't* resume our marriage. I'm sure Lamar would like to hear that it failed."

He shot her a reproachful glance. "That's not fair."

"You're right. It's not. But neither is keeping secrets. I feel shut out and don't want you coming near me at the moment."

"All right." He let out a sigh of resignation. "I'll tell you what's going on—against my better judgment. Sam and Rose don't want us going out to the big boats anymore. They want to bring everything in to a fish camp and sell it to us from there."

"Won't that be easier?"

"Yeah, if you don't mind paying twice the price. Those Sicilians must think I'm a sucker. They want to mark everything up double what we pay off the boats. I can't make any money that way. Neither can Prairie Dog."

"Why do you call him that?"

" 'Cause he comes all the way down here from Kansas. Besides, he looks like one."

"So you and Prairie Dog are sailing out anyway?"

"Goddamn yes. I have just as much right to be out there as they do. It's International Waters. They may own Galveston, but they don't own the whole damn ocean."

"I see," she said. "You're not going to let anybody tell Garret MacBride what to do."

"Why should I?"

So this isn't about business, Hetty thought. *It's a pissing contest between a bunch of boys. To find out who's got the strongest stream.* She was beginning to realize what accessories came along with Garret's make and model of manhood. The same power that attracted her—the engine that ran him with such a roar—could also veer out of control and crash. She remembered the tennis game with Lamar, how he'd refused to back away from it and lost. She didn't want to see that happen again. "Let's call your partner."

"You'll meet him when we go back to Houston, I promise."

"No, I want to talk to him before you make this run. To find out why he's not coming along. Why don't we just ring up, uh—what's his name, Del?"

"Odell." He clenched his jaw, the way he always did when he was trying to assert his will. "I wish you'd let me handle this."

"I don't want to be that kind of wife, Garret. You might as well learn that right now. We tempt fortune together or forget it."

He stared at her speechless, the wounded look being edged out by a new glint of recognition. She could tell he'd underestimated her, hadn't realized how far she was willing to turn the wheel and stake everything on the outcome. Somehow it hadn't occurred to him that he could have a partner in the game, someone to share the risk he'd always taken alone. But she could see it in his eyes now: He was willing to open a forbidden door, invite her into the realms of authority and let her play. He gave her one of those intense looks, the kind that made her mother's prediction come true: "The eye is a sex organ." As she held his gaze and went wet between the legs, she realized: *This doesn't need to cool our marriage down but could heat it up even more.* She went over to him, took the twisted cigarette out of his hand, and kissed his tobacco-scented lips for a long time. Then they placed the call.

"Odell, I'd like you to meet my wife, Hetty." He handed her the receiver. The sound that floated up into her ear wasn't what she had expected. She'd imagined some kind of rough patter, a dark voice rising from the underworld with a gangster's guttural pitch. What she heard instead was a charming drawl, the speech of a Southern gentleman who'd gone to good schools and traveled the world. He used words like *esplanade* and *coterie*. He complimented her, regaled her with stories, and referred to Garret as "an invaluable asset to our enterprise."

"I hear you're not joining him on his little expedition tonight," she said.

"I may be audacious, my dear, but I'm not suicidal. The problem with men Garret's age is that they still think they're invincible. I have failed to dissuade him from this foolhardy jaunt. I'm afraid the burden falls to you now. My dear young lady, whatever you do, you mustn't let him out of that hotel room tonight. Miscreants in Maceo territory have a strange way of disappearing. Our adversaries don't countenance disobedience. Do I make myself clear?"

"I didn't realize my wifely duties would start so soon."

"They have to, if you still want to be able to refer to yourself by that blessed name, rather than another more mournful one that also starts with a *w*. I cannot emphasize this enough. Do we understand each other?"

"I'm afraid so," Hetty said, and slowly handed the receiver back to Garret. He said good-bye, and they spent the afternoon in bed. They felt closer than they'd ever been, wrapped in the covers, listening to the rain.

"You want to know why I chose you over Lamar?" she asked.

"Yes."

"Because I always felt safe with you, Garret. That's why I love you so much. The feel of you, the smell of you. It made me feel secure, taken care of. Like when you took me out to the sandbar. I would never do that alone, but with you, I can set my fears aside and do the wildest things."

"I'll always take care of you," he said tenderly.

"Before today, I would've believed that. But I can't tonight. That's just it, honey. I don't feel safe anymore. I feel afraid. Afraid for your life." She pictured him walking out of the hotel room door into the dark night. Trembling, she clung to him. She couldn't let go of his warm, fragrant body, the body she'd covered with kisses this week, the body she'd learned to adore. The thought of that body never being found again, not even to bury, sliced her heart in half. *The other word,* Odell had said, *the mournful word that also starts with a* w. She knew what the *w* stood for, and she said it. "Don't make me a widow on my honeymoon, Garret. I'm begging you!"

He cradled her for a while in silence. Then he finally said, "Does it really mean that much to you?"

"Everything."

Garret picked up the handset and called Prairie Dog. "I'm not coming," he said. "Be careful."

When Hetty woke the next morning, the bed was empty beside her. She could see a tinge of blue through the gauzy drapes. She lay there, unable to move, fear cutting into her belly like the edge of a dull knife. She was afraid Garret had snuck out in the night and betrayed their pact. But soon, she heard the key turning in the lock. He came in and stood wordlessly in the shadows for a moment. Then he walked over and sat on the bed beside her. He flicked on the lamp and handed her a pair of horn-rim glasses. The grease identified them as Prairie Dog's. But something else spotted them along with the grease. Trickles of dark red. With a shock, Hetty realized it was dried blood.

"They found his boat," Garret said. "But they didn't find him."

She buried her face in her husband's legs and mourned for poor, ugly Prairie Dog, whom she'd only met once.

"I think we need to leave Galveston now," he said, stroking her hair. "How long will it take you to pack?"

"Minutes."

When the bellhop came to collect their luggage, Hetty glanced around the room to be sure she hadn't forgotten anything. "Goodbye, MacBridal suite," she said sadly.

As they drove down Seawall Boulevard, the streets were almost empty in the dawn. The rain had swept everything clean. The summer sun was steaming away the dark clouds in the east, burning its way through. It gleamed in puddles along the side of the road. Hetty kept glancing back, expecting to see a car following them. She prayed that they would make it to the causeway before they were spotted. As they turned northwest, she looked back into the rising sun and tried to draw its light after them. Lots of shadows still lurked down the side streets that could well up and swallow them. Garret didn't say a word, just drove as fast as he dared along Broadway. Hetty could see the causeway up ahead, clear sunlight striking it first. There was only one stretch of highway left. Not a car passed them either way. She looked into the oleanders lining the boulevard to see if any black sedans were waiting there to chase after them. She saw only pink blossoms dragging the wet branches down.

She could hardly let herself breathe until they reached the foot of the causeway. Then they rose into the light, they lifted above the waters and the peril, and they headed toward their new home.

Chapter 6

Hetty wanted to go straight to Garret's place so she could see where they would begin their married life together. She needed the reassurance of a home base, a roof to shelter her from the storm clouds that had gathered over Galveston. She knew that Garret lived in the Heights, a neighborhood she wasn't too familiar with since it lay across the bayou in Houston. She wondered what his bachelor abode would be like. As messy as most men's quarters? Or would he surprise her and dress his surroundings the same way he dressed himself, with a kind of flinty charm? She couldn't wait to unpack, get settled in, and see how many closets there were in the place.

But when they got to the Heights, Garret turned the Auburn into the driveway of a craftsman-style house that rambled back into a deep lot overgrown with twisting post oak trees. Massive square pillars held up a low-pitched roof. Hetty caught a glimpse of a hulking garage in the rear with rooms on the second story. Behind that, the hood of an orange truck hidden in the blue shade of the trees.

"Is this where you live?" she asked.

"Look—I've got to talk to Odell and tell him what happened."

"Can't we go home first?"

"Pearl will fix us some breakfast."

"Pearl?"

"Odell's wife. Pearl Weems. Come meet her."

He led Hetty through a screened-in back porch into a kitchen plated floor to ceiling with white porcelain cabinets. A woman was hunched over the counter in an old dressing gown, beating eggs with a whisk. When she heard them come in, she glanced up with large sad eyes. Hetty assumed this was Pearl but, unlike her name, there was nothing round or lustrous about her. She was more like the oyster shell: craggy, brittle, gray. The eyes were the only soft things about the woman's face, half hidden by hair in need of a good long brushing.

"Can a couple of newlyweds get some breakfast around here?"

"Garret! How many times I told y'all, the wages of sin is death. But nobody listens to me. Thank the Lord you're safe." She wiped her spindly fingers on her apron and came over to give him a hug. "I'm Pearl Weems," she said, extending a cold hand to Hetty. "I am so pleased to meet the new Mrs. MacBride—but not under these circumstances, o' course. Have a seat, y'all. I'll fetch Odell." She slapped into the hall in her faded mules to yelp *"Odellllllll!"* up a flight of stairs. "He'll be pleased you're back safely, though it's a shame y'all had to cut your honeymoon short. You got to live it up to live it down, I always say. Coffee, hon?"

"That would be a lifesaver," Hetty said.

"A lifesaver! Ain't you the one?" Hetty and Garret slid into the built-in breakfast nook while she clattered cups of coffee in front of them and went back to work. In no time, she had the air awash with the keen scents of morning: the sizzle of bacon, the tawny smell of bread turning brown in the toaster.

But those aromas were shortly pushed back by an emanation of bay rum that floated in from the stairs. Hetty looked up and had to smile. Strolling into the room as though promenading along a boulevard rather than simply entering a kitchen came a portly man in a maroon smoking jacket with a gray satin cravat blossoming at his neck. He stopped, walking cane at a jaunty angle, and eyed her over the top of half-moon reading glasses that were inching down his nose. His double chin tripled as he lowered his head to get a better look.

"Honey, this is my business partner, Odell Weems."

"It's a pleasure to meet you," she said, lifting a hand to him.

"The pleasure is all mine, I assure you, young lady." Hetty recognized the cultivated voice she'd heard on the phone yesterday. He strolled over, took her hand, and actually kissed it. "Garret didn't extol your virtues nearly enough. You are far lovelier than we dreamed, isn't she, Pearlie?"

"Odell, you flatterer," she said.

He took a seat across the table. "And smart, too, since it seems you were able to dissuade Garret from his rash errand yesterday evening."

"It's a good thing she did," Garret said. He pulled the blood-spotted glasses out of his pocket and placed them on the sparkling white table.

A silence so profound fell over the group that Pearl padded over to see what was up. They all stared at the smudged horn-rims. Light glimmered through the windows. Hetty felt a deep sense of relief to be sitting there safe and alive in the clear morning sun.

"Prairie Dog," Odell whispered solemnly.

"You men!" Pearl said, shaking her head as she retreated to the stove. "Like to run me crazy."

"What does this mean, my friend?" Odell asked.

"It means we have a problem," Garret said, torching a Camel. "A real problem."

"Perhaps I need to pay a courtesy call to Poppa Rose."

"It won't do any good," Garret said. "The Maceos have got themselves a nice little monopoly. They control everything south of Dickinson."

"They can't do that," Odell said. "It's against the law."

"It's all against the law!" Pearl cracked an egg.

"In answer," Odell said, "I quote that great American philosopher, Henry David Thoreau: 'When unjust laws exist, shall we be content to obey them or shall we transgress them at once?' I say we transgress."

"You know best, dear."

Odell pushed his glasses up his nose to study the bloody horn-rims, then whistled. "So what you're telling me is—we buy off the fish pier or—"

"Or we don't dare cross the Maceo-Dickinson line."

"And the prices on the fish pier . . ."

"Are double what we were paying off the boats. I say we launch from somewhere else—Padre Island. They don't own International Waters."

"They'll find us, my friend. Look what happened to poor Prairie Dog."

"They're not telling me what to do. I've got some big money to raise—enough to drill me an oil well."

Pearl slapped a steaming platter down on the table. "Now that's enough about business, y'all. Let's eat. Nothing's worse than cold scrambled eggs."

While Garret and Odell spent the morning discussing strategy, Hetty let her hostess lead her on a tour of the property. She could tell that Pearl loved escorting guests through a home crammed with all the riches of the Sears, Roebuck & Company catalog. Gloomy, gargantuan furniture clashed with the craftsman woodwork: a dining table standing on massive legs, china cabinets rattling with teacups and gravy boats. Hetty was shown the Queen Anne chairs in the parlor, the glorious new Water Witch electric washing machine in the laundry room. All paid for by what Pearl described as "dark of the moon imports."

"Years back, I was like every housewife—you know, five dollars a month till it's paid? That's when we was Weems Moving and Storage. But ever since Odell's been running liquor, I just order whatever I want. Now that's my idea of an easy payment plan. How about you?"

"Does it ever bother you?" Hetty asked, running her fingers over a mahogany chest. "Knowing your money comes from that source?"

"Did at first. I was against it. I was raised in the Bible Belt—Lufkin, up East." She pointed over her shoulder. "We was always taught, the wages of sin is death, but for now I say, I'm livin' in sin and lovin' it. Come see the den of iniquity."

Hetty trailed Pearl to a side entrance across the driveway that led into the garage. She stepped out of the high sun into near darkness, stumbling for a moment. Garret's brougham lurked in one of the bays and, as her pupils dilated, tall shelves seemed to crawl out of the shadows. Pearl flicked a switch.

Bare bulbs hanging from the ceilings in each of the three bays dropped a dusty light over the scene: a cracked, oil-stained concrete floor, tools hanging on the walls, the smell of gasoline in the air. Exactly what she'd expect a garage to be like, except for one detail: The doors of the brougham were thrown open, the fenders unbolted, the seats pulled out. In every possible cavity glistened bottles, bright new shining bottles slapped with labels. They were massed on the floor, stacked on the shelves three deep, bottles and bottles and bottles. Hetty moved closer and read the labels: Johnnie Walker, Teacher's Highland Cream, the Antiquary 20-Year-Old Scotch, Hiram Walker, Vat 69, Old Crow, Bacardi Rum. She'd never seen so much alcohol in one place. She took it all in, then walked slowly back to where Pearl waited.

"They use this car for deliveries in town. Garret ever shown you his chauffeur's livery? That's how come Odell hired him—looks so fine in it."

"So he *is* a chauffeur?"

"Ain't you the one? He only puts the livery on to impress the clientele. Odell likes to be driven around in style. The big shipments come in that truck out yonder. Got a false bottom."

Hetty walked along the shelves. "This all the stock they have left?"

"Now you know why Garret was itchin' to sail out last night."

"But I don't understand." She turned back to Pearl. "Isn't moonshine easy to come by?"

Pearl looked wounded. "Oh, hon! Odell would never bottle alkie himself. It's got to be imported under seal. He and Garret fancy themselves the elite among bootleggers. That's why they got to find a new spigot pretty damn quick."

* * *

"Now keep in mind I didn't have time to tidy up," Garret said as they exited the Weems' back porch that afternoon. "This elopement all happened so fast." Hetty started for the car, but he turned and led her up creaking steps to the second story of the Weems' garage.

"You live in a garage apartment?"

"A carriage house, please." He opened the door for her to pass through.

What she saw inside confirmed her worst fears. Garret lived amid the vulgar litter that virile men often leave floating in their wake: stacks of cardboard boxes that hadn't been unpacked, clothes flung about on the furniture, trash cans that needed emptying, a ring around the bathtub. The woodwork was blistered with old varnish; the floral wallpaper was starting to curl off in places. Bare bulbs decorated the ceiling; slats drooped in the venetian blinds.

"You expect me to live here?"

"It's just a starter place for us, honey."

"This isn't a starter, Mac. This is a finisher." Garret looked sheepish in the silence that followed. Hetty sighed, not wanting to start a fight. "But there's only one closet."

"Maybe we could get a rack?"

She looked at him dumbfounded. Surely he was joking. As he paced about picking up debris, she studied his face for a moment and decided he was perfectly serious. That was the kind of man Garret was—slap up a rack and make do till we hit our big strike. Women were expected to rough it along with the men, like she imagined they did in the mining camps of Montana. Grit your teeth, hack out a life, and don't complain. It was his Rocky Mountain vigor again, the part of his manhood she found so bracing. She just wasn't sure how it would mesh with her womanhood. Hadn't he noticed how many clothes she had?

Hetty gritted her teeth. "All right, I'm willing to slum it for a while. On one condition."

"What?"

"That you find us a better place to live."

"It's a deal."

* * *

In the middle of the night, Hetty placed her feet gingerly on the floor. Smooth and cool. Stumbling through the dark, she used the bathroom. She worried about what she'd find behind the closed door of the kitchen. *Don't go in there,* she told herself. But as she came out of the bathroom, she found herself turning in that direction—in spite of her vow never to walk across the living room carpet barefoot. *Marriage is compromise.* She found the door and pushed it open. All was black inside, quiet except for that almost imperceptible rustling she'd heard the day before. A scurrying, a ghostly whispering. She stepped onto the linoleum floor, and something immediately tickled the side of her foot. She groped for the light switch. Her fingers found the top button and pushed it. When the light flickered on, she screamed. Dozens of huge brown roaches crawled over the trash and swarmed on the dirty dishes in the sink. The light appeared to terrify them. They retreated in all directions, evaporating into cracks and crevices.

She strode back into the bedroom, hit the light switch, and slammed the door loudly enough to wake Garret. "You've got roaches."

"What . . . ?" He squinted up at the light. "Naw, just a few palmetto bugs."

Hetty snickered. There was no such thing as a *few* palmetto bugs. These weren't the little cockroaches common across the South. No, the palmetto bugs of the Gulf prairies were *monster* roaches—up to two inches long with spindly hairy legs and long, twitching feelers. They flourished in the moist semitropical air of south Texas, building kingdoms unseen right under your feet. She knew they could fly—across the room, into your face. She sat down on the bed.

"That's the last straw. I can't live here, Garret."

"What do you mean?"

"I mean . . . I'm going back to my mother's . . ." She said this with more confidence than she felt inside.

"You are?" He turned and looked at her with the hollow eyes of a hurt child. He sat up and tried to slip his arms around her.

She pushed him away. "Yes. And don't expect to sleep with me again until you find us a better place to live."

* * *

Later that afternoon, Hetty let herself into the Warwick apartment with her old key. She sat her suitcases down in the foyer and removed her shoes, intending to enter the suite like a pilgrim, a penitent. She had to tread carefully here. Although it felt like months had swirled by since her elopement, in reality it had only been a week. Now she was back, wishing she could slip into her old room unnoticed.

She entered the hallway, counted her steps as she walked by her sister's door, then the bedroom she had abandoned a week ago. She turned sideways to squeeze through the heavy *postigo* doors so that their hinges wouldn't creak. She wanted this invasion of Nella's privacy to be a sneak attack, giving Hetty a clear advantage. She tiptoed to the threshold and peeked through the open door. Shutters dammed up the flood of afternoon heat. Only ceiling fans stirred the sultry air, rippling the scarves draped here and there about the room.

Hetty stepped in and spotted her mother immediately, sitting at the *bureau de dame* wrapped in a kimono and painting her face. She didn't see her. Hetty glided forward soundlessly and stood amid the rippling scarves. In the mirror, Nella sensed movement and looked up. Her eyes widened with surprise only for a moment, then glazed over. She pursed her mouth and applied lipstick. She said nothing.

In the silence that followed, Hetty moved automatically to the place where she and her sister always sat when they watched their mother adorning herself—on one of the two quarter-moon chairs at the foot of the dais. She tried to slump back against the hard, straight back. These were not chairs to relax in. The only way to sit in them successfully was the way Nella did: spine perfectly straight, shoulders lifted just slightly, hands floating above her lap, barely touching, head held high—like a figure come to life off a Mayan frieze.

She sat like that now appraising her hair, sleek as patent leather. The lipstick she had applied was the same color as the walls behind the mirror, deep marigold. Hetty expected a tirade of spicy Spanish to come sizzling out of those orange lips, but instead her mother asked coolly, "How was Galveston?"

"It rained the last two days. We came home early."

"If you're here to discuss the weather, Esther, I don't have time. I'm going out."

Hetty fished for something to talk about. It was too soon to mention moving back in. "How was the party at Ima Hogg's?"

"Why do you ask?"

"Just curious."

"I didn't realize you were interested, since you so carelessly threw away the chance to go."

"You're right, Mamá. I did. But I still want to know what it was like."

Nella's eyes grew misty as she gazed into the silvered light of the mirror. "You want to know what it was like? All right, I'll tell you. Every room at Bayou Bend was thrown open to the new gardens. There were flowers all over, inside and out, and the whole place was lit only by candles—thousands of them twinkling. The Houston Symphony played music from the Vienna woods. Will Rogers asked me to dance."

"And the Diana Garden?" Hetty was almost afraid to ask.

Nella finished applying a light dusting of powder and reached for one of the perfume bottles she'd massed on the *bureau de dame*. Hetty had forgotten with what tiny things Nella always surrounded herself—this one had a crystal grasshopper for a stopper. She touched it lightly to her wrists and her neck, releasing into the air the fragrance of distant, exotic flowers filtered through a spring orchard.

She rubbed her wrists together lightly, then slid the thronelike chair around to face her daughter. "Just as you would imagine it. Even better. *¡Glorioso!* You step out of the rear entrance—and by the way, I'm so glad Ima had the good sense to do Latin Colonial. When will people realize that Georgian just doesn't suit our climate!" Nella snapped open a black lace fan and cooled her face. She chatted on in an almost amiable fashion, which puzzled Hetty. Why wasn't she livid, as she'd been on the phone? Had she forgiven her in only a week? Hetty found that hard to believe.

"The view is magnificent—through stucco pillars with just a hint of pink you look across terraced lawns, and there she stands—*la diva,* reflected in a pool of water. She's copied from the Diana of Versailles, you know. She's striding forward, Esther, striding—hunting—reaching for an arrow. She's so—*sofisticada.*"

"Were any of my friends there?"

"No. Charlotte . . . *solamente.*"

"Charlotte?"

"*Sí* . . . someone had to go with Lamar." Nella gave her an impish glance from behind the fan.

Hetty looked away quickly, not wanting her mother to note the look of regret stealing over her face. She hadn't foreseen that her sister would take her place at Lamar's side for the gala that all of Houston clamored to attend. The whole affair had mattered little to her a week ago, but now—in the midst of her uncertainty—she found herself longing to know what the statue of the goddess looked like . . . mirrored in a pool of water.

Nella walked over to the cedar *armario,* whose rustic facade hid a wealth of finery inside. She began flipping through various gowns, and Hetty heard the kind of rustling that brings taffeta and silk satin to mind. Presently, she pulled out a long black tunic and hung it on a hook on the door. She untied her kimono and stepped forward. As she did so, one knee emerged. Hetty could see some kind of strange markings on it. She realized that she had never seen her mother's knees. When Nella saw her looking at them, she frowned. *"Perdóneme,"* she said, pulling her kimono back together.

This was obviously not the moment to ask her about moving back in. Hetty walked out into the hall and pushed the heavy *postigo* out of the way. It banged against the wall, drawing a startled look from Charlotte, who, at that moment, had just emerged from Hetty's room down the hall. Her eyes had the haunted look of someone caught stealing. Hetty moved closer and took in her impressive metamorphosis: Her face was beautifully made up, and she wore her hair like a crown across her head, woven with pearls.

"Hetty . . . ?"

"What were you doing in my room, sis?"

She pulled her dressing gown closer around her. "Oh . . . didn't Mother tell you? It's not your room anymore."

"What are you talking about?" Hetty brushed past her sister and crossed the threshold into her old quarters. Charlotte was right—it wasn't her bedroom anymore. In fact, she wondered if she had walked through the wrong door. All traces of her previous residence had been stripped away. Not one of her possessions remained—not her orange and black draperies centered with the Chinese emblem of happiness, not her four-poster bed, not her Chinese lanterns hung with fringe, not her chest of drawers inlaid with mother-of-pearl. She was unable to move for a moment. Suddenly, she'd become a displaced person, someone whose passport back home had been revoked, leaving her stranded in a strange place. The only things standing in the empty room were two racks of new clothes still tasseled with price tags. Charlotte leaned against the doorjamb, sniffing at her.

"Where's all my stuff?"

"Look in the back hall." Hetty searched her sister's face for a hint of sympathy, a quiver of regret. But Charlotte didn't smile or blink, just stared back with those metallic gray eyes of hers unfazed. The Triumphant Sibling. Hetty blinked back tears as she barged out, forcing Charlotte to step aside. She marched through the gloom of the drawing room, swung the kitchen door aside, and made for the back hall. And there they were: All the possessions she had prized through the years thrown in heaps along the wall, not even boxed up. The lightbulb in one of the lanterns was broken, its shards scattered on the floor. Hetty stepped gingerly so as not to cut her bare feet. A dreadful smell coated everything back here: ripe garbage, rancid grease, the must of things forgotten. Hetty closed the door to shut it out and glanced into the servant's quarters. Lina lurked in there, looking shamefaced.

"I'm sorry, *m'ija.* She made me do it."

"It's not your fault," Hetty said, going over to squeeze her tiny hands.

"Now I call you *Señora.*" Lina stood on tiptoe to kiss her on both cheeks. *"¡Felicitación!"*

"*Gracias,* Lina." She smiled quickly and turned her face away.

* * *

Hetty made her way back into the Mexican quarters. Nella stood on the dais, wearing a long black tunic covered by an equally long evening coat extravagantly beaded in black-and-white seed pearls. She was sliding a matching headpiece over her shining hair.

"Mamá, you gave my room to Char?"

"She needs it as a dressing room now that she's dating Lamar." Nella yanked the headpiece until it was sitting properly, dipping over one cheek, a single teardrop pearl dangling like an earring. The effect was most provocative.

"*Dating* Lamar?"

Nella did a final appraisal of her image in the mirror, then swiveled to look down intently at her daughter from the dais. Hetty felt her knees slacken for a moment as she met the gleam of those black eyes, sharpened by the faintest trace of mascara. She sat down in the quarter-moon chair. When Nella turned herself out in full regalia like this for dinner, no one looked more radiant or assured. "Yes, dear. That's where we're going tonight—to Splendora for dinner."

This time it was Hetty who rose in her seat and lifted her shoulders. Now she understood why her mother wasn't angry. She didn't have to be. It was becoming only too clear how cleverly Nella had finessed this whole situation. She had moved decisively while Hetty was out of town, working her subtle stratagems to match one of her daughters with the Rusk heir. It really hadn't mattered which one. It wasn't the person who was important here, but the prize. With Hetty out of the game, Charlotte had been moved into position as the perfect pawn—eager, malleable, a vessel still open to Nella's adoring ambitions.

Hetty had to laugh. *"Lamar!"* An image came to her mind: She thought of the victorious smile that would play across her mother's lips when she made her favorite winning move in mah-jongg, clicking together a pair of matching tiles bearing the *ma chiang* figure, the house sparrow that gave the sport its name. Nella cast her head back and was now watching her daughter across the white tilt of her cheekbones, her black eyes impregnable within their serene depths of power and elegance. With a chill, Hetty knew she could never return home.

Nella followed her all the way out to the foyer in a frosty silence. Hetty slipped into her shoes and picked up her suitcases.

"Now I'd appreciate it if Pick could carry me home."

Nella took a deep breath. "I'm afraid that won't be possible."

"Oh? Why not?"

"Picktown was fired."

Hetty felt as though her mother had kicked her in the solar plexus. She dropped the suitcases with a clatter and sank down on the large one. "Fired?"

Nella nodded.

"But . . . why?"

"We no longer found him suitable."

"You can't, Mamá. You know as well as I do he supports his whole family. There's no father."

"We've made our decision." The clock chimed five. Nella walked back into the drawing room. "Now I must ask you to leave before Lamar shows up. You've caused him quite enough heartache for one week." Nella sat in her armchair in front of the great Diana screen and began transferring the contents of her handbag to an evening purse. She ignored Hetty, crouched in the foyer.

"You're throwing me out?"

"You've got it backward, Esther. You were the one who abandoned me, remember?"

Hetty stood and heaved up her suitcases, but had no idea where she was going. "How am I supposed to get home?"

Nella continued to look away from her. Hetty could never remember this happening. She found it unbearable. Her shock and frustration turned to panic. She wanted those black eyes on her, seeing her, whether in rage or love she didn't care, as long as they were seeing her. But Nella only looked down as she continued sorting through her purse and said, "May I remind you that the streetcar stops right in front of the hotel?"

* * *

Hetty left the Warwick by the side exit, putting a line of shrubs between her and the doorman. The greenery shrank back, and she was out there, on the esplanade, in the deepening haze of a late afternoon, wandering aimlessly through the clipped hedges, shifting the heavier bag from one hand to the other.

She stopped.

Spread-eagled on the grass before her was the Texas star, bronze centerpiece of the city fathers' master plan. It was pointing in five directions. She had never noticed that before. Clearly five directions. She was astonished. It lay there in the grass, a dark star burned into the earth, an unexpected horoscope pointing with its tarnished rays toward the different paths unfolding before her: back to the hotel. *No longer an option.* East toward the refineries out along the Ship Channel. *Her future?* Due south to the lagoon in Hermann Park. *Time to think.* West toward the trolley stop. *Where would she go?* North to the Heights. *Back to that dingy garage apartment.*

She decided to follow the southern ray into the park, to the spot where she always came to be alone. Skirting the lagoon until she reached the far end, she let the suitcases slip through her fingers and fall to the grass. She sat on one of them, long scarf dangling about her ankles. She pulled out a Lucky and lit it with her shaking fingers, watching the light dropping in spangles across the sheen of the water. She sat there until a length of hot ash cascaded onto her hand.

She was all heat and ashes inside, too. She couldn't get Nella's face out of her mind, looking away from her, sorting through the contents of her handbag. As if lipsticks and compacts were more important than a daughter! As if Hetty were a cast-off, something to be thrown on the floor in the back hallway like her clothes sprawled there in the dust.

The Lucky burned her fingers. She'd hardly smoked it all. Her fags weren't tasting as good as they used to. She threw the butt into the lagoon. It hissed when it hit the water. *The cruelest thing of all,* she thought, *was telling me they fired Pick.* Nella knew what that would mean to Hetty, who had discovered him. Lifting the Waller family out of the poverty they'd sunk into in Settegast had been like dragging six people out of quicksand. What would happen to the children now? It was like Addie and Ollie and Minnie and Lewis were sitting there on the grass in front of her, not saying anything, just watching her with those orphaned eyes. *No one is coming to rescue us,* they seemed to say. *No one is coming to help.*

Hetty's face muscles weren't strong enough to blink back the tears any longer. They trickled down her cheeks until she was sobbing into her scarf. "Oh, Mother! I hate you! I hate you!" she sobbed over and over, but even as she did so, she knew which tip of the star she had to follow. The one that pointed back to the Heights. She had no choice. She had chosen Mac because he was the man she wanted. He had that itch in his soul, the grit and growl in his voice that made him a fighter. And now she needed him to fight for her in a way Lamar never could. She needed him to take a steel bit in his big hands and use it to drill through layer after layer of limestone, to go down to the heart of the earth where treasure lay, to wrest out of rock a kingdom of her own where she would never need her mother and father and sister again. Then let them come begging for her affections! Yes, as she dried her tears and choked down her sorrows, she knew only one direction was possible now. It was clearly there, in the earth. Auspicious and plain. A point, a ray. She had to follow the star whether she wanted to or not. Because as of today, it was no longer just a state emblem. She had made it her own.

And now she knew why it always flew alone.

Hetty moved in and out of the constant stream of walkers flowing in both directions downtown. She had no idea where to catch the Heights streetcar. She glanced about, hoping to find someone to ask.

Then, almost a block away, through a blur of shadowy figures, her eye was caught by a cloud of pastels glowing in the evening light. Three young women seemed to float out of an elegant gray car drawn up at the curb. It took a moment for all three of them to alight on the sidewalk, then they turned and started down the block, coming toward her, unmistakable. They fluttered along in a tight little flock, trailing wisps of silk, parting pedestrians as they passed. Hetty recognized their gait—long sleek legs clicking along on the same beat, as in a dance. Belinda Welch, Doris Verne Hargraves, and Winifred Ilse Neuhaus. She debated whether to face them or flee. She'd been crying and probably looked a mess. On the other hand, she was the first among her friends to wed and that should win her a certain status. These girls would appear naive standing next to her—a *wife,* a seasoned woman who could be blasé about such dreaded rites of passage as the wedding night and the honeymoon. She decided to stand there and let her friends discover her.

Doris Verne was the first to come running up. "My crazy pal. Did you go and get married on us?"

"So you've heard?"

"Of course. Everybody knows. We're all in awe."

"A week ago."

"Congratulations!" She gave her a warm hug. "I can't believe it."

"Sure you can," Winifred said. "In case people don't know she's an elopist. She's carrying suitcases." She kissed Hetty on each cheek.

Lockett's daughter Belinda hung back and watched with eyes the color of ice at dawn. Winifred noticed her gazing at Hetty's waistline. "Put those nine fingers down, Bel. We promise not to count the months, Het."

"Why does everyone think I'm pregnant?" Hetty flung her suitcases to the sidewalk.

"You should hear what people are saying."

"I don't really care what people are saying. My friends know the truth and that's all that matters to me."

"That's right, honey child," said Doris Verne. "And we're happy for you. How was your honeymoon?"

"We stayed in the bridal suite at the Galvez."

"How swanky," said Doris Verne.

"I played roulette at the Hollywood Dinner Club. Guest of the Maceos."

"You know the *Maceos?*" Belinda asked.

"Yeah. My husband introduced me."

"Aren't they . . . you know . . . on the lam?" said Winifred.

"Heavens no! They run everything down there."

The three girls just stared at her.

Belinda checked a dainty watch on her wrist. "Aren't we going to be late for our motion picture?"

"Now *I'm* jealous—what are you going to see?" said Hetty.

"That thing about slave days in old New Orleans," she answered. "*The Love Mart* with Billie Dove."

"The most beautiful woman on the screen!" Winifred said with mock breathiness. "I wanted to catch *The Jazz Singer* in Vitaphone, but these two pooh-poohed it."

"It's just a gimmick, Wini," Belinda insisted.

"I wish I could go with you," Hetty sighed. "I've got to find the trolley to the Heights. Do you know where it stops?"

"Sorry, kid," said Winifred. "I've never ridden on a streetcar."

"I do feel so sorry for you—married and all," Belinda said, planting a quick peck on Hetty's cheek.

"Don't bother, Bel. She's already somebody's love slave, and we're just seeing a movie about it," Winifred said.

As they moved off, Doris Verne squeezed Hetty's hands and murmured, "Let's have luncheon at the club. Call me."

Hetty turned on the lights in the living room of the garage apartment. She called Garret's name, but he wasn't home. Nothing had been tidied up, and the kitchen door was still closed. She set her suitcases down and walked cautiously in that direction. Opening the door a crack, she reached inside and flicked the light switch. A frantic scurrying ensued as the palmetto bugs retreated back into their nests. She left the light on, like a fire to keep wild animals at bay, and slammed the door. She placed a dirty towel from the bathroom across the crack so none of them could shimmy through. In the bedroom, she found a blanket to cover herself on the couch, where she lay down exhausted to wait for Garret. *Maybe I had to come back,* she told herself. *But I don't have to sleep in his bed.*

She left the lights on in the living room, too.

* * *

Garret finally arrives home and tells her to pack. Before she knows it, he's driving them around and around the plaza of a desolate town. Wild dogs follow in the dust and yip at them. The land is as brown and mangy as the dogs, yielding only the thorns of prickly pear cactus. Hetty doesn't understand why they've come here. As Garret circles, she glances into the plaza. Old men sit on massive stone benches talking in Spanish. She knows it's Spanish because they have the heads of gargoyles and their words float out like smoke rings. They are talking about her. Her name floats in the air: Esther de las Ardras. Her ancestors are there, with stone dust on their hands, watching from the quarry.

Church bells toll. Out of the stoneworks, white as marble, a bride walks into the plaza. Her face is covered by a silk shawl caught in her hair with a Spanish comb. The gargoyles lift it to reveal her dusky face: It is Hetty's grandmother, Liliana Ardra y de la Herrera, who has just become Señora Beckman. Liliana goes to the fountain and washes the stone dust off her hands. The water trickling out turns bloodred. The wedding guests all hold their glasses under the spigot and fill them with wine. Hetty looks everywhere for Garret but can't find him.

On the sofa in the garage apartment, aching and alone, Hetty turned over to make sure it was day. She pushed herself up and set her bare feet on the floor. Dust motes swam by the thousands into the sunrays leaking through the drooping venetian blinds, but she didn't care. She was so glad to see that the wild dogs running through her dreams had found the dawn at last.

She dressed and cautiously opened the door into the kitchen. No palmetto bugs in sight. She found a tin of Folgers and set the percolator going. After unpacking, she wandered from room to room, picking up clothes and drinking too much coffee. As mugginess mushroomed in the air, the reek of gasoline drifted up from the garage below.

A pile of dusty books lay on an old shelf littered with pencil stubs, cuff links, and empty cigar jars. She perused the stack, wondering if it had been left by the previous tenant: *The Outline of His-*

tory by H. G. Wells, *Main Street* by Sinclair Lewis, *If Winter Comes* by A. S. M. Hutchinson. Her fingers were drawn to an exotic-looking book called *White Shadows of the South Seas,* but when she opened it, some of the pages fell out in her hands. The glue holding the binding together had been eaten away. She dropped the book and ran out into the sun shuddering. The roaches were eating the books!

When Garret walked in the next night, Hetty was ready for him. She lounged across crisp white sheets on the sofa, freshly bathed, in a pair of satin pajamas. A soft light pervaded the rooms, thrown by new table lamps with silk scarves draped around the shades. Stalks of red gladiolas towered over the coffee table. The furniture gleamed. He stood at the door, a look of pleasant surprise spreading over his face.

"You've been busy," he said.

"I've been in class for two days."

"Class?"

"Home economics with Professor Pearlie. She really knows her mops."

"I'll bet she does." He came into the center of the room, glancing around and sniffing the air.

Hetty impersonated Pearl's East Texas twang: " 'A house without a woman runs wild.' I learned all about Octagon Super Suds, Sani-Flush, Fuller Brush furniture polish, and spray cans of Flit for the roaches."

He smiled faintly. "I take it you're going to stay for a while."

"Not for long. I just couldn't sleep in this rat hole another night without cleaning it."

He loosened his tie, slipped off his chauffeur's coat, and slung it over a hook. He nosed around for a few minutes, used the bathroom, then came back in and stretched out in his old club chair. He ran his hands over the fresh ticking on the arms. "This chair feels different."

"Slipcovers. Another one of Professor Pearlie's tricks."

"You wanted to be back with me, admit it." He came over and squatted on the edge of the sofa.

Hetty could smell his cologne, that manly limy smell she usually liked. Now it just soured her nose, like too much lemon squeezed into tonic. She pulled the sheet closer around her body and pushed him off the couch with her feet. He fell to the floor.

"Why'd you do that?"

"For one thing, I'm beat. I've never worked so hard in my life. Pearl is a slave driver. Today we ran into Munn's to buy lamps and linens and had to carry all the packages home on the streetcar. I just want to go to sleep."

"How can you push me away?" He stood up, reaching into his pocket and pulling out a thick wad of bills. He tossed it onto the coffee table, where it uncurled like a peony in the last stages of bloom. "Look at all this money I brought you."

"Good. I owe Pearl sixty-six dollars and ninety-nine cents."

"I'll pay her."

"Thanks." Hetty poked at the cash, trying to estimate how much it was. "This is peanuts compared to what you could be making in the oil business."

Her words made him bristle. "Sorry if it's not good enough for you, goddammit. Maybe you should go back to Lamar."

"Maybe I will."

He went into the bedroom and slammed the door. She got up and turned off all the lamps, falling back onto the sofa bone weary. She could hear him slamming around. He paced the floor, unbuckled his belt, kicked off his shoes, and then brushed his teeth in the bathroom with the new tube of Ipana she'd gotten. She heard the old bedsprings squeaking and decided they should use part of his wad of money to buy a new mattress. She kept drifting off in the dark and quiet, but waking up and wondering if Garret was asleep. The bedsprings squeaked again. *Good,* she thought, *he's tossing and turning, too.*

Through heavy eyelids, she saw him slip back into the room in his undershirt and shorts, pour himself a drink from a silver flask, and light the little beeswax candles she'd arranged in a candelabra on the coffee table. As a warm haze began to mingle with the scent of lemon oil, she heard him light a cigarette. He sat in the flickering light smoking, and began to talk quietly and earnestly. She could hardly stay awake to concentrate on what he was saying, but found his deep voice oddly soothing.

He talked about his wanderings around Texas to visit the big oil strikes since Spindletop—places like Saratoga, Electra, and Desdemona. He went on spreading his dreams out before her until they crowded the room and pushed the walls out into the far reaches of the night. His deep voice kept pulling her down until she finally went under and didn't wake again until the candles had burned out and all was quiet. A blue haze sifted in from the streetlamps.

She heard the floor creak and saw him come back into the living room and stand over her, this time without his undershirt and boxer shorts. His white body looked so pure and tempting in the pale light.

"You're naked."

"I have a confession to make. You're the only person I would tell this to."

Hetty knew not to say anything. She waited. *I'm watching a deer venture out of deep woods into a meadow. The slightest movement on my part . . . and it's gone.*

He knelt down in front of her. "I don't know how to drill an oil well. I don't know the first thing about it."

"So all those stories about oil towns aren't true?"

"Oh, they're true. I did visit those places. But I always felt like a tourist. I didn't know how to get on the inside so I could learn the secrets of the old wildcatters."

"You will. Every weevil has to learn the business. We'll do it together—okay?"

"So you're not going to leave me and go back to Lamar?"

She shook her head. He rose off the floor. Hetty thought he was going to crush her as he wrapped his arms around her and held on tight. He started to climb on top of her, his confidence renewed. She pushed him back.

"Now *I* have a confession to make."

"Okay. Your turn." He laughed with relief.

"Shall I get naked?"

"I'd like that."

"Can you help me?"

He slipped her pajama bottoms off first, then unbuttoned her top and helped her slip it off. She covered her breasts with her arms because she knew he would look at them. But she wanted to be completely vulnerable, so she overcame her modesty and lowered her arms to her sides. He looked. Her nipples went hard in spite of herself.

"I didn't come back here because of our wedding vows. I don't believe in keeping vows just for the sake of keeping vows. I came back because I had no place else to go. Mamá kicked me out."

"I knew she would."

Hetty described it all to him: her empty room, the piles of stuff in the back hall, the news about Henry Picktown Waller.

"What a—" Garret stopped himself.

"Go ahead and say it—Mamá's a bitch. She'll never forgive me for marrying you."

"It doesn't matter. I want you here with me, Hetty."

"It's not me I'm worried about. We can't abandon Pick, Garret. I've worked too hard to rescue that family from the Ward."

She pulled him up onto the sofa with her, then slid her hands up his arms and around his shoulders. "Promise me one thing. When you drill your first well, I want you to put Pick on the crew."

"So I *am* drilling a well."

"No. *We're* drilling a well."

He hugged her again. She loved the way her breasts felt so warm against his bare skin. "I really love you," he whispered into her ear.

"Why do you love me?"

"Because you're kind. Because you want to help Pick and his kin."

"It's not kindness."

"What is it, then?"

"Survival. I'm their only hope. If I drop the ball, those kids will die."

"Here's to survival, then."

"Amen."

He kissed her tenderly on the mouth. She couldn't stop him and couldn't break away. She promised herself she wouldn't sleep with him tonight, but when he took her by the hand and led her into the bedroom, she followed, telling herself that she was half-asleep and didn't know what she was doing. The silver cord of pleasure that had tied them together in the ocean was still too tightly wound. It wrapped them together invisibly so she could barely breathe.

He sat down on the bed, and she knelt in front of him. He opened his legs. She kissed his thighs, his stomach. Then she buried her face in his fragrant genitals. She began kissing and licking, hungry for his salt taste. When he grew hard, she drove her mouth farther down on his cock, swallowing the whole thing. He sat back on the bed, paralyzed with pleasure. She sucked on it feverishly, up and down, like she imagined a prostitute would do. That's what she was now—Mac's whore. He moaned, and Hetty felt herself, again, simultaneously captivated and alarmed at how deeply his passion fed on the sincerity and disgrace of her submission.

Then they were in bed, rustling through the cool new sheets she'd just bought. His mouth was right at her ear, nibbling, kissing, talking so low she could hardly understand him at times. *Whispering so no one can hear me,* like the song said. *This is what it means to be a love slave,* she thought. This was the real thing. This was what her friends could only dream about, what Wini read about in marriage manuals. Hearing a man's most secret thoughts expressed in these passionate whispers, here in the middle of the night when you can't see his face but can only feel his body wrapped tightly around yours.

The wind picked up and stirred the leaves of the post oak tree that was the only covering for the windows in the bedroom. They seemed to whisper *Nella,* as if she were spying on them. Hetty knotted up, feeling her mother's disapproval like a cold hiss. Then Garret's hand slid down between her legs. She yielded slowly into what was alive and richly warm inside her—more insistent even than the bare lightbulbs and the windows with no curtains and the cockroaches. His tongue worked her until he had stroked Nella and memory right out of her mind, and she went flowing in his heat and was nothing now but a warm liquidlike stream, eddying in the drift of his love.

Then he lay on top of her, heavy, manly. He made love to her for a long time, talking all the while, slipping into obscenities until his voice, like his self, became so triumphant over her that she could only answer in the affirmative over and over chanted in with other phrases, syllables, and half-formed sounds that lost all meaning and became nothing, nothing, but the deepest felt and most urgent sound of surrender in the night.

Chapter 7

On a limp evening in July, Hetty sat next to Garret at the big oak table in the gloom of the Weems' dining room. The dusky shadows and dank air made her feel as though she'd plunged to the bottom of a warm pool. The only light left on was in the kitchen, because lamps would raise the temperature too much. A ceiling fan churned the air to no avail. Her husband was making her sweat even more with questions. "Why won't you call your father?"

"He's not going to help us, Mac."

Garret jumped out of his chair. "Why not? He's an oil man."

"Sit down and have some ham, y'all," said Pearl, carving. "A cold supper for a hot night." Odell sent plates wheeling across the table from hand to hand, heavy and fragrant.

"Don't you remember the last thing he said to you? 'You're not welcome in my home.' " Hetty held her iced tea glass to her forehead and closed her eyes.

Everyone else started eating. After a few moments, Garret asked while chewing, "So what do we do now?"

Hetty was wondering the same thing. She'd checked her wallet last night. She had $7.34 in cash, plus a small balance in her bank account. She set her iced tea down. "Maybe you should get a job working on a crew."

Odell almost choked on his food. Garret looked at her, amazed. "Do you have the faintest idea how much the average worker makes?"

"Not a clue." She nibbled on potato salad.

"I didn't think so. About a hundred a month. I doubt that Kirby Allen's daughter is going to be happy living on that."

Odell regarded her over his spectacles. "As Oscar Wilde once said, 'Anyone who lives within their means suffers from a lack of imagination.' I've said it again and again to Garret, and now I'll say it to you," he explained, looking at her cagily. "You don't make money by working harder. You make money by using your imagination."

A silence fell as Hetty took this thought in. There was only the sound of knives and forks clinking on china.

"So I guess it's back to The Hammocks," Garret spoke up.

"What's The Hammocks?" Hetty asked.

"Our cottage on West Beach in Galveston," Odell said, mopping his brow with his napkin. "Out past Thirteen Mile Road."

"Garret loves that place," Pearl said. "I've seen him disappear yonder for a week at a time. You'll have to take your new bride there, Mac. Don't worry; we do have beds. The hammocks is out on the porch."

"I'll have some more of that tasty potato salad, Pearlie," Odell said. "Yes'm. No one would have suspected that inside The Hammocks we were running a thriving import business."

"We'd leave a light on in the house, see," said Garret, "and that would be the beacon that would guide our boat back to West Beach. Wouldn't be another light for miles. Even the roads run out."

"Sounds risky," Hetty said. "Was it worth it?"

"Let's put it this way, my dear," Odell said, holding his knife and fork in midair and fixing her with a burning glance. "A case of Haig and Haig Pinch costs sixty dollars off the ship and sells for three or four times that on the mainland. I'd say that's a pretty good profit for a few hours' work, wouldn't you?"

His stare made her laugh and admit that he was right.

"I've said it before, and I'll say it again. When Congress passed the Volstead Act they created a business opportunity unprecedented in our lifetime. We just need to find a new spigot, that's all."

Hetty set her silverware down with a clatter. She had just remembered her dream—the one where her grandmother turned water into wine. She recalled what the wine was flowing out of: an old-fashioned iron spigot.

"What's wrong, hon?" Pearl asked.

"Nothing," Hetty answered.

Hetty wrote to her mother the next morning.

Garret was still coiled in the bedclothes asleep, while she stretched out on the couch in her silk pajamas and drank coffee the way she liked it, guzzled, not sipped, with a glut of sugar. She had all the windows open. The shadowy living room felt cool and fresh, but it wouldn't last. Heat was already leaking like silt into the clear night air pooled under the post oak trees.

> *Dear Mamá,*
>
> *Garret and I are settled in our new home, a carriage house in the Heights that Garret rents from his business partner, Odell Weems. Being newlyweds, we don't have a lot of furniture, so I would like to come and get my possessions, if that's all right with you. Garret has a truck we can move them in (a Wichita painted orange of all things!).*
>
> Perdóneme, Mamá. *I'm truly sorry if I've hurt you in any way. That wasn't my intention. You must believe me. I was only doing what I thought would bring me happiness. I'm sorry I deceived you but, at the time, eloping felt like my only way out. If it caused you distress, well—¡lo siento mucho! I apologize; I really do. I hope you will forgive me and let me back into your heart where I belong as your own querida hijita.*
>
> *I'm also sorry if I broke Lamar's heart by marrying someone else. I will call him and apologize. I need to set my accounts in order, as Dad would say. In the meantime, I really hope you'll take the opportunity to*

acquaint yourself with my new husband. You'll find that he's a very fine man. Would I choose anything else? In fact, I would go so far as to describe him as "the next Mr. Esperson." Tell Dad! I know it isn't good form to invite oneself to dinner, but why not have us over for a meal with the family? I sincerely hope you'll consider this. I miss you and Dad! I look forward to your reply.

Con mucho amor,
Esther

She checked the rusty mailbox at the bottom of the stairs every day. The only posts that came were an electric bill and a letter in a big swirling hand addressed to Garret from Arleen MacBride in Butte, Montana. When she asked him what his mother had said, he brushed her off with an evasive answer. At the end of the week, two letters arrived for Hetty, both written on ecru rag with the familiar gray monograms.

NAA

Esther,

Please do so at your earliest convenience. The hotel is complaining about the items left in the back corridor.

Nella

CAB

Dear Hetty,

Mother told me that you are planning to telephone Lamar and beg his forgiveness for deserting him so cruelly. Are you really that blind and selfish? Don't you realize that calling Lamar now would only rub salt into his deep, deep wounds? You cannot break a man's heart as thoroughly as you did Lamar's and then expect him to allay your guilt by granting you instant and complete forgiveness. I may be younger than you, but even I know that life doesn't work that way.

In short, Hetty, Lamar doesn't want to talk to you. If you weren't such a swellhead, you would know that. Please do not attempt to communicate with him in any way. I also have no desire to correspond with you, but I felt it my duty to send this warning in order to shield him from further pain. You cannot expect to maltreat a man and still have access to him as if nothing has happened. You have burned that bridge. Do not attempt to walk back across it.

Your loving sister,
Charlotte

When Hetty stepped through the bronze doors of the Esperson Building two days later, she headed straight for the banking quarters, not knowing what she'd find. She was running out of cash and wanted to check the balance in her account to see if Kirb had deposited her stipend for July. She tried not to let her fingers tremble as she presented her passbook to the teller. He stepped away from the cage, thumbed through a cart of ledger sheets, and must have said something to the bookkeeper at the adding machine, because she glanced at Hetty, then quickly dropped her gaze. The teller came back looking a little sheepish.

"I show this account as being closed," he said, handing the passbook back. "I'm sorry, Miss Allen."

"Isn't there any money I can withdraw?"

"The balance is zero, ma'am."

Hetty averted her eyes. "Well . . . thanks for checking." She tucked the passbook into her handbag and glanced past him. Now two bookkeepers were ogling her and Lonnie, too, who'd stopped wrapping coins to see what was going to happen. Only Kirb was ignoring her completely, pretending to work at his desk at the back of the banking floor.

Hetty went over to a marble island and took out her tortoiseshell fountain pen. In her passbook, under the *Withdrawals* column, she wrote, *My father's love*.

Back in the Esperson lobby, the terrazzo floors were so highly polished, Hetty was afraid she might slip and fall. She took the elevator to the Cupola Club on the twenty-seventh floor. The maître d' looked up. "Miss Allen, how are you?" The club's distinctive crest, a round Greek temple, embellished his blazer.

"Hello, Cooper. Actually, I'm not Miss Allen, anymore. I'm Mrs. MacBride."

"Of course. Congratulations. I should have remembered. Your mother called."

"She did?" A tinge of disappointment pricked Hetty's breast. She was hoping Nella would forget about the open door always afforded the Allen sisters here at the club. Hetty leaned forward and whispered, "I'm still a member, aren't I?"

Cooper shook his head and smiled at her sympathetically. He handed her an envelope embossed with the round Greek temple. Hetty glanced at the application inside, trying not to react to the annual membership dues: $1,500.00. "Meanwhile I'm meeting Doris Verne Hargraves for luncheon."

"Of course, Ross will carry you back." Hetty followed the tall colored waiter to rooms that opened out into air and light. He escorted her through French doors onto one of the six private roof gardens terraced at the top of the building. The brightness was stunning, but the tables were sheltered by a canopy of leafy shadows. Doris Verne stood and hugged her.

Winifred Neuhaus sat sipping iced tea in an outrageous set of white silk beach pajamas and a beret. "Where have you been, kiddo?" she said behind big round sunglasses. "I'm terrified they're going to run out of shrimp."

"Am I late? Look at you!" She gave her a little peck on the cheek.

Ross pulled Hetty's chair out but didn't seat her. "Drink, miss?" he asked in his haughty tone.

"I'll have iced tea, please, sir. I had to pick up an application to the club. Now that I'm an old married woman, I want my own membership." She set the envelope down beside her plate.

Winifred snickered. "You'll never get in."

"Surely they wouldn't turn down an Allen?" Doris Verne asked from under her hat brim.

"They can turn down anyone they want, kiddo. This is the Esperson Building." Winifred crooked her finger and said, "See that cupola?" They craned their necks to look at the round Greek temple rising into the blue heavens four floors above them. "They say Mellie Esperson has her office inside it. She sits up there higher than everybody else in town, looking down on the rest of us, surveying her little kingdom, and making sure her henchmen guard the doors. She may even be watching us now. Somebody wave."

Hetty sat back in her chair, smoking, and tried to relax into the amiable chatter. Winifred went on rattling off esoteric facts about the Esperson Building, confiding that more million-dollar oil deals were made right there in the Cupola Club than in all the boardrooms across Texas.

"That's why Garret and I need to get in."

"You've got to if you want to make it in this gassy town," Winifred said. "My dad signed one of the first leases in the building. I remember him telling Mom, 'Esperson's the place to be.' Okay, let's eat!"

The three of them prowled around the buffet, heaping their gold-rimmed plates with coleslaw, gargantuan Gulf shrimp, and scallops swimming in cream. They took turns talking and eating, catching up on the latest developments in their lives. Winifred gave a report from Belinda Welch, who'd headed to Virginia a week ago and was busy preparing for a big horse show in Lexington. "How's married life?"

"Full of surprises."

"Well, at least you can Fornicate Under Command of the King now."

"Wini!" Doris Verne said.

"What? You do know that's what *F-U-C-K* stands for? It's an acronym. When the king wanted to increase the population of England, he commanded his subjects to fornicate as much as possible. It was their patriotic duty."

"And that's our history lesson for today," Hetty said. "Thanks, Wini."

"You're welcome." She glanced at her watch and signaled the waiter. "I must be off, chums. Getting the hair cut even shorter." As they paid their bills, Winifred fluttered both her tiny hands in good-bye.

Hetty hadn't noticed how much the shade of the canopy had inched across the table. The membership package sat in full sunlight, glaring at her, mocking her. This was the visible sign of her banishment from the hidden realm of No-Tsu-Oh. Now that she was alone with her best friend, she couldn't help but fret.

Doris Verne leaned forward and bathed Hetty in the golden light of her hazel eyes. The sunlight radiating off the white tablecloth gave them a few extra volts of energy. "What's wrong, Het?"

"The reason I picked up an application is that my membership's been canceled."

"Who would do that?"

"My mother, of course. It's all part of her vast campaign of revenge." Hetty told Doris Verne about some of Nella's other maneuvers. "And my dad's cut off my stipend. I'll never raise fifteen hundred dollars."

Doris Verne frowned. "I thought Garret was in oil."

Hetty wondered if she'd said too much. But she didn't care; she had to soothe the chafing in her heart by confessing everything to Doris Verne, who'd always been like a sister to her. For the first time she found herself telling someone the whole truth about her marriage: the flight from Galveston, the bottles hidden under the seat in the brougham, the tacky little garage apartment she'd driven home to in the Heights. "And Garret's family is no help. He won't even talk about his mother. All I can squeeze out of him is that her name is Arleen. I don't know what we're going to do."

"Don't know what you're going to do! Is this a Houston girl I'm talking to?"

"And how."

"Hey—you're not acting like one. You know what they say about us Houstonians. If there's no river to the ocean, we dig one. Why do you think we're named after magnolias?"

" 'Cause we're white?"

" 'Cause we're tough, honey child. My dad always told me that magnolia flowers are pollinated by beetles, and their carpels have to be thick as bark so the beetles can't eat them. 'They only look delicate!' he said. I've always remembered that."

"Garret wants to wildcat, of course."

"Well, there you go! You think Miss Mellie was born in a cupola? You know as well as I do—a gusher lifted her up there. She was just an Oklahoma farm girl who used to scrub her husband's overalls by hand."

"So I should buy some detergent?"

Doris Verne's eyes burned with afternoon sun. "Het, you're a daughter of the Magnolia City and don't you forget it. You just give that husband of yours a little push!"

The following afternoon, Hetty stood mopping her brow in the back hall of the Warwick. The fetid smells that rose out of garbage pails grew unbearable in the soggy July heat. It was so swampy, she'd rather be a mermaid, she decided. She tied a knot in the twine, binding another box, and added it to the pile she and Lina had built through the afternoon. They had almost finished packing Hetty's belongings, Lina carting them over to the freight elevator so Garret could pick them up later at the loading dock. Hetty was hot and thirsty. From the drawing room, the alabaster clock chimed five in the afternoon.

She handed the last box to Lina, who carried it on her head to the elevator. *"Gracias,"* she shouted before making her way through the kitchen and down the hall. She used the bathroom, then noticed that the *postigos* were unlocked. She slipped through and peered into the Mexican quarters. They were empty. She tiptoed in and turned one of the quarter-moon chairs toward the black-and-white photographs on the far wall. She sat and studied her grandmother's wedding portrait, the enigmatic ancestor she'd never known. *What are you trying to tell me?* Liliana looked out at the world the way she had in Hetty's dream, just before she changed the water into wine, the wine that had flowed out of a old-fashioned iron spigot. *Speak to me, abuela.* The eyes glistened, the wedding shawl flowed out of her hair, and her copper skin shone in the searing light of Mexico. All was quiet except for the stir of the ceiling fan. The warm room surrounded Hetty, close and moist, a wild dog's ear lifted to catch a command uttered in Spanish, a distant cry.

Then it came.

Down the hall, the cocktail cart jingled as Nella wheeled it in from the kitchen. She was beginning her afternoon alchemy, the ice bucket crackling beneath her busy hands. Hetty pictured her sitting before the great Diana screen, cooled by a circulating fan, reaching for the bottles—

Of course. It was so obvious. Why hadn't Hetty seen it? It was right there under Nella's manicured fingernails. Her grandmother's eyes seemed to close and then open again in confirmation: *the bottles of tawny liquor Nella's sister shipped to her mother every few months.* The ones that came nestled in raffia, wrapped in golden twine, the ones that commanded a place of honor on the lowest shelf of the black-enameled cocktail cart. *Swish your hands in the water, m'ijita. You, too, can turn water into wine.*

Hetty stood, turned, and walked down the hallway toward the marble floors of the drawing room. She wasn't sure what kind of reception she would get, but she had to try. Nella was always more approachable after her first Manhattan.

"Mamá, could I have a drink before I go?"

Candlelight quivered across Nella's face as she looked up at her daughter in surprise. She said nothing but, with a single contemptuous gesture toward an armchair, let Hetty step into an invisible circle whose rim until now had excluded her and Charlotte.

Instead she was asked, "What would you like?"

"I'd like to try that stuff Aunt Cora sends you from San Antonio."

"How did you know about that?"

"I've seen you unwrapping it."

"I guess my secret is out." Nella's fingers played Braille with the bottles on the bottom shelf until she found the one she was looking for. She poured a splash of nectar into a snifter and handed it to Hetty, swishing it on the way to release the aroma. "Here you are."

Hetty took a quick shot and thought she'd gag. Going down her throat it was like molten lava running out of a crater.

Nella sighed with exasperation. "*¡Imbécil!* It's a snifter. Here—let me show you how your ancestors drank it. If you hadn't abandoned *la familia,* you might have learned this." Nella poured some into an elegant old cognac glass with a gold rim, inhaling it first, then savoring every sip before letting it glide with its wet fire down her throat. Hetty followed her example and was amazed at how many different flavors unfolded from the golden sauce if you took it slow.

"What do you taste?" Nella's voice came as Hetty sat with eyes closed, following the descent of the drink to where her stomach was starting to smile.

"A whiff of wood first, then wood burning—herbs on a mesquite fire—then a hot, sweet aftertaste, fruit sizzling with peppers. Then you swallow the whole fire."

"Mmmm." Nella smiled at her for the first time. "You've got a good tongue."

Hetty tried it again. "This stuff grows on you. What is it?"

"Vino mezcal."

"¿Qué no?"

"Mescal wine. The brandy of Mexico."

"Really? And *Tía Cora* sent it to you?"

"Yes, bless her. She knows how much I like it—and you can't get it here." Nella poured them another round and, as they sipped, she seemed to warm up to the presence of her daughter at the cocktail hour. She told Hetty more about the wonders of this fabled *vino,* why it had been prized for centuries by the upper classes of Mexico and how it came to be imbued with such a varied garland of flavors. "They take the heart of the *agave* plant—the crown of daggers—and bake it for three days in a rock pit before drawing off the spirits. It's still made the old way."

Hetty couldn't get over the novelty of drinking with Nella, growing more amiable by the minute. With her rich soft voice, she remembered for her daughter some of the lore that had been passed down in their family. As Hetty sipped at the *mezcal* and listened to the old legends of its gods, she found herself being transported. Maybe she'd drunk too much or listened too long to her mother's hypnotic voice, but she sensed that the room was taking on a soft haze more golden than mere candle power, a radiance that was brightening her mind. When she heard about *Mayuel*—a mere woman who had first discovered the succulent heart of the agave plant and thus became the mother of all mescal gods—Hetty began to hear the voices of her friends giving her advice. She remembered how Doris Verne had chided her during lunch at the club: "You're a daughter of the Magnolia City!" Then what Odell had said at dinner earlier in the week: "You don't make money by working harder, you make money by using your imagination." She hadn't understood what he'd meant at all, but here—in the radiant air above the brandy snifters—his words took on a new significance. They shimmered across her vision, hovered in the air—*USE YOUR IMAGINATION.*

"So where does *Tía Cora* get this stuff?"

Nella's eyes glazed with a vacant, melancholic light. "There's a man . . ."

"And where does this man get it?"

"*Quién sabe.* Cora knows—Guerrero, I think she said."

"Guerrero? *¡No! ¿En serio?*"

"I think so."

"Grandmother's birthplace?"

"Sí. ¿Porqué?"

"*Ayinada.* Does it have wild dogs running through the plaza?"

"*Es probable.* What Mexican town doesn't?"

"*Sí. Como no.* Where is Guerrero?"

Nella tried to describe the location of the old colonial town: If the edge of Texas were a plow cutting into Mexico, Guerrero would sit right where the plow bit into the earth. "Near Zapata," she said. "South of Laredo."

In her mind, Hetty pinned a red flag along the sharp curve of the Texas border. "Mamá, would you let me have that bottle?"

"My mescal! You're taking my mescal?" Nella pretended to pout. "Well, I suppose. Cora always sends four. Here—take an unopened one."

Hetty held the bottle in her hands. "Do you think people will drink this stuff?"

"Well, you loved it, didn't you? And there's a more refined liquor made from blue agave that you can substitute for gin."

"Really? Is it good gin?"

"Let me put it this way—the Aztecs used their word for *volcano* to describe it."

"Oh, what word was that?"

"Tequila."

Hetty didn't wait for Garret to come and pick up her belongings, but caught a cab at the hotel entrance and headed straight home. In spite of the hot air flowing through the taxi's windows, she shivered along the way. Her grandmother's ghost had entered her with a chill, setting her mind tingling with possibility. She no longer saw herself lying quietly beside her husband, snagged in his bed. She saw herself in motion now, leaping like Diana with the deer, a huntress who was more than Mac's whore. Perhaps she would adopt her mother's deity after all. The ancestors had spoken. Hetty was to take her husband to San Antonio, be his translator, and lead him to hidden treasure. When she strode into the kitchen, she found Garret and Odell huddled in the breakfast nook over a crinkling map of Louisiana, looking for a quick route to New Orleans.

"Not east," she announced triumphantly. "South." She poured them some mescal and demonstrated how to drink it.

"Where did you find this cactus nectar, my dear, this elixir?" Odell asked.

"My aunt Cora sent it from San Antonio. She's an artist and knows about these things."

"And how long has it been since you've visited your dear aunt the artist?"

"At least six years."

"Poor Cora," he cooed. "Don't you think you've neglected her long enough?"

Garret turned onto Flores Street, and they came right through the center of San Antonio, past the white dome of San Fernando Cathedral, which Odell claimed was Moorish. Hetty craned her neck to catch a glimpse of the river, but it was below street level, down in a shady crevice.

Next a street sign flashed in the corner of her eye, Dolorosa, causing a memory to arise from the corner of her mind. She'd been riding in the backseat of another car, six years earlier, sitting between her mother and her sister, touring the Mexican Quarter. The driver had put his arm out to turn left from Santa Rosa onto Dolorosa, when Nella had shouted out, "Don't turn down this street!" and had gone as pale as a porcelain doll. Hetty pulled out her passbook and made an entry under *Balance: Dolorosa Street.*

White columns and porticos began to drift by the window, bringing Hetty back to the present. She knew they were on King William Street in Germantown.

"Cora's studio is on Washington, over by the river." A mailbox glinted on a metal fence when Garret pulled up to the curb. The wrought iron gate shivered as Hetty opened it, and the wind came rustling up from the river through the giant pecan trees. She remembered filling her pockets with the smooth hard nuts when she'd come as a child to visit her stern grandfather, Anton. They would click together as she walked. She heard a distant sound of tinkling from the deep shade. Something in her stirred, ancient yet familiar. She spotted an old wooden sign she recognized—THE COSMOS: WE'RE OUT OF THIS WORLD—and nothing else.

The path ended at a mossy rock wall, a trellis overgrown with some kind of wild grape. She caught the shape of a window in the rocks. It was a river cottage run wild. Then she saw the source of the tinkling she kept hearing. The grape vines had been hung with wind chimes every few feet: a flock of birds, a set of temple bells, and a spiral of harlequins. Everything seemed to be in motion, murmuring and ringing. She rang the caravansary bells.

Her aunt emerged silently out of the garden shadows, slipping off an artist's smock. She was tall like Hetty, her height emphasized by a long black dress and equally black hair that was caught in a Spanish comb and streamed down her back. Silver frosted her temples and tinkled at her wrist. Under her feet, a half dozen cats poured by, mewling and peering up with green, unblinking eyes.

"¡Tiíta!" Hetty called, addressing her with the affectionate Mexican title for Aunty that they'd always used as girls.

"*¡Sobrina!* My dear, dear niece," she answered, hugging Hetty warmly and twirling her around to admire the crepe dress she wore, hung with a long sash. "Weren't you in high school last time I saw you? And here you are married—I hardly recognize you.... Where's that new husband of yours?"

"He's in the car." Hetty led her out, and a search party of cats followed surreptitiously in the leaves.

Garret and Odell must have been busy while she was at the house. The Lincoln had been freshly dusted and stretched out with lustrous elegance in the shade. "There's Garret. And this is his business partner, Odell. I'd like you to meet my aunt Cora. Now let me see if I can remember your ex's name," Hetty said, "Cora Beckman de..."

"Groos. I made the same mistake my mother did—marrying a German! But I paint under Cora Ardra. Never mind our family history—I'm so glad you young people have come to visit the Cosmos." She opened the gate and waved them through. "We're out of this world!"

Apparently no one ever used the front door but entered the long, low-ceilinged living room straight off the veranda. She invited Hetty and Garret to take the old cracking leather wing chairs drawn up before an enormous stone hearth, hung with worn farm tools and old Spanish armor. Odell spread out with some ceremony on one of the sofas. Once Hetty sat down, many things around her looked familiar: aging, flaking mirrors in baroque frames, at least a dozen tarnished candelabra that would all be lit at night, faded rugs underfoot.

"Now let me get you young people something to drink. I'm sure you're dying of thirst after your long drive. What'll it be? Iced tea?"

"Mother served me something the other day you had sent her...."

"Oh, what was that?"

"A brandy from Mexico."

"Vino mezcal?"

"*Sí,* that's it."

"Aha! You've discovered mescal already. You youngsters *are* growing up fast nowadays. So mescal it is. You, too, Odell?"

"Please, ma'am."

She dusted off some snifters and splashed a little golden liquid into them from a decanter kept next to the birdcage. Hetty suspected it was used a lot. "Let's make that four then."

She served them, then planted herself in the middle of a divan crowded with oversized cushions. Hetty studied her aunt as she curled up amid the sun-faded silks. Cora Beckman de Groos, in spite of her marriage to a gentleman of her German neighborhood, had never really assimilated into Anglo society like Nella. She didn't hide her ethnicity but accentuated it with colorful accessories and dress. A silver necklace of coral spread across her black dress. She lifted her glass and waited for them to join her. *"¡Salud, amor, y dinero—"*

They all took a healthy sip and let a collective sigh of pleasure escape.

"So let me look at you two newlyweds." She gazed at them both for a moment, unflinching, appraising them. "I can see you're in love," she said, sipping. "Thank God. Too bad you had to elope, but it was probably the only way."

"Mamá and Dad wanted me to marry Lamar Rusk, of course."

"Of course. Had your life all mapped out for you, I'm sure. But you never loved Lamar. I knew that. Besides—" She whispered to Hetty, pretending that Garret couldn't hear, "This one's choice."

Garret buried his grin in his snifter. They were all inhaling, taking their time, and letting the flames unfold slowly down their throats.

"You don't sound like a Texan, young man."

"No, ma'am. I'm from Montana."

"Montana? Then I take it your family weren't sheep farmers."

"My father was a senator."

"A senator's son? Aren't you a clever girl, Hetty."

"I thought so. But Mother won't even have us over."

"Of course not. You eloped."

"So?" Garret asked.

Cora asked in an aside to Hetty: *"Si sabe que eres mestiza, ¿no?"*

"*Sí,* he knows my grandmother was Mexican."

"Well, there you go. In our culture, elopement is an unpardonable sin. We call it stealing the bride."

"I didn't know that," Hetty said.

"Of course not, *m'ija.* You've been deprived of half your heritage."

"Then is that why Nella's so angry at me?"

"That's part of it, I'm sure. As much as she tries to deny it, Nella's still a Mexican at heart. Plus, my dear niece—you would have to go and marry a MacBride!"

"What's that got to do with it?" Hetty asked.

"My sister has an old grudge against the Irish, I'm afraid."

"Why?"

"Oh, let's just call it a childhood trauma. It's mostly because you eloped. You'll be shunned until your first child is born then showered with forgiveness."

"I don't care what happens, *Tiíta.*" Hetty shrugged. "I had to get away from home."

"You're a true *norteña,* like me. We Ardras come from the north of Mexico, and we'll be damned if anybody's going to tell us what to do. And to make it more complicated, I've also been psychoanalyzed. Have you read Freud, Odell?"

"*Totem and Taboo*. A classic."

"How about you, Garret?"

"No, ma'am," he said sheepishly.

"Oh, you should! He's all the rage right now." She looked at him intently. "There's someone here who trained under Dr. Freud himself."

"Don't they interpret your dreams?" Hetty asked. *What would they make of mine?* she wondered.

Cora chuckled. "There's more to it than that, I'm afraid. It took four years." She continued to peer at Garret.

"So?" He locked eyes with her. "Are you cured?"

"I no longer catch colds," she answered, looking right through him. "And I know people's secrets without being told."

"Uh-oh, I'd better make my mind blank then," Garret said, glancing at Hetty and Odell.

"You have nothing to worry about, my dear fellow," Cora answered, smiling sagely. "What you think you have to hide is all on the surface." She turned to Hetty. "And if your mother weren't so shallow, she'd see that. Now that's a woman who needs to be psychoanalyzed!" A black cat leaped up onto her lap. "Cassandra, my pet," she cooed, stroking her. The cat mewed. "Yes, you know secrets too, don't you?" She whispered into the cat's ears, "Especially about the future." Cora glanced at Hetty for only a moment, but it electrified her. "Enough about these arcane matters. What can we plan for your visit to Unsainted Anthony?" Cora rattled off an itinerary for them that would have taken days, but Hetty insisted they could only stay overnight.

"We'd love to pick up some of that mescal to take home. We've grown so fond of the stuff."

"Tepoztecatl has touched you, I see." Cora gazed at Hetty and narrowed her eyes as if debating something in her mind. She shook her head. "Your mother's going to kill me. . . ."

"Then do it!"

"Okay. I'm sending you to meet Miguel. Mr. Delgado. He runs an ice house in the Quarter. Right on Haymarket Plaza."

"What's an ice house?"

"Oh, don't you have those back home? They're sort of like open-air cantinas. You just have to go and experience one. Miguel can tell you where to find the best brimstone bowl, too. There's so much more to do here than in boring old Houston."

Before they left, Cora gave them a tour of the house. Her pictures of *la familia* weren't hidden like Nella's, but openly displayed in clusters on ranch tables. When Hetty discovered Liliana's wedding portrait, she stopped and gazed at it, the shawl glowing around her head like an aura.

"You should have that, *m'ija,*" Cora said and disappeared.

Garret and Odell followed the sound of a fountain into the back bedroom. When her aunt returned, Hetty caught the scent of a cedar chest. Cora carried something draped over both arms. "This is the *rebozo,* the shawl, your grandmother is wearing in that portrait." She let it fall into Hetty's hands like purling water, its long fringes cascading through her fingers.

"Abuela," Hetty whispered.

"When a *mestiza* weds, she is always given her own *rebozo*. This is an especially fine one from San Luis Potosí, made of Chinese silk."

Hetty hung it on her arms and stepped up to one of the baroque mirrors to survey herself. It was cut very full, with the longest fringes she'd ever seen, the silk faded to a pearly antique white.

"Wear it around your shoulders," Cora said, lifting it, "to show that you are a married woman, and men will respect you more. Mexican men, at least."

"Gracias, Tiíta. Es tan hermoso. I guess I get it because I'm the oldest."

"Ha! I don't think Charlotte would want it. I could never even get her to speak Spanish with me."

Hetty then noticed a photo of two girls in sailor suits, sitting on the ground with their arms clasped around their legs, laughing. "Who are they?"

"Your mother and me."

"Her knees are showing here," Hetty murmured as if talking to herself.

"¿Perdóneme?"

"I just realized lately that I've never seen my mother's knees."

"And you never will. She always keeps them covered."

"Why, *Tiíta?"*

Cora didn't answer. She gazed at the photograph of the young girls, their hair pulled back in knots, and said, "Don't ever ask her about it." She turned and flashed Hetty a smile, saying, "Just go meet Miguel." Then she roared out so the men would hear, "Let me show you my studio!"

She escorted the whole group into a long narrow room overlooking the river. Her recent works in progress startled Hetty: The quaint scenes of life in the Quarter that Hetty remembered had metamorphosed into something surreal—dreamscapes of haunting intensity.

"Your work has changed."

Cora just laughed. "I can't paint the Mexican market anymore. Not since Freud. And here's my latest work. . . ." Cora said with a wave.

The huge painting on the easel, almost finished, had already caught Hetty's eye: A girl hovered in the crucifixion pose, trying to hold heavy books in her outstretched hands. She stood inside a high wall, a prison overlooking the river, or maybe it was a convent because above it nuns swooped from a scarlet sky and only one window in the building blazed with hot light like someone couldn't sleep. The nuns were not pious, Hetty noted. Their black habits flared like the wings of avenging angels.

"I call this one *Sisters,*" Cora said.

Just as they turned off North Flores and crossed over the bridge into the Quarter, the Angelus tolled. Shadows fell off things like black smoke and the last of the sun burned for a bright instant in the retama trees along San Pedro Creek. They parked the car on Milam Square and set out on foot. The men unbuttoned their collars and rolled up their sleeves, welcoming the cool breeze that was beginning to stir the hot, dry air.

With it came the sound of singing, sweet and melodious, somewhere ahead of them, so they wandered down San Saba Street and along Produce Row. The buildings were low and flat, but their insides spilled out onto the walkways from all sides. Color vibrated in the evening light. Strips of paper in orange and blue advertised *grandes ventas*—big sales—in every shop. Storefronts were a jumble of huge paper flowers, clay animals, striped serapes, and racks of papier-mâché Judas figures leering at Hetty out of the shadows. The scent of chili floated in the air from little hole-in-the-wall restaurants.

A dark woman standing in the doorway of a bookstore asked, *"¿Amorosas, señorita?"* When Hetty objected that it wasn't Valentine's Day, the woman explained in rapid-fire Spanish that these cards were imported from Spain to inspire romance on any night of the year. Garret bought two.

Hetty led them back toward the Haymarket, passing rows of chili stands crackling with mesquite wood fires and furnished with long tables lit by tin lanterns, then headed across the crowded plaza toward a sign crudely painted with the words MIGUEL'S IZE HOUSE—AGUA FRÍO. It held a busy corner of the Quarter, its folding garage doors flung open on both streets to let in the night air and the thirsty customers.

"Let me do the talking," Odell told them. "I'm used to dealing with Mexicans. We had some illegals working for us at Weems Moving and Storage. You have to use a lot of flattery with these people. . . ."

A jovial Mexican man joked behind a big red Coca-Cola cooler swimming with sodas and the Mexican soft drinks called *refrescos*. His handlebar mustache drooped under a black bowler hat, and he'd thrown an apron on over his white shirt and black vest. Hetty could see that Miguel's was more than a retail ice outlet: It was a local meeting place, an open-air refreshment stand, and—if Cora was right—the closest thing the Quarter had to a speakeasy.

"Buenas noches," he hailed them as they walked in. *"¿A sus órdenes?"*

"Are you Mr. Delgado?" Odell asked.

He nodded cautiously, immediately suspicious of Anglos asking questions.

"We were sent by Mrs. Groos."

His smile jumped back with the name. "Cora? *Ay, entonces es un placer conocerlos.*"

"Nice to meet you, too," Hetty spoke up. *So this odd fellow is the man my aunt wanted me to meet?*

Hetty ordered a Tamarindo, but the two men pointed to green-tinted bottles of Coca-Cola floating in the melting ice. Miguel flipped a couple into the air and cracked them open on the side of the cooler so that foam came running down the side. He spiked the sodas with a bottle hidden in his vest.

Whatever it was hit Hetty hard and, after her second spiked Tamarindo, she realized that she'd better eat something soon. They had sat down at one of the tables. Voices around her began to echo, and the vapors that would pour out of the ice vault when the door was open began to look more and more like Judas dolls dancing by with fiendish grins.

When Miguel had finished slicing some watermelon for a large family, Hetty approached him. "Cora told me you would know where they have the best food around here."

"*¡Sí!* You must have chili con carne. This you will only find in San Antonio. And in San Antonio, the best chili con carne is made by Señora Delgado. You come with Miguel—bring your drinks, *sí.*" He signaled to an old man dozing on a wooden cane, then led them out onto the street and down to a small wooden house with a door open to the night. Once inside, Hetty looked in vain for clues as to why Cora had sent them here. It was like many of the restaurants they'd passed earlier: a small, simple room crammed with rough wooden tables and benches and an altar to the Virgin glistening with votive candles against the wall. The other diners had finished eating and were sipping coffee. Miguel pulled out a bench for his guests to squeeze in. He shouted directions in Spanish through the serape hung over the door, removing his apron.

Shy and quiet as an animal, a woman slipped through. Her skin was darker than Miguel's, and she kept her eyes averted as she brought them bowls of a steaming red stew, followed shortly by a platter of smoking tortillas freshly baked from corn masa. As she left, Hetty caught a glimpse of bare feet under her long black skirt. Miguel watched them taste the concoction, his smile exploding as they tried to cool their mouths with swigs of Coca-Cola. "*¡Jejeje!*" he laughed.

"*¡Ay, que picoso!*" Hetty gasped.

Once she got used to the piquancy of the stew, she found it delicious, a burning mouthful of *chile ancho* and beef hash, delicately spiced with cumin seeds, garlic, and the leaves of wild marjoram. She finally set aside the wooden spoon and ate it like Miguel did, using the warm tortillas to scoop just the right amount of stew into her mouth. He fetched his guitar to serenade them, singing old ballads about cinnamon flowers, blue doves, and a silver boat.

Once the other customers had left and the candles had begun to dim, Miguel set his instrument aside and confided, "You came for something more than ice, *amigos?*"

"We're looking for mescal," Garret said.

"*¿Vino mezcal? Sí*—I can sell you some. How many bottles?"

"Señor Delgado," Odell spoke up, "I don't think you understand. We're not wanting to buy a few bottles from you. We are looking for the source."

"¿Cómo?"

"La fuente," Hetty said. *The spring.*

"Ah, *la fuente.*" He nodded, then shrugged. *"¿Quién sabe?"* He spread his palms. "Mexico."

Hetty knew he was holding back. She told him their story, all about the stream of goods flowing through The Hammocks that had been dammed up once and for all by the Maceos.

"Of course, we are willing to pay you well for whatever information you have." Odell reached for his wallet and drew out one of the freshly minted hundred dollar bills he'd brought for just such a purpose.

"¿Quién sabe?" Miguel shrugged and left the room.

Odell whispered to Hetty fiercely, "Tell him you're Cora's niece."

"All right!" Hetty whispered. She watched the serape. After a few minutes, it lifted and Miguel peered at them from the gloom on the other side. *"Soy la sobrina de Cora,"* she called to him.

His eyes flashed at her out of the darkness, like black pearls. "You are Esther Ardra Allen . . . ?"

"De MacBride," she said, tipping her head toward Garret.

He rushed back into the room and came over to kiss her hand. "I am honored to meet the niece of Cora Ardra Groos and the daughter of Nella Ardra Allen. Why didn't you tell Miguel?"

"Has my aunt told you about me and my mother?"

"Sí. Mucho." He couldn't take his eyes off her.

Odell spoke up. "Now perhaps you would be kind enough to . . ."

Miguel began speaking passionately in Spanish, his eyes burning into Hetty as he spoke. His words were for her ears only. He told her how much he loved his friend Cora and that he had waited for years to meet her niece, the lovely young *mestiza* from Houston. Now that she was before him, his heart was full, half filled with light, half with blackness. Cora's niece brought him joy, he said, because of her great beauty and her pale complexion. Already, he loved her in his heart. So he would send her to the one free state left in Texas—he pointed at himself and at Hetty—"that belongs to *us*. There we have our *patrón*—and there he is for the people."

Hetty lowered her eyes to break the intensity of his gaze. "There is a *patrón*."

"Oh really? What's his name?" Odell asked.

"*Señor* Archer Parr. He is the Duke of Duval."

Odell's eyebrows shot up again. "An Anglo?"

"*Sí*—" Miguel pulled the bench out and straddled it. "But I tell you—he is for the people. He has helped us take our land back."

"Indeed? *¿Dónde?*"

"In the free state of Duval. That is where you must go if you want mescal."

"I knew it!" Odell slapped the wooden table. "I knew there had to be a pipeline flowing with cactus juice." He kissed the one hundred dollar bill and slid it across to Miguel. "*Muchas gracias, amigo.* I take it you mean Duval County?"

Miguel nodded, folding the bill into his vest pocket.

"Where in hell is Duval County?" Garret asked.

"Just there. In hell. The brush country south of here. Any particular town, *amigo?*"

"Sí, San Diego afamado."

"Famous San Diego," Hetty translated.

"San Dicgo? We have to drive all the way over there?" Garret asked.

Odell chuckled. "The one in Texas, not California."

"*San Diego afamado . . .*" Miguel repeated the phrase, this time singing it. "You see, it is a line from one of our ballads. Here—" He clutched his guitar. "I sing it for you. It tells all about *los tequileros*—the tequila trains."

"It comes in by rail?"

"No, no, *señor.*" Miguel smiled, strumming chords. "Mule trains. One mule can carry eighty bottles."

"And how many mules travel in a train?"

"*Quién sabe*—twenty, thirty."

Hetty could almost hear the mechanism inside Odell's head, counting bottles, as notes came spilling out of Miguel's guitar, launching him into the wailing rhymes of a border *corrido: "Ya la siembra no da nada."* "The crops are not productive; there is nothing more to say." He sang the whole song through in a lisping Spanish, then intoned an English translation for them. It was all about the "proud sons of Guerrero"—who import the only crop that is profitable anymore, *la mejor cosecha,* the one that is *la que dan los barriles,* "given by the barrels."

The last verse, *Pobrecita de mi madre,* he sang over two or three times, like a refrain, a lament. "Down the bars of this dark prison/ Flow her tears, so sad, so sad." His sweet tenor voice hovered over the word for tears, *lágrimas,* and his eyes glistened in the candlelight.

Hetty loved the song and made him repeat it several times so she could write the words down. The melody was simple, and the lyrics were easy to remember because of their frequent rhymes.

He stopped singing. Everyone fell quiet for a few moments as another candle sputtered out. It was almost dark in the room. "Remember," Miguel told them in a low voice, "we Mexicans believe anything south of the Nueces River is still our land. So be careful. And never go into the brush alone. Find your way to the ranch they call *Las Ánimas. . . .*"

"The spirits," Hetty translated.

When they left the Delgado Cafe, there was only a single votive still burning on the shelf underneath the Madonna. It flickered across her face, and Hetty noticed for the first time that she had dark skin, like an Indian. There was also enough light to see the golden stars glistening on the deep blue mantle that cascaded from her head to her shoulders, eddying around the arms lifted in prayer. Hetty was about to ask Miguel about the Madonna of the Stars when he blew out the candle and whispered *adiós.* Then she felt him clutch her arm in the darkness and murmur in Spanish, "Come back to see Miguel soon—alone. I have more to tell you."

Hetty pulled her arm out of his grasp and stepped into the street. She wondered what he meant. The sidewalk was so narrow she had to walk behind Garret and Odell. She looked up and caught a glimpse of the Milky Way streaming over San Antonio and thought about the celestial beauty of Mary's mantle. It was like someone had taken the sky just before dawn, when it's starting to turn blue but stars are still twinkling, and pulled it rippling down to earth, like a circus tent collapsing. She almost saw it floating above her head, settling down around her as the air escaped from under it. Then she realized that Garret and Odell were talking about her.

"Odell, no!" Garret's voice was raised. "You're not taking my wife into the brush country. She's staying here with Aunt Cora."

"But you heard what he said, Mac. Anything south of the Nueces is still Mexico. We need someone along who speaks Spanish."

They were just on the edge of Milam Plaza, waiting to cross.

"Don't make me do it, Mac," Hetty shouted after him. "Don't make me call you a flat tire."

Garret kept going, dodging Model As.

She ran after him, shouting, "Flat tire! Flat tire!"

He was standing at the car. She came up beside him and looked into his face. His jaw was set.

"You're not going. That's all there is to it."

Garret asked Odell to drop them off at one of the stairways leading down to the water. They strolled along in silence, following the flow of the river that washed through the town like a canal imported from Venice. Garret tried to hold her hand, but she pulled it away, hugging herself with her arms. Stone bridges arched overhead, and trees crowded the lush banks: fig and banana, cypresses spreading ancient roots, and weeping willows trailing their endless leaves into the rippling water. They could hear accordion music from a beer garden up above, its yellow bulbs leaving a long wake of shimmering light.

The riverbank became too overgrown for them to continue, so they had to climb back up to street level and follow Saint Mary's south to the King William district. Hetty led Garret up a crumbling staircase, through a gate, and into the back of Cora's stone cottage.

Garret stripped in the dark, and she heard the bedsprings squeak. She lit a candle, then undressed and wrapped herself in a kimono.

She slid into bed and turned her back to him. He moved his body against hers, and she heard something crinkle. He had unfurled the valentine he'd bought her. Its ribbons were tickling her arm.

"Are you my—what was the word? *Amorosa?*"

"I don't know. I don't feel like it at the moment."

He kissed the back of her neck. He let the long valentine stream across her shoulder.

"I thought this was guaranteed to inspire romance. I want my money back." He pulled her kimono up over her hips and wrapped his legs around hers. She usually found that very sensual, but it wasn't doing a thing for her tonight.

"It's not the card. It's you. You're being such a bore."

He kissed her neck again and started that sexy whispering in her ear that he liked to do. *Whispering so no one can hear me.* "I can't take you into the brush, baby," he breathed. "Everything's got thorns. They've got scorpions thick as ants."

She turned and gave him a long kiss with her tongue. He tried to climb on top of her, but she kept holding him down. "Remember the time you took me out to the sandbar and I was so scared?"

"Mm-hmmm." He kept trying to kiss her again.

"I felt safe as long as I was sitting on your lap. As long as I didn't have to touch the bottom. That's what this is like for me, Garret." It was true. She pictured them driving across the prairie until they came to the shore of the brush. Everything would crackle and hiss around them. An ocean without water, dry and fossilized. The chaparral was the coral; the scorpions were the crabs. But none of it would wound her as long as he lifted her up. She'd be like the picture she'd glimpsed today of Mary standing on the crescent moon, above it all. She would wrap herself in an ultramarine mantle glittering with golden stars, and nothing would harm her because she would have the protection of the sky. The sky was male—Nella had told her that once, long ago. It was the earth that was a woman.

He was trying to get his arms around her. She knew if he succeeded she was lost. She pinned them to the bed, straddling him. "Do you understand what I'm saying?"

"Yes, yes. Okay," he whispered, grinding his hips.

"So you'll take me? Promise?"

"Yes, I mean it." He rose on his elbows. "We'll drink and fornicate our way to hell and back. Now let me up."

"Oh no, you don't." She shoved him back down. "Just lie back, *señor,*" she said, peeling the kimono away from her hardening nipples. "*Mamacita's* got *chile* in her veins tonight."

Chapter 8

As they headed south down Route 281 the next day, the river gardens of San Antonio gave way to gray-green hills of brush. Hetty looked through the dusty windows and watched the terrain whipping by: Everything looked as if it had been sprinkled with ashes. Stretching out luxuriously on the soft leather seats, she lowered the window to get a little air. She was not only hungover, but her body was still languorous from all the lovemaking last night. Cora had been right, that back bedroom was the most romantic. She fell into a trance of happiness until the pavement ran out, then every rut Garret rattled over made her head throb a little more. Odell drowsed beside her. To distance herself from his snoring, she hummed the *corrido* Miguel had taught her.

Places drifted by in the haze: Pleasanton, Campbellton, Three Rivers. South of the Nueces River, the Lincoln rolled out onto the Gulf Prairies, as bald and flat as a tortilla. It looked like a steamroller had come along and leveled the land all around. The road ahead seemed endless. *What the hell?* Hetty thought, but didn't say anything.

When they reached Alice, Texas, Garret turned right on Route 96. They headed west for a quarter of an hour—back into the brush. Hetty watched for some kind of sign. Currents of heat blew past like sheets rippling on a clothesline. Mirages of mesquite trees began to appear through the shimmering air. Chaparral arose like patches of fog. When Hetty first spotted San Diego up ahead, she wasn't sure it was real. The twin towers of the Catholic church swam into view. Palm trees rustled overhead.

Garret chuckled. "Look at this godforsaken place."

"My dear fellow." Odell shook himself awake. "We fought a war to wrest this land away from Mexico."

"Yeah? Well, maybe it's time to fight another one and make them take it back."

As Garret drove down one of the avenues, dodging the chickens that strutted freely everywhere, Hetty started to wonder if he was right. She peered out at the buildings they passed: a brick courthouse, a wooden shack called Rodriguez Groc with an awning that had rotted away, a building made from some kind of coarse white block. She was wondering where the stone came from, when Odell read her thoughts.

"That building? It's constructed out of caliche," he said. "A sedimentary rock. You find great encrustations of it here in these arid climes."

They had crept their way down to the foot of Texas, grown dry and callused from constant exposure to the sun.

A chicken fluttered up in front of the car, screeching at Garret. He ground to a stop. "We're nowhere," he muttered.

Hetty looked out the window. And there were the wild dogs. "No, we're in the right place. See if there's a hotel."

Garret turned up St. Peter's Avenue and slid to a stop in front of a two-story frame building laced with a veranda. MARTINET HOUSE, the sign read. Hetty followed Garret through the doors in case they didn't speak English. But the clerk behind the counter was a burly Anglo man. He took one look at Garret's slicked-down hair and said, "Second road to your left, o'er the creek, three miles south. Y'all come to the gates of a ranch. . . ."

Garret just stared at him.

"How'd you know?" Hetty asked.

The man smirked at her. "Lady, I can smell that brilliantine a mile away."

* * *

Once they crossed a creek, the brush engulfed them. The narrow road must have been hacked out with machetes, because on both sides rose impenetrable walls of mesquite trees twisting over the brittle branches of chaparral. Occasionally, a Spanish dagger plant cut through or a pasture opened up. There Hetty saw a windmill turning listlessly or an old cow stretching its neck to reach the beans on the topmost branches of the trees—the only things that hadn't shriveled up in what had obviously been a long dry spell. They were whole colonies of *nopalitos*—prickly pear cacti with their flat round leaves studded with thorns.

Hetty sang the *corrido* to cover the itch of anxiety. She was certain they'd driven farther than three miles and were lost out here where everything had thorns. Were they being set up for an ambush? She was about to warn her husband to turn around when they came to an opening in the brush: a rough mesquite fence, a lane that led straight off to the right. Garret slowed to a stop.

"They wouldn't advertise themselves, of course." Odell smacked his lips.

Garret nosed the Lincoln into the narrow caliche lane, muttering that he wouldn't be able to get the long car turned around. Odell egged him on, and Hetty remained silent, in spite of the doubts she felt looking out at the desolate landscape. Much to her relief, the undergrowth rushed back, and they came out into the *placita,* the "little plaza" that surrounded a South Texas ranch like a moat. In its midst spread the structures she'd been hoping for: barns, loading pens, a great wooden wheel of a windmill turning above the squat rock ranch house. Hetty's faith in her dreams was restored, and she felt an odd sense of connection to the place. She could even see a barren beauty in *la broza,* the underbrush so ashen and wild all around them.

Then they spotted the cars.

Garret whistled. "Look at those wagons!"

On the dry bones of the clearing, a ring of automobiles sparkled like a chrome necklace in the bright sun. Hetty recognized a white Cadillac V8 and a long black Bugatti, but had never seen some of the other exotics.

"There's a brand-new Duesenberg," Garret said.

"You think it's a '28?" Odell asked.

"Looks like it to me."

"What's that one?" Hetty asked, pointing to a luscious model up ahead that was the color of cream.

"That, my dear, is a Hispano-Suiza," Odell said. "Look at the license plate." It was from Oklahoma.

In the shade sat the drivers of these glorious cars, men with their pin-striped vests unbuttoned and their white shirtsleeves rolled up. They stopped their poker game and eyed the newcomers suspiciously. Hetty saw what the fellow back at the hotel had meant: Many of them wore their hair like Garret, sheik-style. But something else they wore brought her anxiety rushing back: shoulder holsters.

Garret slowed to a stop in front of the car from Oklahoma. Hetty leaned forward. "I wouldn't go any farther if I were you."

"Take it slow." Odell motioned him forward.

Garret eased the Lincoln toward the ranch house. Through the dusty windshield, Hetty spotted an Anglo hunched in a chair under the tin roof of the porch, smoking. Only his dusty boots stretched out into the sun. Over by the loading pens, a couple of Mexican ranch hands were stooping over a rectangular pit in the ground, throwing mesquite logs onto hot coals. The man on the porch watched them warily through trails of smoke. Then he came over.

"Is this *Las Ánimas?*" Garret switched off the engine.

"Who wants to know?" He leaned into the window and looked them over.

"Mr. MacBride. And this is my partner, Mr. Weems."

The eyes under the Stetson spotted Hetty in the back. "Who's the woman?"

"Mrs. MacBride."

"You brung your wife here?"

"We're looking for *Las Ánimas*. Are we in the right place?"

The man straightened up and tipped his hat at Hetty. Holsters dangled off both hips. "Miss."

Hetty sat on the edge of the backseat. "Mr.—?"

"I'm the foreman, Jeremiah."

"Looks like you're expecting a pack train," Garret said, gesturing to the other cars.

"This here's a ranch, Mister. You want cows. We got cows." Jeremiah dropped his fuming butt and bruised it with his boot. "Now if y'all excuse me," he said, tipping his hat at Hetty again. "I'd get her out of here if I was you." He walked back to the porch.

"You heard him," Hetty said. "Take me to the hotel."

Brandishing his cane, Odell opened his car door. "Nobody intimidates Odell Weems." He followed the man. Garret hustled after him, leaving Hetty abandoned in the passenger compartment of the Lincoln. She panicked for a moment, then reminded herself, *I'm the one who wanted to come here. Take heart!* She sucked in a deep breath and opened the car door. She made her way across the rocky ground and up the worn steps of the ranch house.

"As a matter of fact, Jeremiah," Odell was saying, "we're more interested in mules. We were told you import mules from Mexico."

The man squinted into the sun. "Oh, yeah? Who told y'all that?"

"A certain Señor Delgado of San Antonio. I think you know him. He runs an ice house on Haymarket Square."

"You mean Miguel? Bowler head? *He* sent you?"

"With his personal recommendation," Odell said. "He gave us some delightful samples of . . . uh, what shall I call it? Donkey piss?"

This made Jeremiah chuckle. "Whoa, shit. If Miguel sent you . . ."

"And, of course, we are perfectly willing to contribute a little"—Odell rubbed his thumb and forefinger together—"*mordida,* as the Mexicans say."

Hetty jumped. She thought she'd felt something tickling the toes that peeked out of her white summer sandals. "I'm afraid of scorpions." She smiled at Jeremiah.

"I imagine they're asleep now, ma'am. You don't need to pay them no mind. Just turn your shoes upside down before you put them on in the morning."

"Is it true you have rattlesnakes six feet long?"

"Tall."

"I beg your pardon?"

"Six feet tall. *El Víbora Seca,* to be real exact."

The name caught Hetty's attention. "The dry snake," she translated.

"He's bringing them mules you're so interested in. You don't want to tangle with him, though. He'd just as soon eat y'all for dinner tonight. Got a taste for barbecued Anglo, which he acquired at the age of fourteen fighting in the Mexicans' civil war. His idea of fun is to bury you up to your neck then trample your head with his horse."

"Charming," Hetty said. "When can we look forward to meeting this person?"

"*Quién sabe*. Smugglers are like your scorpions, ma'am; they only come out at night. Some time after dusk, you'll see them—riding up that dry creek. But I wouldn't expect much. See Baldy over there? The one that never takes his coat off no matter how hot it gets? He's come all the way from Kansas. I'll tell you one thing—he ain't leaving here without enough drink to make the trip worthwhile. He and his men alone own four of these fancy cars. And they all got guns."

Odell and Garret exchanged glances. Garret cocked his head impatiently toward the car. "Thank you kindly, sir," Odell said, bowing. "I'm sure we'll be meeting again."

Rather than take their chances, Odell urged Garret to drive out into the brush and head off the pack train. Hetty insisted on going with them. As the car creaked along the ranch roads a few hours later, she kept busy in the backseat. New luster glimmered in her dark eyes thanks to the right touches of eye shadow and mascara. She crowned them with a cloche that completely swallowed up her hair in cool, white felt. She had thrown on long earrings and lots of beads and unpacked the wedding shawl with its deep antique fringe.

Garret glanced at her in the rearview mirror. "Aren't you a little overdressed for a trip into the brush?"

Hetty just smiled at him and pulled the *rebozo* around her shoulders. She might have to do a little snake charming of her own tonight.

Garret found a narrow dirt road that edged along the bed of the arroyo. They followed it for several miles, losing the creek then finding it again, passing through sandy mesquite flats and low gravel hills. Tree branches slapped into the car, bringing shadows with them. Something howled in the distance. Hetty glanced back to be sure no cars were following them. She rolled up her window and gathered the shawl about her shoulders. She could see why Miguel had warned them: "Never go into the brush alone."

Odell was riding up front, keeping an eye out for the creek, while Garret gassed his way slowly over the gullies that had washed out of the road. But neither foresaw what happened next. From the backseat, Hetty saw the nose of the car rise up, the hood ornament—a leaping greyhound—lifting into the air as they rose over a gravel embankment, then dipped down a slope into the creek bed itself. Directly in front of them were mules, gray as dusk and heavily loaded, trudging along and hardly noticing the car motor throttling down upon them. Garret braked, and the Lincoln slid sideways to a stop in the sand. Hetty didn't wait to be told to duck down, but fell to the floor immediately, making sure the window was open into the driver's compartment.

"Get down," Garret whispered.

"I am down, you idiot. What's happening?"

"They're riding up—pointing rifles at us."

"Let me handle this," Odell said, clearing his throat. He climbed out of the car, shouting, *"Amigos, amigos."* Then Garret's door opened, too.

Someone shrieked Spanish so fast she couldn't follow it, bawling the same phrase over and over. She rose on her knees and peered cautiously over the top of the seat. In the fading light, Garret and Odell were nowhere to be seen, but three Mexicans mounted on horseback pointed 30-30 rifles at the ground in front of the car. Shouts ricocheted up and down the mule train, which had come to a complete stop. They were calling for the *jefe,* the boss. That would be *El Víbora Seca.* She recalled the Virgin of the Stars she'd seen last night at the Delgado Cafe and found a prayer forming on her lips.

Then she heard hooves, galloping fast, and a huge black horse rose out of the creek. She remembered what Jeremiah had told them about the man on its back, how he liked trampling people underfoot. He circled the two bodies in silence, armored with the rugged gear of the *vaquero:* chaps laced with a bramble of scratches from the thorny brush, a bandoleer of bullets slung across his chest, and a leather Stetson cocked over his black eyes. Hetty could hear a faint *amigos* rising up from Odell. They obviously needed an interpreter.

She opened the car door and snaked out a ghostly leg, smooth and white with its silk stocking. The rest of her followed and floated up out of the blue dusk like an apparition, white from head to toe, dripping with fringes and jewels, her eyes deep and beguiling. The *tequileros* peered at her stupefied, the barrels of their rifles dropping slowly through the air. Seca's horse backed up a few steps.

"For God's sake, stay in the car," Garret whispered fiercely.

But she ignored him, stepping out and gathering the blue light around her as she decided what to say. Hetty draped the *rebozo* around her shoulders so they would know she was a married woman. What rose to her lips were phrases from the song she'd learned last night from Miguel. She reached into her purse and pulled out the lyrics that she'd written down. With her rich contralto voice, at first softly, then resoundingly as the Spanish couplets poured back into her memory and out through her throat, she began to sing. *"Ya la siembra no da nada . . ."*

As she sang, Seca leaped off his horse and threw the reins to one of his men. He strode over, stepping across the bodies stretched out on the ground. She heard something jiggling as he walked and looked down—he had snake rattles hanging from his gun belt. What Jeremiah had said about his height was true: He was tall for a Mexican, a good six feet and muscular. She wasn't surprised at the way his face looked as it swam into focus in the twilight—sunbronzed, scarred, with a virile swag of whiskers where he hadn't shaved in days.

"¡Ya basta!" he shouted to silence her. "This song is a joke!" *Of course he would speak English,* Hetty thought. *He's a borderlander.*

"It was taught to me by Miguel Delgado de San Antonio."

"Where I come from, women do not sing such songs."

"But where I come from, they do," she answered. "Why is it a joke?"

"The three men this song was written about? They were trying to smuggle three bottles of tequila across Rio Bravo. They were killed! *¡Por tres botellas de tequila!*"

"*¡Jejeje!*" His men laughed.

Hetty started talking, sometimes in English, sometimes in Spanish. She thanked the bandit for opening her eyes to the humor in the song, but said that it should really have been written about *El Víbora Seca*. He's the one whose fame should be sung about. Only Seca and his men were brave enough to bring the mescal across the river, and that he is well named, for Seca is indeed like a snake that can slither his way through the underbrush and never be found.

The bandit's eyes bored into her from under the leather Stetson. "Who is now crawling on his belly?" He snapped his fingers, and three rifles were lifted back into the air, pointing at the bodies on the ground. "I walk into Texas a free man, and I leave Texas a free man. I am Seca de Guerrero!"

Hetty held her breath. She felt as if she were standing on an eroding cliff and had to quickly find her footing. Those men would pump her husband full of bullets without blinking a dark brown beady eye. She began trembling but knew it would be fatal to show her fear to a man like Seca—it was like staring down a wild animal. She stopped holding her breath and let it fall, deep into her throat where it rose with her voice: "And I am Esther from the family of Ardras who also walked into Texas free! My *abuela,* Liliana Ardra Herrera, came to San Antonio from Guerrero many years ago."

"You are an Ardra?"

"*Sí.* Do you know the Ardra family?"

"*Sí, como no.* Everyone in Guerrero knows of the Ardra family." He squinted at her with new interest.

"We are a very close-knit clan," Hetty boasted. It was a lie. She had never actually met any of her ancestors from Mexico, but Seca didn't have to know that. "*Mi tía,* Cora Ardra, sent me to Miguel Delgado, who sent me to you. My husband and I have come to bring glory to Seca. We have traveled all the way from Houston to find you. The people do not know you there; they have not been touched by the god Tepoztecatl. Doesn't Seca want to be the one who sends the famous brandy of Mexico to los Houstonians?" She poured on more Spanish *adulación* until he stopped circling her, and his growls turned into grunts. She could see a smile playing over his face in the dim light. His eyes melted a little. "But if Seca gives all the mescal to the men from Kansas, there will be none for us to take to the people of Houston. They are very thirsty."

He motioned to the men to lower their rifles. He walked back to his horse and mounted, gripping the reins tightly, and turning the horse to glance at the mule train then back at her. *"Tres,"* he said, pointing at three mules. "Next time, four."

His horse stepped backward, and he disappeared into the darkness.

Hetty sat on a large outcropping of caliche, her feet drawn up from the ground below. Jeremiah had invited them to stay for the barbecue. She knew the flames would keep animals away; she hoped it had the same effect on insects. Darkness had fallen, and that was when the scorpions came out of hiding. She heard a rustling and fancied it was their upraised tails brushing past leaves.

But it was just the two ranch hands coming to turn the thick steaks over and rub more salt and coarse pepper into the brisket. Then the wind shifted, and she caught a whiff of mesquite burning and the succulent sizzling of meat dripping down onto it. She looked around, feeling oddly exposed yet privileged. Garret wasn't too far away. He and Odell had joined a gaslit poker game over at one of the parked cars.

Jeremiah came up to check the progress of the food, his face aglow with orange light. He smiled at Hetty. "Hungry?"

"Starved. Can we eat soon?"

"Yes'm, I believe so." He muttered something in Spanish to the Mexican hands. They went to the other end of the pit and raked dirt off a metal sheet, yanked it back, then picked up shovels and began digging five large round objects out of the coals.

"What are those?" Hetty asked.

"*Barbacoa*. Baked cow heads. For the Mexicans. Want to try some?"

"No thanks. I'll save myself for the bull's testicles."

Jeremiah broke into a grin. "You do that, ma'am. Just don't take any eyes. Seca gets all of them."

Maybe it was the dry air or maybe the aura of menace that hung over the camp making every sense crackle with alertness, but when Hetty was served some of the brisket with a slice of raw onion, a tortilla, and a jalapeño pepper, she swore it was the best food she ever had. She sat there on the rock, her senses adrift, when she noticed someone watching her from the *tequilero* camp beyond the mesquite flames. The horses and mules were all entrenched on the other side of the trough where the exchange of goods had taken place. She knew the eyes instantly, shadowed as they were by the brim of the leather Stetson. Bullets gleamed like war medals in the bandoleer strapped across his chest. She wondered if he slept with it on.

Seca was watching her with a dark glitter in his eyes, and she kept looking away, hoping he'd do the same. But every time she looked back, his eyes were there, mesquite eyes mysterious and full of flames. Then he smiled at her, and she found herself fascinated. What kind of man became a *contrabandista?* What did it take to risk your life daily carrying mescal across the Rio Grande and through the brush to *Las Ánimas?* Only a *norteño* was fearless enough to do something like that, the kind of man cut from rawhide and toughened by living on Mexico's northern frontier. She'd heard about such men all her life. Nella said they were different from other Mexicans—they became outlaws like Pancho Villa. And now here was one of these wild *fronterizos* in the flesh, stalking Hetty as she sat near the fire. She felt her blood stir and stole a glance in his direction. He was walking toward her, fixing her with those eyes again. She panicked and looked for her husband, but he was nowhere to be seen.

"¿Se le ofrece un tequila?" he said, lifting up a bottle in his hand as he came near. He set his plate down on the rock next to her. It

still had a few fatty-looking morsels clustered on it. She was afraid to look too close, for fear she might recognize an eyeball.

"I hear it's like gin," she answered brightly, trying to show him that she had a good line of gab even under these circumstances.

He just snickered. "No, no, *gringa*. Mexican liquor is different. Because you are an Ardra, Seca will show you how we drink tequila in Guerrero. Then you will teach the *norteamericanos,* no?"

She nodded in agreement, afraid to do otherwise.

He carefully laid out his supplies: a handful of sweet little round Mexican limes, a tin of some kind, and the bottle still packaged as it came across the border, wrapped in tissue paper and a protective coating of tule or bulrush.

"Tres," he said. A silver knife appeared in his hands, which he passed slowly in front of her face. It flashed red in the firelight. He picked up one of the limes, fondled its juiciness, and then sliced it cleanly into quarters. He ripped the shucking off the bottle. Pointing to the label, he said, *"Plata."*

"Silver. It has to be silver. . . ." She nodded.

He cracked open the tin and sprinkled a salty-looking ash on the skin between his thumb and forefinger. He lifted it close to her face and said, "In Guerrero, we call this *gusano seco.*"

"Dried snake?" He shook his head. "Oh, I see. Worm. Dried worm," Hetty said.

"Sí. De agave."

"From the agave cactus?"

"Agave is not a cactus. It is a lily."

"So we're not drinking cactus juice. We're drinking the milk of the lily. Wait till I tell Odell."

"Sí. Un momentito." He fell silent and readied himself. Hetty watched closely, taking in every detail. She felt as though she were present at some kind of secret ritual. She had to be able to repeat this accurately for Garret and Odell. He took a large swig of tequila, chased it with a little mummified agave, and then sat down, sucking on a slice of lime and trying to recover his senses. Soon, a deep sigh escaped his lips, and his black eyes opened, slightly glazed.

"Usted . . ." he said, handing her the bottle.

"Gracias."

"De nada." It is nothing.

When she spread her thumb and forefinger, he tickled the delicate skin between them before sprinkling it with the magic worm dust. Lifting the bottle to her lips, she gulped some down, licked up the powder, and chased it with lime juice. It was all she could do to keep from choking. The silver tequila was harsher than mescal, with the subtler flavors refined out, so she welcomed the salty kick of the spicy worm dust and the cool finish of citrus. How many times they did this she didn't know, but she wasn't about to let Seca drink her into the barbecue pit. The fire began to take on a glorious blaze.

"This stuff makes you plenty *bravo,*" she said.

"In Mexico we say, if a rabbit gets a drop of tequila, he spits in the eye of a bulldog."

"And how, kiddo!" She didn't know how to translate that into Spanish.

Seca smiled at her drunkenly. "Esther de las Ardras—*you* are plenty *brava. . . .*"

She smiled back triumphantly, knowing she no longer had to fear the dreaded dry snake of Guerrero. Later, when the fire had died down and no one could see their dark shapes on the rock, she asked him, "Can I buy some of that agave from you?"

He fumbled in the pockets of his coat and fished out a fresh tin. He leaned over and placed it in her hand, which he closed tightly around it. She couldn't wait to tell Odell about the caterpillar crunch. That was the kind of thing that got all his cylinders pumping. Then Seca moved in even closer and turned his face up. His lips hovered less than an inch from hers, and his odor rose up to her nostrils. She'd never smelled a Mexican man before. His scent was different from Garret's, gamier, a wild mingling of southern sweat and leather.

"Gracias," she whispered, not pulling back but joining her breath with his.

Seca breathed the word *nada* into her mouth. In the end, their lips never touched, but she knew that her soul, somehow, had been kissed.

It took them all autumn to get a bustling trade going in tequila. Odell told Hetty he was determined to make it happen by the time Christmas unfolded and holiday decanters demanded to be filled. She did everything she could to help. It was a tough sell at first, as most Houstonians were unfamiliar with the Mexican distillates and went on asking for the labels they'd come to expect from Weems Importing, such as rum from the islands, vintage Old Crow, and the best Canadian Club. Each type of import was aimed at a different market: mescal they sold as a fine brandy, the "favorite of Mexican lords and ladies"; silver tequila was pitched to the flapper crowd as a less expensive form of gin; whereas their more discriminating customers appreciated the subtleties of *añejo*, the most expensive tequilas that were aged in oak barrels for over a year. The tins of agave they saved for the rougher speaks along the Ship Channel, where the dockworkers dared each other to lick up the fossilized worms and slam down shot glasses of the rawest alkie. Everyone liked the prices, as Odell and Garret were able to undersell their competition by a significant margin thanks to the low cost of Mexican liquor brought across the border without any tariffs.

As 1928 bubbled over into 1929, people all over Harris County began referring to Garret and Odell as the Tequila Kings. The bartenders even invented cocktails using the exotic new ingredients: Milk o' the Lily involved cream in some way, and the Dry Snake was a popular mix of citrus, salt, and silver garnished with a coiling twist of lime.

Hetty enjoyed their success thoroughly. Never had she known a New Year so spangled with promise, a winter so cushioned with luxury. Her husband was making thirty times the average salary, so she no longer had to restrain herself. There were new fur coats to snuggle into, new rings sparkling at her fingertips, new gowns of a breathless elegance to wear out dancing at clubs where the bandleaders were their customers. Garret spent $488.99 on one ring alone, hoping to show her that Lamar wasn't the only one who could afford to buy diamonds. The flow of money reached flood stage, and they spent it recklessly, happily, feeling wildly rich and more in love than ever.

Christmas day dawned mild and sunny, as it often did in Houston. On a trellis overlooking the driveway, climbing roses bloomed, while in the still-green post oak shading their bedroom, she heard a redbird trilling his traditional spring song. The screen was broken on one of the windows of their bedroom, so Hetty reached through and hung a Japanese lantern in the branches. She would light a candle in it to signal when she was feeling amorous, which was often.

Garret wanted to go on living in the apartment over the garage so he could be near the thriving business downstairs. Hetty agreed on one condition, that she could take some of the thick wads of cash he handed her every week and give the place a little more swank. She wanted a whole new kitchen and bathroom. As soon as the renovation was finished, she promised Garret, they would start saving toward a well. Odell had told them about a mysterious new syndicate that promised to discover "an ocean of oil" somewhere in Texas. Garret wanted to get himself a lease in the field right away, but Odell refused to disclose the location of this important new find. He seemed to enjoy tantalizing Garret with the news, saying only, "I have bought myself a share." Meanwhile, Hetty hired Henry Picktown for the heavy work of updating their carriage house, spending the cold rainy months of February and March picking out paint colors and going on shopping sprees downtown at Munn's.

At nine a.m. every morning except Sunday, Pick showed up for breakfast, then spent the day sanding woodwork and stripping off the old, faded wallpaper. They lacquered the walls the color of lipstick and the woodwork black as mascara to match Hetty's Chinese dresser. He added a closet in the bedroom, muscled her new golden oak kitchen cabinet up the stairs, and helped the plumber wedge clean white fixtures into the bath. While Pick worked, he sang one of the spirituals he'd learned singing in the choir at Elijah Missionary Baptist Church, his deep-set voice booming over the drum of rain on the roof:

O, poor sinner
Now is your time
O, poor sinner
What you going to do when your lamp burn down—

The apartment was finished by mid-April. Hetty began having the Weemses up for Sunday dinner every week to toast the completion of the weekly run to Duval County. She gloried in the new elegance around her, spreading out elaborate feasts on a round pedestal dining table. Even Pearl was impressed by the luster of the service Hetty set, gleaming with candlelight across diamond-cut crystal and Stieff sterling silver. Oriental carpets spread underfoot, a portiere hung over every door, and music drifted by from a new Silvertone Radio. Hetty was in her element. Small though they were, these four rooms became home. She could call them "a carriage house" now with complete confidence. She even mailed in the application for the Cupola Club.

In early May, Garret and Odell were late coming back from a liquor run. They always returned by Friday afternoon, in time to unload the Lincoln and make deliveries for the evening shift. When they hadn't returned by five p.m., Hetty began to fret. She called Pearl to see if she'd heard anything.

"What can't be cured must be endured, I always say. I wouldn't worry if I was you, hon. It's probably just the pack train being late." Pearl chattered for a while, her words taking the edge off Hetty's fears. But she still spent a restless night, curling into the sheets, listening for the sound of footsteps on the stairs. She had good reason to be worried. She had just that day read in the *Post-Dispatch* that Congress had passed a law elevating the selling of liquor to a felony punishable by ten years in prison and a ten-thousand-dollar fine. She remembered the name because it sounded so innocuous. The Jones Act.

By Saturday afternoon, she was beginning to get calls from their clients. Garret had tutored her in the language of liquor dealing. She was never to offend the customer by using direct speech; she was to keep everything vague and impersonal while still delivering the necessary information. Some of the voices she recognized; others were strange. Most were polite; a few were rude and pushy. She would have stopped answering the phone altogether, but every time it rang, she hoped to hear her husband's voice on the other end.

Later, she turned on the radio and tried to distract herself. She stretched out on her new chaise lounge and listened to "the RKO Hour," then caught an episode of *Amos 'n' Andy*. Andy was giving Amos a hard time about not working.

"Where yo' taxi?"
"At de mechanic."
"Is dat automobile broke?"
"Nosir, it fixed."
"Den how come yo' ain't driving it?"
"Ain't got de money."
"How yo gonna make de money widout de taxi?"
"Yo' gonna float me a loan."
"A loan? I tell yo' what. Yo' don't get dat car out yo' gonna be alone awright. All alone."

Laughter relaxed her and, without realizing it, she drifted off, dipping into a shallow sleep in a warm bubbling pool, waking only hours later when the phone echoed through her hypnotic dreams. Static crackled from the radio. Half awake, she turned the knob off and fumbled for the receiver, thinking it would be Garret at last.

Instead, it was Pearl. "Any news?" Hetty asked sleepily.

"Nothing but bad to tell," Pearl sobbed.

Hetty threw the receiver back onto its sleeve and slid off the chaise, wide-awake. She shoved her feet into shoes and rushed down the stairs. It was a clear spring evening, the air soft, slightly scented. She looked up. The crescent moon cut its way through the stars, razor-sharp. Gleams of white light glinted along the driveway, which was empty. No brougham. *Pearl must have gotten a phone call,* she told herself. The big house loomed over her, lightless from the looks of it. Hetty felt her way to the screen door, edged into the kitchen, and stood perplexed.

Darkness chilled the room. Only one ceiling fixture had been flicked on, out in the hallway, driving a stake of light across the breakfast nook. Garret sat there alone, his face in his hands. *What's he doing here?* Then, something moved in the shadows. A hand, all bone and nail, grappled onto Hetty's arm.

"Nothing but bad to tell," came the strangled voice. Hetty put her arm around Pearl's frail shoulders and felt them shaking. She took the woman in her arms and held her tight while she cried. She kept glancing over at Garret for an explanation. The skin on his hands had been torn. She held on to Pearl while the sobs came choking out, stroking her back. "They got Odell, hon," she was finally able to say. Hetty lowered Pearl onto a kitchen stool in the dark and went over to Garret. She slid her hands into his and pulled them away from his face. She gasped. It was horribly scratched.

"Honey, what happened? Where's Odell?"

His eyes were lowered. He wouldn't look at her. "Odell's still there," he said in a dry, hollow voice. "They almost got me, too."

Pearl rocked back and forth, repeating, "I've rolled snake eyes again." Then she started moaning. Hetty held Garret, not knowing what to say. The moans welled in the gloom, raw and distressing, then settled into quiet weeping that ended with a hostile whisper. "You left him, didn't you?"

Anguish twisted Garret's face as he looked across the room. "I'm sorry, Pearl. I'm really sorry. But there wasn't anything I could do—you got to believe me."

"Just tell us what happened," Hetty breathed.

"I need a drink first."

Hetty went into the dining room and retrieved a bottle of mescal from the sideboard. She found some snifters in the china cabinet and poured them each a generous shot. Garret downed his in two gulps. In a tense, ragged voice, he tried to explain to Pearl what had happened.

"First of all, the pack train was delayed. It didn't get there till yesterday—late afternoon. We made the exchange as usual. Odell was over at the trough paying Seca. The car was backed up to the live oak tree—the one we always parked under for shade. I had climbed into the trunk to lift up the false bottom when I heard a shout: *¡El lobo!*"

"The wolf—" Hetty whispered.

"Then there were gunshots. I crawled into the cavity where we put the bottles and pulled the false bottom over me. I lay there in the dark, breathing axle grease, trying to figure out what the hell was going on from the sounds. There was a lot of gunfire, back and forth. I heard screaming in Spanish, horses running by. Then, everything became quiet. Deathly quiet."

"What happened to Odell?" Pearl asked.

"I couldn't see what happened. That's what I'm trying to tell you. I just lay there, utterly still, hoping they wouldn't discover me. I was afraid to breathe too loudly. Then the other sounds started."

Hetty took a long shot of liquor before asking, "Other sounds?"

"Yeah." Garret swallowed. "The sounds of the wounded men. It was awful, honey. I've never heard such piteous cries. They must have been in unbearable pain. I just kept thinking, a few minutes earlier and that might've been me out there, bleeding to death. They would cry out, begging, then I'd hear a dull thud, and the voice would be silenced. Before long, all was calm again. I waited until the voices drew away and I knew it must be growing dark. I slipped out without a sound and made sure no one saw me. I peered around the hood and saw rangers in the lighted windows of the ranch house. Two others patrolled the cars, making it impossible for me to drive away. I hid behind the tree, then tiptoed into the brush."

"The brush?" Hetty knew what that meant.

"Yeah! The brush. Chaparral up to my hips, no gloves on, hardly any light left. That's why I got scratched so bad." He groped in his pockets, wincing as his wounds stung. "You got a smoke, honey?"

Hetty was about to say no, when a bony hand lifted a red pack of Lucky Strikes into the light. "Thanks, Pearl." Garret latched on to a cigarette with obvious relief, gulping smoke a couple of times before going on. Pearl sat opposite them in the nook.

"I looked for a *sendero*—paths they cut along the fences. I made it into town, went to Rodriguez Grocery. The store was closed, but I knew he lived in the back. I knocked on the rear door. Severino answered—that's Mr. Rodriguez. I must have looked a fright because he crossed himself when he saw me. I had blood dripping down my face. But he knew who I was and let me in. He told me some things. The raid came from *los federales,* he said. They sent in Lone Wolf Gonzaullas, a sergeant in the Texas Rangers. The Mexicans fear him more than anybody. One of their own that defected to the other side. He led the raid. It's part of a crackdown."

Hetty nodded. "It was in the paper. Running's now a felony. The Jones Act. But why did they kill Mexicans?"

"Told to. The governor's declared war on *tequileros*. He made an announcement, Severino said. They are now considered an armed invasion of the United States, to be destroyed like any other foreign army would be. That's why they sent in the Wolf."

"They're serious about this, aren't they?" Hetty said, lighting herself a Lucky.

" 'Fraid so. It was a slaughter. Just like that song said—they hunt them down like rabbits."

"Did they get Seca?" Hetty asked.

Pearl cursed in the darkness. "I don't care about some snake. What happened to Odell?!"

"The Anglos are alive. All of them."

"Thank God, thank God," Pearl moaned.

"Sheriff locked them up, but nobody believes they'll be there for long. Not in Duval County."

"So Odell can come home soon?"

"I think you can count on it, Pearlie. *El Patrón* will get them out. When I heard Odell was all right, I figured the best thing I could do was leave town. Severino doesn't have a phone, and I couldn't be seen at the hotel. That's why I didn't call. He drove me into Alice, where I caught the afternoon train just as it was leaving."

"And the car?" Hetty asked.

Garret sniggered. "I think you can kiss that good-bye—five thousand dollars' worth of machinery. Along with a small fortune in mescal."

They talked for a long time, drinking mescal and passing the Luckies around, reassuring each other in the arms of light that reached down through the smoke floating over their heads.

* * *

Hetty came to believe in omens, in a startling conjunction of events that seemed to be connected in some mysterious way. A tan envelope arrived by post the very next day embossed with a Greek temple. She knew what the letter was going to say before she ripped it open: "The board has reviewed your application for membership in the Cupola Club. We regret to inform you that, at this time . . ."

She crumpled the letter and let it drop to the floor. "It's over," she said under her breath. She reached for her handbag, took out her passbook, and made an entry under *Withdrawals: My place in society.*

The next few months were an exercise in survival. Odell was still in jail, and his "pipeline flowing with cactus juice" had dried up. Hetty had to ration their money carefully to make it last. She was shocked when Garret revealed their bank balance: $1,030.75. Panic flashed through her like heat lightning. *We've been clearing over $3,000 a month since Christmas! Could we really have run through $11,000?* She dug into a drawer of her new antique secretary and found the stack of crinkled receipts for all the items she'd bought: the chifforobe and tea cart, the Victrola and fancy smoking stand with its built-in humidor, the Silvertone Radio with its own console table, her chaise lounge, the grenadine portieres she'd hung over doors between rooms, the Oriental carpets and marble pedestals, the vacuum sweeper and the hand-painted china lamps from London, the twelve-piece sets of silverware and crystal, the Lalique candelabras, the ceramic baking dishes, the pressed glass water bottle in her new electric Frigidaire. She hadn't really kept track of how much she'd spent. Each purchase had seemed effortless at the time, a tiny extravagance to brighten the gray winter days, but when she tallied the prices, Hetty realized that her manic campaign of redecorating had cost them $4,897.99, not counting the labor she'd hired. Then there were Garret's tailor-made suits and the jewels he kept bringing her in velvet cases: the jade pins and cameos, the long drop earrings, those endless strands of pearls. She could account for everything but a couple of thousand dollars.

He wouldn't tell her what he'd done with it. She accused him of gambling it away at the tables down in Galveston. They had a huge fight, and he walked out. She never found out what happened to the money. He kept insisting that, any day now, he'd be able to start making runs back to Duval County. Hetty wasn't so sure. Gun smoke from the San Diego massacre still haunted the air of South Texas—hatred and fear made it gather and thicken until it began to move like a dust storm across the whole state.

When she'd walk to Sander's Grocery on Oxford Street to do her shopping, Hetty would scan the headlines of the newspapers displayed in a rack at the front of the store. Almost all of them ran front-page stories about the capture. She soon realized that the widespread publicity was making it impossible for *El Patrón* to drop the charges against his prisoners. Pearl waited weeks for an arraignment, only to find out that no bail had been set and that the men were to be detained indefinitely in San Diego. The weather got hot. Hetty lay in the chaise lounge in her new living room with a circulating fan brushing over her, back and forth, listening for the sound of distant thunder. She kept expecting the heavens to break, unleashing one of those torrential downpours Houston was famous for. Something catastrophic had to happen. First, the US District Attorney got involved. This was the moment the government had been waiting for, they learned: a chance to demonstrate publicly that the controversial new Jones Act *would* be enforced, that Hoover's administration would be the first to really do something about America's drinking problem.

The D.A.'s team swept in, moving the venue out of corrupt Duval County, where a conviction would be highly unlikely. The prisoners were all transferred to the jurisdictions in which they resided, in Odell's case, Harris County. The brutal truth became inescapable: Odell *would* have to stand trial for the illegal selling of liquor and, since it was a criminal offense, the case would be pushed through the courts in under ninety days. His only hope was to face a sympathetic jury, but alas, it was not to be.

As Hetty sat beside Garret and Pearl in the county courthouse, she grew sick of heart when the members of the jury filed in. Women with pinched faces and ramrod straight posture, men in the somber suits worn by ministers. It was high August. The courtroom was sweltering. Nobody would have much patience in this kind of weather. Odell went down in a matter of days. The maximum sentence. Ten years in prison and a ten-thousand-dollar fine. He looked pale as the verdict was read; he'd lost weight from repeated bouts of dysentery in jail. But when they went to visit him in the penitentiary at Huntsville, he was still trying to piece together scraps of dignity, quoting Thoreau: " 'Under a government which imprisons any unjustly, the true place for a just man is also a prison.' "

Pearl was out of her mind with grief. She was given ninety days to raise the staggering fee. She had no idea what to do, she told Hetty, bumbling about in a confused state, weeping on and off, snatching at bits of advice that came in censored letters from her husband.

"Oh, Lord, why wasn't I a crib death?" she asked over and over as she paced the kitchen floor in her old mules. "I told Odell not to go into this business. The wages of sin is death, I said, but he just wouldn't listen."

By October, the two women had managed to pull together a fairly comprehensive portfolio of Odell's investments. It looked like there would be more than enough to pay the fine and still leave some money for Pearl to live on for a few years. Hopefully by then Odell would be out on parole for good behavior, and they could resume some kind of life together. He wrote and instructed her not to liquidate anything until she absolutely had to.

That's why she and Hetty were puzzled by phone calls that started coming in from local brokers in the closing days of October. There had been a plunge in the market, they said, so Pearl needed to sell off some of her stock to provide additional "margin."

"Ain't got a head for business, sir," she said at one point and handed the phone to Hetty. The man on the line explained that Odell, like a lot of small-time investors, had bought stocks with a marginal down payment and had let the brokers finance the rest of the purchase price through loans. It was a scheme Odell had kept secret from his wife, a way to stretch his assets by speculating on the bull market. Pearl either had to come up with more "margin," meaning ready cash, or sell some of her stocks at reduced prices. She had no choice. She told them to sell.

That was on Friday. On Monday, Hetty bought the late edition of the *Houston Post-Dispatch* and took it over to Pearl. There had been an even bigger drop in securities that morning. Pearl had been getting more phone calls demanding "more margin." Then Tuesday morning a frantic letter arrived from Odell, dated Friday, telling her to sell everything immediately. She tried for hours to get through to the brokers, but the lines were busy, busy, busy. Later, they turned on the radio and heard the devastating news: The market had gone through the biggest crash in history, slumping by billions in one day. Pearl grew glassy-eyed as she listened, wondering vaguely how much money she'd lost.

The next morning, Hetty went over to the big house and kept dialing all day until she finally got through to one of the brokers. After talking to him, she didn't know how she was going to break the news to Pearl: The securities Odell had invested in were not only worthless, he owed money on top of it for "margin."

Hetty shoved her pride to the back of her mind and called her father at Citizen's Bank of South Texas. He couldn't talk to her—he was batching up the accounts. But she called back every fifteen minutes until she got him on the phone.

"Yes."

"Dad, it's Hetty."

"I know." His voice sounded weary.

"I'm worried about your bank. Are you all right?"

"Keeping my head above water. Barely."

"It's really that bad?"

"The worst break in history. The market's down ten billion. Everyone I know is being hit. It's a disaster."

"Can't the banks do something?"

"We waited too long. Nobody expected this. Now we just have to let prices seek their own level. I—" His voice trailed off. Hetty could hear shouting in the background.

"Listen . . . I need a favor for a friend. Dad?"

"Yes?"

Hetty outlined Pearl's problems and asked if Citizen's could help her out. "I wouldn't ask for myself, of course."

"I'm afraid there's nothing we can do," Kirb said brusquely. "Investors like Odell are part of the reason this happened."

"She's going to lose her home, Dad. Can't you—"

"I said there's nothing we can do." More shouting in the background. "Now I really must go. Good night." He hung up on her. The dial tone stung her ear. *I bet if I were Charlotte,* she thought, *you'd help me.*

By November, when the court fine came due, the market had bottomed out completely and Pearl had no way to raise the ten thousand dollars. Her house and its furnishings were auctioned off under a sheriff's sale. They brought in a little over six thousand dollars.

Hetty sat in the kitchen with Pearl after the auction was over. Though night was falling, neither stood up to turn on a light and neither spoke. They didn't know what to say. They just sat there in the breakfast nook, smoking, waiting for Garret to return with beer and sandwiches. Hetty felt spellbound with grief. Her dreams had not led them to treasure, as she'd hoped, but to trouble. To a man in prison, to two women left speechless here in a darkened room.

Hetty's devastated dreams made her remember the old Magnolia Park. She wasn't sure why she was thinking of that now, sitting here in the dusk, but she was. Nella used to tell her and Charlotte stories about it. She and Kirby had conducted their courtship out there, taking the trolley to the turning basin in Buffalo Bayou. They would stroll through the sixty acres of parkland, attend concerts at the bandstand, have picnics in the shade of three thousand seven hundred and fifty Magnolia grandiflora trees that had been planted there by the developers. Nella said the air for miles around hung heavy with the sweet perfume of those giant white blossoms, often thousands of them blooming at once. This earthly paradise, she told her enraptured daughters, was designed to rival Central Park in Manhattan and Woodward's Gardens in San Francisco, making Houston known coast to coast as the Magnolia City. Hetty begged Nella to take her there so she could experience such a place for herself. When Hetty was old enough, she finally did. All around the turning basin loomed refineries, factories, warehouses, and shipping docks. The magnolia trees had been razed years before to make room for industrial development. Hetty never forgot the acrid smell of smoke that had replaced the heady aroma of those delicate white flowers.

Why was she thinking of that now? She wasn't sure. Somehow the events of the last few days made her mourn all over again the destruction of such a magical forestland east of Houston. Hetty thought she heard something roaring in the distance, like chain saws at work. Or maybe she was just remembering Pick's deep voice intoning the words of that hymn he sang as he painted—the one about the lamp burning down. She left Pearl alone in the kitchen and made her way through the twilight to the apartment. Stumbling about like a blind woman, she felt her way into the bedroom, thinking, *We are no longer the Magnolia City. What's to become of us now?* She opened the window beside the bed and took the Japanese lantern out of the post oak tree. She held it in her hands as she sat on the bed and sang in the darkness, the misery in her heart welling into the words of the hymn:

O, poor sinner
Now is your time
O, poor sinner
What you going to do when your lamp burn down.

Chapter 9

The last great storm of 1929 came like a whisper out of the Caribbean and ambushed the Texas coast. People had already shelved their storm shutters for the winter and burned their candles at the last crabbing parties along the bay. Late editions of the *Houston Post-Dispatch* broadcast the news: TROPICAL STORM UPGRADED TO HURRICANE: Headed for Mexican Coast.

As she sat in her living room packing, Hetty absentmindedly scanned the headlines while wrapping her new china in the day's paper. Tankers steaming out of the Ship Channel had radioed the news—something unfriendly was brewing out there, spawned in the incubator of the equator, nursed on the warm breast of the Caribbean, and bawling as it crawled its way westward toward the nearest land. It had an empty, inhuman heart: a pocket of air pressure so low that winds from all directions poured down the wall of its eye like Niagaras of air. The earth's rotation made it turn, spinning off across the glassy sea like a child's top out of control. It bounced into Tampico and back out, careening here and there in a bad temper, stopping only to suck more heat out of the sea and spur its winds to over a hundred miles an hour. It wore a wide whirling sombrero of clouds, hundreds of miles across.

Already, down at Galveston, Hetty read, they were seeing the long coasting waves that glide into shore before the squall itself, the ones that move like those scenes she'd seen in motion pictures where they slow the action down and everything seems to hang suspended in time. Like she was. The rooms of the garage apartment around her were emptying bit by bit, draining her old life away. All her new clothes had disappeared into trunks, the carpets had been rolled up, the drawers cleaned out. She had taken all her portieres and curtains down; through the bare dusty panes, the clouds that passed beyond the post oaks never changed. They just kept revolving, around and around, waiting to see what the storm would decide to do.

Drainpipes gurgled and eaves dripped as Hetty flapped along the driveway under a Chinese parasol. Her galoshes were unbuckled as usual, and a canvas raincoat two sizes too big hung halfway off her shoulders. Raindrops big as bullets ricocheted all around her. She made her way up the back steps, dropped the parasol upside down on the porch and, knocking lightly, slipped into the Weems' house for what would surely be the last time. Pearl was moving to a Victorian rooming house on Studewood.

The kitchen had been cleared out completely. The only sign of where they used to sit at the breakfast nook were scuff marks on the table. A dirty glass had been left in the sink.

"Pearl . . ." Her voice echoed against bare walls.

"Yoo-hoo," came a thin reply. Hetty followed the sound down the hall, through leaded glass doors. She found Pearl slouched wearily on boxes stacked in the living room. Around her, the few possessions she had left huddled, everything else sold to pay debts. "In here having a pity party. Pull up a box."

"It would have to rain on top of everything else." Hetty found a perch on a wardrobe trunk. "I hear the bayou's flooding."

Pearl sighed. "Like my mother used to say, 'First it's all roses, roses, then thorns, thorns.' "

"You didn't happen to find that certificate, did you? From the oil syndicate?"

"Lord, I have messed up." Pearl stood as though every bone in her body ached. She tore open a box on one of the piles and dug around until she found a manila envelope. "I meant to give this to y'all."

When Hetty opened the flap and let the contents slide out, she found a letter from the Joiner Oil Syndicate in the Praetorian Building in Dallas, a certificate to a one-acre share and a scientific report entitled "Geological, Topographical and Petroliferous Survey of Rusk County, Texas." "Sure you don't want to keep this for yourself?"

"Ain't worth spit to me without Odell."

"I'll accept it on one condition."

"What's that?"

"That you become a partner with us."

"Well . . ." Pearl looked out into the sky and chuckled. "I do hail from Rusk County, you know."

The slanted coast of Texas sent the hurricane veering into land just shy of Port Arthur, so they missed the worst of it. But there was still plenty of tempest to endure. After moving the last of their possessions into a new garage apartment, Garret cut open some of the cardboard boxes and taped them over the bedroom windows. Hetty got to the corner store just in time to grab a few emergency rations. They plugged in her hand-painted china lamps and stretched out right on the mattress because they couldn't find any sheets. The storm roared all afternoon and all night. Garret spent the time napping and reading the papers from the oil syndicate, but Hetty lay wrapped tightly in a blanket, listening to the ominous sounds outdoors, afraid even to go to sleep.

"You don't know what it's like," she told him when he teased her. "You didn't grow up here." His clear blue eyes shot her an amused glance, his slick black hair glistening with pomade in the lamplight.

She turned her back to him, knowing he couldn't understand her weather phobia. He hadn't been suckled on stories of Gulf storms like she had. The granddaddy of all such stories was the one her mother Nella told her about the terrible Galveston storm of

1900, the hurricane that had launched the new century with the greatest natural disaster in American history. It hit suddenly on a Saturday in September. When the big breakers started to roll in, crowds took the trolley out to the beach to see them. There was a party atmosphere, Nella said. Then the winds began to rise, reaching 145 miles per hour in only a few hours. A fifteen-foot surge of water swept over the island. Thousands of homes were turned into kindling. Some said the death toll reached six thousand souls; others placed it as high as twelve thousand—nobody knew for sure because they had to burn the corpses quickly to stop the spread of disease.

Hetty remembered how she and her sister Charlotte used to cry when their mother told them the story of St. Mary's Orphanage. It had been right on the beach at 69th Street. The gale had blown it down like a house of straw. In a desperate attempt to save lives, the nuns had lashed themselves to groups of children. Hetty wondered what sounds the orphans made right before they died. She smelled something burning and realized that Garret had lit a cigarette. The thought of her husband smoking in bed as if nothing had happened comforted her and, haltingly, she let the wind carry her away.

She woke later in darkness. She could hear waves, giant ones crashing one on top of another. The winds began ripping boards off, and a wild light came in with the rain so she could see where she was. A crucifix hung crookedly in the wind. She wanted to get up and run. But she couldn't. She was tied down. She could feel Charlotte squirming beside her. Hetty called out. But her voice was lost in the loud crack that broke open the wall between them and the sea. Hetty saw a veranda float away. She craned her neck to look out at the ocean . . . and there it was. A fifteen-foot wall of water. All the girls were told about it when they first came. It spread itself above them like a cobra about to strike, moving from side to side, taking its time. And now she knew what sounds the orphans of St. Mary's made right before they drowned. They didn't die praying, as she'd always hoped.

It was cold, that's what she remembered most about the wave when it finally hit. The cold. It took her breath away. She couldn't move. She wondered where her mother was, if she'd heard about the storm. She tasted the salt in the water as it thundered over them.

"Mommy!" she cried. "Mommy! Mommy!" Hetty longed to be back in her mother's arms, to stop this headlong roll into the cold shock of womanhood. The wave shook her over and over, as if she were being scolded. But it was Garret shaking her—Garret had hold of one shoulder while her other shoulder was still being sucked down into the black vortex. "Help," she cried to him, but the sound got dammed up in her throat as a moan. *I must save Charlotte!* she thought.

"Honey," he called. "Honey, what's wrong?" He was on the shore. He could save her. She wound an arm around his neck and let him pull her out of the ropes to a bright place of morning.

"Hey. You were moaning in your sleep."

She looked around their bedroom wildly. The only thing flooding the room was sunlight. Garret had ripped off the cardboard. She could see clear sky opening up. "I was tied down. . . ." The effort of pulling herself and Charlotte out of the ropes made her tremble. She clung to Garret until her fear subsided. "Nella left my sister and me at the orphanage. I was so scared."

Garret stroked her arm. "It's all right. I'm here. The storm's over. And guess what. I found the coffeepot."

"That's progress."

The calm blue sky settled Hetty, and she kissed her husband's neck. He let her slide back to her pillow and sat up on his side of the bed, where papers spread around, crinkled. "I've been up drinking coffee and reading this report from the Joiner Oil Syndicate."

"Look good?"

"I hope to tell you!" He handed her a scientific journal. "Look, here's an article written about East Texas by two Humble geologists. I'm telling you, honey, they're going to discover one of the largest oil fields in the world. Listen to how he describes it—a treasure trove all the kings of the earth might covet," Garret read from the report. "This is big. And we've got a one-acre share." He kissed the certificate. "Now I hope you'll call your dad."

"You know he won't talk to me," she said, pushing out of bed.

She wormed her way around stacks of cartons in the living room and peered through the window. Tree limbs scratched the street everywhere, and wires sagged. "We'll never get a telephone now," she muttered.

Garret yanked on his pants and snatched up the envelope on the bed. "All right! If you're too proud to call your parents, I guess I'll have to do on my own, won't I?" He jammed his shoes on and tied the laces. "I've got ways to raise money. You just watch." He slammed his hat on and wrenched the door open, dragging his raincoat behind him.

For the rest of the day, Hetty distracted herself by unpacking one box after another. Stacks of them sagged against the walls, making the apartment even more oppressive than it was. All her new furniture had been crammed into the middle of the living room, barely leaving a space to sit on the davenport. She'd never be able to fit it all into these two small rooms. Half the stuff would have to be stored downstairs in the garage. Hetty looked around and sighed. No one would ever refer to this place as a "carriage house." She could still smell the old tenants in the air. The closets were scaled for dwarves and, for her new china, there were only a few cramped cupboards in the kitchen. She looked at the floor under her feet in horror. *Linoleum! My carpets will clash with the pattern!* To try and bring a little warmth into the rooms, she unpacked her fringed shades and set a couple on the china lamps. But it was pretty hopeless. Mostly the place needed a good cleaning and a fresh coat of paint on the gray plaster walls.

Garret came home late smelling of whiskey. He fell asleep across the bare mattress with his clothes on. She rifled through his wallet. It was empty. He woke with a headache around noon and emptied two or three cartons, leaving bottles strewn on the floor in a search for aspirin. When he left that afternoon, Garret had the same look of impotent rage in his eyes. He wouldn't tell her where he was going, but he took the checkbook with him. Hetty couldn't stand to stay in the apartment alone.

Miraculously, her landlady's phone was still working. Hetty slouched in the hallway while the woman eyed her from the kitchen—a lumbering lady named Mrs. Cobb. Whiffs of rancid chicken fat lingered in the air. Hetty took the phone book off its nail and looked up a Courtlandt Place number.

"Good afternoon. Hargraves residence." The sweet mellow Southern tones identified the voice immediately as Doris Verne's.

"Hi, kiddo, it's Hetty."

"Hey—whatever happened to you? I haven't seen you at any of the parties."

"Shame on me. I guess I'm turning into a boring old married woman."

"Not at all. Why do you think the rest of us are running around like mad women? We're looking for husbands, honey child."

"Fools," Hetty said with a laugh and caught up on all the latest buzz before describing to her friend the scenes she'd just had with her husband. Doris Verne suggested that Hetty bring Garret to Ima Hogg's benefit. "What benefit?"

"You are out of touch, girl. Ima Hogg's giving a concert. Fifty dollars a plate."

"What would I do without you, kiddo? Give me the number to call!"

Hetty scribbled it on Mrs. Cobb's notepad, ripped the page off, and tossed the earpiece back onto the phone. After a hasty thank-you, she raced on her toes out the back and up the stairs, where she began ripping open carton after carton. She nosed about until she found the box she was looking for. She lifted out handfuls of jewels: long strands of pearls with a pink blush, the good ones off the floor of the Sea of Japan; her moonstones; her jade scarabs; her amethyst bracelets—the stuff that would bring some kind of quick money from the hock shops down on Preston Avenue. She pulled more and more out, piling them up, until she had enough to fill two dinner plates.

In the damp December night, fog floated over the bayou that snaked through the deep forests of River Oaks. Rising like ghostly fox fire out of the woods came globes of light rolling through the mists: the headlights of cars, one long, elegant automobile after another. They came up from the east, from the city, sweeping around the curves of Lazy Lane, their beams striking across white pillars and moss-hung trees, all slowing down to turn at the same place: into a narrow lane that looked like it disappeared into the woods unless you knew that it led to the most talked about new house in Houston, the pink stucco mansion perched on a crook of Buffalo Bayou. The family who'd carved the exclusive subdivision out of the woods around the country club—the Hogg brothers, Will and Mike, and their sister, Ima—had saved this choice spot for their own fourteen-acre estate.

In some long, shaded driveway, Hetty and Garret sat parked in the Auburn, watching the cars pass behind them. She was trying to make Garret understand why they didn't just rush up to the mansion at the appointed time. "Our blood veins are like our bayous," she explained. "Slow moving." An hour on an invitation was only a suggestion. It was much swankier to mosey in on the verge of being late than to stand around waiting for something to happen. Besides, she was still trying to recall everything she'd been taught about the behavior of well-bred Southerners at social occasions—don't take your seat before the hostess does, don't unfold your napkin all the way, never sit closer than four or five inches to the table, never ask for seconds. She described the nine or so courses they could expect tonight and what utensils were proper for each.

"You really expect me to remember all this?" Garret chuckled. Hetty found his amused smile catching. She was in a splendid mood, anticipating the auspicious moment when she would step across the wide threshold of Bayou Bend with a proper invitation in hand. She hadn't even minded hocking some of her best jewelry. "I *know* it's silly. But tonight it's important. We have to look like we know what we're doing."

He watched the lights in his rearview mirror for a few moments. "Haven't enough cars passed by?"

"Oh, all right. I just hope we don't arrive before my family does. I have to upstage my mother tonight."

Garret backed out of the driveway and followed the red taillights of another car into the narrow woodland road. The fog obscured everything. Then, a strange pink luminescence glowed through the black trees. Bayou Bend rose into view at the peak of a circular drive. They waited their turn to drive up to the arched entrance, where a colored attendant opened the door and Hetty stepped into the spangled air. Out of tall French windows, light and music lapped at the darkness welling under immense oaks. She heard the purr of soft voices, sniffed wood smoke trailing out of four towering chimneys. In the blue haze, the spreading stucco walls took on a ghostly light, unfolded into pale pinkish white wings on either side of the two-story central quarters. She glimpsed an elegant wrought iron railing, a round window, and then Garret took her arm and led her, entranced, into the long entrance hall that led all the way to the gardens in back. Her vision blurred as she passed through the crowd: Massive antiques loomed darkly along the walls while above, like angels, girls in white crepes gazed down at them from the twisting railing of the grand staircase. Hetty spotted Diana Dorrance and her date up on the landing. Garret escorted her through one spacious room after another, past crackling fires, under scrolled pediments, his report from the oil syndicate tucked carefully under one arm.

As she strolled along, inches taller than the boyish girls who flitted about in their short little gowns and white gloves, Hetty was glad she had dressed the way she did. She had her hair cut daringly short in a waved shingle and long metallic earrings dripped like shimmering minnows from her earlobes. Her eyes were streaked with their exotic and secret pedigree: a bloodline flowing back to a mestizo grandmother whose blood had been cut with German genes, then thoroughly anglicized, leaving Hetty with a slightly foreign look no one could place. She was just sorry there weren't more familiar faces around to appreciate her appearance.

She was also disappointed to find the dining room dim and empty. She circled the round tables, scanning the place cards set on top of damask napkins on the gold-rimmed plates. Garret found their place first. "Here we are. Next to your mother and father!"

"What?!" Hetty strode over. "That'll never do. Let's see—" Glancing around to be sure no one was in the room, she quickly rearranged the white cards. "That's better. Put you next to the Yoakums. Cleveland Yoakum's a promoter. Could bankroll your scheme in a heartbeat if he chose to. His wife's in between you, so you'll have to charm her first."

Maids started lighting candles, so she knew it wouldn't be long until dinner was called. They made their way back into the entrance hall, where Hetty noticed people revolving around two balding, robust men standing in front of a massive Remington painting of a cattle drive. She heard one of them referred to as Will, and realized that these were the Hogg brothers themselves. She pointed them out to Garret and murmured into his ear that their father, Jim Hogg, had been one of the original investors in the Texaco Company and that they themselves had discovered oil on their old family home, the Varner Plantation, where all you had to do, legend said, was strike a match near the ground and a flame would appear. Hetty sidled up to the group and had just presented her husband when another group of partygoers arrived with a flurry at the door. There was a lull as everyone turned to see who the latecomers were. Nella stood in the archway, pausing for a moment to let all eyes take her in. She looked sumptuous all right, in cinnamon satin with silver brocade, a cape of monkey fur falling off one shoulder. Kirb led her in grandly, followed by the rest of the Warwick party: Congressman and Mrs. Welch, their daughter Belinda with a new beau. Hetty made sure she and Garret were standing in between the Hogg brothers as they approached. When Nella spotted them, a look of sheer terror flared for a moment in her eyes but was quickly doused by her icy composure.

"Esther, I—what a surprise to see you here," she said, brushing her lips against her daughter's cheek and only nodding at Garret.

"I didn't think you'd want me to miss another party at Bayou Bend, Mamá. You do know Will and Mike Hogg, don't you?"

"Of course, dear. You gentlemen must excuse our tardiness, but it's such a piece out here from the Warwick."

"Then you'll have to become neighbors," Will replied, shaking Kirb's hand vigorously. "What a pleasure to see you here, Mr. Allen."

"Mighty pleased, Will, I—"

"I'm afraid River Oaks is too country for me, Mr. Hogg," Nella cut in. "You remember our neighbors at the Warwick, Congressman and Mrs. Welch?" Greetings ricocheted around the circle, but Kirb ignored Garret altogether. Through the crowd, Hetty saw Lamar lead Charlotte through the front door. She tried to catch his eye. *What shall I say to him once we're face-to-face? How will he treat me?* Her high spirits were in danger of being ruffled when she was rescued by a woman in a shimmering gown who appeared from the dining room, ringing a bell. It was Ima Hogg. She had a golden head, an air of importance about her. When she turned to lead the procession in to dinner, she walked as though she were drawing a rustling train behind her.

Once she took her seat, everyone else followed and, as the oyster course was served, the women began the Ritual of the Glove Removal. White gloves were tugged off finger by finger and placed on laps under half-folded napkins. Hetty slipped her kid casings off her hands and bunched them up at her wrists. She thought it was much sexier that way. And so, apparently, did the congressman at her side, who ogled her aslant. She made sure Garret noticed her picking up her oyster fork, which for some esoteric reason she had never understood was placed on the side with the knives rather than with the other forks.

Silence circled the group as everyone enjoyed the tang of fresh Gulf oysters. Over the sparkling waters fizzing in champagne flutes, through the tall candles, Hetty peeked at her parents. Nella's gaze was sunken in her oyster dish, afraid to surface. She looked mortified. Kirb did glance over, but the kind of look he shot Hetty made her wonder if her lipstick was on crooked. Cleveland Yoakum swilled scotch around in a highball glass. Clare Yoakum's round face swam out of the dimness and drawled, "I hear Ima's playing has real power."

"But does anyone take her seriously?" Garret asked. "I mean, you know, with her name."

Lockett drew up and spoke in a stage whisper. "Young man, if you're going to attend parties at Bayou Bend, the first thing you have to learn is that Ima doesn't like people discussing her name." The white satin ruffles at her wrist swished as she wagged a finger at him. "It's been such a burden to her."

"I can tell you're not from these parts, young man." Clare Yoakum turned to him. "Her father was our first native-born governor. And one of our best. James Stephen Hogg."

"She grew up in the governor's mansion—" Lockett said.

"And slept in Sam Houston's bed!" Nella added, finally looking up.

While the congressman rattled off the reforms pushed through by Governor Hogg, Clare leaned over and murmured to Garret, "I'm most curious to know where you're from, sir. You don't sound like a Yankee."

"No, ma'am, I was born atop the richest hill on earth—in Butte, Montana. And my name is Garret MacBride."

"Why, I don't believe I've ever met a Montanan before. Just can't imagine what it's like way up there in the West. What do you mean by the richest hill on earth? I thought we had that here—down in Beaumont."

As they worked their way through the fish course, Garret talked in that earnest, intimate voice he sometimes used on Hetty in bed, the one she found so hypnotic. He described the vein of copper fifty feet wide discovered under his hometown, the white peaks lost in the clouds, the dozens of glaciers grinding through the mountains, and how, as a boy, he'd sometimes be awakened in the middle of the night by a spooky light outside his bedroom window: the aurora borealis. Hetty had never heard Garret talk so much about his native state and found herself leaning in to catch every word. At one point, she caught a glimpse of Clare's face in the candlelight, her dull eyes sparked with fascination. Good, Hetty thought, caressing her husband's thigh under the tablecloth, now if we can just get that spark to leap over to her husband.

As the entrée was served, thin, pink shavings of the finest Texas sirloin, Clare ignored her plate and blinked at him, bright-eyed, lifted for a moment out of her perpetual lethargy. "Y'all should stop talking about politics and listen to these stories," she said to the rest of them. "Where have you been hiding such an interesting beau, Hetty?"

Lockett's voice shot across the table. "He's not her beau, Clare. He's her husband."

"Husband? Hetty, dear, I don't remember reading about your wedding."

A few awkward beats drummed by as Hetty tried to think of a response. Her mother was stunned into silence, and Lockett watched them with cat's eyes, ready to pounce. Garret maneuvered through the moment smoothly by saying: "You wouldn't have, ma'am. I just kind of lassoed her, Montana-style."

"How sweet. Now tell me the truth, was it love that brought you to the Lone Star State?"

"No, ma'am, I'm afraid it was more mundane matters. I feel a young man has to have good prospects before he thinks about romance."

"I'm glad you're being sensible. Most youngsters seem so irresponsible these days. What is your line of work, sir?"

"Import-export pays the bills. But as far as I'm concerned, the future lies in petrochemicals. I came to Texas to wildcat."

Clare laughed. "Petrochemicals? How cute. Honey, here we just call it plain old oil." She pronounced it *all*. "Did you know my husband's an *all* man?"

"I'd love to meet him. I'm sure we'd have a lot in common."

She tugged on her husband's sleeve. "Honey, Kirb's son-in-law wants to talk to you about petrochemicals. Is that what we have here?" She and Lockett giggled. Cleveland gave a slight nod of his head, thick with silver hair.

"Mrs. Yoakum is right, sir," Garret said, reaching across her plate to offer a handshake to Cleveland. "I wanted to tell you where the next big strike is going to be."

Cleveland Yoakum didn't shake Garret's hand or even look at him. He sat without moving, bullish, emitting a deep chuckle that was burnished with scorn.

"I'm serious, sir. In fact, so serious, I brought a report for you to look over from my syndicate in Dallas. Backed up by a scientific article. There's an ocean of oil waiting to be discovered, and we know where it is." Garret slid out the papers he'd been hiding under his napkin and held them above Clare's plate. Everyone froze, as if Garret had just stood up and dropped his pants. Hetty held her breath. Several beats passed.

"Well, at least look it over, Cleve," Clare said, seizing the documents and plopping them down in front of her husband. "I like this young man."

Hetty could hardly keep her hands from folding together in prayer as new courses glided in front of her soundlessly: lamb with mint sauce followed by a raspberry sorbet and a baked squab that oozed with apples and raisins when she cut it open.

Cleveland ignored his food as he leafed through Garret's report. He began rasping with laughter again. "Haven't you told your son-in-law about Dad Joiner, Kirb?"

"What's that . . . ?"

Nella sneered as she passed the papers to her husband. "Business? At dinner?" She dipped her fingers into the crystal finger bowl that had just been placed in front of her.

"I want to get this settled, Nel," Kirb said gruffly. He flicked through the pages, squinting in the candlelight. "Umm-hmm, just as I thought. It's Lloyd's report. We've seen this before, haven't we, Cleve?" He chuckled, tossing it back.

"Then you know about Rusk County?" Garret asked.

"According to Doc Lloyd," Cleveland pitched his deep voice to address the whole table, "East Texas is floating over a vast sea of fossil fuels and all anybody's got to do is dig down a few feet and start spooning it out."

"You've read the report?"

"Young man, do you know what Doc Lloyd's real name is?"

"No, sir."

"Joseph Idelbert Durham. He's not a geologist at all. He used to sell patent medicines made from oil."

"But his survey—?"

"Oh, he knows the lingo, all right. He's just in the wrong field. He should be writing fiction." Cleveland shared a knowing snicker with Kirb.

"But all those salt domes and—"

"Have you ever been up yonder, Mr. MacBride?"

"Umm, not exactly . . ."

"Well, you won't find any salt domes in Rusk County, believe me."

"No?" Garret took a breath. "Okay, maybe he was wrong about that part. But what about the Cook Mountain formation? They're sitting on a gold mine up there, I tell you. I just know it."

"A mountain in East Texas?" Lockett exclaimed, sending laughter scattering on both sides of her. "Hetty, dear, you'd better send your husband back to Montana if he's looking for mountains."

"The best part of all," Kirb said, "is how Lloyd picked Rusk County. He drew a line from every major oil field in Texas and Oklahoma and they all converged in East Texas. He called it the apex of the apex."

"The apex of the apex," Cleveland sputtered, rattling with laughter.

The candle flames wavered as the men chortled till they coughed. Hetty wished someone would blow them out so she could shrink back into darkness. The laughter was scalding her ears. She glanced at Garret, then down at her finger bowl. She couldn't meet the eyes of anyone at the table and couldn't bear looking at her husband's face, at his stare of embarrassed confusion, at his lips trying to open to speak, turning to her for an answer.

"Y'all are being rude to poor Mac here," Clare said, trying not to laugh along with the others. "Cleve, can't you put forward some advice at least."

"Only this," he said, pulling out a pen and scribbling across the cover of the Joiner report. "If you're really serious about the oil business, young man, call this number. This fellow will get you a job as a cat skinner on the derrick floor." He reached in front of his wife and dumped the package back in front of Garret. "In the meantime, don't send me any more wild schemes. I don't want to see your face again until your hair is so saturated with crude oil you can't get the smell out no matter how many times you shampoo."

"Yes, sir," Garret murmured. Everyone watched him in silence. He stood and lifted the report off the table. "Go ahead and laugh, but you're all my witnesses. I still believe in Dad Joiner. I still believe we'll strike oil in East Texas." Clare pulled him back down into his seat and took the papers from him, hiding them under the table. She smiled at Garret indulgently.

Someone placed a delicious-looking dessert in front of Hetty, but she couldn't bring herself to eat it.

It wasn't long before she felt people rising around her and saw shadows passing by the candle flames that had drawn her eyes in, mesmerized. Garret left to join the other men for a smoke, and she would have just sat there watching the maids clear the tables had not Lockett come over and squeezed into a chair beside her.

"I'm so glad I found you alone, Esther," Lockett murmured in a conspiratorial tone. "I'm liable to bust! This is very confidential."

"Oh—what's that?"

"My dear, I'm sorry it's taken me so long to get back to you on this matter. After tonight, I fear I may be too late."

Hetty snapped out of her trance and turned to face Lockett. "What matter?"

"Well, if you recall"—Lockett leaned in even closer, her eyes impaling Hetty—"I feel responsible for introducing Garret to Houston society. So I felt it my duty to investigate his family. I finally found out why Garret's father didn't finish out his term in the Senate. You need to hear this."

"No, I don't." Hetty stood and slid out of her chair. She heard Lockett shouting after her, "But, my dear, it's just not going to wash."

The music throbbed around Hetty's head, but she didn't want to let it in. Ima's skill was evident: Her fingers skimmed the keys as though she were brushing velvet, letting the soft etudes fall into the hushed hall, sending the sonatas pounding down the aisles of chairs that had been jammed into the drawing room of Bayou Bend. Hetty had rushed in at the last minute, alone, taking a seat too near the marble mantel. She thought the first half of the program would never end; she couldn't breathe and the heat from the fire made her face feel even redder. Finally, the last note echoed through the wide room, and applause stirred itself out of the silence that followed. As soon as people stood, not a beat later, Hetty leaped up and threaded her way quickly down the aisle. She wanted to find her husband and leave before she had to face any of the people they'd sat with at dinner.

Hetty's head swarmed with confusion. She had to get out of the crowded rooms and needed a cigarette in the worst way. She prowled the parlors and porches, keeping her face averted, avoiding friends she saw at a distance. She spotted Doris Verne and Winifred heading upstairs at one point but didn't follow them. Instead, she wormed her way down the hall to the threshold of the Pine Room, where the men went to smoke. Ordinarily, she wouldn't hesitate to barge right into that male enclave, even bumming a smoke off a startled stranger, but, tonight, she didn't want to draw attention to herself. She hung in the doorway, watching the men moving about in their black evening wear, pouring themselves enough brandy to get through the second half of the concert. Kirb was at the gravitational center, passing out cigars like calling cards. Then, in a corner, she spotted Mac, or rather heard him first. His flask was out, of course, dancing in the air above the heads of the men who surrounded him. In a voice too loud even for this room, he was offering the group some "good stuff! Don't worry, it's Canadian."

She panicked when she saw Lamar veering toward her. She stepped back into the dim hallway and turned away. But a shadow fell across her feet, and she heard his voice chasing after her.

"Why didn't you call me?"

"What do you mean? Where's Char?"

"She went to the ladies' lounge to powder something or other."

"Char always was big on powdering." Hetty turned to face him. His bow tie was askew as usual. His eyes studied her intently.

"You're awfully flushed!" he said. "Embarrassed to face me?"

"It's so hot in here. All those fireplaces. Didn't Mother give you my letter?"

"That's all I get? A Dear John letter? I deserve more than that."

"Char told me not to call you."

"Since when have you done what Char wanted you to do?"

"She said you didn't want to talk to me. That I no longer had access to you."

He shook his head.

"You mean that wasn't true?"

"Just the opposite. I need some answers."

A couple brushed by them. "This is not the place to talk about it, Lamar."

"Where *can* we talk about it?"

"I don't know. Some place more private than this."

"How about the Diana Garden?"

Give me your answer in the Diana Garden. Suddenly, Hetty remembered the note Lamar had sent her with his proposal, tied to a silver quiver filled with little golden arrows. "All right."

He steered her through the central hall and under the colonnade in back. In the foggy dark, they felt their way down a series of grass terraces and across a long slanting lawn to a grove of trees where the goddess, draped in soft light, was reflected in the cold waters of a pool.

Hetty found herself falling back into the easy intimacy she used to share with Lamar, reaching into his tux pocket to pull out his pack of cigarettes and bending close to him when he offered her a light.

She drew the smoke in hungrily, letting it settle her nerves. "Ummm. You always have such delicious cigarettes."

"Only the best." He chuckled.

She shivered. He slipped out of his tux coat and draped it over her shoulders. "Thanks—I guess I *have* to answer your questions now."

"There's only one," he said, lighting his own cigarette. Plumes of smoke rose like confessions. "Why?"

"It just felt like the right thing to do. Nella had me feeling so trapped. Did I hurt you as bad as Char made out?"

"I have to admit I was stunned when I heard the news that you'd eloped. I couldn't believe Mac had won you away from me."

"I didn't give you much of a chance, did I, my poor little Lam?"

"No, you didn't. You disappeared out of my life just like that."

"I'm sorry. Will you ever forgive me?"

"I've waited a long time for that apology. I don't know." He seemed overcome for a moment. He looked away.

Hetty touched his cheek with her fingers. "Dear Lam. How can I make this up to you?"

He gave her a penetrating glance. "Kiss me." He was still the trickster, she could see, daring her to do forbidden things.

She lifted her face to him. He moved in to kiss her on the mouth, but at the last moment, she turned her lips and kissed him on the cheek. Then she gave him a long, loving hug and whispered in his ear. "It broke my heart to return those beautiful gifts you sent me. Thank you so much."

"Did you like them?"

"They were beautiful," she said, pulling back. "Where did you ever find the silver quiver with the golden arrows?"

"Didn't you know? We own a jewelry store."

"Oh . . . that's convenient."

"I really thought that quiver would win you over."

"It almost did. It was a very hard decision—I hope you know that."

"You still haven't told me why you chose him over me."

Hetty thought for a moment before she answered. "Garret needs me more than you do."

"That's not true. *I* need you, too."

"No, you don't. You just *want* me—that's the difference."

"Don't you mean *wanted* you? You are unavailable now, right?"

"Right. Sorry."

He ground his cigarette out under his toe. "How is your marriage?"

"Oh, fine," she said quickly. "Just fine." She looked across the water at the statue. "That's quite a piece of work, isn't it?"

"Ima commissioned some sculptor in Florence to carve it. It's copied from the Diana—"

"Of Versailles. I know. Mamá told me. She's quite enamored of the huntress."

They sat on a stone bench while Hetty gazed at the white marble figure spotlighted in a curve of yew trees. It was as if Diana were striding across the pool, reaching for an arrow to hand to Hetty. She could have dashed out of the yews only a moment before, searing a path through the misty woods with the cold fire of the moon. She was quick, this goddess, and merciless. Too hard and merciless for Hetty. Her face was turned away in profile, sharp, her eyes hammered with sheer grit out of the hard white marble. Hetty felt her shame cool in the night air as the bold light from the goddess blazed across the water. *What can you teach me?* she wondered. *What gifts do you give my mother? Icy shafts of willpower? Enough to endure the kind of life she's had to live?* Hetty took a final drag and threw her butt into the water. *Sssst!*

"I'm lying," she said. "My marriage isn't fine, as everyone could see tonight." She told him what happened at dinner.

"I wondered why the men at your table were laughing so hard."

"Now you know," she said, feeling the goddess urge her on, "they were laughing at us. Cleveland was ruthless."

"Cleveland *is* ruthless. They don't call him Cleve the Cliff for nothing."

"I was hoping Garret would wrap up a deal tonight and instead, look what happened. Dad sat there and let Cleveland make fools of us. I'm sure Mamá was pleased."

"Why didn't you come to me?"

"You?"

"Yes, me. My last name *is* Rusk."

"You'd still be willing to help me?"

"I'd do it for Charmaine."

Hetty laughed. "So you haven't forgotten?"

"I'll always remember my little Charmaine."

"Even after you've married my sister?"

Lamar chuckled. "You'd be my sister-in-law then—even more reason to help you."

"But—what could you do?"

"I don't know. I'd have to think about it. Give me your phone number. There's a pen in my tux pocket."

They heard a bell ringing from the back door. Hetty scribbled her new phone number on his pack of cigarettes. "I hope you're not doing this just to get my digits. I am unavailable, remember?"

He broke out into a crooked grin.

When they stepped back into the central hall of the mansion, Charlotte was on the lookout for Lamar. The moment she spotted them, she strode right over and entwined her arm into his. "Where have you been? I've been looking everywhere. We won't get a seat for the second half." She was wearing a choker made entirely of diamonds. *Probably borrowed from their jewelry store.*

"We'd better go in then." Lamar tried to tow her away from Hetty.

"You'll need your coat, Lam," Char said, whirling him to a stop. Hetty stood there paralyzed. She'd forgotten that she was wearing it. Her sister came over and yanked it off her shoulders. She held it open so that Lamar could slide his arms into the sleeves. She brushed off the shoulders and turned him around to button it up, examining the coat while she did so. She turned him toward the drawing room and pushed. "Get us some seats, you scoundrel. I'll be right in." He staggered off.

As soon as he was out of earshot, Char turned her chilling gray eyes on Hetty. "You haven't changed a bit. You're as horrible as ever."

"And you're still a flat tire, sis. I went outside for some fresh air—you know, a smoke, that's all. Lamar happened to come along. I was cold. I asked for his coat. It wasn't his fault." *Why am I lying?*

"I'm sure it wasn't his fault. You make him do these wild things. That's why you need to stay away from him. It's not regular." She lifted her chin with a haughty thrust, a thousand diamond prisms glittering across her pale white throat.

"It wasn't true what you said in your letter, by the way. Lamar did want to talk to me."

"Now the truth comes out. You've been talking to him!"

"All I did was apologize for hurting him. He needed to hear that. What harm can it do for me to talk to him? I *am* married now."

"Oh! As if you'd let that stand in your way. *Your* name should be Ima Hogg!" Char's shrill voice echoed through a sudden silence that had fallen over the hall. She clapped her hand to her mouth, then whispered vehemently to Hetty before rushing off, "Leave my boyfriend alone, damn you!"

As she watched her sister strut off, her white dress bristling with chandelier light, Hetty realized why she was lying. *I'm trying to protect Lamar from Char. Why should I care?*

Chapter 10

The call came during those dead weeks after New Year's. Hetty usually spent the mornings ironing clothes in one crowded corner of the living room. The air hung heavy with steam and smelled of gas from the radiant heater that hissed nearby, the only source of warmth in the tiny apartment. The iron thudded as she tried to get the wrinkles out of Garret's work clothes. He had surprised her by following Cleveland Yoakum's advice and trading in his crisp white collars for khaki ones. He had knuckled in to learn the oil business as a roustabout on a rig over in La Porte, even surviving the first week of hazing that could make life utterly hellish for a weevil down on the derrick floor. He choked back his temper and made it through. It was exhausting work. She didn't mind that he came home worn out and dirty, but she hated the way he fell right into the easy-spending ways of the oil workers. Garret came stumbling up the stairs in the wee hours Saturday morning, reeking of Jack Daniel's. He'd sleep all day, leaving her lonely and bored on the chaise in the living room. As she lay there, she would hear his footsteps echoing in her memory, down the back hall of the Warwick—the day she'd agreed to elope. Those hollow footfalls would always haunt her: *He's coming for me. Should I run or stay?* Her feet wanted to run, she remembered, but her heart wanted to stay. She would always wonder if she'd made the right decision.

Then, one Wednesday morning as she stood pressing Levi's, the phone rang. Hetty set the iron on its metal stand with a clink. She walked over and stood looking at the shiny black handset, shivering as it rang. The phone number she'd scribbled on Lamar's pack of cigarettes had nested in her mind like a row of spiders, scratching at her doubts and hopes. Would he spin her a silk ladder, after all—or simply weave another one of his glistening webs to entrap her before she knew what was happening? The phone rang. And rang again. She picked up the handset and paused a moment before saying, "Hello."

"Hetty? It's Lamar."

She lost her breath and had to sit down on the chaise lounge to catch it again. "Hey, kiddo. I was wondering if you'd call."

"Why wouldn't I?"

"I don't know. I thought maybe you'd lost that pack of cigarettes."

He chuckled on the other end. "Don't tell your sister, but after the concert, I went into one of the bathrooms at Bayou Bend, tore your number off, and put it in my billfold." A moment passed while he let that sink in. "What are you doing?"

"Laundry. Garret's on a rig."

"Tell him to work his way up to driller," Lamar said.

"Driller?"

"So he can attract the attention of my people."

"Your people?"

"Interest owners."

"Who are they?"

"Oh . . . some folks I know who buy interests in oil wells. Garret can sell shares to raise the money he needs. We'll put together a consortium."

"So that's how it's done?"

"Yep. I'd be happy to introduce you to these folks."

Hetty wasn't sure how to respond. He was throwing out the first glistening thread. Where would it lead? "Lamar, that's so decent of you! I really appreciate this. When can we all meet?"

"I'd prefer to introduce you first, Hetty. Garret can be—well, you know, an embarrassment."

Suddenly the glistening thread felt sticky, but she had to agree. "Yeah, like that night at Bayou Bend. He's still raving about Dad Joiner and the big strike they're going to make in East Texas. I finally told him he wasn't to mention that name again in this household, but I can't guarantee what he'd say at a meeting. What did you have in mind?"

Lamar's voice dropped into a more intimate tone. "Would you have dinner with me?"

"Dinner, huh?" Hetty stretched out on the chaise and tried not to sound too eager. The truth was she longed to see Lamar again in person, to meet furtively in some dark, swanky restaurant and continue reciting the rough saga of her marriage. There was something so inappropriate but irresistible in talking to him about Garret. But she wasn't sure what it might lead to—and how she would break the news to her husband. Then she remembered Garret's weekly benders with the other roustabouts. "Could it be on a Friday night?"

"Sure thing, kiddo. How about next week?"

"Next week, then."

Lamar took her to The Montrose for dinner the following Friday. After improvising martinis from a flask, he snapped open a silver-and-black-lacquered cigarette case and offered her a Turkish Murad—preferred, as he liked to point out, by the transatlantic cruise set. She inhaled deeply as she sat back, letting a rush of excitement flow into her head. She hadn't felt this alive in months.

Lamar made the perfect audience for the melodrama of her marriage. She told him about everything, beginning with her honeymoon in Galveston and ending with her recent snub by the haven of Houston's oilmen, the Cupola Club—feeling more a need for sympathy than status at the moment. His warm, discreet support made her open up even more, until she found herself saying silly things like, "God, how I hate linoleum!"

"It's not you," he agreed. "Listen, kid, I'll take you to the Cupola Club. Let me be your entrée."

The thought brushed her lips like a fresh coat of lipstick. She smiled. Later, she would blame it on the combination of Murads and martinis. As the evening wore on, she found herself sharing with him her deepest doubts about her marriage. She laughed, cried, and confided, her cheeks flushed and glowing.

"Perhaps I made a mistake marrying Garret," she said at one point. The consequences of such a confession were too tantalizing for them to discuss openly and were allowed to dangle dangerously above, out of the reach of their conversation. But she noticed Lamar growing serious, putting his wry humor on hold, and looking her straight in the eye as she catalogued her disappointments with her husband. "I think you're absolutely right not to introduce him to the investors right off."

"I'll let you charm them first," Lamar said. "Which you will—they're all men."

"Who are these fellows?"

"A bunch of Texans who hate Yankees."

Hetty threw him a puzzled glance.

"They want to invest in a real Texas oil company, not one owned by Rockefeller."

Hetty giggled drunkenly. "One like Splendora, you mean."

"You laugh. But we are the only pure Texas company left."

"What about Humble?"

"Rockefeller owns half of Humble."

Hetty looked at him wide-eyed. "Go tell it to Sweeney!"

"It's true."

"When did this happen?"

"Right after the War. The Blaffers, the Fondrens, they all sold out. Everyone but my dad."

"So Chief Rusk is the only real honest-to-God red dirt oilman left in Texas, is that what you're telling me?"

"Yep. Another reason not to introduce Garret to the investors right away. They'll see he's not from these parts. You've got to impress them first—you know, daughter of the founders and all that.

I think our next dinner should be at the Cupola Club. You've got to haunt the place if you want to meet the right folks."

"You'll really take me there?"

"How about next Friday?" Their thighs touched under the table. Their eyes met. The alcohol in Hetty's bloodstream rose like a slow-moving river, wide and sleek. She felt like it flowed from her eyes into Lamar's, then banked back into her body out of his thigh.

"I don't have anything I could wear to the Cupola Club," she said.

"Then I guess we'll have to go shopping."

It had been almost a year since a man had uttered those magic words to Hetty.

After lunch Monday afternoon, Hetty found herself being led by Lamar across Texas Avenue, the invisible border beyond which the dress shops waited. She was surprised there weren't all kinds of red caution signs along the road as the streetcar rumbled by. Once they stepped up onto the curb, she knew she was past the point where she could fend off any fashion temptations. When they came in front of Everitt-Buelow, where she used to shop with her mother, there were embroideries on display of such haughty elegance they made her heart ache with deprivation: one-of-a-kind smocks across which delicate Japanese lilies shimmered in shades like lilac and teal blue. Lamar remarked on their beauty, but Hetty only shrugged and looked away, thinking to herself, *It's been so long since I could afford a dress like that. ¡Ay, dios mio!*

As Lamar pulled her toward the entrance, she wondered how he planned to slip unseen by floorwalker Ellison. No sooner had they stepped into the fragrant first floor, then the gentleman appeared, tipping his hat and greeting them both by name.

Hetty avoided his eyes, but Lamar shook his hand warmly and said, "Afternoon, Ellison—has Miss Allen been in lately? Do you know what she's been looking at?"

"Not lately, sir."

"Then it's up to you, Hetty. You'll have to help me pick out a gown for your sister. You know me—all thumbs."

Hetty smiled. "I'd be glad to, Lamar. I should know what Charlotte likes by now."

Ellison waved them by. They kept the charade up as they headed toward the salon at the back of the second floor, the one appointed with couture gowns for evening. One thing unraveled into another; they were shopping their way along, trying on jewelry, sniffing perfume.

"Shopping for Charlotte," Hetty told all the saleswomen and the customers they recognized.

After rifling through lush embroideries for spring, she turned. And spotted it. A dress slung across a mannequin in a halo of light. Her heart stopped beating when she saw it, and when the blood surged back into her ears, it thundered like the first chord on an organ in a church. A low-cut gown in black and red sequins. It was more black than red, and black was her color. The red ran down it here and there like a scandal breaking. Like melted roses. She took it into a dressing room and tried it on immediately. She looked at herself in the mirror, the spangles clinging to her like scales on a fallen mermaid, her white breasts exposed just enough over the extreme décolletage. She knew it was the right thing to wear. Black, for things hidden, for the night. Red, dripping through it. Just a little. Bringing in the warning, the ripeness, the burn. *The blood.* What they were doing wasn't wrong. It was just risky. Very risky. As Lina liked to say, *"Cria cuervos y te sacarán los ojos." Breed ravens, and they will take out your eyes.*

He bought her the dress. "Charlotte will love it," he said.

He not only bought her the dress, he insisted she get some sexy new black lingerie to wear under it. Late Friday afternoon, Hetty stood naked in her bedroom and drew them on piece by piece: the black satin bra and panties, the chemise that slid over her silk stockings like whispers in bed. The dress she swung out of the closet, heavy as a coat of mail. She stepped into it and slid the zipper up. It enclosed her curves like the arch of a night sky where all the stars were red. Hetty's hands smoothed the dress over her midsection. It gurgled. Her stomach was corkscrewed from hunger and nerves. She tried to remember her favorite dishes at the Cupola Club. "Shrimp," she murmured and buttered her lips with the brightest red lipstick she could dig out of her drawers.

Footsteps creaked outside on the steps. In the mirror, she saw someone stumble through the dark living room. Fear corkscrewed her stomach even more. A light came on. "Anything to eat?" Garret asked. "I'm famished."

"Garret! You scared me to death! I thought you were a burglar." She raised her voice to cover the guilt that was clutching her throat like a velvet choker. *He's caught me dressing to go out with Lamar!* "The only thing we have to eat is bacon and eggs, since you didn't leave me any money to shop. I've had breakfast four times since yesterday."

In the silence that followed, she swiped at her hair then slapped the brush down. He tiptoed into the bedroom and began unbuttoning his shirt.

She stayed busy in the mirror, jabbed on a dangle of onyx earrings. "I thought you went out with your oil buddies on Friday night."

"Bunch of them are working. Refinery fire. It's good money, but I was too tired."

Hetty went over to the closet, unzipped a bag, and hid her breasts inside the sable stole that had capped the afternoon's shopping Monday. She bent to pull on her sandals then drew up, ready for the night, a tall lustrous column of sable and sequins.

"Where are you going?"

"Well . . ." Hetty took a deep breath. "I'm having dinner with Lamar actually."

"Lamar? Why?"

"He's offered to introduce me to some interest owners."

"What's that?"

"People who want to buy an interest in an oil well. This is for us, Garret."

He brushed past her. "This isn't for us—you just tell yourself that so you won't feel guilty."

"How come you know me better than I know myself?"

"No, I know men. Because I am one." He sat on the bed and took off his boots. "You don't need to do this. I'll make us the money for a well."

"How much have you saved?"

Garret was silent as he shrugged his shirt off.

"Just as I thought. You're gambling all our money away. That's why I have to do something."

He looked her up and down. "Where'd you get that stole?"

"If you were ever home, you'd know, Garret. It's been hanging in the closet."

"It has?"

"Yes! Haven't you noticed? I've got to go."

He came close enough to smell her perfume. "Can't I even have a little smooch? You look so gorgeous tonight. Is that a new perfume?"

"Yes. I have to keep those interest owners interested." She spread the red fingernails of her right hand across his chest to hold him back. "No kisses for weevils. I'm mad at you. Besides, you're too greasy."

With her nails, she drew red trails across his pectorals and noticed for the first time how they'd beefed up in the last month. The musk of his sweat made her head swim. *God, I must be in heat,* she thought. *I want to jump him, grease and all.*

Garret puffed his chest out and let her caress his nipples. "Be careful," he said, gazing straight into her eyes. "I don't like this."

She held his gaze. "I can take care of myself."

She could feel his eyes on her as she walked to the door, hips rippling, the layers of silk whispering to each other over her thighs. *Check your calendar, Hetty,* they seemed to say.

It was all so smooth. That's what she loved about going out with a Rusk. That short little name gave her instant entrée to exclusive spots like the Cupola Club. When she stepped up to the velvet rope this time, there was no embarrassed silence while they fumbled through the membership book.

"Cooper." She nodded. "How are you? I'm here for the meeting with the Rusk consortium."

"Of course, Mrs. MacBride. I'll carry you back myself."

The whole procedure was as smooth as the marble floors they walked across as the maître d' personally escorted her through dim hallways to a secluded suite hidden behind one of the Esperson Building's massive bronze doors. Cooper offered to take her stole, but she shook her head no, shy about unveiling her neckline. At the table, Lamar waited behind a blaze of candles. As the maître d' withdrew, Lamar instructed him to bring the investors back one by one as they arrived. The door clicked behind him with finality.

The smoothness turned from silken to slimy. Hetty held back at the door, reluctant to walk over. "A private room?"

"You look disappointed," Lamar noted.

"I was looking forward to dancing."

"We can dance." He pointed to a Victrola. "I even have your favorite record, 'Charmaine.' "

"I haven't heard that in years." Another step in.

"What's wrong, Het?"

"Mac came home tonight."

"So he knows you're here?"

Hetty nodded, peering at Lamar. "I had to tell him. He warned me to be careful. He doesn't trust you."

" 'Course not. He's expecting me to act like him."

Hetty sighed and let her eyes wander over both rooms.

"Why don't you take your stole off and stay a while?" When Hetty hesitated, he said, "I'm not Mac, kiddo." He got up and pulled her chair out for her.

She sat down but didn't remove her stole. "All right. Just until the investors arrive." She was hungry, so they ordered right away, substituting shrimp for oysters at her request. Hetty took a deep breath. There was something perilous in such rich privacy. She didn't want to examine the label, but she knew it must be very expensive champagne because the bubbles didn't burn her tongue, they just glided over it like the lightest surf leaving a little foam on a beach.

After they'd popped the second cork and she could see the flush coming into Lamar's cheeks, she relaxed a little.

"Don't I get to see the dress I bought you?"

"Promise to stay on your side of the table? It's low cut."

"All the better to sway the investors, my dear. It's all part of my devious plan."

Hetty let the sable stole slowly slide off her shoulders, revealing the breasts that the sparkling dress showcased so well. Lamar tried not to look at them.

The courses flowed with a quiet grace across the table. Hetty relished every bite. She hadn't eaten like this since their dinner at The Montrose. Lamar slid his chair along the curve of the round table and put his arm around her, looking down at the dress he'd bought her. He toyed with the slab of onyx that dangled suggestively from her ear.

After dinner, one of the waiters put some music on. The song he'd promised her played, and she had to smile in spite of herself, humming along as the brass floated on the air, the endless sweet melody haunting the room. Lamar matched the falsetto voice of the singer as he crooned the words:

I wonder why you keep me waiting,
Charmaine, my Charmaine . . .

"Play it again!" Hetty squealed, getting up to dance. Her slippers glided across the polished floor, and she began to feel as if she were hovering two inches above it. After a few more songs, Lamar wheeled her around and laid her out like an odalisque on the chaise lounge. She was too intoxicated to resist.

"You broke your promise," Hetty said, wagging a finger at him playfully.

"I'm a naughty boy."

He dragged a chair over from the table and watched her as he had many times in the past, his eyes flicking back and forth in a nervous mixture of longing and confusion.

"Why are you staring at me?"

"I always found you so gorgeous, Het. Especially tonight."

She let her eyes swim, letting his image shift out of focus. "Only because you can buy me the clothes that make me look that way."

"Let me just have one kiss," he said, sliding onto the chaise again. "I deserve that much."

Her arms held him back. "What if the other men walk in on us?"

"Don't keep me waiting any longer, my Charmaine." His kisses traveled down her neck, toward her breasts.

"What do you want from me, Lamar?"

"Right now, it's to see you in those French silks I bought."

Hetty's dress was so low cut, she felt as if the tops of her nipples had been peeking out all evening, so it was a simple maneuver for Lamar to hitch his thumbs into the neckline and pull it back. He immersed his face in her cleavage. Then, somehow, before she knew what was happening, he had gotten her breasts out of the black silk bra and was kissing her nipples. They went erect in spite of herself, killing the last bit of hope she'd been holding out.

"There are no other investors, are there, Lam?" She said it as much for herself as for him.

"Why do you want other oil men? You've got me."

"So there's no consortium of interest owners?"

"I'm the consortium. Consort with me." He started sucking on her nipples.

"Wait a minute—I thought we needed to sell shares to raise money."

"We don't need to do that at Splendora. We have the money to do our own drilling."

She pulled his head away from her breasts for a moment. "Let me get this straight. You're going to finance a well for Garret and me?"

He looked her in the eyes. "I'll do whatever it takes to have you. You know how it works in business, Het. You scratch my back, I'll scratch yours."

"I have a feeling scratching your back is going to be a little complicated."

"No, it's simple. I've booked a room at the Rice. Come spend the night with me."

She sat up. "You booked a room?"

"Well—I—" Lamar stammered. "Dad keeps one there."

"I can't be gone all night. What'll I tell my husband?"

"Just tell him you met a financier. You won't be lying."

"Lamar!"

"Com'on, Het. Believe me—Garret won't care what you do, as long as you come home with the money for his well." His mouth headed for her breasts again.

"Hold on, buster," she said, pulling her bra back up. She slid past him off the chaise and adjusted her dress. He came after her. "Just hold on a minute here." She lifted her hands to stop him. "I need to visit the ladies' lounge."

Hetty wandered through the hallways until she found the powder room. Dance music drifted by from the ballroom. She went into one of the marble stalls and sat down, her head reeling as much from Lamar's proposal as from champagne. She needed to think clearly for a moment, which was hard to do under the circumstances. She couldn't pretend to be surprised that there were no other investors. Wily Lamar. Somehow he'd snagged her, as he always did. Why had she come in here instead of just walking out of the club? *Maybe part of me wants to be Lamar's mistress. Maybe it would suit me—donning the robes of a concubine as easily as this dress I'm wearing tonight. The red running through the black. The luxury. The gossip. And wouldn't Charlotte seethe when she found out?!* Hetty stood up. Then sat back down. Her husband had made his sacrifice, going to work as a weevil on a rig, killing himself five days a week to learn the business. Now it was her turn to make a sacrifice. *But it has to be on my terms, not Lamar's. There's a little detail we have to work out first.* Hetty used the toilet and marched back into the room.

Lamar had stretched out on the chaise, watching her with a crooked smirk on his face.

"Okay, I'll do it."

"That's my Charmaine," he said, getting up.

"But there's one condition."

"Yep?"

"You have to break up with Char first."

"Let's leave Char out of this, Hetty."

"No way, buster. I can't have sex with you as long as you're still dating my sister."

"You can't?"

"Of course not, Lam. Break it off with her. Then I'll go with you."

"That could take some time."

"Why? You could call her right now." When he hesitated, Hetty felt the heat of irritation rising in her heart. She wanted to complete their transaction that very night, before she lost her nerve. She wanted him to acknowledge the sacrifice she was making by giving up something that was important to him, too. She needed to know how he really felt about her.

But Lamar just stood there, looking confused. "I don't want to do it over the phone," he said. His reluctance angered Hetty and made the champagne go flat when he poured her another flute.

Her impatience reached a head when he finally drove her home. She directed him to Heights Boulevard, a couple of blocks over from where she lived with Garret. She had been inflamed by the evening and had found Lamar endowed by the candlelight of the Cupola Club with a new aura of power and charm. She wanted something from him. Something to verify the risk they had taken. Something more than his trickster games. She wanted him to lay a claim on her—wanted it badly. So badly that she felt the outcome of the rest of her life could depend on it.

But he only sat there stiffly in the Bearcat, not sure how to proceed. She remembered petting with Garret in the Auburn. Garret always knew what to do at moments like this. She wanted Lamar to act like Garret. Instead, all she got was a lingering kiss on the mouth and a promise to call her once he'd talked to Char. After slamming the car door a little too hard, she had to find her way two blocks home in the dark.

She marched up the stairs, nerves sharpened for a confrontation. Instead, she found cleanliness and quiet. The dishes had been washed; the trash emptied. On the dining table sat unexpected gifts of contrition: red roses and a round blue music box such as one might buy in a dime store. She lifted the lid. It played "I Love

You Truly." The tinny, quavering notes made her anger shift mysteriously into tenderness, touched by the very crudeness of the gesture. When she walked into the bedroom, she was undone completely.

Garret had fallen asleep waiting for her, the covers thrown off. His face was clean-shaven, sober, his black hair slicked back and glossy. A shaft of unshaded light fell across him at an angle from the bathroom's bare ceiling bulb. She was reminded of a statue from Nella's tome on classical sculpture—*The Dying Gaul,* the fallen warrior vulnerable yet still so virile in his defeat. That was Garret.

His naked white body in its sleep was marble-innocent, a broken god, so in need of rescuing. She reached out, appalled by the lust she felt for him, but still too intoxicated to resist it. She had wanted Lamar to lay his claim on her, and he had failed. She knew that Garret could give her what she wanted—after all, he was her husband. He had not betrayed her. He loved her truly, like the music box said. Was this whole thing with Lamar a big mistake?

When she woke Garret, he buried his face in the cleavage showcased by her low neckline. She stood, unzipped the heavy sequined dress and let it slink to the floor, then lifted the chemise over her head. She lay down and let her husband remove the black satin bra and panties that another man had bought, moved by the way he clung to her when she was naked, skintight, like a frightened child.

She clung back, slaking her lust on him, wondering the whole time if Lamar would really break up with her sister.

In the three weeks following that night, Lamar began calling Hetty almost every day after Garret left for work. She stretched out on the chaise and waited for the phone to ring, falling behind on her housework and ironing. They would talk for two hours at a time. She snuggled up with the warm fragrant receiver nestled against her ear and fantasized. Would she become his mistress? Is that what this was all leading to? Why not his wife? His wealth lapped at her dreams like azure water. It was vast as an ocean, deep and mysterious. It was the source of his power over her, giving him a radiance that was more than human. He would come for her, she believed, and release her from her poverty. In the Rusks' private yacht, he would cruise up the muddy Ship Channel and bear her away to some island where the water was clear. She just had to reside on her chaise lounge and wait.

Hetty sat one morning studying the telephone cord, coiled with promise. It rang. After they talked for a while, she got out a calendar to fix a date for their tryst.

Suddenly, she noticed another date she had penciled in. For a moment, she thought that she'd gotten an electric shock off the telephone, such a flash of horror flitted across her nerves. It knocked the receiver out of her hand. Lamar's voice crackled in concern. But she could only watch, speechless, as the receiver dangled out of control, twisting the wire into writhing tubelike forms.

She felt her hands instinctively cradle her abdomen. Otherwise, she was petrified.

Her period was a week late.

In the last cold quiet nights of February, the air stirred. Hetty listened to it rising around her as she lay sleepless beside her husband or sat alone in the afternoons watching the lace of bare branches flicker across the floor. March set the whole world into motion, blustering winds pulling at her wherever she went. But deep inside her, nothing moved. She waited through two windy weeks and prayed every night to wake up and find a bloody stain on her nightgown, the monthly flow. But as the weather swelled, the stillness inside her only grew deeper. Nothing broke. Nothing was lost. There was a breathless hush at her nub, like the quiet at the bottom of the ocean. A mystery. And a curse. *I can't be pregnant,* she kept telling herself. *I'm only late. Lamar and I need more time to figure things out. And we'll have that time. We have to.*

But soon she was over a month late. There was a feeling inside she couldn't ignore, the languor of new life. She began taking naps in the afternoon. Her face changed. A trip to Nella's doctor confirmed her fears. She told Lamar before she told Garret. He didn't take it the way she'd hoped he would. His voice grew cold over the phone.

"You slept with Garret?"

"We're married, Lam. I sleep with him every night."

"You wanted me to break up with Char and you slept with Garret?"

"You *haven't* broken up with Char. It's been weeks, and you just keep talking about it."

"But you wanted me to."

"Are you still going to do it?"

"Well, not now."

A long pause stretched out over the telephone lines. In her other ear, the radiant heater sputtered like it wasn't putting out enough heat. The guarded tone in Lamar's voice gave her a chill. "Think about what you've done here, woman—"

"I didn't mean—"

"For God's sake! Now *he'll* be the father of your children, not me."

"Lamar, listen—"

But he didn't listen. He hung up on her and never called back. She knew what to expect next and, right on cue, it came: the news of Lamar's betrothal to her sister. There would be a long engagement, no doubt, leading up to a grim Protestant ritual. *If that's what Lamar wants, he can just stew in his own juice. See if I care.* Hetty tried to exile him from her mind. But then one day she opened the *Houston Post-Dispatch* to the Society Column and was stunned by what she read: RUSK/ALLEN NUPTIALS SET FOR JUNE. They were to be married in less than three months! She wrote in her passbook under *Withdrawals: Lamar's love.*

The wedding itself was a series of small shocks for Hetty. She and Garret arrived at Christ Church at four p.m. on a hot June afternoon, presenting their card of admission in the vestibule. As they were escorted down the aisle, Hetty saw instantly that Garret was underdressed. He'd worn his best double-breasted pinstripe, but all the other men sported cutaways and spats. Everyone watched them as they approached the pew where her parents were sitting. Heat rose into Hetty's cheeks with a fury. She felt huge now, her feet so swollen she had to wear chunky shoes that tied. She kept her eyes down and tripped as she tried to sidle into her seat. The sight of Nella reminded her that the Spanish use the word *embarazada* for pregnant. Suddenly she understood why. She sat down and turned her back to the congregation, but could hear whispering behind her, imagining that people were commenting not only on her husband's attire, but on her less-than-fashionable maternity outfit. *Lockett should be happy,* Hetty thought. *Now we do look like shanty Irish.*

As Cora had foretold, once Hetty was with child, Nella forgave her for eloping with Garret. She was overwhelmed with a torrent of attention such as she'd never known. Nella threw her a shower in the suite at the Warwick, inviting all her debutante girlfriends. She received so many gifts, she had to store them in the garage underneath their apartment. Nella bought her new maternity clothes, paid her doctor bills, and insisted that Lina come to comfort her through the long hours of labor. Hetty's water broke right on schedule one evening in October as a huge harvest moon glided into the somber sky. Everything looked ghostly on the streets as Garret drove her to St. Joseph's. When he turned toward the hospital, she saw a sign drift by in the gloom: Pierce Street. He lifted her into a wheelchair at the entrance. As a nurse wheeled her down the antiseptic white hallways, she looked toward the windows for a glimpse of the moon: It had lost its golden color but still rode huge in the night sky. Hetty fancied that its pull had ruptured her waters, like the tides it towed out to sea every night.

Lina came into her hospital room later and pulled down the blind. "Don't gaze at the moon, *m'ija*—you'll give birth to a sleepwalker!"

Time passed. Hetty wasn't sure how long. She couldn't get comfortable; she was beginning to sweat. Even through the drawn blinds, she felt the moon drawing her behind it as it inched along. She could hardly keep from crying out at times when the pains cramped her up and she couldn't stop them. She felt slightly delirious and had trouble concentrating on anything. She just tried to endure.

Lina propped her legs up with pillows and stroked her knees. Hetty whispered, "Have you ever seen Mamá's knees?"

"Sí," came a whispered response.

"What's on them?"

"Cicatrices."

Scars, Hetty thought, knife blades flashing in her mind. "From what?"

Lina grew silent. "That happened in San Antonio. Ask Cora."

Hetty hoped she would remember to do that. Right now, she felt trapped in an undertow of pain that crested into huge waves sweeping her away. Then something seemed to go wrong. The labor pains were coming fast now. Hetty was delirious with them, moaning and clutching at the pillows. Nurses stood over her, shaking their heads, asking questions. She felt fingers inside her, stretching her.

Lina came and sat on the bed beside her, trying not to look concerned. "*No te preocupes, m'ija,* but the baby's feet are coming down first."

"Just hurry up and get it out!"

"*No podemos, m'ija.* The head has to come down."

Contractions strangled Hetty so she couldn't breathe. No one had prepared her for this kind of torment. She remembered the injection she'd read about that was so popular at hospitals. "Twilight sleep!" she screamed. "I want twilight sleep! Lina!"

Next thing she knew, she was being lifted onto a stretcher and felt cold air passing as she was carried through hallways. When she finally felt the prick of a needle in her arm, the pain didn't go away all at once. It took a while. "Just wait, miss," some nurse told her. An eternity of torment passed until the pain started fading slowly like music getting softer and softer until she could hear it no longer. There was only white noise all around until a red balloon floated up into the sky and she was gone.

When she woke, the pain was back, deeper and sharper. A baby was screeching nearby. She groaned and looked around the gray room. In a shaft of afternoon sun, Garret paced back and forth holding a bundle in his arms.

"It's finally out?" she asked.

"You had a Cesarean."

"That's why my stomach hurts so much. What flavor is it?"

He came over to the bed and raised the infant proudly. The child's face was a tangle of discomfort, red and bawling. "It's a boy. What shall we call it?"

Hetty remembered the street sign she'd glimpsed on the way to the hospital. "Pierce," she said, reaching up. "Let's call him Pierce."

Chapter 11

While Hetty was in the hospital, time went out of focus. Light and dark drifted in and out of her window, hazy in the ebbing of twilight sleep. Gray clouds dusted the sky. She kept the curtains drawn all the way back, watching for a flash of lightning, listening for a drumroll of thunder. Anything to sweep away the gloom. It wasn't that she was lonely. St. Joseph's Infirmary crawled with efficient nurses anxious to tutor her in the intricacies of childcare. Visitors appeared almost daily to snap her out of her daze: Nella and Lina, her friends one by one, Garret dropping in after work with a warm fragrant bag of Chinese food. Kirb came by one night after batching up the bank. He seemed delighted to have a grandson to carry on the Allen line. He even called her princess again. To her surprise, Charlotte actually visited twice, holding Pierce proudly and confessing how much she wanted one of her own. Hetty sat up on mounds of pillows and radiated the glow of motherhood. But after visiting hours, when they brought the baby in, she held him away from her. His crying and helplessness only depressed her. She longed for someone to come and take care of the child so she could sleep. But she didn't dare ask. She could feel her throat tighten up just at the thought. Her secret sadness was like the scar that had disfigured her belly: She showed it to no one.

The day Garret took her home, Pearl came over and helped them settle in. They set up the crib, hauled out the diaper pail, and unpacked some of the baby blankets she'd been given as gifts. When she opened the GE and saw that Pearl had stocked it with food—a meat loaf and a whole ham, a bowl of potato salad, and a gallon of refrigerator slaw—she choked up. That would happen to her a lot in the days to come. She would cry at the slightest nudge, sometimes from joy, usually from a piercing but unidentifiable distress.

The following Saturday, fierce cries fished Hetty out of a deep afternoon nap. She had fallen asleep breast-feeding Pierce on the chaise lounge. He was having one of his rare fits of colic during the day. She tried feeding him, but he wanted nothing to do with her nipple. She changed his diaper, tossing the soiled one into the already overflowing pail that she hadn't had the energy to empty. The whole apartment reeked from it. Hetty settled into the rocker, seesawing the baby in her arms. He cried all the louder. She stood up and heaved him to her shoulder, wincing at the pain in her abdomen. His howls scorched the close air of the apartment, making her cheeks burn. She swore under her breath and stomped into the bedroom. She set the baby in his cradle and ordered him to go to sleep. That enraged him all the more. His face was beet red.

"If you don't stop that right now, I'm going to start screaming, too." And she did. She started screaming back at him, pitching her voice louder than his, appalled at what she heard herself saying. "You think YOU have something to scream about? YOU? Because of you I have this horrible scar—my nipples aren't even pink anymore. They're dark brown! *Do you hear me?!* Dark brown! Now—*YOU!*—won't even sleep when you're supposed to. Well—*YOU!*—can just stew in your own juice—see if I care!"

Trembling, she went outside and sat on the rickety stairs, a Lucky hanging defiantly out of one corner of her mouth. The baby screams weren't as loud out here. She smoked the cigarette to a nub, then went down into the garage and rifled around in the boxes of gifts for a rattle or pacifier that might distract him. His crying leaked through the ceiling like rancid water. She found his Uncle Wiggily Game, his Magnetic Fish Pond, and a Chick-in-Egg Rattle. She settled on the Steiff barking dog Nella had given him, the one with the natural-looking glass eyes and the baby-size bark. Then she went upstairs and waved it in front of his scrunched-up face. She made it bark. He caught his breath. She placed it in his tiny hand, but he bawled and threw it out of the cradle.

"Fine. Just *FINE!* That was my last offer." She went into the kitchen and pulled out the bottle of champagne crazy Wini had brought her. She wasn't supposed to drink while she was nursing—they told her at the hospital—but she didn't care anymore. *Let the little bastard drink champagne straight from my tits—maybe that'll knock him out.*

Then inexplicably, the squall blew itself out as suddenly as it had begun. Silence pounded at her ears. She tiptoed into the bedroom and peered into the crib. Pierce had fallen into a ragged sleep, his breathing shallow, his face forlorn. Hetty clutched at her throat and went over to the phone.

"Pearl," she whispered into the receiver, hoarse from screaming, "something awful happened with the baby." She confessed what she'd been afraid to tell anyone, that she hadn't wanted the baby in the first place and now was leaving it abandoned in its crib to cry its eyes out. "Him, I guess I should say," realizing that she'd been referring to Pierce as "it."

The receiver crackled with laughter. "You just got the baby blues, hon. I went through the same thing."

"You had a baby? You never told me that."

"Like to run me crazy. We lived in a fourth-floor walk-up when my Little Pearl was born, and there was a fire escape outside our window. I kept looking at that window, thinking I'd step out there and drop the baby off the fire escape."

The big lump in Hetty's throat found its way into her eyes. "I thought you'd report me, and they'd come take my baby away from me," she said, tears dribbling down her cheeks.

"Aren't you the one!" Pearl said, clucking. "There's a mother in you somewhere—y'all just need to dig down and find her."

* * *

Sunday morning the sun managed to work a chink in the cloud cover. Hetty was awakened by sunlight on her face for the first time in weeks. Sleep floated around her like chiffon scarves. She stretched in slow ripples and realized that she'd actually slept through the night. Pierce hadn't wakened once. She unbuttoned her nightie and let the golden sunlight flow over her engorged breasts like warm oil. It made her milk come in. She could smell Garret on the sheets but couldn't see him anywhere. He would enjoy the sight of her naked in the sun. They hadn't made love in so long, the poor guy must be desperate. He'd probably gone down to the corner newsstand to get the Sunday paper. In his undershirt, no doubt. She couldn't break him of that habit. She also couldn't convince him to pick up the *Post-Dispatch* so she could read about her friends. He always got the *Chronicle* for the oil news. Hetty heard tiny sounds coming from the crib and rolled over to lift Pierce out and pull him to her breast.

She was almost asleep again when a stampede of footsteps shook the stairs. Garret busted in shouting, "I was right, goddamn it! I was right."

She could hear him slap his hat down before he came in. Sure enough, he was wearing his sleeveless undershirt. He hoisted the Sunday paper with one muscled arm like he was waving a letter. It would take two hands for Hetty to pick it up. He slammed it down on the bed and dangled the front page in front of her eyes. "Look at this," he said. Huge block letters blared out the headline EAST TEX WELL A GUSHER! Then in smaller letters: *Dad Joiner hits pay dirt in Rusk County.*

"What?" Hetty pulled herself out of the snuggle with the baby—who had dozed off—and sat up in bed, yanking the section out of her husband's hands. Garret hovered above, waiting for her reaction. Her lips moved as her eyes sped along the lines:

> Henderson, Texas. A new oil field was discovered in Texas last night when the Joiner well #3—the "Daisy Bradford"—was brought in. Some 5,000 persons were present to witness the bailing in. The ground

> shook, witnesses said, as oil shot almost to the top of the derrick. Today oilmen have determined that the well is flowing at the rate of 5,000 barrels a day. The well is named the "Daisy Bradford" as a tribute to the woman who let Dad Joiner drill on her farm and believed in him when all others said it was folly.

Hetty looked up. "Old Dad did it?"

Garret yelped, "Yes!" and slammed his fist into the air, dancing about to a chorus of yahoos. "I knew it! I just knew it!"

"Shhhh! You'll wake the baby." But it was too late. Pierce was startled by the tremors rumbling across the floor. She lifted him up to Garret. "Here, do diaper duty while I read on."

Garret sang to his son as he struggled with the safety pins: "Daisy Bradford had a farm . . ." Hetty scanned the front page again—the letters were huge, the kind they save for announcements of war or the first flight across the Atlantic: JOINER, HERO OF THE HOUR.

> The producing formation has been definitely identified as the Woodbine Sand, which is the source of other famous pools of recent years in Texas, such as Mexia, Powell, and Van. The Woodbine Sand, noted for its great flush production and rich gasoline content, has been the goal of countless wildcatters.

Hetty could almost smell the rich deposit, then realized it was the baby poo from the diaper Garret had just peeled off. He went into the bathroom to retrieve a wet washcloth. Hetty pulled her nightie back on. "So it *is* the Woodbine Sand?" she asked as he came back out.

"Yes, sir! Exactly like I said. Now maybe your goddamn father will believe me."

Hetty watched her husband swaddling their child in layers of white cotton. She'd never realized how sexy it could be to watch a grown man changing a baby. The thick fingers fumbling with safety pins, the darkly tanned arms cradling the soft white flesh. Garret, always fit, was now strapping from hauling pipes and breaking joints eight hours a day. He bent over Pierce in a pool of sun, a new light of confidence around his head. Her legs stirred with desire for the first time in months.

"So you'd better pack your bags, Hetty," he said, lifting his son into the air with one hand as easily as the newspaper, "because we're going to East Texas."

"Of course we are, kiddo," Hetty said, lying back and letting her enormous breasts fall out of her nightie. "But first—come here."

All through the holidays that year, Garret planned his invasion of East Texas. He crawled over maps of the region like an ant, surveying the dimensions of Joiner's lease, wondering where their one-acre share might be. "We've got to get up there," he'd tell Hetty, twisting a Camel in his fingers and dogging her to call her father.

Hetty decided she'd better put in an appearance at Nella's Christmas party, cradling Pierce in her arms and wearing a sweater that showcased her bust line. Lamar noticed it at once, steering his new wife over to where Hetty sat on the sofa. Charlotte wore a mysterious smile.

"You look like the cat that swallowed the canary," Hetty said. "You're not . . . ?"

"Yes!" she squealed, breaking out into a broad grin.

Hetty squealed back. "When did this happen?"

"I don't know. I wasn't there," Lamar said, trying not to be too obvious about eyeing Hetty's abundant breasts.

Charlotte slapped him on the head. "We're due in July."

"I'm sure Rachel will be happy," Hetty said. "She finally gets that Rusk heir she's been waiting for." A swarm of elegant guests eddied around them in Nella's drawing room. Charlotte sat down beside Hetty and looked at Pierce longingly. "Would you like to hold him, sis?"

"May I? I have to practice." Hetty slid the baby into her arms.

"Ohh, sugar, come to your aunt Char," she cooed, her cool demeanor completely disarmed by the little pink face surrounded by its creamy bunting. When Pierce smiled at her, she got a little teary-eyed and gazed at him in a kind of rapture. "If I had one of these, I'd never put it down." She sighed.

"Well, you'll have one soon. And by the way, it's not an it." Hetty laughed. "They do have genders."

"Sorry, him. You must be so in love, Het."

"In love? Wait till you have to change a diaper."

She rocked Pierce back and forth. "But it's that sweet-smelling baby poo, isn't it?" she crooned.

"I hope to tell you!" Hetty said. "See what you have to look forward to, Lam?"

"I've already made a deal with Tuggie," Lamar said. "No diapers." They all laughed, even Pierce.

Hetty leaned over to watch the baby giggling. She slipped her arm around Charlotte and hugged her ever so slightly. She was not rebuffed. *A rare moment of closeness!* she thought. *Maybe becoming mothers will finally turn us into sisters.*

Charlotte wouldn't give the child up until their father came over and demanded equal time. Cora had been right: Pierce was proving to be Hetty's entrée back into the family circle. She watched as Kirb's face melted into grandfatherly smiles. The child worked his simple alchemy.

Hetty waited for Charlotte and Lamar to be drawn into the festive crowd, then leaned closer. "Well, Dad, I guess you've heard about the Daisy Bradford."

"I know what you're going to say next."

"I'll try not to rub it in too much."

"There's nothing to rub in," he said, cooing to the child.

"Dad! Why can't you swallow your pride and admit that Garret was right?"

Kirb sat back, his eyes cagey. "How do we know it's not just a lucky strike?"

"Oh, never mind, Dad. I don't know why I was expecting anything from you." Hetty stood up. "It's time to feed the baby."

Kirb gazed down at his grandson, not ready to relinquish the child. He unzipped the bunting and grabbed one of Pierce's tiny hands, shaking it lightly. When the baby smiled at him, he babbled nonsense back. Then he sighed and heaved the two of them off the sofa, passing Pierce into Hetty's arms. While he was bent close, he murmured in her ear. "I just need more proof, princess. Then you'll hear from me."

Hetty said nothing to Garret, thinking it would be well into January before her father called. But on the Monday following Christmas, after sweeping up fallen tinsel and torn wrapping paper, Hetty took Pierce for a stroll down the block and picked up a copy of the *Post-Dispatch* from a coin box. There on the front page was the news they'd been waiting for: Another well had been discovered near Kilgore, the Lou Della Crim, only nine miles north of Joiner's. "Excitement High," the headline read. "Opens Extensive Territory." She showed it to Garret when he got home that afternoon and, that very night, her father telephoned to say he was arranging a meeting with none other than Cleveland Yoakum. It was to take place during the New Year's Day brunch at the Cupola Club.

On Wednesday, Nella called, asking after the baby. She lowered her voice and added, "Tell Garret not to get his hopes up, dear. Your father twisted Cleve's arm to come to this luncheon, but never forget he's a Texas oilman. A slab o' granite."

"But, Mamá, haven't you heard? Another well was discovered."

"I don't care if they found diamonds in the drill stem. You won't get past Cleve the Cliff. And by the way, we only call him that behind his back. To you, he's Mr. Yoakum."

"I'll remember that, Mamá."

Nella lowered her voice. "This is so unlike your father. I think he's doing it because of Pierce."

"Pierce?"

"Oh, haven't you heard? Charlotte had a miscarriage. She's not going to be giving us that grandson."

Hetty gasped into the phone. "At Christmas? How awful. She was so elated at your party."

"*Pobrecita*. You should call her, *m'ija.* She's in a bad way."

Hetty wondered if that was a good idea.

Later that afternoon, after putting Pierce down for a nap, Hetty got up the nerve to dial Splendora's number. The phone rang and rang. She was about to hang up when a familiar but irritated voice answered. "Rusk residence."

"Tuggie?"

"Speakin'."

"It's Hetty."

"Miss Hetty? Well, I'll be. But hold on, you ain't a miss anymore, I hear. And a mother, too. How's your baby boy?"

"Wonderful, thanks. What are you doing answering the phone?"

"You tell me. Like to rung off the wall. And me with so much dirt to scratch. Wait'll I get my hands on some niggers."

"I'm calling to talk to Charlotte. How is she?"

Tuggie lowered her voice. "She not doing good. Just lie on the sofa listening to radio. And Chief shunning her. Poor child. She'll be glad to hear from you."

"I hope so. Can you put her on?"

"Yes, ma'am." Hetty heard a rustling, then Tuggie's contralto voice booming through the vast rooms. *"Charlotte! Phone!"*

Clicking followed by a whispered, "Hello."

"Charlotte, it's Hetty. I heard the news. I'm so sorry. How are you?"

"All right." There was a long pause. Hetty didn't know what to say. She heard sniffling, then, "I just feel so blue."

"I can imagine."

"Can you? Can you really? Did Lamar tell you?"

"No, Mamá called."

"I thought he might have come to you."

Hetty wasn't sure how to respond to that. A loud protestation would sound like an admission of guilt. She tried to keep her voice steady as she said, "I don't think I've seen Lamar since the wedding."

"I know he's disappointed."

"A lot of women lose their first child. You'll have another. Is there anything I can do?"

"No, thanks. I've got Tuggie. She's been a big help."

"How about I bring Pierce by to cheer you up?"

Hetty heard more sniffling. "I . . . I don't think I could witness your happiness right now."

"Oh . . ." Hetty stammered. "I didn't mean it that way. I just want him to get to know his aunt."

"Use me another time. Not now."

"Char . . ." Hetty sighed. "I wish there were something I could do."

"There isn't. You're making it worse, actually."

"Oh . . ." Hetty never knew how to talk to her sister. "Then I'd better go. Let me know if you need me—for *anything*."

"I don't . . . but thanks." There was a hollow click.

Hetty left the stroller at home. She knew the New Year's brunch at the club was always a lavish affair and didn't want to try and wheel her way through the ice sculptures and the silver tea sets. She wrapped Pierce in a creamy wool and satin blanket, and herself in her long silver fox. Garret got his papers in order and knotted on a crisp four-in-hand silk to set off his pin-striped suit. Hetty glimpsed him in the bathroom, parting his hair precisely down the middle, adding an extra splash of luster to make it shine even more.

As a waiter led them through the vast dining hall, she nestled Pierce against her fur coat. Cleveland Yoakum didn't rise when they approached the table. He sat there stony as the Sphinx, Bloody Mary in one hand, Cinco cigar in the other. As her father hailed them and drew out a chair for her to sit in, Cleveland nodded a head thick with white hair in their direction. She noticed that he was wearing a diamond-studded bolo instead of a tie. That didn't surprise her, but the plate of half-eaten ham and eggs in front of him did. He had helped himself before they arrived. Hetty's mind stung with the Morse code he was telegraphing by that gesture: This young couple wasn't important enough to wait for, even if *she* was Kirby Allen's daughter. Even now he hardly acknowledged their presence. Hetty ignored him right back, leaving the baby with his grandfather and sidling up to the buffet for some of the club's famous creamed crab over toast.

When she returned, Garret was thanking her father for the invitation and turning to Cleveland. "Mr. Yoakum," he began (she'd warned him not to use his first name), “I’d also like to thank you for that contact with Humble.”

A guttural grunt was the only reply.

“I’ve been on a rig for over a year now.”

A long silence. Then a deep drawl: “Learned anything?”

“I think so, sir. I started as a floor hand, worked the motors for a while, and this fall was promoted to driller.”

Cleveland looked at Garret directly for the first time. “Driller?” *Drillah?*

“Yes, sir, Mr. Yoakum.”

“So you think you know how to drill an oil well?”

“Yes, sir.”

“But do you know the difference between a driller and a wildcatter?”

Garret hesitated. “Is this a trick question?”

Kirb spoke up. “Wildcatters usually hire someone to do their drilling.”

Garret looked a little chagrined. Cleveland flicked his cigar into an ashtray and stuck it in one corner of his mouth. Out of the other, he said, “Let me put it this way. Now that you’ve given Kirb a grandson, I suppose you’ll go on working at Humble?”

Garret glanced at Hetty. “I know that’s what I should do, but I just can’t. I’m going to East Texas.”

Cleveland’s chest heaved with laughter. Garret went over to the buffet to get some food.

“Before you arrived,” Kirb said, “we were placing bets on whether Garret was wildcat material or not. Cleve is surprised he’s kept the same job for a year.”

Hetty glanced at him with a puzzled look.

“You see, ma’am,” Cleveland said, “the wildcatter’s problem, he’s plum farsighted. Can’t see what’s right in front of him ’cause he’s always looking out yonder . . .”

“That’s Garret all right,” Hetty said.

Kirb kissed his grandson on the cheeks and smiled beatifically. “We have to hand it to him, Cleve. He predicted the strike in East Texas when the rest of us were scoffing.”

Cleveland stoked his cigar. "We never reckoned they'd find the Woodbine Sand up east."

Garret heard the tail end of the sentence as he sat down. "The Woodbine? Now there's something to talk about! It was right where Doc Lloyd said it would be, at thirty-six hundred feet."

Garret's boast drew a flinty glance from Cleveland. "Didn't prove a damned thing." *A damned thang.*

"With all due respects, Mr. Yoakum, how can you say that? It proved that Doc Lloyd wasn't the charlatan everybody said he was but, indeed, a great geologist."

"It proved he was damned lucky, that's all." He took a swig of scalding hot coffee, black as crude. "But this new well, this Lou Della Crim, makes me think we have an oil field on our hands."

Hetty handed Garret a fork so he'd eat something.

"Twenty-two thousand barrels is nothing to sniff at," Kirb said.

"It was the cleanest wildcat ever drilled in Texas," Cleveland announced. "They didn't spill a drop. The temperature was only seventy-four degrees. Now that's what I call an elegant oil well. None of this gusher crap like you had with Joiner and his crew. This one was all done scientifically."

"Maybe so, but the frenzy's started," Kirb said, rocking his grandson in his arms. "The day after the well came in, they say the people of Kilgore woke up and found thousands of boomers swarming into town."

Garret's silverware clattered to his plate. "Damn! I've got to get up there before it's too late."

"We've got to get in there before the big boys buy up all the leases, that's what we got to do," Kirb said. "And we have to be quiet about it. That's why I invited Mr. Yoakum to brunch today."

"Um-hmm," growled Cleveland.

"You see, Garret, Cleveland thinks he could get together a consortium of interest owners willing to gamble on East Texas. I'm one of them, in fact. We're just looking for an operator that can do the job."

"Give me a chance, gentlemen," Garret said with reverence. "I know I can do it."

Cleveland ignored him and drawled, "Strictly speaking, it's not a wildcatter we're looking for, Kirb. The field's been discovered. We just need somebody to get in there, buy a lease, and drill us a well without messin' up."

Garret fumbled with his papers. "We don't need a lease, sir. I've already got a one-acre share. Look—" He waved the certificate in front of them.

"Forget that swindler, son," Cleveland said. "You got to go up yonder and find yourself a dirt-poor cotton farmer and offer him more money than he's ever seen in his life. He'll sign whatever you stick under his nose. East Texas is so poor the roaches are starving to death."

"I hope you'll take a chance on me. I can show you—I'm a good investment." Garret reached for more papers.

"Investment?" Cleveland's chest rumbled with amusement. "Let me tell you how I invest. I'm like the red-eared slider trying to cross the road to get to the other side. Turtle don't move unless he sticks his neck out. Say he hears a car coming. If he pulls his head back in, he gets run over. That's my philosophy of investing. It's just that simple, son."

When Pierce started to fuss, Kirb gave him up reluctantly. Hetty excused herself and found a dark corner of the bar where she could breastfeed in private. Garret emerged after a while and hustled her into a waiting elevator.

"Did you eat anything?" she asked, but his lips were pressed together tightly. Then the bronze doors slid shut, and he erupted with shouts, jumping around and making the car shake as it descended.

"Twenty thousand dollars!" he trumpeted.

"What? He's going to raise twenty thousand dollars? Whatever for?"

"That's how much it takes."

"So much money! Don't you have to put up some kind of collateral?"

"He made me promise to pay the investors back if the well's a dud. He wants it part of the contract."

Hetty's voice went cold. "Oh . . . I see." A few floors passed in silence. "Couldn't you have asked me first?"

"It's only a precaution. It doesn't mean anything."

"No?" Hetty's breath came hot. "You've put us twenty thousand in debt in the middle of a depression, and it doesn't mean anything?"

"Stay out of this, Hetty. I'll pay back the twenty thou in no time, I promise."

"How?"

"The Lou Della Crim paid for itself in twenty-four hours."

"It did?"

"Of course. Oil's selling for a dollar five a barrel."

"That doesn't sound like much."

"Honey, the Lou Della Crim came in at twenty-two thousand barrels."

"So?"

"Twenty-two thousand barrels a day. You can multiply, can't you?"

She thought about it for a moment. Then felt a sudden sinking in her stomach that wasn't from the elevator falling to a stop. The doors hissed open and the polished pink marble walls of the lobby flashed into her eyes. Garret disappeared into the light.

Hetty ran after him. "That's twenty-two thousand dollars a day!"

He shouted over his shoulder. "That's a million dollars every couple of months. Six million dollars a year."

"You mean we could be making six million dollars a year off one oil well?"

He stopped and turned to her. "Goddamn, Hetty, what do you think I've been talking about all this time?"

She sank onto a bronze bench at the foot of a towering Corinthian column. Looking up at Garret and past him at the portico that soared three stories above them, she had a vertiginous glimpse of power, of the thrust that had raised the Esperson Building above the simple prairie dust. It wasn't the money that made her dizzy, it was that glimpse of a life so far off the ground, close to that high place where her sister now dwelt like a goddess with Lamar. In a small voice, she said, "I guess I never really thought about the numbers."

He glared down at her, his hands gripping the portfolio he'd presented to Cleveland Yoakum. He'd scrubbed himself for this meeting, but still the thumbnails were outlined in black from the crude oil that had soaked into his skin. *Lamar's hands would never be soiled like this,* Hetty thought. Yet his manicured fingers had taught Hetty how to play dirty tricks on her husband. She felt sullied by him, guilty by association. Only her baby had saved her from outright deception and, now, she could see how false her heart had been. To be faithful, after all, meant just that: to have faith, to believe enough in your marriage to stay with it no matter what. She had given up too easily, had given in to temptation, and failed Garret as a wife. But it was not too late. She could still serve her husband obediently and, in being true to his vision, cleanse herself. Ignoring the people passing by, Hetty grabbed one of his hands and began kissing it over and over.

"I'm sorry, Garret. I didn't understand." She held his palm to her cheek, the fingers thickened by labor. "Do you forgive me?"

"For what?"

"For misjudging you. You were the one all along. I just couldn't see it." She began kissing his fingers one by one. She felt like kissing his feet but was drawing enough attention from patrons circling through the revolving doors nearby. "I promise to make up for it. I'll do whatever I can to help you. I'll be like Mellie Esperson scrubbing her husband's overalls by hand."

"I don't think it'll be that bad."

"But I'd do it. I want you to know that. I'll do whatever it takes."

"Just believe in me. That's what I need."

"I do. I believed in you the first time I met you. I just forgot somehow. I lost faith. I'm sorry. You were the one I loved, Garret. You were always the one."

He didn't say anything. He took the baby out of her arms and set him on the bench. Then he lifted her up and gave her the kind of deep kiss with his tongue that they hadn't shared for a long, long time. She snaked her arms around his neck and held on tight.

The crowd at the elevator tried not to watch out of the corner of their eyes.

* * *

The cold snap of Christmas eased into a January thaw wet with winter dew—although *thaw* wasn't a word Texans used readily since there was rarely any actual snow or ice. But it still felt like the world was melting as the Auburn drove under the dripping porte cochere of the Warwick Hotel late Sunday morning. The door came open before the car even rolled to a stop, and a long slim leg slipped into an unbuckled galosh flopped down on the damp concrete. Hetty jumped out, asking the doorman to announce her arrival as she paced back and forth with a slapping sound. She was spent from packing, feet itching to travel, annoyed that Nella had asked them to stop by on their way out of town to accept a little going-away present.

"It'll be a bottle of perfume," Hetty had told Garret that morning, "or something equally useless in the oil patch." At the moment, he sat in the car with Pierce asleep on the seat beside him, tracing roads on a map with his finger.

Hetty heard a chugging sound and turned as the Wichita flatbed truck came swinging around the circular driveway. She loved its bright orange paint, which jiggled against the blue light that spread over Hermann Park behind it with its bare branches and still-green lawns of lush Saint Augustine grass. The truck's windshield was tilted open, and Pick braked to a stop at a distance. At her suggestion, Garret had hired Henry Picktown Waller for eight dollars a day as his derrick man. Pick kept his hat lowered over his face, not planning to budge out of the cab during this meeting with his ex-employer. But next to him, Pearl had already swung the demi-door of the Wichita open and was alighting on the running board. She'd been unusually optimistic since Hetty had insisted that they offer her a ten percent interest in the well. She hailed from Lufkin, so was thrilled to be heading back to "God's country" as she called it.

She dashed over, Lucky Strikes in hand. They lit, sending up a flurry of smoke and nervous chatter. "My, it's wet," Pearl said. "Another morning like this, and you'll have to haul out your Japanese parasols. Two heavy dews mean a rain."

"I hope not," Hetty said. "I don't want our things getting soaked."

Just then both of the great bronze doors of the hotel swung open and a parade of bellhops began marching out, lugging an array of parcels down the grand staircase. Nella followed shortly, freshly made up and aglow in her cape of monkey fur.

"Mother, what is all this? We don't have room for anything more."

"I'm sure you can stuff it in somewhere, dear. You won't need the boxes," she said, signaling for two of the bellhops to unfurl a large kit of canvas and metal poles.

Hetty drew back. "What is it?"

With glee, Nella said, "A tent! Waterproof!"

"We're not going camping."

"No? Where do you think you're sleeping tonight?"

"In a hotel, of course."

She laughed and turned to Kirb, who had followed her out wrapped in his gray tweed overcoat. "They think they're sleeping in a hotel tonight." More laughter. "But wait—here's my greatest find." A little wave of her hand brought a second nest of hemp ropes and flaps unrolling from the arms of two more bellhops.

"Another tent?" Hetty asked.

"This one's for you and Garret and the baby. It's an Auto Tent. You set it up right beside your car—see, this flap gets pulled over the roof and turns your car into a drawing room." She had the bellhops demonstrate. This brought Garret grinning out of the driver's seat. "Good morning, Garret darling. How do you like your new home? One of the things I hate about camping is there's never a comfortable chair to sit in."

"If this is a joke, Mother, I don't find it very funny."

Nella just smiled at her and had more packages unwrapped. Kettles began clanging, and canvas ducking snapped.

"Hey, look at this!" one of the bellhops shouted. The rest of them joined him, kneeling around some kind of lamp.

"Another gem," Nella said. "A carbide spotlight. I've thought of everything. Folding cots, a kerosene stove for cooking."

"Now that we'll use," Pearl said.

Garret was drawn to the group of squatting men who had unfolded the handles of the lamp and were trying to figure out how to work it. He was able to show them right away, after a quick fiddle with cans and fuses. In a twinkling, a fierce bluish light scalded the wet streets.

"Where'd you learn how to do that, honey?" Hetty asked.

"In Butte," he said. "Down in the mines."

He turned the spotlight on her, and a searing light shot out, penetrating her very bones. All of them drew in their breath as he shone it up and irradiated the whole porte cochere. He aimed it at the truck, and Pick was frozen in its beam, horrified.

"The light travels three hundred feet, they told me," Nella said, not recognizing Pick or, if she did, not wanting to acknowledge his presence. Garret dimmed the lamp, and the Negro face faded back into obscurity.

"That one's for fun, but here's something serious." She kicked off the top of a shoe box and hauled out a pair of high hobnail boots. "Friendly Fives! Only five dollars a pair and de rigueur in the oil patch."

"We're wearing galoshes, in case you hadn't noticed, Mamá."

"Trust me, dear, you'll want knee-highs."

"Why?"

"Because whenever a new oil field is opened, it rains."

"Mother, you're embarrassing me."

"It's true, oddly enough." Her father stepped forward, snapping the brim of his Borsalino. "I remember Will Hogg telling me stories about rowing in a boat down the main street of Beaumont after Spindletop came in. It'll rain; you can count on it. I hear it's already started."

"I told you so," Pearl said. "But is that true, really? It always rains when they strike oil?"

Nella nodded sagely. "In biblical proportions."

"Why is that, do you suppose?"

"Madame," Nella said, lifting her eyes above their heads and gazing off into the skies glowering down at them. "When we invade the stillness of the earth, the heavens know."

Chapter 12

As Garret followed the braid of roads to the northeast, Nella's words wove themselves through her daughter's thoughts . . . "the heavens know." Harris County receded behind them, its grasses thinning like hair over bald spots of sandy loam that started to line the side of the road. Pines began to appear, clumps of them tangled together in black silhouettes against the slate of the sky. Hetty's eyes followed them up . . . and there it came. The rain. Cold sheets of it washed down from the clouds onto their windshield, swallowing up the Wichita truck on their tail. Garret would slow down until an orange speck would flare up in the distance, getting closer and closer until it chugged up on their rear. Mists drew into the trees, giving the forests a Nordic look.

Hetty shivered, a thrill of cold and expectation. She was heading north to a whole new life and had no idea what it would be like. In spite of having Kirby Allen for a father, she'd never been in an oil field, just seen one from a distance. She wondered what she and her husband would find. Would this rain really go on for forty days and forty nights? That sounded like another one of Nella's fables, yet everything about oil was, she had to admit, a little magical. The way the Indians revered it for its miraculous healing powers. The way diviners and fortune-tellers told men where to drill. The gushers that thundered up from deep in the earth like volcanic geysers. The sudden riches. The lives that were changed. *How will mine change?* she thought as she looked out the window.

It was slow going with the truck on their rear. Places appeared out of the mist as they climbed up rolling hills in the incessant rain: Pearl's hometown of Lufkin . . . then Nacogdoches . . . Henderson. The pine trees thickened, and night seemed to rise out of them when Garret finally found the left turn that would take them into the town of Kilgore itself. They slid off the pavement onto the muddy track of Main Street, finding it clotted with traffic both coming and going. A necklace of headlamps was strung ahead as far as Hetty could see. They eased along, following the curve into downtown, rolling up the windows to shut out the acrid smell that floated in the air. The rain let up a little as it grew darker.

Soon, there were so many cars parked along the street and so many people walking about, it was almost impossible to move. A sign floated by, Brown's Drugs, and they caught a whiff of hamburgers sizzling inside. Garret and Pick pulled over wherever they could—the whole town seemed to be one big parking lot.

Nothing had prepared Hetty for what she found when she stepped out of the Auburn onto Kilgore Street. First, she sank an inch or two in mud. Then the noise hit her: engines sputtering, horns honking, wild laughter, men shouting across the street, a constant roaring in the distance as of giant forces being released. She quickly shut the door so it wouldn't wake up Pierce. Crowds milled about as if they were waiting for a parade to start or for the next gusher to rain black drops over them like confetti. Everyone seemed to be talking, no one listening. Roughnecks waded along the streets in their rubber boots, clothes blotched with grease. There was the smell of rotten eggs in the air, mingled with cigar smoke from the knots of businessmen standing around on the sidewalk bargaining under lowered hat brims.

Garret came around the car as Pearl wiggled out of the crowd. "Y'all ever seen anything like it?" she shouted.

"So this is what a boom town looks like!" Hetty said.

"This is it." Garret grabbed her arm. "I think we've hit pay dirt, honey. Look at the air. Aren't those silver dollars falling from the sky?" Hetty glanced up and saw what he meant: There was something incandescent about the night, the raindrops sparkling in the car lights, the flares burning like giant candles all around.

They pushed their way up to the sidewalk, out of the muddy street. "It's standing room only," Pearl said. "We'd better get to the hotel if we hope to find a room tonight."

"I'm not sleeping till I strike oil," Garret said.

"But I hope we're still eating. I'm starved," Hetty said. She went to get Pierce, and they edged their way into Brown's Drugs. There was mud tracked an inch thick on the floor and bodies waiting three deep at the soda fountain. They waited in line beside a gaunt man with a frizz of red hair on his head. He kept eyeing Garret and finally leaned over and shot into his ear, "Got any leases to sell?"

Garret shook his head.

"I'm buying all I can today from anybody. It's at four hundred dollars an acre and going up every hour." His swollen eyes kept jumping around the room, checking who was coming and going. "And to think, a few months ago they couldn't give this worthless land away." He spoke with a nasal twang Hetty couldn't place.

"You don't sound like you're from these parts," Hetty said.

"Jersey, baby."

"You came all the way from up there?"

"Damn right. This is the only place in the country there's any action. Name's Kozak," he said. "You folks new in town?"

Garret shook his hand. "MacBride. Just drove in."

"You may be too late." He stepped up to the marble counter and asked for a ham sandwich and a slice of pecan pie.

"I'm not worried," Garret told him. "I've got a one-acre share."

"I hope it's downtown."

"Even better. Out on Daisy Bradford's farm."

"Ha! Next you'll be telling me it's on Joiner's lease."

"As a matter of fact, it is. We're members of his syndicate."

"Yeah, yeah, baby, you and everybody else."

"Next!" the soda jerk shouted. Hetty leaned on the marble counter and ordered six hamburgers and four chocolate shakes. There was a dim reflection of the crowded room in the mirror behind the stacks of gleaming soda glasses.

"I just need to find Dad himself. You don't know where he is, by any chance?"

"Nobody does. Disappeared."

"You mean my certificate's no good?" Pearl asked.

" 'Fraid not, sweetheart."

"Don't worry, Pearlie. Cleve already told us it was worthless. Said we should talk to farmers."

"Shhhh!" Garret hissed, frowning.

"Cleve?" Mr. Kozak's weary eyes lit up. "Cleve Yoakum?"

Hetty gave him a proud nod. "He's our backer."

"Then you got nothing to worry about, baby. That's what he said? Talk to farmers?" He scratched his sandy hair. "Of course! They had a drought here, lasted for years. Why didn't I think of that? Talk to farmers. It's so simple. But I guess that's why Cleve is the Cliff." The man grabbed his sandwich and tucked it tightly under his arm like he was afraid somebody was going to steal it. "Thanks for the tip, baby. And let me give you one. You're wasting time on that Joiner business. Don't believe me, check it out yourself at the title company. It's just down the street." He elbowed his way through the crowd.

"Are they open?"

He shouted back over his shoulder. "You kidding? They never close!"

When their order was ready, they added trimmings to their hamburgers and sacked everything up. Pearl took food to Pick, who was reluctant to get out of the truck. Garret wouldn't eat until he'd settled the claim on the land. He set off in the crowd with his portfolio of papers as the rain swelled, sending Hetty and Pearl to squeeze into the bench seat of the Auburn. They pulled their hamburgers out of the crinkling wax paper, smelling of onions and pickles. Pierce woke up, and Hetty put him to her breast while she nibbled, covering herself with the *rebozo* Aunt Cora had given her. Thunder cascaded over the town.

When they finished eating, they lit up Lucky Strikes and wiped off the windows so they could watch the parade of people going by. Their favorite sight was the odd woman strolling by in gaudy beach pajamas, twirling raindrops off a parasol.

It seemed to take Garret forever to return, diving into the driver's seat soaked and shivering, saying that the title company had verified that Joiner's shares were useless—all the leases long ago spoken for. He had sold more land than was available. Everybody was filing claims against him. It could be months or even years before affairs were settled.

"Wait'll I write Odell about this," Pearl said.

"You heard what Kozak said, land's going up every hour. Where am I going to find a lease?"

"Talk to farmers—but not tonight. First we need a hotel room." She rolled down the window and asked a passerby where the hotel was. He pointed ahead of them. Garret swerved out, waving for Pick to follow. The traffic didn't look too bad in that direction.

They soon found out why. A block or two down the street, the drenching rain had softened the mud even more and the Auburn seemed to float for a moment and then sank to a stop. Garret could only get the tires to spin a little, adding the smell of burning rubber to rotten eggs. He scrambled out and shouted, "Goddamn it!" as he went down. Hetty stepped out the other side and saw the muck rising over the running board. She could feel something thick and icy spilling into her galoshes, oozing between her toes. She looked back at the truck, but it had stopped short of the mire.

Pearl peeked out and said, "I guess we'll need those knee-highs your mother sent after all."

"Oh, shut up!" Hetty whispered under her breath.

Hetty isn't standing on mud any longer. She is barefoot on smooth cool sand where the morning sun glimmers through pine shadows. She hears a ripple of water nearby, sees it sparkling out of the corner of one eye. Out of the other, she sees a hill rising into the light. She looks up. Two pine trees bend together overhead as if to mark the spot. Their brown needles lie scattered at her feet like the pickup sticks she and Char played with as girls.

She grabs a handful and throws a pattern. They turn colors, all pointing in the same direction . . . toward an Indian woman sitting on a throne at the foot of the hill. Her black garments are polished and hung with many fringes upon which white beads glisten. She surveys

Hetty with the arrogance of a tribal queen, triangles tattooed at the corner of each eye, a black line from brow to chin dividing her face exactly in half. Without knowing why, Hetty approaches the throne and kneels. "Drink this," the mysterious woman murmurs, "it will make you well."

She lowers a clay vessel filled with the blue-black water the Indians traveled far distances to find. It is so dark Hetty can see her own face reflected in it and, above her head, the visage of the Indian queen crowned by the moon and stars. But isn't it morning? She drinks, tasting its bitter medicine. The earth rumbles, and a baby starts to cry. The woman descends from the throne and stands holding Pierce in one arm, the vessel in the other. Hetty knows she is to choose. She reaches for her baby and, when the Indian turns her back and walks into the forest, Hetty sees that her train is made of many turkey feathers. They smell gamy like Garret. He hasn't bathed for three days now. She puts Pierce to her breast. Her milk comes in and draws her eyes open. She wakes.

Garret bent over, pulling on his shirt. It was dark inside the Auto Tent, where they'd been sleeping, but a cold light leaked through the windows of the car. Garret tried to stand but bumped his head on the canvas ceiling. Pine needles crunched under his feet, the only thing between them and the mire they'd been forced to camp on. She couldn't hear rain at the moment, but everything was damp. Their clothes were piled on suitcases, boots and shoes on the floor of the Auburn. Cots and the cradle took up most of the room. Garret yawned and crawled out through the car seat. Hetty tried to get comfortable while she nursed, but found herself all cramped up with the memories of the last two days.

After getting stuck in the mud the other night, they'd pulled on Nella's knee-highs. Hetty had been glad to have them, but hated her mother for being right. When they'd waded down to the Kilgore Hotel, she'd known it was hopeless the minute she walked in. The lobby had been full of cots! With people lying in them! They had laughed, of course, when she'd asked for a room. The same stinging laughter she'd heard from her parents that made her feel so small and naive. The clerk had sent them over to the Cot Houses on Commerce Street, horrid places with no heat or light where you could rent a bed for an eight-hour shift for fifty cents. It was hardly a place for a family, the beds occupied by itinerant workers who moved from one oil field to the next.

They would have driven to another town, but the rains simply made the roads impassable. Eventually, someone told them they could camp down in the Hollow, which sounded romantic until they got there. A dark, stinking place where all kinds of riffraff had taken up residence under a forest of loblolly pines. The headlights of the truck revealed dwellings made of cardboard boxes, houses hammered together from tin cans and scrap lumber, people huddled under old blankets over steaming fires. At first, Hetty had refused to enter the Hollow, but it started raining even harder and everyone was exhausted and their car was bogged down in a sinkhole back in town and she simply had no choice. Pick steered the truck carefully through the ramshackle "town" until they found an empty spot on the outer fringe that they could claim as their own.

That first night had been horrible, trying to raise the tents in the heavy rain, everything soaking, the baby screaming. More than once Hetty was ready to call it quits and go home, but her husband's grit got her through. Garret stood in the rain, soaking wet, and told her, "I'll never give up, never."

It had taken a team of four mules to pull their car out the next morning, its lower half encrusted with mud like a plague of barnacles. Still, they'd pitched Nella's amazing Auto Tent over it and had been a bit dryer and more comfortable last night.

A shopping trip yesterday with Pearl made Hetty realize how difficult life in Kilgore was going to be. Garret had dropped them downtown, which had looked so vibrant their first night, but now revealed itself to be a sodden, depressing mess, little more than a string of low brick buildings facing the railroad tracks. There were long waits to buy groceries, mail a letter, or get a telephone line for long distance. Hundreds of umbrellas bumped along the few sidewalks, and derricks were being hammered together in every block. Just crossing the street was a major operation. A glass of water cost as much as a Coke and still tasted funny. Warm showers could be had for fifty cents but only in the back of Tulsa's, a barbershop near the train station with a distinctly masculine clientele.

"I've had it!" Hetty lost all patience when her shopping bag split open as they stood in the rain outside Brown's Drugs waiting for Garret. "We have to pay to go to the bathroom and because we're women we can't even take a goddamn shower."

"Now don't go borrowing trouble," Pearl said, stooping to rescue the groceries. "We just need to get us some big tin washtubs. That's all we had to wash ourselves in when I was a girl."

"Great! I can hardly wait." Hetty sighed, glad that she'd followed her hunch about bringing her friend along. The rain seemed to reach right down to Pearl Weems's East Texas roots and bring them cracking back to life. She was putting out feelers, taking charge. Under a tarp Pick had slung between two pines, she'd already set up kitchen—firing up the kerosene stove and unpacking Nella's cook kit. At the Great Atlantic & Pacific Tea Company over on Main Street, she'd shown Hetty all the best brands to buy: Marrett's Potted Meats, hominy grits by Red and White, lard from the Wickham Packing Company. "There's lard and then there's *lard,*" she'd said, picking out a meaty ham bone to throw into a pot of black-eyed peas for supper last night.

Now she was out there fixing breakfast. Hetty could smell the pungent fumes of bacon and coffee. She finished feeding and changing Pierce, then rocked him back to sleep in his cradle. She sat there letting the chill creep over her, losing heart, wondering how she was going to endure another cold, wet day of camping. And another haunted sleep. The divining rod of her dreams had dipped last night, and she could still feel it quivering inside her. The gleam had gone, and she had no idea what it meant. She never did. Forcing her stiff body up, she pulled on a sweater and worked her feet into the knee-highs. She slid across the car seat and stood up outside, stretching.

Garret heaved a satchel between them on the seat of the Wichita and throttled the engine into motion. He'd heard that farmers out along Caney Creek were selling leases cheap. They got up to Commerce Street without bogging down and stopped at Tulsa's on the way out of town.

"Want a shower, kiddo?" he said, kicking the door open.

"Don't tempt me." Hetty looked at him askance.

There was a lot of activity both inside and outside the popular barbershop. Pipes were being unloaded off freight cars, while a team of twenty mules hauled huge boilers down the street on a wooden wagon. Model Ts followed in its wake, sporting license plates from Arkansas, Alabama, Kansas, and New Mexico. Through the gleaming windows under the spinning candy cane, Hetty watched the men of the oil fraternity getting their brogans shined while they traded leases and waited for an empty barber chair.

After an hour, Garret emerged transfigured: clean-shaven, hair slicked back, tie freshly knotted. He had to leap from the sidewalk to the running board of the truck to keep his pin-striped pants from getting spotted. The minute he entered the car, she practically threw the baby at him. "Here! I hope he spits up on you." She had to walk two blocks and pay a dime just to use a toilet.

When she returned, Garret backed slowly into traffic and followed it across the railroad tracks. Keeping the truck in the lower gears, he dodged potholes and mud traps as best he could. Hetty was still tossed about quite a bit. She held Pierce close. Town buildings gave way to farmhouses fanned out all across the open hills. Garret drove through several cotton farms, but decided none of them would do because there was no ready source of water.

"You got to have water," he said, "for the slush pit. That much I know."

Then, about the time Hetty felt hope slipping away from her, Garret found a little crow's foot of a road that paralleled Caney Creek. He passed a mailbox with the name Hillyer spelled out in black paint that had dripped down. He backed up and turned into the drive. The farmhouse was on a hill, a wing of smoke lifting out of its chimney. Down below, a flock of weeping willows bare as bird claws grew on either side of the water. Garret followed their line until he reached the creek, glistening over a sandy bottom. Hetty gazed at the brown pine needles scattered on its bank and had a moment of déjà vu. A trace of sunlight emerged. She looked across. The stream here flowed around an embankment that rose on the opposite side. Hetty's eyes followed it up. And there they were. The two pines bent together. "Drill over there," she said, pointing.

Garret cranked the Wichita into its lowest gear and climbed the hill to the farmhouse. They followed along the barbed wire fence that held back a few grazing cows and parked in the spidery shade of an old gum tree that rose above the chimney. Smoke hung like moss in its bare branches. Down the dog run that split the house in half, Hetty saw two children in overalls dodge into the backyard.

Garret took the satchel up to the front door and knocked politely. A chicken clucked by when the farmwife peered out, face as weathered-down gray as the old clapboard house, frowning at Garret while he talked. Hetty watched as she retreated into the parlor. More chickens strutted forward, but not too close. They scattered when the farmer came around the corner, wiping his fingers. He smiled as he shook hands with Garret, his rusty face corroded from years of hot Texas sun.

"Hollis, Oleta, y'all come in here." The farmwife leaned out and shouted down the dog run. "Them's oil people." The children came running, and she gathered them under her arms and ushered them inside.

If Hetty listened carefully, she could hear snippets of what Garret was saying to the farmer:

"Lease ten—"

"Hundred dollars per acre—"

"A bonus of two—"

He didn't get much response from the man, until he opened the bag and showed him the stacks of bills. The farmer staggered back as if there were a rattlesnake in there, instead of more cash than he'd probably ever seen in his life.

Garret's hands moved as he talked, and the farmer shrugged and looked away, or just smiled and nodded. His wife materialized behind the screen door occasionally to shout comments: "You ain't forgetting what your cousin told you, are you, Roy? Jessie let them drill a well on his land and the salt water ruined his vegetable garden."

"Not on your farmland—" Hetty heard as Garret pointed down toward the creek, and the farmer craned his neck to look that way. Then he eyed the satchel and circled it warily.

The wife appeared at the door again.

"Don't forget what they bring with them. Those painted women in beach pajamas. That's probably one of them sitting in the truck."

Garret had told Hetty to stay in the Wichita and let him handle the negotiations with Mr. Hillyer. But she couldn't hang back any longer. She wanted more than anything to see a derrick rising beside those two bent pines from her dream, pumping down through the sandy soil by the creek. It was the place to strike oil; she knew it even if nobody else did. Now she just had to convince the owners of the land that she was right. For once she was glad she hadn't worn any makeup and wouldn't be considered one of the "painted ladies." She probably looked downright bedraggled next to Garret, but maybe that would win her some points from the Mrs., who was, like Pearl would say, plain as a mud fence. She cracked the door open, cradled Pierce in her arms, and stepped down.

Garret eyed her warily. "This is my wife and our new son, Pierce."

Hetty smiled at the woman behind the rusty screen. "No beach pajamas."

"Sorry, ma'am," the woman said. "I'm Ada Hillyer." She stepped outside, a faded apron hung over her gingham wash dress.

"We're the MacBrides," Hetty said.

Ada shook their hands. "Don't mean to be unfriendly. We're God-fearing people, Mrs. MacBride."

"I know. That's why we're here. My husband's looking for a quiet place to do some exploration away from that mess. We're just a family, Ada, like yours."

"What makes you want to drill way out here?" Mr. Hillyer asked.

Garret stammered to come up with a reason, not wanting to say, "Because your land is cheap."

Hetty hesitated, listening to Garret ramble on. She never told anyone about her dreams, not even her husband, for fear that they would stop. She felt the bud of a blush about to open on her cheeks. What would these simple country people think if she told them what she'd glimpsed before waking this morning? But they were churchgoers; they read about such things in the Bible. Maybe they *would* understand, even more than her own husband. She could tell that his arguments weren't convincing anybody. Mr. Hillyer was shaking his head. Ada was squinting sideways, all wrinkled in doubt, hands plunged in apron pockets. Hetty decided to speak up. "Excuse me, Garret. I want to tell the Hillyers about the dream I had this morning. I saw two bent pines growing next to a creek. Then an Indian woman appeared."

"Honey, I don't think these folks—"

"An Indian woman?" Ada interrupted. Her eyes flashed as she turned to Hetty. "What did she look like?"

Hetty described her shiny, fringed dress and the clay vessel with the blue-black water. "She said it would heal me if I drank it."

"And it would." Ada spoke with conviction. "Were there any markings on her face?"

"Yes, a line right down the middle. And a triangle at each eye."

"Judas Priest! That was a Caddo Indian you saw." She blinked at Hetty in amazement. "You hear that, Roy? This lady had a dream about a Caddo Indian woman."

"Well, I'll be . . ."

"Does that mean anything?"

"Mean anything? Lady, East Texas is Caddo country. When the Spanish granted this land to my great-grandfather, there were still Caddo on it. They came to the creek for the sour dirt, used it for rheumatism. That woman you dreamed about—was she wearing a cloak?"

"Yes—I'd forgotten about that. When she walked away, I could see it."

Ada eyed her intently. "And what was it made of?"

Hetty strained to remember. She knew she was being tested. She saw the figure walking away from her . . . into the woods. She saw the pine shadows shimmering over the cloak . . . saw it mottled . . .

"Turkey," she said. "I think it was turkey feathers."

Ada's hands fluttered out of her apron pockets and landed on her face. "My God, it's her. Dead out."

"What are you saying, woman?"

"Roy, it's a sign."

"But, Ada, the farm. You were always so hidebound . . ."

"I know I was. But there's something I never told you. That hill over there, other side of them two pines. That was one of their mounds."

"Mounds?"

"Yes, Roy. Where they had their ceremonies. Don't you see? It's a sign from above. Like in the Bible. This is consecrated ground. God is speaking to us through the Indians." Her hands worked themselves around her neck as she breathed the surprise in and out. "Lord, Lord, what a day." She raised her shoulders and looked to the sky. Hetty could see she was turning the matter over in her mind. "Well . . ." she said after a few moments. "Folks say Daisy Bradford had a dream telling Dad Joiner where to drill. I could be like her." She cocked her head at Garret. "If we do let you drill a well, mister, would you name it the Ada Hillyer Number One?"

"What else?" Garret said. "But why stop there? We could have the Ada Hillyer Two and Three and Four. Tell you what, ma'am, as well as paying to lease your land, I'm prepared to give you folks a one-eighth interest in every well I drill."

The farmer hitched up his pants. "A one-eighth interest now?" He squinted, trying to wrap his mind around the fraction.

"It's generous," Hetty said. "You'll be rich as Croesus."

But Ada wasn't listening. Hetty could see she had no idea how much money they were talking about. She was gazing past them, watching her own local dreams write themselves across the sky. "I could be in the papers like the others," she said, almost breathless. "Like Daisy. Like Lou Della Crim. My grandchildren would read about me in history books. The Ada Hillyer Number One. I like the sound of it."

Roy hunkered down and peered into the leather satchel. He cleared his throat. "It is an awful lot of money."

Ada pursed her lips and put her hands on her hips. "Well . . . I could use a new cookstove."

* * *

Once Garret had drawn up the abstracts and secured the lease at the title company, the Hillyers couldn't have been more helpful. They invited the whole party to move out of the Hollow and pitch tents on the farm within walking distance of the outhouse. Ada gave Hetty fresh-churned butter and showed her how to dry clothes East Texas style, on the barbed wire fence so she didn't need clothespins. Near the future well site, they let Garret and Pick throw up two shotgun houses, which you could buy in a kit for seventy-five dollars—long, stringy things with no hallways, just one small room opening into another.

"I reckon I can share a house and a bathroom with a black man," Pearl said. "Seeing as how it's Pick."

As soon as the simple frame houses were finished and woodstoves installed, the men unpacked the Wichita while the women tried to dry the furniture out and get some kind of kitchen set up. They bought new beds for everybody at the Horn Brothers' Furniture Store on Main Street. Hetty didn't even mind the sound of the rain drumming all night on the tin roof as she slept in a real bed with clean sheets for the first time in two weeks.

Garret could hardly rest until he'd put together the two crews he'd need to run a double shift. He drove into Tulsa's and came back with a report of the men he'd hired: two brothers named Elwyn and Jim who knew how to run the motors, backed up with four floor hands who'd just arrived by rail from the Oklahoma oil fields looking for work. That meant he could finally sit down at the dining table and savor the moment he'd anticipated for years—ordering plans for a derrick out of the National Supply Company catalog.

The next day, Mr. Hillyer hitched up his mule team and followed the Wichita into town to help haul back all the supplies they would need: fresh pine planks from a local sawmill, thousands of feet of pipe, drill bits that looked like fishes' tails. Hetty, Pearl, Ada, Oleta, and Hollis lined up in front of the barn that afternoon, all agog as the farmer's wagon rolled by hoisting the traveling block that would nudge the bit through tons of solid rock. It was huge, like a hippopotamus or beached whale. "Weighs as much as a freight car," Garret boasted from his seat on the bench. Hanging from it was a giant iron hook.

"Looks like something God might lower from the sky," Ada said in awe, "to raise the righteous."

Hetty could see how happy Garret was orchestrating all this frenzied activity. He was no longer just a weevil working the decks; he was now the foreman, ordering the other men around, standing back as they hammered the derrick together, making it rise a hundred feet or more over the tops of the pines, like the skeleton of a great obelisk.

Garret didn't want to admit that he'd chosen the spot to drill based on Hetty's dream. He put it down to creekology, the tradition that a prime spot for finding oil was laid between a creek and an acclivity, one of the geological terms he'd picked up in his reading, a fancy name for a hill. He told her that the first oil well dug in America, the Drake Well in Pennsylvania, had been discovered that way and it was still good enough for him. He spurned the use of diviners and the even more scientific doodlebugs, special instruments guaranteed by their operators to pinpoint reservoirs under the earth. No, Garret depended on the time-proven folk wisdom of wildcatters, who studied the coils of rivers and creeks. Just as serpents had always guarded great hordes of treasure, so the snakings of a creek bed around a bend or hill, if you knew what to look for, could reveal the secret geology at work deep in the earth. Still, Hetty suspected that her dream and Ada's reaction to it might have exercised some gravitational pull as Garret had scoured the bank with a pine branch and drawn an *X* in the sand at a point between the water and the hill that might have been a Caddo mound.

Once the drilling started, it was relentless. Sixteen hours a day with hardly a break for food and coffee. Darkness fell early, smudging the line between January and February. Garret's second shift had to work mostly by electric lights strung up on the derrick. Hetty saw them shimmering in the creek as she walked through the black pines, bearing supper on a metal camp tray. She could hardly coax Garret to stop and eat, or get enough sleep. She would wake up at midnight, alone in bed.

The longest days came when they had to "make a trip," as the workers called it, pulling each length of pipe out of the hole and unscrewing it in order to change the drill bit that had grown dull from days of cutting through limestone and chalk. During these pauses, it was quiet enough to hear the spirituals intoned in a deep baritone by Pick from his perch in the sky. Hetty would stand in the cold twilight and listen to him sing of hammers ringing and the Rock of Ages. She got to know his favorite by heart:

While Jesus was hanging upon the cross,
The angels kept quiet till God went off.
The angels hung their harps on the willow trees,
To give satisfaction till God was pleased.

One night during a trip, Garret left his supper steaming on the tray she had set on the edge of the platform.

"Eat it while it's hot," she called up to him.

"Can't. Got to get kelly out of the rathole first."

Hetty frowned. So that was why he stayed at the well so late. They had a woman in the doghouse. "And just who is Kelly?"

"The kelly," he shouted at her, as they lifted a long stem of pipe out of its sleeve at the corner of the derrick. "That's what spins the bit."

"It's named after a woman?"

Elwyn guffawed. "She's like a woman, too. Eight-sided." As they lifted it into the air, Hetty could see that it was indeed hexagonal in shape.

"So that's what keeps everything turning?" Hetty asked.

"Yes, ma'am," Elwyn said, grunting as they joined the kelly to the drill stem. "Fits down yonder into your kelly bushings."

Kelly Bushings, Hetty thought. *If I ever change my name, that's what it will be. Kelly Bushings.*

On a murky afternoon in February, as more rain lurked at the edge of the sky, Hetty clutched the newspaper she'd bought and ran down the slope from the shotgun houses. She crossed the crude bridge they'd built over the creek. "Look at this," she shouted above the roar of the steam engines. The men only glanced at her, their breaths streaming around them like gossamer scarves.

"Later, honey," Garret said, as he helped Pick, ninety feet up, guide a string of pipe into its stand.

"I think you want to read this now," she shouted again, unfolding that morning's edition of the *Kilgore News Herald*. She and Pearl had just returned from an expedition into town with the Hillyers, and she'd snatched up the paper with the article everyone was buzzing about. Garret raised his eyebrows at her and wiped his nose on the dusty sleeve of his coat. He signaled the motorman to bring the steam engines hissing to a stop.

Silence settled like early frost over the crew, as all four of them gathered around to read the headlines she held up: NEW GUSHER IN LONGVIEW! Lathrop I Blew in Last Night at 18,000 Barrels.

Garret shrugged. "I'd rather read about the Ada Hillyer blowing in at eighteen thousand barrels."

"You didn't read far enough. They hit the Woodbine Sand clear up in Longview. . . ."

"They did?"

"Don't you see what this means?"

"No, ma'am," Elwyn the motorman said, the two roughnecks behind him shaking their heads in tandem.

"It's one big field!"

They looked at one another, frowning and cursing.

"Don't you see? The Daisy Bradford lies miles south of here. And now the Lathrop I many miles north. All tapping into the same formation—the Woodbine Sand." She turned the paper toward her and read:

> "The discovery of the Lathrop I has led geologists to realize the scale of the field discovered last October by Columbus Marion Joiner. The prediction by geologist A. D. Lloyd that an 'ocean of oil' lay under East Texas appears to be true after all. They estimate the

> length of the reservoir to be over forty miles long and up to twelve miles wide, making it almost certainly the largest oil field ever discovered in North America."

Garret just stared at her. They all stared at her. "Read that last part again."

"You heard me right . . . the largest oil field ever discovered in North America." Hetty found herself laughing hysterically. Garret scooped her up and spun her around, howling in her ear while the men bellowed all around him. As she whirled, she caught a glimpse of Pick's dark head leaning over the board high above, watching them.

"If you think it was bad in town before"—she gasped as he set her down—"you should have seen it today. Pandemonium. You know what the word on the street is, Mac?"

"Tell me, baby."

"They're saying it's impossible to drill a dry hole anywhere around Kilgore. That means the Ada Hillyer's got to be a gusher!"

The men all started a wild dance on the derrick floor, swinging off the mud hose, hugging each other, slapping hands. Pick shouted down, "What's happening, y'all? Tell me what's happening."

"Get down here, Pick boy," Garret yelped. "We're going to celebrate." He disappeared into the doghouse, where the supplies were stashed. Hetty could hear him in there yapping and rattling around until he emerged hoisting a fruit jar in each hand. "Here you go, boys. Let's all get drunk." He pitched one to Elwyn.

"Yes, let's!" Hetty screamed in delight. In her mind, she saw hundreds of derricks sailing like the masts of ships over a vast and ancient black sea of petroleum. "Just think of it, honey. There's going to be wells all the way from here to Longview."

"And a bunch of them are going to be mine!" Garret said, taking the first swig and passing the jar to Hetty. She nearly gagged on the raw corn whiskey.

March spun up from the south, soughing in the pines. Garret called her to the well one warm, windy day and showed her a core sample he'd pulled from deep within the earth.

"It looks like brown sugar," she said.

"That's oil-saturated sand. We've hit the Woodbine."

He refused to come to bed that night. Even after the crew went home exhausted, he and Pick kept on drilling with the help of Mr. Hillyer, who was anxious to bring the well in. Hetty stretched out on the chaise lounge and tried to sleep, but the rush of wind in thousands of pine branches kept her mind astir. She finally got up and stepped outside for a cigarette. On the hill, through tossing foliage, she saw a light burning in the kitchen of the farmhouse. She gathered Pierce up and headed for it like a beacon, pushing up the road against the wind. When she came to the door, she saw Ada sitting at the kitchen table, sewing under an old copper lamp. She knocked.

"You can't sleep neither?" the farmwife said, as she got up and opened the door to invite her inside.

Hetty shook her head no, yawning as she passed. "My baby's the only one who's going to sleep through this."

Ada took Pierce and rocked him in her arms, humming something that might have been a lullaby or hymn. Hetty reached for a high-backed chair and sat down at the old wooden table. The kitchen was the largest room in the house—and the most popular. A long wall of whitewashed, built-in cabinets divided itself by a double porcelain sink. The doors of a primitive American pie safe had been left cracked, and Hetty could see rows of Mason jars inside with their lids clamped down. Ada nestled Pierce in a rocking chair over in the corner.

"Let me make some coffee," she said, reaching for a burlap sack full of beans. She poured some into an old iron grinder bolted to the drain board and turned the handle. A rich brown fragrance followed the fresh coffee into the room and was met by the crackle of fire in the woodstove. She put the kettle on to boil.

"We wives might as well hold our own wake as sleep alone in bed," she said, bringing out her best china cups. They settled in for the night, talking and nibbling on biscuits and jelly with their coffee.

Hetty looked through the dusty windows at one point and saw

the sky turning blue. The wind had settled down, and dawn started to creep with its startling light over the hills.

"That day I told you about my dream . . ." Hetty spoke after a long silence. "You said it was *her*. Who were you talking about?"

"Well . . . I've never told Roy about this. Men, they don't understand, but the Caddo, they had some powerful women among them. The right woman, they let her rise to the top. I expect that was Santa Adiva that appeared to you."

"Santa . . . ?"

"Adiva. The Great Lady. My mother used to tell me stories about her, which she heard from her mother. Folks say she had a large house . . . with many rooms. The whole Caddo Nation brought gifts to lay at her feet. She was married to five Indian men."

"All at once?"

Ada threw her a mischievous glance. "Um-hmm."

"Now that's my idea of being queen."

"It's the turkey feathers, that's how I knew. Only the highest of the Caddo were allowed to wear the cloak." She went on telling some of the tales about the Great Lady and her powers. *We have no goddesses in America,* Hetty thought as she grew sleepy. *That's our problem.*

Then something flashed in the corner of her eye. She looked over. Mr. Hillyer was drenched in sun, peeping in. "Miss Hetty," he called, cracking the door. "Your husband wants you down at the site. Right away. He says to bring one of your scarves."

Hetty's chair fell to the floor as she stood up. "Oh, my God. Is he hurt?"

"No, ma'am. He says y'all don't want to miss this."

"Don't worry about the baby," Ada said. "I'll bring him along presently."

Hetty skipped out the door, sprinting through the morning hills lacquered with light. She took a detour home and grabbed the first thing she could find draped over an easy chair—the wedding shawl. She pounded on the door of the other shotgun house on her way to the creek.

When she arrived at the derrick, the crew was standing over the well core, waiting for her. Garret signaled for her to step up. "Don't anybody dare light a cigarette," he said. Hetty could hear a hissing sound.

"Now hold your scarf over here." As she did so, the shawl floated up like a parachute. Pearl joined the group shortly, followed by Roy and Ada, holding Pierce up so he could see his mother.

They stood there in a circle, nobody speaking, watching the shawl drift about in the currents of gas, its fringes swaying, knowing that behind this gentle wafting a giant eruption was about to follow, a shiver that would travel up the earth's spine and burst out with such fury it would send the cap splintering through the crown block and hurtling hundreds of feet into the clear blue sky.

"It won't be long now," Garret said.

Chapter 13

Hetty and Pearl spread out a blanket on the bank opposite the well so they could watch the show. Ada came and went all morning, thinking of more people to ring up on her party line. The day opened into a warm, sunny noon.

After lunch, a caravan of dusty Ford trucks came creaking in—one dented bumper after another—and parked in the meadow beyond the willows. So many God-fearing folks assembled along the shores of Caney Creek, Pearl said it looked like a baptism was about to take place—the men lean and crooked in overalls, the women nodding about in starched-brim sunbonnets.

Hetty bought lemonade from Hollis and Oleta, who'd set up a makeshift stand. As she passed with the cold glasses in her hands, the crowd parted to let the Baptist preacher through, his fearless wide-open eyes blinking with zeal.

The crew spent the afternoon crawling over the well like worker ants, clamping down valves, checking the pipes that ran to the large holding tank Garret had just purchased with an advance from the interest owners.

After dinner-on-the-ground, the crowd grew restive in the fading light. Ada brought the neighboring farmers, the Gosses, over to meet Hetty and Pearl. They owned the farm just south of the

Hillyer spread. Clay Goss seemed dubious about drilling on his land, but his wife, a rosy-cheeked woman named Wavie, glanced at Ada's well with undisguised greed.

"Why not, Clay?" she kept saying over her husband's objections.

Finally, the motorman, Elwyn, flicked on Nella's carbide lantern and spotlighted Garret on the derrick. All heads turned together in that direction.

"Let 'er blow, son!" Wavie Goss shouted. "It's getting dark." She was followed by a blast of encouragement.

"Hold on, folks." Garret raised his arms to quiet them. "I want to thank everyone for coming out today to this historic moment. But I'm here to tell you—after consulting with Cleveland Yoakum, my promoter—I've decided not to let the well blow in."

A wave of grumbling swept through the air, and Ada's frowning face emerged from the edge of the crowd. Garret spoke directly to her, explaining how much money they'd saved by not letting the well spew its wealth onto her farm. She lifted her shoulders in a shrug, while a swarm of relatives congratulated her.

"What's the readin'?" Wavie Goss yelled.

Elwyn handed the log to Garret. Everyone grew silent with anticipation. Hetty stood. "The Ada Hillyer Number One is a good steady producer with an average flow of"—Garret checked the numbers in the logbook again, then glanced back at the crowd—"four hundred barrels a day." There were confused murmurs. A sigh of disappointment rose in the dusk.

Pearl grappled onto Hetty's arm. She heard a worried voice in her ear. "How much was that well up yonder in Longview?"

"Eighteen thousand barrels."

"A day?"

Hetty turned to Pearl, nodding.

"And we've got four hundred?"

Hetty took her hands. "I'm sorry, Pearl. The oil game's always a gamble."

"Oh, don't worry for me, hon. My share seems like a small fortune—twelve hundred a month! In hard times, too. But what about Garret?"

Hetty sighed and let go of Pearl's hands. She pushed through the crowd, pulled herself up onto the derrick floor, and approached her husband, who wore black streaks on his face like war paint. She wanted to kiss him, long and deep, but he shrugged her off and jumped down into the shadows of the doghouse.

She followed him. "I'm sorry, honey."

His face tilted into the intense light from the lantern for a moment, showing what he'd hidden from the crowd. He looked close to tears. "I've been running the numbers through my head ever since we read the gauges," he said. "Ten percent to Pearl, twelve point five to the Hillyers. I'll be lucky to have eight thousand a month to pay in royalties."

"It could be worse—we could have a dry hole on our hands."

"I don't know which is worse—a dry hole, or a well that doesn't give you enough of what you need."

She could hear him spitting again. Flecks of tobacco hit her face. She could imagine him twisting the cigarette in his hands. "Look, honey, I know you're disappointed, but we'll just do the best we can. Let's vow to put every cent toward paying back the consortium—we'll go on living right where we are." She slipped into his arms and was enveloped in the earthy aroma of oil-soaked skin. She held him while she told one of the stories Chief used to recite when Nella would have the Rusks over for dinner. "I remember him bragging about living in a shack on the field in the early years. He had to pawn his best gold watch just to pay his crew's wages. We're not that bad off, see? We've got the Cliff behind us."

"More like in front of us," Garret said, dodging into the doghouse to avoid the onlookers, who were becoming unruly.

Hetty had an idea. She hoisted herself up onto the derrick and stood in the bright light of the carbide lantern. "Four hundred barrels a day," she shouted to quiet people. "Now I know that doesn't sound like much compared to some of the other gushers we've had around here. But, Ada—where are you?" She searched through the crowd until Ada stepped forward. "Look at it this way, it's over twelve thousand dollars a month."

"Thanks be!" yelled the preacher, raising his hands into the air.

A few cheers followed, and Hetty watched Ada's apron flap in the air as she jumped up and down.

"Now listen to me, folks," Hetty shouted over the commotion. "I'm going to give you a rare treat. You're going to come up here one at a time and place your arms around what my husband likes to call the Christmas tree," she said, pointing to the branching valves that had been clamped down on the well head. "I want you to feel that East Tex crude just pouring into the holding tank over there."

This appeased people as they lined up to take their turns. The ritual lasted until well after dark. Hetty was the last to hug the Christmas tree. It hummed under her hands, a steady flow of wealth that would continue even while they slept.

The next day, as soon as Garret left the house, Hetty sat down and wrote out an application to the Cupola Club, giving Cleveland Yoakum as reference and reporting that their monthly income now exceeded twelve thousand dollars. She left Pierce with Pearl and drove into town, standing in line for an hour to mail the letter. As she was coming out of the post office, a muddy, white Ford truck chugged by with an oil company's name painted on its door. Not something she would normally notice, but the logo was painted in golden yellow, with rays crowning a rising sun. She recognized it at once. *Splendora.* The next thing she knew, she was sitting on the post office steps, trying to find her breath again.

All through March the nights were filled with light: an eerie glow in the east from wells flaring off their gases, a brilliance ballooning in the sky like a second sun when a well cratered, swallowing the rig and all the men working on it. But the most colorful lights came on after dark out on the Gladewater highway, the neon pinks and blues, the strands of yellow bulbs over the beer gardens.

One night Hetty and Garret made the party at Mattie's Ballroom when the famous Sax Kings hit town, drawn by the oil boom. It had all been described to them by Elwyn, who came here for the taxi dance. There was the booth outside where Mattie Castlebury sat on high, selling five-dollar rolls of tickets to a horny lineup of roughnecks. Couples were fifty cents. Inside, swirls of fabric turned the whole place into a giant sheik's tent, fringed in gold and hung with spangles of stars that revolved in the soft lights. The lighting was designed to cast a romantic hue on the faces of the taxi dancers. *They look so young and fresh,* Hetty thought as Garret elbowed her to their table—farm girls trussed up in satins to try and make a living dancing for three minutes a time with any man willing to pay the price.

She and Garret blessed their success with bottles of good champagne he'd obtained in town at great expense. When he popped the corks, the bottles spewed multicolored bubbles into the air. He drew Hetty to her feet, and she moved along to the new and bigger sounds of jazz that flowed like rich cream over the shining dance floor.

Later on, when the band took a break, a colored group filled in whose lead singer's lizard eyes looked familiar to Hetty.

"Isn't that?"

Garret looked up. "I'll be damned. It's Brown Sugar." The crooner had sung at Andy Boy's the night that Garret had taken Hetty there against her mother's wishes.

Later, coming back from the men's room, she saw him stop at the side of the stage and light up a Camel, watching the singer through clouds of smoke and getting a sideways glance in return that Hetty thought lasted just a few beats too long.

She kept him away from Brown Sugar the rest of the night, tailing him to the pissoir, dancing almost every number with him, sitting in his lap like she used to, and teasing him to the point of torture. Back home in bed, Hetty crooned in the dark, caressing him in slow motion like she thought a brown woman might.

When the tan envelope bearing the Greek temple finally landed in the Hillyers' mailbox, Hetty didn't open it for hours. Waiting until they sat down to dinner, she slit it with her steak knife and let the words glide into her mind like silk. "The board has reviewed your application for membership in the Cupola Club, and we are pleased to inform you . . ."

She handed it to Garret. He read it and shot her an amused glance. "I think this calls for a party, don't you?"

"We'll invite all those people who laughed at us—Cleveland, my parents."

"Don't forget Lamar. I want him to see that we can get into the Cupola Club on our own."

She coaxed Pierce to eat more mashed potatoes. "I'll go on one condition. You have to take me to Neiman Marcus first."

"I thought we were going to put every penny toward paying off the consortium?"

Hetty plopped down the baby spoon. "Oh, Garret, what am I going to do with you? You don't just mail your first royalty payment to someone like Cleveland Yoakum. You present it to him in person. Over dinner, along with a whiskey sour and a very good cigar. You want me to look like the wife of an oilman, don't you? Especially in front of Lamar."

"I sure do."

"There. You see. This *will* go toward paying off the consortium." She passed him the salt.

So they made the pilgrimage that all the new oil rich made—on the Texas and Pacific Railway from Shreveport, the sharp smell of cold new metal ringing in the air as they steamed westward. Hetty watched the Piney Woods recede and the blackland prairies stretch out on all sides, flat . . . flat . . . flat. The monotony made her drowsy. As she yawned, she wondered why she kept spotting more and more Splendora trucks in Kilgore. Was Chief Rusk moving in? Or worse, Lamar? She'd been afraid to tell Garret about it, even though there was nothing the Rusks could do to harm the Ada Hillyer. She knew everything would be fine. She'd left her baby with Pearl, their oil well under the care of Pick. Hetty lay back on the seat and drifted. Then, sometime after lunch, a city of towers lifted out of the cotton fields, immense, like magic. Hetty's heavy eyelids fluttered. Was she seeing things?

It was Dallas, suddenly there.

They stepped out into the vastness of Union Station, checked into the Adolphus hotel, and shopped for a whole day at the famous store on the corner of Main and Ervay. Garret followed Hetty as she prowled through the spacious salons, trying on English tweeds, cinema satins, and the new afternoon dresses that dropped the hem almost to the ankle. For him, she picked out linen suits, Borsalino hats, and shoes made of soft kangaroo leather. Before they went to dinner, she insisted he soak in a hot bath while she scrubbed to get the last traces of black crude from under his fingernails, out of every pore.

While waiting for their clothes to be altered, they went sightseeing on the State Fair grounds, glimpsing eels and anemones at the aquarium, and a twelve-foot skeleton of *Mosasaur tylosaurus* at the Museum of Natural History, an aquatic lizard which had drifted through these parts when Texas was an ancient sea. At night, they found a speakeasy near the hotel where the bartender suggested they try a Dry Snake, the hottest new drink in Dallas. They had to laugh when he brought the cocktails, crowned with limes sliced to look like snakes, remembering their part in the creation of this concoction. Hetty spoke wistfully about Odell, knowing what a kick he'd get out of the name.

After bellboys carried their stacks of striped boxes down the grand staircase at Neiman's and their new steamer trunks were loaded onto the train, Garret rifled through the sales tickets to see how much they'd spent. The total came to over eight hundred dollars. Hetty shrugged off her new English tweed jacket and settled into her seat for the ride to Houston. "That's only two days of oil," she said. She thought in barrels now, not dollars.

On the evening of April 1, the maître d' of the Cupola Club slipped Hetty and Garret through the velvet rope and into the wide dining room where the drone of conversation and the clink of silver rebounded off pink marble walls. She walked arm in arm with her husband, beaming smiles at strangers who looked up from candlelit tables. She'd poured herself into one of the cinema satins she'd bought and wore her hair in the latest style, curled at the back of her neck.

Their guests rose in a body as they approached their table—the six people Hetty had chosen to witness this moment of intimate triumph: her parents, her sister and Lamar, Cleveland Yoakum and his wife, Clare. The men shook hands, the women planted kisses on each other's cheeks, and Hetty, assuming the head of the table, called for champagne. No flasks here: In the secluded precincts of the club, alcohol was served freely.

She found herself playing the hostess with ease, describing their adventures in the oil patch, engaging in folksy repartee with Cleveland. Lamar was boastful as usual, describing the dimensions of the house he was building for Char in Courtlandt Place, who, in turn, supplied a lot of technical details about the architecture and construction, determined to hold her own in this company.

Following the first course of anchovy toast and clams, a champagne glass rang out. "Now, y'all, hush," Clare Yoakum said, "it's time somebody proposed a toast." She wavered as she stood up. The glass trembled in her hand. "I want to remind everybody of the last time we had dinner together at the Hoggs. Garret here charmed me with his stories of Montana, but y'all laughed at him when he tried to tell us about the ocean of oil in East Texas. He didn't give up, though, and that's my idea of the true wildcatter. They never give up, no matter what. My wish for y'all is that the petrochemicals flow as freely as the champagne does tonight."

"Amen," Cleveland shouted as eight glasses sparkled in the air. Garret stood next, his cheeks flushed, his eyes radiant. "Thanks, Clare. What you say may be true of men like Dad Joiner, but I guess I was just lucky. I hit pay dirt with my first well. Here's to the Ada Hillyer Number One. May there be many more."

"Hear, hear," Kirb shouted as they all raised their glasses.

"And now I have a little presentation to make to your husband, Clare." He reached into his suit coat and pulled out a cigar wrapped in a white linen envelope, which he handed with a flourish to Cleveland. Cleveland threw back his head of white hair and read the label. La Corona Belvedere. He lit it immediately, filling the air with a woodsy reek. Only then did he open the envelope, glancing at the slip of paper inside and tucking it into his breast pocket.

Nella watched him across the table as she nibbled on a wedge of toast. "Com'on, Cleveland, don't we ladies get to know what you gentlemen wrap around cigars these days?"

"It's nuthin," he mumbled. "Just a check for eight thousand dollars."

"Ah," Kirb said, "the first royalty payment. A nice way to deliver it, Garret."

"He got the brand right," Cleveland said, stoking his favorite kind of cigar. "But the payment's a day late."

Garret's smile faded as he sat down. Cleveland looked genuinely stern. He blew smoke rings out over the table.

Clare cackled. "Oh, I get it, honey. It's April first."

"I can get it in by the thirty-first if that's what you want, sir."

Clare cackled again. "April Fool's, Garret, April Fool's."

Cleveland blew more smoke rings. "Son, I don't care if it comes in on the thirty-first, the first, or the fifth, wrapped around a cigar or a dried pig's turd, as long as I get a check for eight thousand dollars next month, you hear me now?"

"Yes, sir, I do. I want to pay back the consortium as soon as possible, so they'll back me in another well. East Texas is sitting on a gold mine like you've never seen."

"Keep your britches on, son. You just make your first well pay off. Then we'll talk."

"Yes, sir, Mr. Yoakum."

Through the *O*s floating in the air, Hetty watched as Cleveland turned the full power of his gaze on Garret and said, "Call me Cleve, son."

Garret flushed. "Thank you, sir. I mean—Cleve. I'd like to say—I really want to do more deals with you, Cleve. What'll it take?"

"I already told you. Just be sure that turtle gets across the road."

"In other words, don't pull my head back in?"

"That's right. And you'd better buy up the offset location."

"What's that?"

"The farm next door. You don't want someone drillin' south of you."

Garret looked at Hetty. "Didn't you meet the farmwife next door?"

She nodded. "Yes. A greedy woman named Wavie Goss. I guess we'd better pay a call on her."

Noiselessly, fresh utensils appeared at each place, and the fish course was borne to the table on a huge, steaming platter. As they were served, the talk turned to Nella's recent travels. She had sailed abroad again, this time to study the public spaces of European cities. She had joined Will Hogg's Forum of Civics to help devise a city plan for Houston. She came back filled with visions of wide boulevards festooned with fountains and statues.

"Mamá wants a Pont Neuf over every bayou," laughed Charlotte.

"And why not? We have a chance to turn this city into something grand, the Paris of the South," Nella said. "But we have to act now, before it's too late. Look what happened to Magnolia Park."

Cleveland sniffed the air. "Is this swordfish a little old, Kirb, or do I smell the putrid odor of zoning?"

"The fish is fine."

"Well," Nella admitted, setting down her fork, "there'll have to be some zoning, of course. You can't leave these things to chance."

"Who said, 'Bad taste leads to crime'?" Charlotte asked. "Stendhal, I think."

"Well, you would know, dear. And I agree with Mr. Stendhal. Those of us with a little knowledge will have to make the decisions for the rest of you, that's all there is to it."

"I'll be damned if you will," Cleveland boomed out. This sparked a debate about the role of government in the life of Texas. Everyone had something to say about it except Hetty, who sat back and breathed in the fragrant air, scented with rosemary, beeswax, and cigar smoke. She looked around the room, her eyes resting on the white lilies at every table surrounded by gleaming china and crystal. She forced herself to forget the shotgun house they would return to tomorrow and wiped it out of her memory for tonight. Someday they would live in rooms like this, she told herself, crowning the skylines of cities.

The musk of wild meat drew Hetty out of her reverie. The entrée had been placed smoking at her side circled with swirls of Duchess potatoes. She clinked on a glass to interrupt the wrangle over zoning and announced, "I have a special treat for you tonight. Real oil field fare—a stuffed opossum."

Clare cackled loudly, and Char wrinkled her nose.

"Oh, com'on," Hetty said. "You have to be adventurous in the oil business—right, Cleve?"

"It smells good," Lamar said, sitting right next to it.

Hetty signaled for colored attendants to carve and serve the game along with warm glasses of claret. People took timid bites at first, then decided it was every bit as good as venison.

After lemon sorbet to clear the palate, everyone sat back satisfied. Nella grasped the moment for one of her grand gestures. She passed a white box garlanded with silver ribbons Hetty's way. Inside were fossils of fern leaves and spirals of shells, polished like jewels.

"Mamá, they're beautiful. Thank you."

"I thought you'd like to see where your oil is coming from."

"Are these Texas fossils?"

Nella nodded, her eyes smoky with mystery. "Pass them around, and I think you'll see." The fossils, pale and pockmarked with ancient life, migrated from hand to hand. "It all started with creatures like these," she told them, "once upon a time when there was an ocean where we're sitting now."

Hetty ran her fingers over one of the spirals. She tried to imagine the world that Nella described, seething on that seafloor. She pictured amphibians slithering up onto beaches, ferns arising, dragonflies buzzing. And, of course, cockroaches—huge ones!

"There were scorpions ten feet long," Nella laughed.

Hetty studied the shell fossil through eyes glazed with champagne. She could imagine it swimming out of her hand as her mother described the animals that followed it in evolution—the sea serpents, the sharks, the great lizards that floated through the waters like whales. Hetty looked up. Her eyes quivered. The chandelier shimmered high overhead, a constellation of stars glimpsed from underwater. "But how did these become oil? Remind me."

"They died. The sea bottom became a giant graveyard, swallowing everything. Sediment sealed it in. The juices of all these life-forms, their fatty oils, became bottled up. Waiting . . . just waiting . . ."

"Whatever for?" Clare asked.

"The secret ingredient." Nella paused to pick up her champagne, which had started to go flat.

Kirb tapped his fingers together. "Heat and pressure."

"That's right," Nella said after taking a sip. "Thanks to the alchemy at work deep in the earth, the fat from all those critters became transmuted into East Tex crude. It's resurrection by hydrocarbons."

"I'd forgotten," Hetty said, "that oil came from living things."

"I thought you could use a refresher. Millions of beings sacrificed themselves to make you rich."

Cleveland chuckled. "Nella," he boomed out, planting his elbows on the table. "I never cease to be amazed at the bullshit you come up with. Millions of beings—Jesus! Oil's just muck."

"Oh, really? Then why do they call it buried sunlight?"

"That's what they call it? Buried sunlight?" Hetty was amazed at the words coming out of her mother's mouth. The champagne was adding a halo of significance to everything.

"That's not what I call it. It's just plain old black gold to me, right, Mac?"

"I'm with you," Garret said, adding with relish the name "Cleve."

Nella smiled across the table at them both. "Maybe you men should think about what you're doing, trespassing on the mineral kingdom like that. You know what the Hopis say—when you dig treasure out of the earth, you invite disaster."

"But it's all right to use it, isn't it?" Clare asked. "What would we run our cars on?"

"'Course it is," Cleveland said. "Ye shall have dominion over the earth, the Good Book says."

"Over, Cleve, not under."

At this point, both Char and Garret excused themselves from the table. While Nella and Cleveland debated loudly, Hetty turned to Lamar. "I've seen some Splendora trucks in Kilgore. What's up?"

"You really don't expect me to tell you, do you?"

"So something is up. Now that men like Garret have done all the work, Chief thinks he can just walk in and take over."

"What makes you think it's Chief?"

Hetty just watched as he grinned at her with his crooked smile. She was speechless for a few moments, then caught her breath. "Congratulations, Lam. I'm sure you'll do quite well."

"It's a good opportunity for me. You know, show the old man what I'm made of."

"Not to mention the rest of us." She felt Lamar's eyes following the movements of her body in the clinging dress as she slipped out of her chair and fled to the ladies' lounge.

Charlotte was still at the mirror when Hetty emerged from a stall. The colored maid turned on a faucet and handed Hetty a towel. She washed her hands, then splashed herself with some of the perfume on the counter. Charlotte was applying pink lipstick. "I love that dress, sis."

"Thanks. It's from Neiman's."

"Oh, we're shopping at Neiman's now, are we? Quite a change from pawning your jewels to get into Ima Hogg's."

"I hope to tell you, sis! I'm glad those days are over." Hetty reached into her purse, groping for lipstick. "Looks like we're both going to be oilmen's wives."

"Welcome to the club."

Hetty enjoyed the camaraderie with her sister as they preened in front of the mirror. Now that they were on an equal footing financially, she hoped for more of these unspoiled moments of sisterhood. She pulled out her vermilion lipstick and remembered how they used to fight over it. Charlotte was always "borrowing" Hetty's things and forgetting to return them. She always acted like an only child. That led to many a screaming match. *Never mind,* Hetty thought, as she smiled at her sister in the mirror. Their girlhood battles now felt childish, and she wanted to exile them to the past. Hetty's mood was expansive enough tonight to enfold all of Charlotte's little jealousies and wipe them away like lipstick taunts on a mirror.

"Thanks. I feel so lucky."

"Just how lucky?"

"What do you mean?"

"Com'on, you can tell your dear sister. How rich are you?"

"It's only our first well, Char. Give us a chance." Hetty clicked the vermilion lipstick open and pursed her lips.

"You don't have to be modest with me, Het. Everyone knows those East Tex wells are real gushers. How many thousands of barrels rich are you? Lamar's dying to know."

"You know as well as I do, it's never enough."

"But how many? Tell me."

"Mind your own potatoes! Do I ask you how much money Lamar has?"

"You don't have to. Everyone knows that I married into one of the richest families in Texas." She pivoted to raise an eyebrow at Hetty . . . waiting.

Hetty tried to hold her hand steady as she glided a gash of color over her lips. A little bled onto her chin.

"Never mind." Charlotte shrugged and started out of the room. "I'm sure I can pry it out of Dad."

Hetty could hardly focus on Clare as she engaged her in a long Southern good-bye. Her eyes drifted to her sister at the other end of the table, clutched in a tremulous tête-à-tête with their father. She dipped her head to drop a question into his ear, laughed at the response, and looked askance at Hetty. Then she fluttered over to Lamar, briefing him behind her hand. As soon as he heard what she was saying, he turned and sneered at Hetty down the long table. She ignored their chatter and took Garret's arm to lead the group out of the dining room. Charlotte managed to wedge herself in at the elevator, as Hetty felt a wet kiss quiver on her cheek, then hot breath in her ear. "Dad told me your little secret," Charlotte whispered. "Four hundred barrels a day. I just had to tell Lamar." She giggled. "He was amused. That's pocket change to someone like him."

Hetty remained silent on the elevator ride down. Her stomach felt an odd jolt when they reached the ground floor. She'd tried to hold out an olive branch to Charlotte, only to be slapped in the face with it. She felt scratched and bloodied and walked out of the Esperson Building without even saying good night.

As soon as they got back to their suite at the Rice Hotel, Hetty began undressing Garret. A torrent of champagne hadn't been enough to douse the burn of Char's laughter and the threat of Lamar's news. Only the sounds of lovemaking would do it, filling her ears with pleasure and the kind of cries that rose after midnight. She had the more powerful man now; she knew that and so did Char, which is why she was being so catty. When Lamar had shaken her hand in greeting, his fingers had felt smooth and limp. He held on to things too loosely, and lacked the grit of greed that drove Garret to plunder and dare beyond all common sense. She loved men like her husband, loved their desperation and sweat, the edge in their eyes, their legs thick as tree trunks, the hands roped with veins. There was only one way to set the sneering ghost of Charlotte to rest: by reaching between Garret's legs in the dark tonight and pulling up the stalk of his strength, letting him bury it inside of her over and over until her own throat cracked with the sounds that were wilder than laughter, harder than scorn.

Just as they were falling asleep, she whispered to Garret, "I have everything I want now, baby." She curled up against him and fell into dreams of delicate tendrils brushing against her skin, fern fronds, mosses, and spores. From a dark corner of the room, lurking in the air currents stirred up by the ceiling fan, something with slitted eyes was watching her.

The fur slips off Hetty, and she stands in the high, thatched house that is shaped like a beehive. In the center of the thatched room lies a large bed of skins where, in the dim light, bodies writhe in a ball like mating rattlesnakes. Santa Adiva is making love to all five of her husbands at once. The men's naked bodies are coppery, tattooed. They gleam with sweat as they work at pleasuring their queen. They take turns plowing her, loosening the carved bone pins Hetty threaded so carefully into her hair.

Hetty cannot look away, even though she feels she should. Adiva's slit gets stretched by the men until it turns into a cleft in the earth. Hetty peers into it . . . dark and cavernous. She smells crude oil and sees the blue-black water seeping up. Orgasmically, the earth shudders, releasing the buried sunlight of centuries. It streams up from miles down and irradiates the high, thatched roof. Swimming up in the beams of light are the ether bodies of animals buried in the sediment long ago. They escape by the billions and dance in the light: the frogs and the salamanders, the anemones and the mollusks, the snails and the lungfish and the wide-winged dragonflies, hooting together a great hymn of sacrifice and calling for Hetty to redeem their deaths.

Then one of the giant scorpions crawls out of the hole and crouches on the floor of the hut. He is ten feet long. Slowly, he rotates until he spots Hetty. She lifts the flap at the door and flees outside. She runs as fast as she can. Hetty reaches the first shotgun house and rips the door open, slamming it behind her. She runs through the room where Pearl lives, through the makeshift kitchen, into the back room, Pick's room. But he is not there. His clothes are gone; his furniture stripped away. The scorpion stands in the middle of the bare floor, choking the room. Hetty clings to the wall; he flexes his stinger, swings it in the air.

Hetty woke up sweating. Her head felt too heavy to lift, but she could tell it was early morning by the blue light leaking through the curtains. Ada would be in the kitchen, doing chores. Pearl would be rocking Pierce and singing to him. She lifted the phone and gave the operator the number, leaving a message for Pearl to call her back.

A *brinnng-brinnng* woke her up again an hour later. "Nothing but bad to tell!" Pearl's voice broke with static.

"Is Pierce all right?"

"Oh, the baby's fine. Say hello to him."

Hetty heard cooing and shouted, "It's Mommy" over and over into the receiver.

"He loves playing with the phone," Pearl said. "You should get him a toy one."

"I will. Hey—what's wrong?"

"I was going to wait until you got back."

Hetty shook Garret's shoulder. "Honey, something's wrong. Tell me, Pearl."

"Oil's down to ninety cents a barrel."

"What? That can't be! Garret, this'll wake you up," she said, pushing the receiver to his ear.

Chapter 14

In the week they'd been gone, Hetty had forgotten how an oil town smells. The minute she stepped off the train in Kilgore, the stench hit her. Rotten eggs being poached in a pit full of grease. A blue haze carried the stink across the traffic clogging Commerce Street, the air echoing with the sounds of hammering and sawing. Pick appeared out of the crowd on the platform, welcoming them back with his warm smiles and handshakes. He swiveled Hetty's steamer trunk up onto one shoulder as if it weighed nothing, stowing it in the back of the Wichita. The three of them squeezed into the cab, and Pick honked his way into the stream of vehicles. Derricks seemed to be sprouting everywhere. Hetty counted over a dozen in one block of downtown alone.

"There weren't this many wells here when we left—were there?"

"No, ma'am." Pick chuckled. "They's coming up like weeds all over." He slowed down as he passed Brown's Drugs and pointed to the eaves that had been chopped off to make room for a rig. Turning onto Main Street, he rounded a corner cluttered with bricks and debris.

"Isn't that where Horn Brothers' Furniture Store used to be?" Hetty asked.

"Sure was."

Garret whistled as he craned his neck to look at the vacant lot. "They're tearing down buildings to drill wells?"

"Yes, sir, too many. That's how come crude's gone down in price, they say."

"Yeah, but fifteen cents a barrel overnight? Sounds fishy to me," Garret said.

"How can the price of something go down that fast?" Hetty gritted her teeth.

"Mr. Hillyer, he came over the other day, and he says, you milk too many cows, price of milk's going to go down."

The acrid fumes swam into Hetty's brain, sparking her exasperation. "But don't they need oil?" she said. "There's a depression, for God's sake. I don't get it!"

"I bet you the Majors are behind this," Garret said. "They're trying to fix prices so they can buy it cheaper."

The Majors—a term of scorn Hetty had heard other drillers use to describe the big conglomerates like Humble and Texaco. She thought of Splendora and wondered if Chief had anything to do with rigging the price of oil. Or maybe it was John D. Rockefeller. Didn't Lamar say he owned half of Humble? She wanted to blame somebody for this! "That's what the Majors always do. And it's not fair to men like you, honey. We finally get our big break, and they're trying to take it away from us."

"They can't hurt us," Garret said, pulling out a notepad and scribbling figures on it. "Look at this. I can still pay back the consortium in two months. Then we drill again," he said, his eyes checking and rechecking the columns of numbers.

It was easy to forget about the price of oil once they got back home and found spring scattering itself over the floor of the pine forests. Rugs of red clover unfurled across the meadows, while long runners of evening primrose paved the side of every road along with pink and yellow buttercups. Other colors began to lace themselves through the deep evergreen of the pines, the light green of budding hickory trees, and the broad handspans of oak.

Pearl and Ada busied themselves in the cool mornings putting in a spring garden, while Hetty caught up on her laundry, hanging the clothes out on the barbed wire fences where they dried quickly in the bright sunny afternoons. Pierce crawled around in the meadow, calling to her. She barely had time to feed him and change his diapers, much less play with him. There was so much to do. He had to content himself with his new toy telephone, which tinkled and talked to him when he pumped the receiver. At night, she and Garret fell asleep to the kind of chirping Hetty associated with crickets.

Every couple of days, their trucker, Mr. Smackover, roared down the creek bank in his muddy Ford tanker, uncoiling his hose while Pick cranked up a centrifugal pump to milk out the eight hundred barrels of oil that had collected in the iron udder of the holding tank. He was their best source of news, reporting what price the Majors were paying for crude on any given day. Garret drove over to the neighboring farm one afternoon and tried to buy mineral leases from Clay and Wavie Goss, but they said they were holding out for the best offer.

By the next week, Hetty had settled into a routine she planned to follow for two months, based on Garret's revised budget. The family was in the middle of lunch one day when a timid tapping on the door drew Garret out of his chair to answer it. From the table where she fed Pierce, Hetty could look through two doorways and see Pick out in the noon sun, squinting, shirtless, sweat giving his black skin the luster of her onyx earrings. Garret gestured for him to come in. He shook his head.

"What is it, Pick?" Garret asked.

"I thought you should know right off, Mr. Garret. Smack just left. Says the majors ain't paying ninety cents no more."

"Oh, shit!" Garret spat out after swallowing a mouthful of food. "What's it down to now, eighty?"

"No, sir." Pick took a deep breath.

"Eighty-five, seventy-five?"

"No, sir."

"What then?"

Pick took a step backward. "He say . . . fifty cent is all."

Garret slammed the door, then opened it again. Pick stood in the brightness, flinching. "I don't believe you! You're lying!"

Hetty felt her lunch turn over in her stomach.

"No, sir. He say."

"I don't believe it. It's oil field rumors!" Garret slammed the door in Pick's face and stomped back into the bedroom. "I'll be damned if it's fifty cents." Hetty could hear bangs and thumps as more doors were slammed and objects were thrown. She tensed for the sound of breaking glass. Garret strode out with a leather jacket on, keys clenched in his fist.

"Where are you going? Aren't you going to finish lunch?"

"Tulsa's. I've got to find out the truth. This has got to be a rumor!" When he slammed the door behind him this time, Pierce started to bawl.

Hetty put the baby down for his nap later in the day and went to look for her husband. She found the Auburn slid to a stop in the sand beside the derrick. Footsteps led across the creek bank and the bridge toward the doghouse. She found Garret slumped there in the gloom, a fruit jar of corn whiskey in one hand, a half-smoked Camel in the other. Butts littered the dirt floor.

"Should you be smoking so close to the well?"

He crushed the cigarette under his boot then reflexively fired up another.

"So it's true?"

"Yeah."

She sat down on a barrel and pried out one of his Camels. They smoked in silence for a while. Hetty was able to draw the truth out of him in bits and pieces as he used the whiskey to blur the bloody edge of his rage. It seemed that in cracking open the sluice gates of the world's largest field, the boomers were inundating oil markets all over with a crude so rich in gasoline content it was driving prices down around the globe. Like any treasure, it lost its value when it became so abundant.

"But I don't understand that," Hetty said. "If there's too much oil, why don't they just store it and use it later? It's not going to spoil or anything."

"They're saying it's not worth much anymore."

"But how can they? The oil hasn't changed. This is East Tex we're talking about—the sweetest oil on earth. How can it suddenly be worthless?"

"Goddamn if I know. Because somebody says it is. Probably Chief Rusk. I saw a whole convoy of Splendora trucks in town."

"I'm afraid it's not Chief this time."

Garret cast her a baleful glance.

She nodded sadly. "Lamar told me at dinner. He's going to start major drilling."

"Christ! That's all I need—Lamar breathing down my neck."

"It's not fair!"

"I know. This is what they did to my dad."

"Who did *what* to your dad? You've never talked much about Termite."

"They killed him. And now they're trying to kill me," he said, staring dumbly off into the treetops.

During the month of April, Garret's quota of Camels rose from a pack and a half a day to over four. He chain-smoked feverishly as he watched oil prices sink faster than a fishtailed drill bit hitting soft sandstone. Fifty cents the second week, forty cents the third week, thirty cents the fourth week until, by May Day, the unthinkable happened. Prices bottomed out at fifteen cents a barrel.

Hetty could see his head reeling with each new drop as he revised the terms of the contract on paper: at forty cents three more months to pay off the consortium, at thirty cents, six more months. When the scale hit its lowest point, he couldn't bring himself to do the math, knowing they were probably looking at a year or more of debt and delays. He spent a lot of time out in the doghouse.

Hetty's daily routine pulled her through: preparing meals, feeding the baby, and helping Pearl boil diapers in a big iron pot outdoors. The chores allowed her to keep reality slightly out of focus in her mind, looking to the day when oil prices would start to rise again. This was only a temporary setback, she told herself—but when she tried to picture her penthouse back in Houston it receded further and further away in her mind's eye, as if seen through the wrong end of a telescope.

"Surely it can't get any worse," Hetty joked one night at supper, trying to cheer her husband up. "If it goes down anymore, we'll be paying *them* to haul the stuff away." Garret didn't laugh.

They had just gotten up for breakfast one morning the next week, when they spotted Ada tramping down the hill from the farmhouse, her face grim. Garret skivvied on some overalls, but Hetty stepped out into the blue dawn in her nightgown. The grass was soaked with dew.

"This here," Ada croaked, holding a paper away from her as if contaminated, "come last night. Why is it addressed to me?"

Garret took the document from her and opened it. Hetty leaned over his shoulder to read. It was a proration order from the Railroad Commission of Texas. They had divided the oil field up into sections and set a pro rata for each well to try and bring prices back up. The quota for the Ada Hillyer Number One was two hundred barrels a day, half its usual production. A clause at the bottom warned that anyone caught defying the order would be fined one thousand dollars daily for each day of noncompliance.

Hetty stepped away in the wet grass while Garret read it again, his jaw set. It didn't take her long to do the math in her head. At fifteen cents a barrel, their current production of four hundred barrels would yield over a thousand a month to pay Cleveland's consortium, which meant they had some hope of paying him off this year. But at half that, it could take two years or longer. Hetty started to shiver in the morning mist. Cold crept into her bare feet. She glanced past Garret at the shotgun house, so stunted and crude, sitting crookedly on its cement blocks. It was all they had; all they were likely to have for some time. *Now we're living like shanty Irish,* she couldn't help but think. Perhaps if she painted it, planted some flowers . . .

Garret handed the paper back to Ada, and they all stood staring at it in her hand, their faces ashen in the gray light.

* * *

Mr. Smackover sat as close to their kitchen table as his big belly would allow. He was a ruddy, balding man with rough, swollen hands and a voice like a rasp filing down a pine plank. He had tracked mud in on his boots. Hetty slid a plate of hot biscuits his way and opened a jar of honey. He sliced one immediately and spread it with a thick layer of Ada's fresh-churned yellow butter. Garret had invited Smack in because he had a scheme for skirting the proration order. Hetty dipped a biscuit in milk and started spoon-feeding Pierce while she listened to Smack's husky words scratching the air. "What you say—y'all got a problem with bootlegging?"

Garret bellowed.

"Smack, you're looking at one of the original Tequila Kings right here," Hetty said and told him a little about their adventures running Mexican hooch down in the brush country.

"I ain't talking about whiskey. I mean"—he lowered his voice to a hoarse whisper—"oil, running hot oil."

Garret jumped out of his chair. "Is there a way to do that?"

"I done started. Found me a teapot up in Gladewater pays six cents a barrel, no questions asked."

"What's a teapot?" Hetty asked.

"One of them refineries that skims off the white gasoline from the crude. You know, Eastex—that stuff you can buy so cheap at gas stations around here."

"Six cents a barrel?" Hetty's eyes locked into Garret's, both their brains tabulating the same sums.

"It's better than nothing," Smack said, gulping down more biscuit. "I got mouths to feed just like y'all." He nodded toward Pierce in his high chair.

"It's a deal!" Garret grabbed Smack's thick hand and squeezed it.

"Long as *you* pump the oil it is."

Hetty yanked their hands apart. "Then it isn't. I've already watched Pearl lose her husband to jail. I'm not losing mine."

"But we have to do this, honey. It'll keep us afloat till prices come back up."

Both men watched her as she steamed black coffee into her cup. "I don't want you doing the pumping, Mac."

"But I don't. That's Pick's job."

Smack leaned forward and spoke in a gruff whisper: "There you go. Have your nigger meet me at the well. They'll never spot him in the dark. I ain't never seen a man as black as Pick. It's like he's carved out of coal or something."

"Onyx." Hetty smiled, spooning sugar into her coffee. "But I don't want Pick getting into any trouble, either. I feel responsible for him."

"I'm sure he won't mind," Garret said. "It's no different from what he does during the day."

"Just tell him what we East Texans say. You can grow more cotton in a crooked row than a straight one."

"Okay, I'll ask him," Hetty said, staring into the dark brown whirlpool in her cup.

Garret lifted his coffee. "Here's to survival."

Hetty touched her cup to his. "Amen."

The next night, Hetty made her way down to the well under a full moon, looking for Pick. The light was incandescent, mother-of-pearl, and everything moved in slow motion as if taking place under water. A black shadow lay under each pine. The truck docked at the holding tank, a pirate vessel Hetty thought, waiting to be loaded with contraband. All someone had to do was crank up the pump, open the valve, and cross a forbidden line. The creek gurgled now and then. The underbrush rustled. Otherwise the night was utterly still.

Then the air eddied around her. Hetty gasped. Pick was standing right beside her, not a foot away, in the thick shade of a pine. Wearing black, he was virtually invisible.

"Pick?" she whispered.

"Yes, ma'am."

Hetty held her breath in the cage of her teeth. Did she dare let the question escape? Inspectors combed the field, checking every well, handing out cease and desist orders. One could be lurking in the trees right now, watching them. On the other hand, if they didn't pirate some petrol soon, they might have to let Pick go completely. Then what would happen to Addie, Ollie, Lewis, and Minnie? She listened to the black man so close beside her—steady, quiet. He knew what was coming. He was ready—she could sense it.

Hetty parted her lips and let the words fly out. "Would you be willing to pump hot oil for us at night?"

"Yes, ma'am."

"Looks like you're the one. I didn't even see you come up."

"I know."

She looked across the watery floor of the pine forest. Mr. Smackover came floating around the truck . . . furtive . . . afraid. On nights like this, he would drive all the way to Gladewater with his headlights off. "Be careful, Pick," she turned to say, but he had vanished.

Covered by the camouflage of night, into the damp dawns of July, Mr. Smackover continued running his truckloads of hot oil up to the teapot refinery in Gladewater. He was never caught. Hetty seldom saw Pick during the day, assuming he slept through the sultry afternoons in his room at the back of the shotgun house, waiting until dark to slip on his black clothes and emerge unseen to practice his nocturnal occupation.

At dusk every night, he'd stop by Hetty's for a strong cup of coffee to keep him awake, and he'd sit down and talk about "my well." His proprietary pride grew the more he cared for the Ada Hillyer, even crawling down into the tank to clean out the sludge coating the bottom.

"Time to go milk my well," he'd say as he swallowed the last mouthful of Folgers and pushed his chair back from the table. Thanks to the extra money he generated, Garret was able to make small royalty payments to the consortium, cover the interests held by Pearl and the Hillyers, and keep food on the table. He gave Pick a raise.

But not all independent drillers were so lucky. Many wells were shut down by proration, and many men were put out of work. Mr. Smackover brought them the reports every night as his truck glided, motor turned off, down the hillside. Roughnecks grumbled in the shadows of the Cot Houses, he said, and there were murders down in the Hollow. The whole town of Kilgore seethed with discontent.

"Don't y'all dare go in there at night," he warned them over a midnight shot of corn whiskey. The three of them huddled around an oil lamp, their shadows huge on the ceiling. "You'll get robbed, or worse. Things are so bad they called in some Texas Rangers to keep law and order. And guess who the ringleader is—none other than Sergeant Gonzaullas hisself."

"Ohhhh!" Garret moaned. "Not Lone Wolf Gonzaullas?"

"Ain't we lucky? Everybody's scared of the Wolf."

"We know. He's the man who put Pearl's husband away," Hetty said.

"A sneaky bastard!" Smack's voice grated at the darkness around them. "Appeared out of nowhere up on Pistol Hill, horse black, Stetson white. They say his pistols are studded with pearls. A shiver runs through the whole of Gregg County. And it should've. That night, he and his sidekick raided Newton Flats, the dance halls, the Hollow. Chained a bunch of folks up on his trotline."

"His trotline?"

"Well, yes! There ain't no jail in Kilgore, you know. Just last fall it was a sleepy little no-count town. So Lone Wolf takes over an old abandoned church, and he chains the transgressors up on his trotline. I pray the Lord I never land in there. You have to sit up all the time. You can't sleep. The only bathroom is a tin can they pass along the line."

"Do we have anything to fear?" Hetty asked.

"Naw." Smack shook his head. "Not from Lone Wolf. He's a perfect gentleman, I hear. It's his sidekick you got to watch, Poke Pritchett."

"Poke?" Hetty laughed at the name.

"Short for Poker Face 'cause he never shows no emotion. A frozen heart carrying a rifle. He'll shoot you without flicking an eyelid."

"That ranger sounds deranged," Hetty said.

"Just stay out of his way. He ain't after oilmen. Not yet, anyway."

* * *

In the middle of a humid July night, Hetty was awakened out of a sweaty sleep by an explosion. Even through the tiny window of the shotgun house, she could see the flash of light in the sky over Kilgore. It was so bright she glimpsed the face of the clock on the bedside table: 2:34 a.m. She nudged Garret, but he only rolled over and went back to sleep. After the radiance died down, it continued to flicker against the low-lying clouds like heat lightning.

They learned what had happened the next day from Mr. Smackover. He brought them a copy of the *Kilgore News Herald* dripping with giant black letters—**HUMBLE'S INFERNO**—under a picture of a churning lake of mud right in the middle of town. The well had caved into a crater, the article said, after being blown up by a charge of dynamite.

"The parties responsible for the latest oil field disaster have not been identified," Smack read to them over sweating glasses of iced tea leaving puddles on the kitchen table. "Ha! Like it's some big secret!" he scoffed. "They shut us down and let the Majors go on drilling. I'd like to dynamite a few wells myself." Although the order from the Railroad Commission had prorated existing wells, he explained, it had not prohibited the drilling of new ones.

"Yeah, but who's got the money to drill a new well?" Garret said.

"Humble, that's who!" Smack bellowed.

"And Splendora," Hetty added.

He continued bringing them front pages crammed with columns of breaking news: More wells were dynamited, a public meeting in Longview turned into a riot, a special session of the Texas Legislature was called down in Austin. As if things weren't bad enough, August made its entrance with a heat wave in tow, one of the worst anybody could remember. It felt like the breeze panting through the pines blew off a nearby forest fire.

Hetty found it impossible to stay in the shotgun house much after lunch and started hosting a daily picnic beside Caney Creek, a little downstream from the oil well. She and Pearl and Ada would stretch out along the shady bank on a red-checkered tablecloth and sip iced tea while they dangled their feet in the cool water. Hollis and Oleta waded into the deeper places, but Pierce was confined to the sandy shallows where he splashed around sans diaper.

It was during their second picnic that Hollis discovered what an ample supply of frogs the creek provided. He began tiptoeing along the water's edge, ferreting sleepy frogs out from under leaves or logs.

About this time, Hetty felt something tickle her foot. She looked down and shrieked. A frog with spots was trying to crawl out of the water via her leg. She shook it off and lifted both feet straight out of the water. "Now I'll get warts on my feet!"

The other women cackled.

"Why are you laughing at me? I thought toads exuded some kind of poison from their skin that gives you warts."

"Ain't you the one?" Pearl snorted. "First, that ain't a toad, it's a leopard frog, and secondly, that's an old wives' tale. Frogs are the most harmless creatures in the world."

"Sure are," Ada said.

"Where do you learn this stuff, Pearl?" Hetty began drying off her legs.

"You forget, hon, I'm from Lufkin. My brothers used to go gigging for frogs, so I know all about them. Lord, they'd bring in a mess of the things, leave the sink all bloody, then fry up them frog legs that'd still be twitching when they threw them in the hot grease. But I could never bring myself to eat one. I loved them too much."

"Loved them!" Hetty arched an eyebrow.

"Yes, you come to. They're such magical things. I mean, just think. They start out as tadpoles, and before you know it, they crawl out of the water just like a butterfly out of a cocoon." Pearl's spindly fingers spread like wings. "And they make such music at night!"

"Is that where all the noise comes from? I thought it was crickets or something."

"You been in Houston too long," Ada said.

"That's the frog chorus you're hearing—the sound of East Texas. I let them serenade me to sleep every night. Some of them sound like they're plucking a banjo, others a bass fiddle. Then there's the whole percussion section—all the clicks, buzzes, pops, and whistles. It's the males that make the noises." Pearl leaned back on one bony elbow and murmured to Hetty, "They're love songs, you know."

"You mean, every night . . . ?"

"In these parts"—Pearl nodded, stealing a glance at Ada—"all summer long."

Hollis came over to his mother, proudly clutching a reddish-brown frog bleating like a lamb.

"Show it to the baby, son," Ada said.

He set it down on the sand in front of Pierce, who reached for it and watched it hop away, lifting his little hands into the air and chortling with delight. He pointed toward the exiting frog and burbled. Hollis brought it back again, and the game was repeated. This went on for an hour or more. The shade deepened.

Ada unwrapped a tea towel and passed around little sweet wisps of divinity. She began telling them Caddo legends about frogs and turtles that she'd heard from her mother. "They bring fertility," Ada said. "Caddo women gave birth all alone in special huts beside streams, to be near the frogs. They would sing you through your labor, making the pain easier to bear."

"Beats a midwife any day," Hetty said. That night, she began to distinguish the sounds Pearl had described to her: the deep manly croaking, the plucking and sawing, the peeps and trills. The love songs of the frogs rose and fell in sensuous waves, interweaving—the call of the waters, as soothing as tides washing in and out at the shore. Hetty smiled and snuggled into her pillow, letting the sounds lull her into sleep. *Dear God,* she prayed, *please don't let me fall in love with frogs.*

One blistering afternoon, as Garret helped Hetty pack her picnic basket, Smack barged into their kitchen, red-faced and sweating, brandishing the day's paper with the headline: OKIE FIELDS SHUT DOWN!

"Alfalfa Bill's gone and done it, goddamn him," he shrilled, referring to the Oklahoma governor's decision to call in state troops and halt production statewide until oil prices rose again to a dollar a barrel.

"What'll we do if they shut us down?" Hetty reached for Garret.

"Texans won't hear of it." Smack slapped his thigh with the paper.

That week, a group of Humble geologists announced the final dimensions of the field around them. Smack unfolded the pages of the *Kilgore News Herald* across their kitchen table, and they all stared at the map in disbelief: The East Texas Oil Field not only flowed under Gregg County, where Kilgore, Longview, and Gladewater were situated, but also stretched itself out into Upshur, Smith, Rusk, and Cherokee counties, five in all, its size a staggering one hundred and forty thousand acres—which made it officially the grandest trove of petroleum to be tapped in the history of the world. Over one thousand wells had been drilled since December, the paper said, and Dad Joiner's Ocean of Oil now flowed with one million barrels of rich East Texas crude every single day.

The frantic pounding came as Hetty was setting the table for dinner. She thought the door of the shotgun house was going to fly off its hinges. When she opened it, Roy Hillyer was hunched there, his jaw trembling as he said, "Our church is on fire."

Hetty and Garret followed the Hillyers into Kilgore, the tornado of black smoke visible from miles off. They had to park blocks away; there was such a tangle of traffic crawling toward the spectacle. They stepped into the crowd of people pushing forward, necks craned to see what they could already hear, the snapping and crackling of a clapboard chapel in flames. Hetty held on to Ada's arms, which were clammy with dread.

When they reached the blockade, the heat was so searing in the August evening Hetty had to shield her face with her hand. What they saw set Ada and the other Baptist women to keening: Only the skeleton of a church was left, flames eating at the bones of the building like a brood of fiendish maggots. Ashes floated in the air. The half-charred page of a hymnal drifted before Hetty's eyes. *On a hill far away,* she could make out. A single fire truck fed water into the blaze, which evaporated instantly into steam.

When the last colored glass window popped, the wall where the altar stood fell backward like a sinner being saved at a Revival meeting. Then the whole roof caved in, beam by beam. It all crumbled to the ground, scattering red sparks over the onlookers. This sent a final gasp rippling through the crowd until all became silent, so stunned was the town to see the Baptist Church, their rock of ages, evaporating before their eyes. Ada fell to her knees, whispering prayers. Fumes scorched Hetty's lungs.

"Why would anybody burn our church?" Ada moaned when they lifted her up. She commiserated with some of her fellow parishioners, all asking the same questions: Who? Why? When the light started leaking out of the sky, she asked Roy to take her home, terrified of being downtown after sunset.

"I want to see Humble's inferno before we leave," Hetty said.

"We'll go, too." Roy nodded with a firm grip on his wife's arm.

They elbowed their way toward the other vapors rising over the rooftops a few blocks away. As they turned onto Main Street, Hetty spotted a white Stetson bobbing above the heads of the crowd. They pushed their way out into the middle of the street and nearly collided with a huge black horse. Hetty saw a flash of pearls out of the corner of her eye, then a set of broad shoulders high above her, a dashing Latino face under the rakish brim of the hat. He was towing a group of prisoners in chains, the latest harvest for his trotline. His black stallion pawed at the dirt, trying to get through the mass of bodies shuffling away from the fire.

Without hesitation, Hetty stepped up to the horse, standing on tiptoe to address its rider. She felt like she was gazing at a deity in the sky.

"You were at the San Diego massacre, weren't you?"

"Yes, ma'am."

"You were the one who killed all the Mexicans—your own people."

"With all due respect, ma'am," he said, tipping his white Stetson at her, "the men I killed were outlaws who'd invaded our country illegally."

"Was El Víbora Seca killed?" Hetty still feared that the Dry Snake had been slaughtered along with the other outlaws at *Las Ánimas.*

He picked up the lisp in her voice and sniggered back in Spanish, *"La culebra muda su piel varias veces."*

A snake sheds its skin many times. She knew it. *He was alive!*

Then she heard Ada's voice quiver in her ear, "Ain't that last one a woman?"

Hetty's eyes followed the scraggly faces of the prisoners until she came to a head that was held higher than the others, a set of black eyes that weren't downcast but peered at her with the haughty slant of a lizard, dark gashes of anguish that welled unashamedly in the dusk. Hetty was shocked to recognize Brown Sugar. She was used to seeing the tall willowy body in sequins, commanding a pink spotlight, not staggering behind pimps and thieves in a faded housedress.

"It's that blues singer," Hetty murmured back. She was being egged on by another Ranger at the back of the line, a cold-eyed man cursing at the crowd. *This must be the infamous Poker Face.* "Mr. Pritchett," Hetty shouted at him. His head jerked around. "You've chained up a woman!"

"Out of the way," he snarled and spurred his horse.

As she was shunted forward, Brown Sugar's mournful gaze cut into Hetty's breast, tearing at her heart until she realized that the heavy lids were looking past her. At Garret. He and the blues singer were exchanging a glance that Hetty didn't like and wanted to interrupt. She inched her arm around her husband and drew him away, saying, "It'll be too dark to see the inferno soon."

But the singer cried after them: "Help me, Mac!"

Hetty stopped. "What's she talking about?"

"I don't know," Garret said, looking after her.

"Help me . . ." she pleaded, then was pulled into the crowd and disappeared.

Hetty felt uneasy as they moved forward through the milling pedestrians. "How come she knows your name, honey?"

"We were friends back in Houston."

"You were?"

"Don't you remember? Andy Boy's was one of our customers."

"Oh, that's right." Hetty wanted to dig deeper, to find out what he meant by "friends," but Nella had once warned her never to perform archeology on your husband's premarital amours. Once you start excavating, she said, you might not like what you find. *Leave it buried,* Hetty told herself.

They came up to the edge of the crater and looked across a pit the size of a small lake roiling with angry black mud. Nothing was left of the derrick, the doghouse, or the tank. Everything had sunk into the hellish mire. All Hetty could see in the fading light were the sulfurous vapors dancing about and the eerie yellow flames escaping as the earth opened a fissure now and then. She tried to peer down into the cracks, but all she could make out was blackness.

Ada, however, was looking skyward. "I see them!" she wailed.

"See what?" Roy asked.

"The faces. The faces in the fumes. Look—up there!" Hetty followed her finger and tried to make out features in the billowing smoke.

"It's a sign, Roy," Ada said. "Hell's coming right out of the earth and taking over our town." She turned away and shivered as darkness closed in on them. "Something's got to be done, y'all. The money ain't worth it."

Chapter 15

On a close night the next week, Hetty had trouble falling asleep. Garret was already drifting in the ebb and flow of steady breathing . . . in and out . . . in and out. But she couldn't seem to follow him, legs fighting against the damp sheets. Then she realized what was wrong: It was too quiet. The frogs weren't singing. She wondered why. Was mating season over for the summer? Had a plague of snails lured them into Ada's garden? She listened for the slightest peep or twang. Nothing stirred. Only an ominous hush, undercut by the distant chundering of a few oil rigs pumping out the last of their day's ration. She rolled over into the shadows and let them clothe her in unconsciousness.

Later, she dreamed of swaying in a hammock slung over the creek. Pierce slept above her, in the treetops, in a cradle made of spiderwebs. He kicked off his blanket. She looked up at his silhouette in front of a gigantic moon. He had frog legs instead of baby feet.

The bedroom window shuddered and woke Hetty up. Someone was rapping on it. She pulled herself to the ledge and peered out. There in the blue light of dawn, Roy Hillyer waited with his head bowed.

"Roy—what's wrong?"

"It's finally happening." He kept his face averted from her window.

Since their church had burned last week, the Hillyers had warned Hetty that some sort of doom was imminent in East Texas. Beetles would devour the pines, hogs would turn rabid, and first born would die. There were signs everywhere, they said: the diabolical faces appearing in the smoke above Humble's inferno, another church burned down in Kilgore (this time the Presbyterian), brawls in the streets almost every night. Angry locals were threatening to take the law into their own hands. And some did. So many more wells were dynamited that the Humble Oil Company had been forced to organize a private police force. In a newspaper article only yesterday, the governor had declared the whole area to be in a "state of insurrection."

"Did you hear some news?" Hetty asked.

"We got a call. Trains and trucks been slipping into town like thieves in the night."

Hetty gasped. "Troops?"

Roy nodded. "Ada says you better come up for breakfast and follow us into town."

"Oh my God—yes!" Hetty shook Garret awake and slipped into the first clothes she could find. She knocked on the shotgun house next door, knowing Pearl wouldn't want to miss anything. After some quick eggs and coffee up at the farmhouse, they found themselves following Roy's Model T on another emergency trip into Kilgore.

"Something's up all right," Pearl said, as Garret slid to a stop in traffic inching toward the new City Hall. They had to park blocks away and push through mobs of people. Hetty staggered, trying to keep up with the others and carry Pierce at the same time.

Police had cleared the intersection, but the sidewalks around City Hall were hives of buzzing rumors. Several trains arrived at the depot in the middle of the night, someone said. Somebody else swore they'd seen convoys of trucks heading this way from the base in Palacios. "Governor been swamped with telegrams," another man boasted. "I know—my sister works at Western Union." Everybody seemed to have an item of gossip or two to add to the buzz.

Only when a trumpet rang out from down the street did the bystanders grow quiet and pivot their heads in that direction.

Hetty sat on the curb and held Pierce in her lap, craning her neck to see past the legs of men standing on tiptoe. She heard the rumble of marching feet and felt a chill of fear. Then she saw them, six Texas Rangers on horseback flanking an officer in full uniform on the back of a great steed. Her heart turned to quicksand.

"It's the brigadier general!" someone shouted.

He led his horse with arrogant strides into the intersection while, behind him, a wall of olive drab drove forward as several companies of the National Guard marched into Kilgore. Exclamations and gasps shivered through the crowd like ill winds, followed by a thunderous *thump!* as hundreds of boots stopped all at once in front of City Hall. The brigadier general dismounted and was escorted by several officers onto the steps.

He said he had an announcement from Austin and began to read in a commanding voice. All murmurs grew quiet as his words rang through the streets: "Therefore I, Ross Sterling, Governor of the State of Texas and Commander-in-Chief of the military forces of this state, do hereby declare martial law in the counties of Upshur, Rusk, Gregg, and Smith—" A howl from the crowd was shushed by those wanting to hear more. "Effective at six a.m. on the seventeenth day of August, 1931, and I hereby invest Brigadier General Jacob Wolters with supreme command of the situation to shut down without delay each and every producing crude oil well in the region—"

Cheers clashed with hoots in the air. Hetty could hear Garret cursing loudly. Pierce began to cry. The crowd became more boisterous, making it harder to catch the rest of the proclamation, but one ominous phrase droned its way into Hetty's ear as the general finished reading: "And to further take such steps as he may deem necessary to enforce and uphold the majesty of the law."

A breathless pause hovered in the air, then people swarmed the streets, shouting, grabbing copies of the order being passed out by soldiers. Hetty held Pierce close and rocked back and forth, as much for herself as for her baby.

Garret came back clutching a leaflet: "They're calling us criminals," he bawled. "Look at this! '*Reckless, unlawful, and criminal handling of producing wells—*' " He read out more phrases in a disgusted voice, then crumpled the paper up and stomped on it several times in the mud.

Criminals. Hetty's mind chewed on the word. *So that's what we've become in the eyes of Texas.*

"What'd they expect us to do?" Roy Hillyer asked. "Go back to raising cotton?"

"It's a hell of a situation," Pearl said. "Sixteen-cent oil and two-cent cotton."

"I'm relieved in a way," Ada said. "Things were getting so bad."

"You think things are bad now?" Garret sneered. "This'll put thousands of men out of work."

"Here I go—rolling snake eyes again," Pearl said.

Roy scratched his head and sighed. "Going to be a tough winter, y'all, just when we thought we'd landed on easy street."

On the way home, Garret turned to Hetty and said, with a cold fury in his voice, "I'm not turning off the well till they make me." Shaking inside, she agreed that they should wait for the order to be delivered, sharing his hope that the army might somehow overlook the Ada Hillyer Number One, concealed as it was in a creek bed so far out of town. But that afternoon, two national guardsmen appeared at the farm with the proclamation, standing as witnesses while Garret tugged on the great wheel of the gate valve that would dam up the flow of crude.

When Smack came to collect the last of the oil that night, they walked down to the tank with him. Inching her way through the gloom, Hetty climbed up on the derrick. She hugged the Christmas tree, remembering how it used to hum under her hands. Now it felt cold and lifeless. Through the black net of pine needles, she gazed at the sky over Kilgore. Everything smoldered, dark and quiet. Over a thousand wells had been choked off in one day. She could find no flares flickering against the clouds, nothing around for miles to break the stillness of the night. Not even any frogs.

The frogs. She found them the next morning when she fled down to the creek to get away from Garret. He'd been up all night scouring the account books, filling the whole house with smoke from his incessant cigarettes, grumbling that he had to find a way to keep going. She couldn't take it anymore, her heart heavy enough as it was.

On a carpet of pine needles, she unpinned the dirty diaper off Pierce and released him into the cool water without even washing him. He paddled around for a few minutes, then sat back and began pointing at the sandy shore, babbling.

She found a leopard frog a few feet away, surprised when it didn't hop out of her grasp. She perched it in front of the baby. He crept forward and poked it. Nothing happened. It sat there stonily. He tried again. No hopping. He began to cry and picked it up by its limp leg. Hetty saw that the frog was dead.

She kicked off her shoes and waded into the creek. The next frog she spotted was floating on its back, yellow belly flashing in the mottled sunlight. Farther upstream, she found a flotilla of three frogs in the same position. Then she searched the banks on both sides. All up and down, under the willow trees, frogs had crawled halfway out of the water and surrendered, their big round eyes dumbfounded with death.

Pierce meanwhile was bawling, heartbroken that his toy wouldn't play hop along with him. "Oh, kiddo," Hetty cooed at him. "That's why they're not singing anymore." She hoisted his naked body into her arms. "Let's show Daddy."

She let Pierce drop the dead frog in the middle of the kitchen table. A puddle spread around it. "Look what your son found," Hetty told Garret.

"We're going under, and you're worried about a dead frog?"

"It's not just one. There's more, a lot more. Are we killing them?"

Garret followed her back to the creek, where he tasted the water. "It's salty," he said, glancing upstream. He fetched his knee-highs out of the doghouse and yanked them on, wading into the creek. "I'm going to investigate."

Hetty rocked Pierce until he stopped crying, then tried to distract him with the smooth pebbles she fished out of the sandy bottom.

Garret came back a half hour later, sloshing toward them, looking worried. "You won't believe what I found!"

"What now?" she called, stepping in barefoot.

He balanced himself in the current and pointed. "The creek bends to the south, through the Goss farm. I followed it onto their property and came upon pipelines dumping salt water right into the creek. Dead frogs all over the place. A massive die-off. I guess they had no place else to go."

"Salt water?" Hetty frowned for a moment, then remembered her mother's gift of fossils. "Of course—from the ancient sea. But who . . . ?"

"I snuck along the pipeline until I found myself in the middle of a big oil field, with crews drilling a string of new wells. Not far from here."

"I guess Wavie Goss got her better offer after all."

"She sure did. There was a whole fleet of trucks parked there from one of the Majors."

The creek suddenly felt cold on Hetty's feet. "Trucks?"

Garret nodded. "Guess what name was splashed all over them."

It felt like an electric shock stunned the water. Hetty fell back onto the bank as an emblem flashed through her mind: a golden crown capping the initial *S* like a rising sun. "Splendora!" She gasped, clutching her cheeks. "Oh my God—Lamar."

"You knew he was here."

"Yes, but"—Hetty caught her breath—"I never expected him to be this close. You'd think Chief would grab a prime spot farther east."

"Nope. He's in our offset location." Garret pointed through the trees. "Right over there."

Hetty looked into the distance, trying to spot some derricks. "But why?"

"Been thinking about that all the way back. Remember the map Smack showed us? The Woodbine slants westward, so a little south of here you'd be closer to the deep of the field. But that explains the salt deposits. Some of their wells have obviously watered out."

"And you saw them operating? Why aren't they shut down like everybody else?"

"Because it's Chief Rusk, honey. He probably paid off the sheriff, damn him."

"But he can't bribe the whole National Guard, can he?"

"I hope not. If your sister weren't married to him, I'd turn him in like that." Garret snapped his fingers.

"I wouldn't let that stop me. It's not fair."

"It sure as hell isn't." Garret kicked at the water, capsizing a dying frog as it floated by.

The next day, Hetty heard a horse whinny on the farm road. She went outside. Lone Wolf's Stetson, so white in the August noon it blinded her for a moment, flashed above his black horse. Another Ranger was with him, a tall gangly man. As he rode closer, Hetty recognized the glare fixed on her from under his swooping hat brim. It was Poker Face. She tried to meet those stony eyes without blinking but, after a couple of breaths, had to look down, the grief she'd choked back all week surging far too close to the surface.

"We've come to inspect the Ada Hillyer Number One," Lone Wolf said.

"I know," she said, keeping her voice steady. "I'll get my husband."

She scooped Pierce off the kitchen floor and followed them down to the derrick, where they dismounted to do a thorough inspection. They made sure the well wasn't humming, checked the pipes and gauges, and even made Garret remove the manhole cover so one of them could climb the ladder and peer into the huge tank.

Lone Wolf clunked around the site in his boots. Hetty couldn't help gazing at the pearls studding the six shooters slung on his slim hips.

"These look like fresh tire tracks," he said.

"They're from last week." Garret folded his arms. "When our trucker came to pick up the last load of crude."

Lone Wolf poked around in the dirt with the toe of his cowboy boot, his spurs clinking. "I'll let it pass this time," he said, stepping into his stirrups. "But don't let me catch your well running, Mr. MacBride. General Wolters has asked the Rangers to help enforce martial law. And we intend to do just that." He steadied himself on the automatic rifle riding in his saddle holster. "You've had your warning. Good afternoon." He turned his horse to leave.

"Just a minute, Sergeant," Hetty said. "I have something to show you." She could hear their saddles creaking as the riders walked their mounts down to the bankside, now crawling with flies and ants feasting on the carcasses. "The whole creek has become one big frog graveyard. Do you know why?"

"No, ma'am."

"Salt water from the wells on the Goss farm. What do you plan to do about it?"

The two men chuckled at each other. "I don't think Governor Sterling is too worried about salt water, ma'am." The horses shied away from the insects and turned back up the hill. Pierce squirmed in her arms so she set him in the sand at her feet.

"You know as well as I do, it's Splendora. Why haven't you shut them down?"

Lone Wolf stopped his horse but kept his back to her. "The governor didn't prohibit drilling, ma'am, just producing. You can drill all the new wells you want. You just can't run them."

"You call that fair? We don't have the money to drill another well. We can't even buy food. What are we supposed to eat?"

She could see Poke's hat tip back in amusement as he rode forward. "Try frog legs," he said with a snigger.

"It's not funny!" she shouted. "I bet you'd never arrest a member of the Rusk family—the frog killers! Have they paid you off, too?" The words flew out with an angry sob.

Poke halted his horse and turned it slowly back to face her. He trotted over until he was floating above her, circling her, scowling down. "Look here, ma'am, if anybody breaks the law, we'll take the proper action. We're Rangers. Splendora's done nothing illegal. If you folks don't have the money to keep going, you'll just have to shut down your operation and go home. We won't allow squatters."

Squatters! She couldn't believe her ears. Poke spurred his horse so close she had to jump out of the way. Both riders broke into a gallop on the road. Dust whirled behind them.

Hetty buried her face in her hands, so overcome with the aching inside that she hadn't even heard Pierce shrieking. She spun around to find him. He had toddled over to a dead frog, red ants swarming up his forearms, stinging. She carried him into the water as the swamp smell of rotting flesh hit her. *We've let everybody down, baby,* she thought as she washed the ants away. *Pick won't be able to send money home to Momma anymore. Pearl will be destitute again, and the Hillyers thrown back to scratching out a living on the farm. Worst of all, we won't be able to pay Granddad back his investment in the well.*

She lifted Pierce, dripping, and hugged him to her breast. His screams tore through the raw places in her heart.

Poke's voice echoed in the air. "You'll have to go home..." She'd been avoiding those words all week, but now they were out. He'd said them. And she had to face the truth.

Garret drifted over and moped at her. "He's wrong."

"No, Garret, he's right," she said, letting her heartache come to its brim. "We have to go home." She started sobbing along with her baby, the salt from both their eyes dripping without check into that from the ancient sea.

Hetty enlisted Pearl to help her pack. They began the next night, waiting until the sun had set and the air had begun to cool. Pearl shuffled over in her faded mules, bearing in her hands the offering of an apple pie. When she placed it in the middle of the table, Hetty caught the smoky scent of fresh-ground nutmeg.

"I thought we could use some sugar, so here's a pie I done this morning," she said. "You know me, I always bake when the sun goes up." She patted her apron pocket. "And here's a letter from Odell."

"How is he?" Hetty lifted a crate onto the counter next to the most recent editions of the *Kilgore News Herald*.

"Nothing but bad to tell. He sent a message to Garret."

"Really? You can read it to him if he ever emerges out of the doghouse."

"Hitting the fruit jars again?"

"I hope to tell you! Spending what little money we have on corn whiskey. Why do men do these things?"

"They'll run you crazy. Where's the baby?"

"Asleep, thank God. Maybe we can get some work done. Why don't you cut the pie?"

Hetty unfolded big sheets of newspaper that rustled when she wrapped plates in them. She tried to ignore the headline: Wolters Tells Guards to Shoot at the Waistline. As she worked, she skimmed the smaller articles reporting the growing unemployment all through East Texas. She worried about Pick—he'd left them that afternoon to hunt for work up in Longview.

A truck drove by outside. A few minutes later, she heard a loud rap at the door. Pearl went to open it.

"Now look here, y'all—" Mr. Smackover planted himself in the middle of the room with his hands on his broad hips. "It ain't time to put the chairs in the wagon yet. Mac said you was packing up. I come to tell you my teapot's back in business."

"Sit down and have some pie," Pearl said, scooping wedges onto dessert plates.

"Don't mind if I do, Pearl." Smack sat ponderously at the table.

"But wasn't he shut down?" Hetty asked, continuing to pack while the others ate.

"He was. Everybody was," Smack said, chewing. "But there's always a way to sneak around the law. The guy was living in a shotgun next door, so he joins the two with a makeshift porch and declares it his residence. Strings up a barbed wire fence, so nobody can enter but us truckers. And he's getting away with it. Put out a call for petrol. I say we start running hot oil again. It'll keep us alive during martial law."

"I'd love to, Smack, but how?" Hetty said. "We're surrounded by an army."

"Pay them no mind. I still say you got a right to the oil out of your own damn well."

"That's what Odell says in his letter." Pearl slid the pages out of her apron pocket. "He says we need to capture our oil while we can."

"He's right. Boss Ross is in cahoots with the big boys. Why—Governor Sterling was one of the original partners in Humble Oil."

"I didn't know that," Hetty said.

"Throws a different light on it, don't it? They're trying to run us little guys out of business, that's all that's happening here. And you're cooperating!"

"Odell says, if y'all don't capture your oil, somebody else will."

"What are you talking about?" Hetty asked.

"It's all in the letter here. I'm trying to tell you about it."

"Read it to us, Pearl," Hetty said.

"Well, not the first part, that's personal," she said, swishing the pages through her spindly hands. "But here—" She began reading. "My best wishes to both Garret and Hetty. I heard about the governor ordering troops to your parts. It's been all over the papers they allow us to read here. Do not be disheartened, my friends, this too will pass. In the meantime, don't give up. Don't let them wipe out the lone wildcatter like yourself, Garret. You can be sure that's exactly what the big oil companies are hoping to do—just like they killed the cattle business by closing down the open range. Let's keep Texas free! There's something you should know about the production of oil. It's governed by an old English common law called the Rule of Capture."

Pearl looked up at them. "He's got it capitalized," she said, "so it must be kind of important."

She read on. "If I kill a deer on someone else's property, it's poaching. But if the deer strays onto my property, he's fair game. Now, why is it important to know this? Because oil also migrates. It moves wherever the pressure takes it. From what I've read of the Woodbine, it flows from west to east. The Ada Hillyer Number One is located, I think you said, at the western edge of the field. So the more the Majors pump out of the reservoir, the more likely oil is to flow away from your location. The advantage the Majors have is that they can continue to drill new wells, and you can be sure, as soon as martial law is lifted, they're going to bleed all the oil right out from under you. So I—"

"Wait," Hetty said, lifting a white china plate, "read that last part again."

"As soon as martial law is lifted they're going to bleed—"

The plate Hetty was holding fell with a crack. "Oh my God!" Her heart skipped a beat. She had to grasp the edge of the counter as a wave of light-headedness swept into her brain.

"What's wrong?" asked Pearl, poised to read more.

"I just realized what's happening here." She moved her hands away from shards of china and held on.

"Where?" Smack looked around the room.

"Right under our feet. That's what Splendora is planning to do—bleed us to death." Hetty turned to face their puzzled expressions. "Don't you see? If Odell's right, that means no more oil is going to flow into this section. It's all going that way." She pointed toward Kilgore. "Damn him!"

"Who? Odell?" Pearl asked.

"No! Lamar!" she said, going white-hot inside. "I knew something was up. He's been too quiet." Hetty pulled a chair out and sat down until her head stopped swimming. The others just stared at her. "All this time I thought we were safe. Wasn't I the little fool?"

"Safe . . . ?" Pearl asked.

"I thought Lamar couldn't do anything to harm the Ada Hillyer, but the bastard found a way." She remembered the way he had looked at her when they all dined together at the Cupola Club. Like he had a secret he was bursting to tell her. Now she knew what his secret was. The trickster had struck again. He had turned the oil field into a giant playing field, moving derricks around like chessmen with one purpose in mind: to checkmate the queen. And, as usual, he was cheating. The thought made Hetty boil.

Smack pushed his plate away. "What all can he do?"

"Plenty! Why do you think he set up shop southeast of us? Don't you think he knows about the Rule of Capture? Of course he does. He's got the best geologists and lawyers working for him. He knows exactly what he's doing."

"Y'all really think he'd make a move on account of—"

"You obviously don't know the Rusk family like I do. Help me put these dishes back in the cupboard, Pearl. I'm not about to let Lamar rob us of our oil. We're turning our well back on." She tossed pieces of jagged porcelain into the trash.

"And how do you plan to do that?" Pearl asked.

"I'll do it myself if I have to. As Smack says, there's always a way to sneak around the law. I'll open the pipes at dusk and turn them off at dawn. Nobody's coming out here in the dead of night to check the well."

"That's the spirit." Smack clapped his hands. "Just remember, I don't pump. Y'all have to get the motor going."

"Just leave it to me, Smack. We've got to suck all the oil we can out of that sand before Splendora gets their greedy clutches on it. What do you say, Pearl? Are you with me?"

"Tell me what to do, hon. You know best."

"Send Odell a big kiss for me. We're going to capture our oil, by God! And I dare Lone Wolf to gun down a couple of women with those pearly pistols of his."

A lurid crimson light woke Hetty the next morning. Tugging on the same dress she'd worn for two days, she went and knocked on the door of the other shotgun house. While she waited for a response, she looked through the pines. A bloodred sun festered through a gash in the clouds. *You haven't beaten me yet, Lamar. Just wait.*

Pearl answered in her nightgown.

"Did I wake you?"

"Oh, you know me, already blowin' and goin'."

"Would you mind watching Pierce and making us some coffee? I think Garret's going to need it."

"Glad to, hon." She looked past Hetty. "Oh my! Red sky in the morning, shepherd's warning."

Hetty walked into the plush of pine needles on the ground, soggy from a heavy dew. The red light of the wounded sun bled into the world. The whole sky was inflamed with it. She crossed the bridge over the creek, still rife with decaying frogs. Peering into the doghouse, she spotted Garret in the purple shadows of the morning. He had fallen into a stupor on a piece of canvas stretched over heaps of rope. Empty fruit jars littered the floor. Hetty bit her lip. It wasn't that long ago she'd dreamed of sleeping beside him on a bed spread with cool Egyptian cottons. If Lamar were here now, standing by her side, he'd be happy to see his rival so fallen—curled like a child on coils of rope in this rough-hewn wooden shed. Lamar would shoot her one of his lopsided grins and offer her his arm in triumph. *You bastard. Get off our lease!* she would snarl, the eyes of dead frogs watching him with hatred as he crossed the bridge.

Hetty knelt and stroked Garret's cheek, craggy with a two-day's growth of beard. He stirred. "You don't have to sleep out here, honey." As he stretched, the odor of rancid sweat rose in the air. "Come have some coffee."

She pulled him up by the hand and escorted him across the bridge. As they stepped onto the floor of pine needles, she steered him toward the tank at the bottom of the hill. "Show me how to start this pump," she said.

"Why?" He yawned.

"Just do it, please."

"You crank it like the old Model Ts." He stooped to pull out the choke, then twirled the handle like a lasso through his hands until the machine coughed into life. He inched the choke back in. It looked easy. "Why do you want to start the pump? There's no oil in the tank."

"There will be. Come have some coffee and I'll explain."

While Garret sipped at a steaming cup and lit his first Camel of the day, Hetty sat across the table and told him about her discovery. Pearl gave him Odell's letter to read, then went to fetch Pierce, who'd started crying in his cradle. After Garret had finished the letter, Hetty said, "That's why I've changed my mind about leaving. Lamar is robbing us blind."

Garret sat there glowering, staring vacantly into space as if old ghosts were rising in front of his eyes. "I've changed my mind, too. Now I think we *should* go home."

"And let Lamar win? I thought you said you'd never give up."

"No—I said only one thing would ever make me give up, but it could never happen here."

"Does that mean it *has* happened?"

"It's about to." He got a haunted look in his eyes. "We need to leave here before we get swallowed by an anaconda."

"What are you talking about, Mac?"

"The best thing we can do now is sell the well against future profits. It'll produce again someday."

Hetty just stared at him.

"I'll take the log into Tulsa's and see if I can find us a buyer. We still owe five thousand to the consortium."

"I don't care. I'm not caving in to my sister and Lamar."

"I thought I was in charge of the well here?"

"But you're not taking charge. You're lying out in the doghouse getting drunk."

"Stay out of this, Hetty." He walked out with his cup of coffee and slammed the door behind him. That was Pearl's cue to appear with the baby. Hetty hefted Pierce on one arm and said, "I don't understand your father. Don't you dare grow up to be like him."

"That's an Irishman for you," Pearl said. "They're friendly, but they never tell you what's really going on inside."

Even though Garret had warned Hetty to stay out of the business dealings, she just couldn't. She watched through the front window all day to see if he'd drive into town as he'd threatened. But neither vehicle budged. Nothing happened. Garret took his dinner down to the doghouse and didn't return. After putting the baby to sleep, Hetty decided to take matters into her own hands. She imagined tiny gurgles rising from underground as their oil slowly drained away. After opening the valve on the well, she called Smack and arranged for him to make a pickup early the next morning. She had such bad dreams that when the alarm went off at four a.m., she was lying there awake waiting for it, castigating Lamar in her mind. She made her way down to the tank with the help of an electric lantern. She tried a few times to get the pump going but just couldn't seem to crank the cold motor into life. She gave up and went to the derrick, turning the beam of the lantern into the doghouse. Garret was asleep with a grease-stained wool blanket pulled over him. She flashed the light at his eyes.

"Mac, get up. You've got to start the pump for me. I can't do it."

Garret threw off the blanket and shielded his eyes. "Will you let me figure this out?"

"What? Give up and go home? Let Lamar beat you?"

"He already has."

"What kind of a man are you?"

"Go to hell."

"I mean it, Mac. I'm really disappointed in you. I didn't know you were a quitter."

"That's not fair!" He sat up, his eyes red and swollen in the lantern light.

"Why not? I notice Lamar didn't give up. He found a way to steal our oil. He found a way to win. And if we let him, he'll gloat about this for the rest of his life."

"So let's sell it and deny him the satisfaction."

"No! That oil is ours. I don't want anybody else to have it."

Garret slid off the canvas and stood to face her. "You don't want Lamar to have it, you mean."

Hetty faced him down. "No, as a matter of fact, I don't."

They stared at each other in silence, their faces ghostly in the quivering beam.

Finally, Mac looked away and asked, "What happened that night?"

"What night?"

"The night you went out to dinner with him?"

"What are you talking about?"

"I think you know what I'm talking about. What happened?"

"I conceived Pierce, that's what happened. You should remember—you're the father."

"Nothing else happened?"

"No."

"Then why is Lamar so interested in our little oil well?"

Hetty tried not to look guilty. She glanced away, then met her husband's bloodshot eyes and held his fretful gaze without blinking. "I think he's getting his revenge on me, Mac."

"So nothing *did* happen that night?"

"No, nothing happened. That's why he's angry."

"But he did try to get into your pants?"

"Well, of course. But he didn't succeed."

Garret drew back his hand as if to slap her. Hetty flinched, but he stopped himself in time. "I knew it. Why would you go out to dinner with him in the first place?"

"He offered to help us . . . I was hoping . . ."

Garret's uplifted hand twisted into a fist. "What about me? Didn't you wonder how I'd feel about it?"

"Is that still eating away at you? After all this time? We've had a baby together. We've struck oil together. I'm with *you,* Mac."

"But you're not with me. You're fighting with him."

"I was hoping you'd fight *with* me."

"That's not the wise thing to do, Hetty." Garret brushed past her and stepped out of the doghouse. She aimed the beam into the darkness, catching his profile cocked back at her. "I can't stay here any longer. I'm leaving. If you love me, you'll come with me." He extended his hand.

She watched his fingers opening to her, golden in the light streaming out of her electric beacon. She felt split in half, one hand longing to reach out to his, the other holding the lantern so tight her knuckles were aching. She just couldn't let go. "You're asking me to give up everything. I won't do that. I'm staying."

"You made your choice then."

He started to walk away, but she spotlighted him. "Mac, if you're really leaving me, let me have one last going-away gift. You owe me that much."

"What?"

"Start the pump, dammit."

Garret packed his clothes and was gone by dawn. He left her the Wichita truck and twenty-five dollars in cash. Hetty tried to find out where he was going, but he wouldn't tell her. He left without saying good-bye.

Later, she set the alarm for four a.m. even though she probably wouldn't need it. She lay there in the dark and quiet, her mind ablaze. She thought of Humble's inferno, the well that someone had dynamited during the war over proration. Everything had caved into the fiery crater, even the roughnecks. She wondered what they saw on their journey down to hell. Yes, it was true what people said about war—it *is* hell but not because of what you have to do. It's the way it makes you feel, that's the hellish part. You fall into the crater. Churning with deep dark heat and hate. Hetty remembered reading in the safety manual at the Warwick Hotel that fire isn't as bright as people imagine. Fire is pitch-black. Which is why it's so hard to escape.

When the alarm woke her, Hetty was tempted to turn on the carbide lamp Garret kept on the derrick floor, but she was afraid its searing light could be seen from a distance. Instead, she flicked on the electric torch just long enough to locate the pump, covering it with her fingers and letting one thin ray of light through. It x-rayed her hand, turning her skin bloodred.

She knelt and grasped the metal crank, spinning it as hard as she could. She knew it was up to her now. The cold motor refused to sputter into life. In the distance, she heard a rumble and saw two yellow lights weaving down the hill toward her. Smack cut his motor and let his truck roll slowly toward her, gravity bringing it to a rest nearby. He killed his parking lights and waited in the cab.

Hetty tried over and over to rev up the pump, her arm muscles burning with the effort. But she just couldn't get it churning fast enough. She smelled gasoline. Perhaps she had pulled the throttle out too far and now it was flooded. She rested for a minute, then she went at it again.

In between attempts, she heard the scrunch of the truck door opening and looked up. The sky was beginning to turn a dark blue.

"I've got to go!" she heard Smack wheeze.

"I know! Just give me a chance," she spit back.

She tried several more times until her arm cramped. She rocked back and shook it out, tears of frustration misting her eyes.

She heard another snuffle. "I don't dare wait!" Then a sound following it from the other direction, unmistakable: pine needles being crushed underfoot. Not like twigs snapping. A softer sound. Almost a whish. The needles whispering against each other. It came again.

"Shhh!" Hetty looked around but couldn't see anything. She

heard Smack slide back into the truck and pull the door almost shut with a groan.

She held on to the handle of the crank and didn't move a muscle. Only her eyes roamed through the murk. She couldn't see anything moving, even though the swishing sounds approached very close, then stopped. Hetty began to tremble inside, realizing what a spot she'd put herself into. Terror sent absurd notions spiraling through her mind. *I've been caught red-handed,* she thought, laughing darkly at the literalness of her fingers turning the color of blood over the flashlight. *I'm sitting here with a tank half filled with oil, my hand on a crank, and a trucker waiting for me to turn on the pump. What more evidence do they need?* She shuddered. *Will I be able to take Pierce to prison with me?*

Her hand holding the crank disappeared as something warm and dark covered it.

"Why are you milking my well without me, Hetty?"

Her lungs sucked in air again. "Pick! You scared me to death."

"Smells like that motor flooded."

"I was afraid of that." She slipped her hand out from under his, straining to make out his dusky face as he knelt beside her. "I thought you were off looking for work?"

"Ain't none. Anywhere. I been up to Longview and over to Tyler. What you doing here in the middle of the night?"

She told what she'd learned about Lamar and the Rule of Capture. "That's why I need to get this pump going. Smack's waiting."

"How come Mac ain't doing this?"

"He left this morning. He quit on me, Pick."

"That ain't like Garret. What's going on?"

"I'm not sure. All I know is, I can't let my sister and brother-in-law steal my oil right from under my feet. Would you help me, Pick?"

"I could sure use the work."

"You got to pump oil for me again. I'm desperate. They won't catch you. You're invisible at night."

"Not anymore. I been seen."

"By who?"

"I rode a freight car back here from Tyler and was heading down Commerce Street. I was trying to stay in the shadows, but a Ranger spotted me. Gets down off his horse, wants to see my hands."

"Your hands?"

"That's how they tell if you're a worker or a pimp. He asks me where I been working. I say on the Ada Hillyer. He asks me what I'm doing in town. I say just looking for work. He say, 'There ain't no work for white men much less niggers, so you better get out of town, boy.' I say, 'Yes, sir.' He say, 'I mean it. I don't want to see your coon face again.' He had the coldest eyes I've ever seen on a man."

"Uh-oh. That was Poke Pritchett."

"That's when I walk out here. I got to hide."

"I'm sorry he called you those names."

"You can't protect me from that, Hetty."

"Maybe not, but I don't want you ending up on Lone Wolf's trotline."

"It don't worry me."

"It's not much fun, from what I hear."

"That's all right," he said, standing up. "My mother always taught me, son, your home's in glory with God, and life on this earth is filled with trials and tests. Just bear them patiently and you're sure to be called home someday. She used to sing, *'We'll run and never tire, we'll run and never tire, Jesus set poor sinners free.'* " Pick's hands came together in prayer as he sang in his fervent baritone.

Hetty stood. "We're all being tested right now, that's for sure."

"Lone Wolf ain't no test for me. It's the other man I'm scared of."

Hetty heard the truck door grinding on its hinges again and knew that Smack was going to leave if they didn't start pumping some oil soon. She covered Pick's hands in hers, shielding them and at the same time feeling their strength.

"You need to do this for Addie, Ollie, Minnie, and Lewis. How else are you going to keep them alive?"

"I reckon there be no other way."

"All right, my man, get this goddamn pump going for me. And pray to Jesus your soul to keep."

* * *

After a week, Smack rewarded Hetty with fifty dollars in cash. At six cents a barrel, that was all she could expect to make. Enough to stay alive, buy some groceries, and have a few dollars to spread around to all the people she owed. It would keep her operating during martial law, but Hetty wondered if it was worth the toll it was taking on her nerves. She was edgy during the day and woke up at four every morning listening for the sputter of the pump. She lay there in complete darkness, sprawled across the bed, still smelling Stacomb on Garret's pillow. She wanted to choke the pillow till her nails split and beat it on the headboard until all the feathers ruptured like pestilence across the floor. *How could you leave me!* A ragged pulse beat in her ears; her guts went hot. She couldn't fall asleep again until Smack's truck had rumbled back up the hill and off into the dawn. She fantasized the sound of Pick's screams as he was dragged off by the Rangers in chains. But none ever broke the silence. He did his job flawlessly, in secret, in quiet, in utter darkness.

With Smack's fifty dollars in hand, she paid Pick and took Pearl and the baby into town. Hetty didn't want anybody to know she had money to spend, so sent Pearl into the Great Atlantic & Pacific Tea Company and then into Brown's Drugs for hamburgers and milk shakes. She lifted the *rebozo* over her head to hood her face and tossed the long fringes off her shoulders.

"I never thought a chocolate shake would be my idea of a good time," she told Pearl, relishing the savor of the meat after endless suppers of purple peas and cabbage.

"One of Odell's favorites," Pearl said.

"How is he? Any more letters?"

"Not this week."

"Sure wish he were here. 'Specially now that Garret left."

"Look at us," Pearl said, taking the last bite of her hamburger and shaking her head. "Both without our menfolk."

"Amen," said Hetty.

Pierce fell asleep as they drove home through the dusk. Pearl unpacked the groceries while Hetty put the baby to bed. She held him in the crook of one arm while she pulled back the clean white sheets and the light cotton blanket he slept under at night. She laid him down in the darkness, cradling his head on the pillow. He burbled as she drew the sheet up and tucked it under his arms. Then his breathing fell into the gentle tides of infant slumber. She cloistered herself at his cradle for a moment, holding his tiny hand, envying the deep peace of his untroubled sleep.

She was lifting the cotton blanket when her fingers froze in midair. A gunshot split the night in two. Three more followed it in quick succession. The air ripped apart to let the sounds through, then closed back into an unnatural quiet. She drew her hand out of the crib and stepped into the kitchen. Pearl's eyes glittered at her in the dim lamplight, knowing what Hetty knew—Pick would have slipped down to the derrick as darkness had fallen, opening the valve on the well so the tank could fill in the night. They both ran for the door.

A ghostly halo of light hung over Caney Creek.

"Oh no!" Hetty gasped, pulling the shawl closer about her. Pearl took her hand and led her slowly down the hill.

The whole derrick was luminous from the acetylene flame of the carbide lamp someone had lit. As it sat in one corner, its powerful white light flashed off the reflector plate and blazed through the twilight. Poke Pritchett stood in front of the lamp, which made the shadow he cast colossal as it stretched over the pine planks and fell down into the creek bed. He had a rifle crooked in his hands. Hetty could smell gunpowder. She made out other figures holding rifles in the shadows: Lone Wolf Gonzaullas, a few state troopers. She heard a horse whinny behind them. They had come over the Caddo mound, she could see, slipping soundlessly through the pine forests behind it. They were all looking at something, but the carbide was so blinding, she couldn't see much. She shielded her eyes, and that was when she saw it: A body was lying at the foot of the Christmas tree. The one they'd just shot. She didn't dare give it a name.

Pearl tried to steer her away, but she broke free and shinned her way up onto the derrick floor. The pine planks moaned as she walked on them, the light etching every detail into startling clarity. Pick lay crumpled like a dirty rag doll ahead of her. One arm was flung toward her, his head turned away. Everything was so black and white in the intense light of the acetylene gas, but Pick was blackest of all as he lay there unmoving in the shadow cast by the Christmas tree. It wasn't until she stood right over him that she saw the other color: red. She could make out four gunshot wounds splattered across his torso and saw in her mind the headline she'd read in the paper last week: Wolters Tells Guards to Shoot at the Waistline.

Hetty stood there unable to move, unable to draw her eyes away. The blood soaked into his clothes and trickled through the cracks in the pine boards. She wanted to take her shawl off and stanch the wounds before it was too late, but she couldn't move. What she saw was turning her to stone. Feeling faint, Hetty realized she hadn't been breathing. She gasped for some air, but choked on the smell of gun smoke.

Reaching toward her friend, she tried to shout, "Help him!" but her voice only came out as a scratch. Lone Wolf wasn't listening anyway. She could hear him behind her talking to Pearl, explaining how this man was found illegally operating the well after being told to leave town. "But he works for us," she said, again in a scratch that nobody heard.

Hetty had to do something. She knelt beside Pick and unwound the wedding shawl from her shoulders. She hefted his body up and worked the shawl underneath him, then drew it as tight as she could across his chest to stop the flow of blood. Red splotches like poppies fanned out across the white silk. She hoped she wasn't too late. She didn't like the way his head lolled back so lifelessly. If only he'd wake up and talk to her. She tried to hold his body upright while she wound the shawl around and around him, but he was so heavy. He kept sagging back.

Somehow, by lifting first his shoulders, then his hips, she got the last wound covered and tied the *rebozo* in a knot. She kept tying and retying the knot to get it tight enough to stop the flow of blood and save his life.

A shadow fell over her hands. She looked up and saw the boots with the silver spurs. "He's dead, ma'am," Lone Wolf told her in a gentle voice.

She crawled around and cradled his head in her lap, stroking his cheeks that she always thought were like the smoothest onyx. "Are you sure?"

"Yes, ma'am."

Poke added in an icy tone: "We can't let a goddamn nigger break the law and get away with it."

Touching Pick's face all over, Hetty brushed his still warm lips and noticed that his eyes were open a crack. She closed them for the last time, holding his head to her breast and rocking him, back and forth, back and forth, in her arms.

The sheriff came in a truck to take the body. "Do you want your shawl back?" he asked her.

"No, I want him buried in it," she said. Two troopers lifted the body out of her arms and rolled it off the derrick. She heard it hit the ground with a lifeless thud. They heaved it into the back of the truck like a sack of feed.

When everyone had left, Pearl helped her down off the derrick and turned to douse the carbide lamp. "Wait," Hetty said, walking along the sandy banks. She took off her bloody pearls and tossed them into the willow trees, where they snagged on a high branch and hung there glistening like a string of stars, like seeds. As she watched them sway, she remembered the final words from Pick's favorite hymn, the one where the angels always hung their harps in a willow grove:

Go down angels to the flood
Blow out the sun, turn the moon into blood.
Come back angels, bolt the door
The time that's been will be no more.

The thick heat of deep August burned on, but Hetty didn't feel it. She didn't feel anything. She lay under a damp sheet on the chaise lounge and forgot to flick on the circulating fan even in the steamiest part of the day. While Pierce played at her feet, she pulled the sheet over her head and tried to sleep. When it was too hot to sleep, she gazed into the white blankness inside the sheet and counted the trickles of sweat running down her face. If Pearl brought her food, she mashed it up and fed it to Pierce. She lived on iced tea and Lucky Strikes. She wouldn't talk to anyone. People came and went, hovering over the chaise, but they were like shadows catching at the corner of her eye.

One evening, Ada's weathered face appeared in Hetty's line of vision, above a steaming plate. "I brought you something special from my garden. It'll strengthen your blood."

Hetty looked down. The plate was piled with gashes of beets, oozing with red juice and butter. She hardly made it to the bathroom in time.

It was the red she was trying to forget. Didn't they know that? Red running through black. That's why she slept so much. She had almost succeeded in numbing her mind into amnesia when Pearl made the mistake of showing her the front page of the *Kilgore News Herald* dated August 31, 1931. She held it up right in front of Hetty's eyes so she had to look at it. There was Henry Picktown Waller, laid out on a platform somewhere, her white wedding shawl still wrapped around him, stained with its poppies of blood. The huge headline read: **A WARNING TO ALL**. That set Hetty back for days. She would just lie there on the chaise and stare off into space, lighting cigarettes and forgetting to smoke them. She had no idea how much time passed in this manner.

Then one night, cool air wafted through the window. An early September norther. It soothed her feverish brow, and Hetty felt herself falling into an endless, dreamless sleep where she realized that oblivion was the deepest blessing of them all. Eons passed, and then she saw light, pure white light with blue pine shadows flickering through it as she opened her eyes and gazed at the wall above the chaise. Someone had thrown a blanket over the sheet in the night. The rich fumes of strong coffee teased her nose. She felt hungry. A rocking chair rolled to and fro on the wooden floor, and the words of a lullaby floated on the morning air:

Golden slumbers kiss your eyes,
Smiles awake you when you rise,
Sleep, pretty baby,
Do not cry,
And I will sing a lullaby.

Hetty stirred. Her head emerged from the thicket of bedclothes to see Pearl rocking Pierce, still wrapped in his blanket and half asleep. She staggered off the chaise, yearning for her baby so much she almost snatched him away. Pearl handed Pierce over and vacated the rocker. Hetty took her place, falling into the same swaying rhythm but unable to sing. She looked at her baby's face and thought about the words of the lullaby. Hetty glanced at her friend, sitting in a smolder at the kitchen table. She looked more spectral than ever from the ordeal they'd been through. "I don't know what I'd do without you. You've been keeping watch over both of us."

"Somebody had to." Hetty could hear the censure in Pearl's voice.

"Don't judge me too harshly, Pearl."

"I leave that to God, hon." She threw Hetty a wan smile.

"Right now, it's all I can do not to duck back under the sheet."

"I know."

"I could feel that newspaper sitting there on the table. That's why I couldn't get up. I heard the pages crinkling as you and Ada read about Pick when you thought I was asleep. You tried to cry quietly so I wouldn't hear, but I did. I knew what waited for me out here, and I couldn't face it."

Pearl lit a cigarette and took little quick puffs off it. "I just can't believe it come to this."

"You think it's my fault, don't you?"

Pearl didn't say anything, just lifted her cigarette to her mouth.

"Well, it *is* my fault."

"Hon, you can't—"

"Oh, yes, I can. I was the one who sent him out there in the night to break the law. That's what you're thinking. And I can't blame you for reproaching me. How could I do such a thing? I was so blinded by my—my rage at having my oil stolen. I should have made him go home. Garret was right—we should have all left days ago. He reached his hand out to me, and I couldn't take it. Now I don't even know where my husband is." Hetty's buried grief suddenly surfaced, trembling in the room.

"I know where mine is. In prison."

"I'm sorry, Pearl." Hetty felt tears falling down her cheeks.

"Don't you start in. You'll get me to crying, too. Heartache's catching, don't you know that?" She rose and showed Hetty some packages of Diamond Dyes that had been sitting on the kitchen table, along with a tin of Polyshine. "I've been cleaning out Pick's room. I found these. They're black."

Hetty gazed at the objects quivering in her friend's thin fingers. The shock started wringing all the blackness out of her mind as she understood what Pick had been doing with the dye, how his onyx skin disappeared into the shadows so she sent him out there night after night to be invisible and save her oil. He'd dipped his clothes in Diamond Dyes for her sake. "He was trying to make himself disappear," she said.

Hetty and Pearl stood looking at the Wichita flatbed truck, its orange paint splattered with splinters of mud. "Think you can drive this bus?" Pearl asked.

"I sure hope so."

Hetty opened the demi-door and pulled herself up. Pearl came in the other side, Pierce wiggling in her embrace. Hetty had to stretch her leg to reach the clutch. She pushed it in, turned the key, and hit the starter button. The cold motor churned.

"Pick always pulled out the choke first," Pearl said, pointing.

"Damn. Choking is my downfall," Hetty said. She pulled it out halfway and tried the starter again. After a few attempts, she got the motor racing and ground the gears into first. Her white sandals were so delicate, she had to pump a little harder on the heavy accelerator as they headed south. She and Pearl had spent the last two days packing up the shotgun houses and burning all the soiled work clothes. "Oil leaves such stains," she'd said.

"Don't burn the suit Pick wore to church," Pearl had said. "I think we should keep that."

As they stood over the smoldering ashes, Hetty had gotten a call on Ada's party line from Nella. Her mother's tinny telephone voice had delivered bad news: Both the Warwick Hotel and the Esperson Building were being sold at auction. She and Kirby had no choice but to move out. They wanted back the money they had sunk into the consortium. "I'm not living in a bankrupt hotel," she had announced. Hetty realized that she had to sell the well, her last remaining asset. The Hillyers were in agreement with this, as long as they still called it the Ada Hillyer. That's why she and Pearl were now chugging down a narrow dirt road that twisted through acres of fallow farmland turning brown in the August heat. They passed the Goss house and barns, then rolled into pastures full of the roar and clatter of wells being drilled. She pulled up to the field house, a rough clapboard shed with a tin roof and the Splendora logo on the door.

"Wait here," she told Pearl.

The grizzled crew working a derrick nearby looked surprised when she stepped out of the muddy truck carrying an oil well log. She had spent an hour grooming herself, and she knew her dark eyes looked especially radiant in the shade of her large white brimmed straw hat. All the men kept their stares clamped on her as she strolled their way, her blue chiffon dress fluttering in the breeze. Someone whistled. Only one man was wearing a white shirt and tie to show that he was boss. He turned to see what all the men were gawking at and broke out into a big grin when he spotted her.

"You finally found me!" Lamar shouted.

"It wasn't easy," Hetty said, stepping up to him daintily. "What are you hiding?"

"Treasure, of course."

"That's what I came to talk to you about. Could we go somewhere private?"

He gestured. "Step into my elegant office, ma'am."

A circulating fan tried to stir up the sultry air in the field house, making the maps pinned to the wall flap now and then. Red flags punctured the paper where wells had been drilled. Hetty did a quick count while Lamar threw open the roll-top desk. Almost two dozen. *He's not wasting any time.*

Lamar's wooden office chair squeaked when he sat down. Hetty lounged back on an old, stained leather couch, pulling her dress up an inch or two and crossing her legs. She lit a Lucky and blew the smoke in his direction. "I've decided to sell the Ada Hillyer Number One. I'm willing to let it go for five thousand. You'll make that back in a few weeks once they lift martial law."

Lamar squinted his eyes. "Another well? Maybe. We've got plenty of our own, as you can see."

"Afraid of becoming too rich?"

Lamar laughed. "One of my deepest fears, my dear." He leaned back in his chair and put his hands behind his head. "I'd have to think about it."

"Oh, don't be such a flat tire, Lam. Do it for old times' sake. I need some quick cash."

"All right. But I'd want to buy it from Charmaine, not from Mrs. Garret MacBride."

"What does that mean?"

"You'll have to sweeten the deal."

"Oh?" Hetty held his gaze while she drew a long velvety drag off the Lucky.

"Come to my hotel room tonight."

I can't believe he just said that. "No way, Buster. This is strictly business."

"You and I both know that's not true."

"You really think I'm that easy?"

"I think you're that desperate. Besides," he said, rolling his chair over to her. "What I'm talking about here is not a one-night stand." He ran his hand over her curving calf, smooth and fragrant with lotion. She had no stockings on.

"Oh? I get to stay for two?"

"You get to stay forever, Hetty."

She dropped her cigarette on the crude wooden floor and squashed it with her sandal. "What are you talking about, Lam?"

He edged his chair in until his knees were prying hers open. *Should I pull away or see where this is leading?* "I'm not going to be coy anymore. When I saw you walk up today, Het, after working all morning with those greasy weevils, I thought—damn! That's the woman I've always wanted. You just looked so cool and pretty under that big hat. Like you never sweat or something. I said to myself, she's too good for that Irishman she married. She ought to be my wife."

"But you've got one. The last time I checked, bigamy was still against the law in Texas."

"I love Char. She and I are one of a kind. But she's had two more miscarriages. I don't know if you've heard."

"No. I'm the black sheep, remember?"

"The doc says she has something called an incompetent cervix. Can't hold a fetus in. It looks like she's not going to be able to have any kids."

"I'm sorry, Lam."

"I won't lie to you. It's a big disappointment. I would have to marry the sister with the incompetent cervix."

Keep the line of gab going. "Well, we could always move to Utah. Become Mormons."

"I'm serious, Het. Once I pay Splendora Oil for their expenses, all the profits from this field will be mine. We've hit a deep deposit here. Chief wants me to spud in thirty wells. Do you have any idea what the revenue on thirty wells is going to be someday? I'm poised to become one of the richest men in Texas. Maybe even in America. You could be my queen. You weren't made for poverty, Hetty. You need money, and lots of it."

"And you need children, and lots of them."

"You got it. Chief wants heirs, and I'm his only shot. Think of what you and I could do together. You're so juicy, kiddo. You could give me the sons I want, the sons of Splendora. I'm sure there's nothing wrong with your cervix. We could start one of the great dynasties in Texas. Come with me, right now. I'll take the day off."

He buried his face in her hands, and she stroked his brown hair. *Can I really afford to turn this down?* she asked herself. *With less than fifty dollars to my name? I'm a free woman. I could say that Garret left me. I could bed Lamar without a pang of guilt and solve all my problems. I would never see that shotgun house again. I could live in utter luxury while I show them all up, including my sister.* Hetty's thoughts poked at her heart to see if they could stir up any interest, but there was only the white blankness from under the sheet, paralyzing everything.

"It's funny, my little Lam," she said tenderly. "There was a time I would have jumped at an offer like this. Thank you, it's very flattering. But I can't think about it now. I have to get this well sold first."

Lamar leaped to his feet and sent his chair spinning. "God, woman! It makes me want you all the more!"

"Well, buy my well, and I might consider giving you a kiss." Hetty stood and smoothed her skirt.

"I'll only buy it from Charmaine."

"She's not selling."

"Goddamn, you're hardheaded, Hetty. You know I'm your only shot. I don't need to buy your little well. I'll get the oil from it anyway. And nobody else is buying leases now. Just give me what I want."

So he finally admitted he's stealing! Hetty forced herself to hold back her rage, the rage she had felt when she found out that he was draining her oil right from under her feet by the Rule of Capture. She put on a poker face. "You're nuts. I've got a good producer that could make a lot of money for the right investor." She picked the log up off the couch and waved it at him. "The equipment alone is worth five thousand. I don't have to sell to you."

"But I want to buy from you. Like you said. For old times' sake."

"You know, Lamar, you could have what you wanted, if you just knew how to get it."

He glared at her, pure frustration frosting his eyes. "Can't you give me a hint?"

"Well, buy the Ada Hillyer for starters. Just a business deal between old friends. That'll show me you really care."

Lamar shook his head. "Not without the fine print."

"Well then, if you won't do it for me, do it for Kirb and Mamá."

He sniggered. "Oh, now we're bringing in the in-laws hoping to rouse my sympathy!"

"I'm hoping to rouse your sense of decency. My folks need their money back. The Warwick's being sold at auction. Nella thought you might buy the well as a favor to her."

"I don't think your mother needs any favors from me."

"Please, Lam. They're your wife's parents." Hetty hoped to see a haze of guilt spread over Lamar's face, but what came instead was the self-righteous smirk that made her want to slap him.

"Let's leave them out of this, kiddo. Like you said, it's just a business deal between old friends."

"Okay. So you'll buy the Ada Hillyer from me?"

"Depends on which me is selling."

"Hetty MacBride," she said proudly.

"Not without the fine print."

From under the hat brim, Hetty shot him a rueful glance and turned away. "That's the deal breaker, I'm afraid, that fine print."

"Okay, then, Mrs. Shanty MacBride! Run back to your shotgun house. Live in squalor. See if I give a goddamn."

"Going . . . going . . ." She edged toward the door.

She could hear his exasperated breathing.

"Gone!" she chirped and slid through the door.

He pried it open behind her and shouted, "One hour with you naked. My final offer!"

Hetty held on to her composure as she sauntered back to the Wichita, climbing into the truck as gracefully as possible. She waved at Lamar as she revved up the motor and backed away. She didn't exit the way she'd come in, but headed straight into the field. As soon as she was out of his sight, she tore her picture hat off. "Men!"

"Lamar wouldn't buy?"

"Oh, he wanted to buy all right. Me along with the well."

Pearl's mouth flew open. "You don't mean it? Lord! That man's got horns holding up his halo."

"That's a good way to put it." Hetty fumed as they bumped along the rutted road, slick with grease spread from the wells. "It wouldn't hurt him to help me out for once. It's pocket change to him. If he really cared about me, he'd do it—wouldn't he?"

"I should hope so."

"That means he doesn't really care. He's playing with me."

"He's showing his colors, that's what he's doing."

"He sure is: puke green. He and my sister deserve each other, that's all I can say." Hetty drove deeper into the field.

"Are we taking the long way home?"

"I just want to spy on Splendora a little. See what they're up to." She drove along the line of derricks, through the blasted meadows.

Black grime covered everything. A wide circle spread out from each platform, a good hundred yards around, choking all vegetation. Only one scraggly plant had wedged its roots into the dry red dirt on the fringes. It was creeping in, taking over.

"That's what we used to call goat weed," Pearl said. "It's a terrible nuisance."

The drilling petered out as they approached a swampy part of the woods, but they could see pipelines snaking into the wetlands, pumping salt water. As she came around a curve, what Hetty saw caused her to brake in the middle of the road and climb out. Pearl joined her, carrying Pierce. They looked down into a cesspool that used to be a marsh. Everything, cankered with death. Hetty could hardly stand to breathe. A foul stench arose out of the stagnant water, reminding her of the dead frogs in Caney Creek. But this was much worse than a few dead frogs. As far as they could see there were acres of dead trees. Leafless hickories encrusted halfway up with salt. Rotting willows. Yellow pines. A skeleton of a forest. Utterly still, deeply decaying. The only things that moved were oil slicks shimmering across the surface like mother-of-pearl in the sun. Mixed in with the reek of death was another odor, heavier than air, a harsh chemical smell that scorched Hetty's nostrils as she breathed it in. She stood there, choking, shaking her head. *Lamar's legacy to the world,* she thought. *A dead forest.*

Pearl clucked. "This ain't God's country anymore. It's the devil's."

"Amen," Hetty said. "And I want to get as far away from it as I can."

Hetty drove straight to Tulsa's barbershop on Commerce Street in Kilgore. She tucked her hair into the white picture hat and applied fresh pink lipstick in the dusty rearview mirror.

"Pray for a miracle," Hetty told Pearl before leaving her in the cab with Pierce. Standing under the spinning candy cane with the log in hand, Hetty peered into the shop. It was filled with the usual crowd of men, most of them in shirtsleeves and ties. There was a group huddled around the table stacked with *Collier's* magazines, sweating out a poker game and wiping their brows every now and then with striped handkerchiefs. A sign hung on the door by a little chain: OPEN. Hetty wondered how "open" Tulsa's would be to a member of her sex. She took a deep breath and stepped inside.

The brisk scent of aftershave cut the air. A ceiling fan whirled. She scanned the room from under the wide brim of her hat, meeting the eyes of the poker players unflinchingly as they looked up scowling. The chatter died down. All you could hear was the *slap-slap* of the shoeshine boy, buffing leather.

Hetty was careful to speak with an easy grace. "Gentlemen! I apologize for trespassing on your territory, but I understand this is where one comes when one has a lease to sell."

Snickers ricocheted through the room. "We all got leases to sell, lady," someone drawled. "Why don't y'all buy ours?"

"I understand that, sir. I realize that leases aren't worth much these days. It's the well I'm talking about. I have a rig I'm willing to sell against future profits for only five thousand dollars."

"We like the rig you're wearing better," a gruff voice barked from the back of the shop and was followed by cheers.

"Thank you, gentlemen. Now that you've had a chance to express your taste in fashion, is there anyone here who's ready to talk business? I don't have all day."

Silence floated under the ceiling fan, broken only by the flap of cards being dealt.

"You come to the wrong place, ma'am," the man in the barber chair finally said. "We all got wells we can't operate."

The barber agreed. "Right now"—*rat now*—"they're about as handy as last year's bird nest."

"Not this one."

"Yeah? What's any different about yours?"

"My promoter is Cleveland Yoakum."

One of the card players spoke up, a Yankee from the sound of his voice. "The Cliff?"

She walked straight over to him. "That's right. Buy my well and I'll make you partners with the slab o' granite himself."

"You really think we're going to buy a rig from someone wearing little white sandals? You ever been on a derrick, baby? You know anything about them?"

"Of course. My husband and I drilled the Ada Hillyer. I can name all the parts of the well and how much they're worth." She looked him straight in the eye, hoping he wouldn't call her bluff.

"Oh, yeah? Name one." He stood up, while the other players exchanged amused glances.

"Well . . . let's see . . . where shall I start?" Hetty said, buying herself some time. She called up the derrick in her mind and scanned the image. Then she remembered the cold February dusk when Scott had introduced her to her alter ego and alias, Kelly Bushings. "There's always my favorite part, of course, the kelly. Named after a woman."

"And what does the kelly do?"

Hetty rolled her eyes to heaven in mock exasperation. "The kelly makes everything turn for the drilling. It fits into the kelly bushings. It's always hexagonal in shape."

"Well, not always," the man said, cocking an eye at her and then sitting back down. "Sometimes it's square." He played his hand, then looked back up at her. "What's the production on the well? You got any proof?"

"Here's the log right here," she said, lifting it from under her arm.

He seemed impressed with that. When it was his turn again, he folded his cards and announced, "I'm out, baby." He grabbed his winnings, then walked over and swiveled the door open, gesturing for the lady to go first. His fuzzy red hair had just been neatly trimmed. "Kozak, ma'am. I don't know if you remember me," he said as she passed outside.

"You sound familiar."

"I'm the guy from Jersey." It came to her, a flash from their first night in Kilgore: the rain, the smell of hamburgers sizzling on the grill at Brown's Drugs, the way this carrottop honked his words through his nose.

"Now I remember. You were the one trying to buy all the leases in town."

"And your husband thought he had a share in Joiner's syndicate."

Hetty felt herself blush a little. "We didn't know much back then."

He turned away from the barbershop. "You knew more than I did. Talk to farmers, you told me. I took your advice and did quite well."

"Really? Then you owe me a favor." As they ambled along the sidewalk, she cocked her head at him coquettishly.

"Five thousand would be a mighty big favor, baby."

"Come on, Kozak, you're a gambler. Take a chance on this. I'll not only make you partners with Cleveland, but hook you up with his whole consortium of investors."

He screwed up his mouth and shrugged. "It's tempting, baby. I'll come out and have a look." He dipped his head under her hat brim and winked. "Besides, I like a woman with a little nerve."

It took another day to complete the transaction with Kozak. They'd settled on four thousand dollars. Hetty signed the well over to the Kozaco Company, glad she insisted on being full partners with Garret. She asked for a certified check, which she took straight down to the First National Bank on Fredonia Street and cashed, buying a money order for three thousand dollars made payable to Cleveland Yoakum, then dividing the rest of the money up into three stashes of $333.33 each that she stuffed into bank envelopes provided by the teller.

In the cool of the following morning, they lifted Pierce, still sleeping, out of his cradle, said a long good-bye to the Hillyers, loaded up the last of their things, and slammed shut the tailgate of the truck. When Hetty set her purse down on the seat, a packet of letters peeked out along with the bank envelopes. She'd found them yesterday when rifling through the doghouse for the logbook on the well. Letters Garret's mother had written him, all signed *Arleen* in big fancy loops. Why was he hiding them out there? She was dying to read them but didn't have time right now. Perhaps they'd explain why he left.

By lunchtime, they were well on the way south. Hetty found the clumsy Wichita exhausting to drive on the highway and almost fell asleep as the day grew hotter. In her drowsiness, though, she was suffused with warm relief as the prickly branches of the pines thinned out and smudges of post oak trees began to whip by in the corner of her eye. There was now something malignant in the dark green of the Piney Woods, trees that grew needles instead of leaves.

They spent the night in the room Pearl had kept at her boarding-house in Houston, then drove to the Settegast slums after lunch to tell a mother that her son was dead. Hetty pulled up in front of the Waller house and turned off the motor. Late summer sun drenched the treeless street. The cab of the truck quickly turned into an oven. Hetty glanced toward the house. The porch glowered back at her. Thistles grew three feet high in what passed for a front yard. Two bare wooden steps waited for her to climb them. She began to sweat. She looked at Pearl.

"I hope you're not expecting me to tell her," Pearl said, dabbing the moisture off Pierce's forehead. "I've never met the woman."

When the windshield began to steam up and the steering wheel was too hot to touch, Hetty pulled out the choke. "I'll go see Cora. I always think better at my aunt's river house." Hetty pushed the starter button.

Chapter 16

The sound of a fountain trickling woke Hetty up. Sunlight flickered on the bed beside her. The day was warming up. It must be late in the morning, perhaps even noon. She could hear birds chirping—dozens of them out there in the trees. Through the French doors, the smell of the San Antonio River floated up to her with the morning mists. She rolled over and stretched. Her bladder felt extremely full. How long had she been sleeping? She had no idea. She remembered taking Pearl back to the rooming house, then dropping off the money order to Cleveland Yoakum and telling him he'd have the rest of the money in a few weeks. She remembered driving to her aunt's house in San Antonio and walking up to the front door to ring the caravansary bells. She remembered sitting on her aunt's sofa sipping mescal out of a snifter, but not much after that.

Hetty stumbled barefoot down the cold tiles of the hallway until she found the bathroom. When she came out, sounds drifted in from the living room: It was laughter, but not bored adult laughter—the gleeful giggles of a child at play. With a little shock, she recognized the voice. It was her own son, Pierce. She felt so distant from him! Other sounds formed a fugue with the giggles: the ringing of bells, the swishing of a rain stick being tipped to simulate the sound of raindrops falling on dry earth. Hetty stood in the shadowy hall and smiled: Cora had hauled out the old wooden *baúl,* the one Hetty had explored with rapt curiosity when she was a girl. It hid many treasures under its creaking lid, from antique toys to various rattles, whistles, and drums from places like Cameroon or Peru. She peeked around the corner, and there they were: her aunt and her child on the tattered Persian carpet of the living room, Cora's long pigtail snaking on the floor, four cats batting at the toys Pierce held up. The late morning light had trickled down through the pecan trees and was dropping in spangles onto the carpet, shimmering here and there. *Jesus,* Hetty thought, *it's been so long since I've heard laughter.*

Hetty went back to her bedroom and dressed, then stood at the door of the living room. Her son hardly noticed her. "I'm sorry, *Tía,*" she said, walking in. "I didn't mean to oversleep."

"Don't be silly!" Cora jumped up and opened her arms wide, making her silver bracelets jingle and slide. "Come here, *m'ija,* and give your aunty a big hug!" As the arms enfolded her, Hetty caught a whiff of coconut oil and cumin. She held on tight, the earthy smells making her feel welcome. "You always have a home here. Coming to the Cosmos was the right thing to do. I'm on summer break from the college, so we're at leisure. My only project is to finish some paintings for a show. Now—you have to tell your *tía* everything, but first"—Cora held her at arm's length and looked her up and down—"I've got to feed you. *Ay,* you're skin and bones!"

"I'm embarrassed, that's what I am."

"Don't be. *Siéntate, siéntate.*" Cora led her over to the sofa and nestled her amid the faded silk cushions, then disappeared into the kitchen. Pierce called to her. Hetty stepped over and pulled out some hand bells from India to distract him. Then she lolled back on the sofa and lit her first Lucky of the day. The smell of corn tortillas warming in Aunt Cora's kitchen was a bittersweet form of *tormento.* She was so glad she'd followed her instinct and come to the river house where she and her baby would be safe for a while.

Soon, Cora emerged bearing a tray steaming with hot coffee and the fresh tortillas that had scented the air, surrounded by bowls of beans and vegetables garnished with guacamole and salsa. Hetty thanked her aunt, then sat up and rolled herself a couple of dripping burritos, practically swallowing them whole without chewing.

The play, meanwhile, continued at a giddy pace on the floor. Cora would reach into the trunk and hide the next toy behind her hand, making the baby stand and peer over her fingers to see what it was.

"Thanks for entertaining Pierce," Hetty said. "I'm sorry about last night."

Cora smiled up at her. "My dear girl, you were in no shape to take care of anyone. You were completely exhausted. *¿Qué te pasó?*"

"*¡Ay!* Where to begin . . . ?" Hetty lit another Lucky as she began to retell the whole saga of the Ada Hillyer Number One. The words poured out along with the smoke from her cigarette. Hetty hadn't realized how much she needed to share what had happened with someone, and Cora—always so *simpática*—made the perfect audience for her recital of tragedy in East Texas. She felt compelled to tell the story again, confessing her doubts to her aunt and even owning up to her own complicity in the crime. "I let things get out of hand, *Tía.* It's my fault Pick was killed," Hetty said, shuddering.

"My dear little niece," Cora said, coming over and taking Hetty's hands. "You mustn't blame yourself. You didn't kill your friend. The men who pulled the triggers on those rifles did."

"I feel like I pulled the triggers. I feel like I parted the pine branches so they could take aim. I was an accomplice to the crime."

"Listen to me, niece. Pick was killed because he was a Negro, that's the simple truth. Ever since the Texas Rangers were formed, they've had it in for people of color—any color. There were wholesale slaughters of Mexicans in the valley—I've seen pictures. Bodies piled up in a mass grave. All because the Rangers thought Texas should be a country for white men."

"Is that true?"

"*¡Sí!* Poker Face killed Pick because he knew he could get away with it. And that's not your fault."

"It's not?"

"No. You're not to blame yourself any longer. I won't let you." Warm sympathy flowed out of her eyes and enveloped Hetty.

"But I feel like I have a noose around my neck that's choking me."

"That's your guilty conscience tugging on you. Have you told his mother?"

"I couldn't face her. Would it be all right to send the news in a letter, Aunty?"

"Would you want to receive news like that in a letter?"

The light in Cora's eyes changed. It shifted to a look both distant and austere, a coolness that set Hetty on edge. "I can't tell her in person, *Tía*. It would be too hard."

Cora continued to watch her with pitiless clarity in her gaze. "It's up to you, of course, but if you hope to get that noose off your neck, you'll do it. You'll go and tell her the truth."

The afternoon was old by the time Hetty rolled up to the Waller house in Settegast. The porch looked gaunt as she stepped across its warped floorboards, the front door wrinkled with flaking white paint. Hetty stood there a long time before she knocked. The children must have been down the street playing, because Velma answered the door alone.

"Miss Hetty?" she said, looking over her shoulder to see if Pick stood behind her. "Is my boy done up east?"

All Hetty could do was nod. She asked if she could come in.

The windows were open in anticipation of the cool evening, but there were no screens, so flies buzzed about. Turnips were cooking somewhere. A green brocade sofa, tattered and stained, slanted across the small room across from a cabinet missing one leg. They sat at either end of the sofa. Hetty leaned against the arm and turned in Velma's direction. Her face, as black as Pick's, was pitted with eyes used to bad news, permanently stained with disappointment. "I have something to tell you, Velma," she started. "It's not good. I'm sorry." *No euphemisms,* Hetty had promised herself.

Velma's face contorted. "About my Pick?"

Hetty nodded. "I'm afraid he's . . . dead."

Velma shuddered and began wailing. "Oh, Lord! Dead? Pick dead? Don't let it be! Don't let it be!" Her cries scalded Hetty's ears as she lost control and rocked back and forth on the sofa howling, "Oh, Lord. Oh, Pick! Pick!"

Hetty slid over and touched her while she swayed and moaned. Velma's plaintive cries threatened to dredge up Hetty's own guilty grief, but she swallowed it back as hard as she could.

Hetty heard whispering, and the children filed in from the rear of the house, drawn by their mother's howls. Lewis hung back in the door while Addie and Ollie held on to each other in their gingham dresses, eyes large with fright. Only Minnie came up to her mother and asked what was wrong.

"Pick is dead!" Velma sobbed out. Addie and Ollie looked down, ashamed, and Lewis frowned at Hetty as if she herself had murdered his brother. Minnie tried to hold her mother to stifle her violent howls, but Velma threw her arms wildly in the air to fend her off. Hetty slid back across the sofa and clamped her heart shut. The looks on the faces of the children were cutting too deep.

"Who killed my boy?" Velma asked, wiping her eyes with her fingers.

"A Texas Ranger," Hetty said, wishing she had a hankie to give the poor woman.

"How come? He was a good boy."

"They said he was pumping oil illegally." Hetty took a deep breath and tried to keep her voice steady. "I'm afraid it's partly my fault. I asked him to do it. He wanted to keep working so he could send money home." Hetty took out one of the bank envelopes containing $333.33 and set it on the sofa between them. "I want you to have this."

Velma glanced askance at the bulging envelope, then glared at Hetty out of swollen eyes. "You think you can buy me off?"

Minnie walked over to Hetty with a look of uncomprehending hatred and began hitting her on the leg, over and over, harder and harder. Hetty didn't try to stop her.

When she got back to the rooming house, Pearl asked how it went.

"As bad as I thought it'd be. The children were there." Hetty told Pearl how they'd reacted. Her leg still ached where Minnie had beaten out her rage. Minnie never could hold back her feelings. But Hetty had deserved the thrashing the child had given her. It had been a kind of penance—just not enough of a penance. The commission Cora had given her hadn't worked. She was still stalled in her sin, the whole world choked with it. Hetty felt like one of those wells they'd seen in the Splendora field, surrounded by barren earth where only goat weed would grow. She carried its greasy mud on her hands and smeared everything she touched. Things died around her; sidewalks cracked under her feet. She was toxic with guilt. Even the children could see that.

"I don't know how I can let someone like Velma Waller upset me so much," Hetty complained to Pearl.

"It's the children, you said so yourself." To ease Hetty's distress, Pearl went over to her closet and pulled out something dark. "I done messed up. I forgot to give you Pick's Sunday suit. Take it to his mother tomorrow. Try again."

Hetty spent a ragged night with Pearl. When she pulled out her pack of Luckies in the morning, she found the stash of letters from Arleen MacBride, peppered with flecks of tobacco. She scanned a few while she smoked. The big swirling handwriting was difficult to decipher at first, but she managed to extract some essential details. Arleen had been forced to take in boarders. The once-grand residence of a senator was now little more than a rooming house, but the situation, Hetty noted, was highly romanticized by the letter writer. Arleen talked as if she were a society hostess and these were her celebrated guests. Hetty could find no clue as to why Garret had been so careful to hide his mother's letters away. She stuffed them back into her handbag half read.

After breakfast, she drove back over to the Ward. When Velma opened the door a crack, Hetty held up the clothes and said, "I've brought Pick's Sunday suit. You don't have to let me in."

She passed the hanger through the door and turned to go when Velma said, "Com'on in, ma'am."

The house felt cooler in the morning air, and the children were nowhere to be seen. Hetty sat at one end of the couch while Velma spread the suit between them as if Pick were sitting there himself. She kept fingering the gray wool, smoothing the wrinkles out of it. Hetty spotted the bank envelope over on the cabinet. It had been opened.

"Velma, about the money, I—"

"I'll take it." She didn't look up at Hetty.

"I'm not trying to buy you off. It's what we owe Pick. He would want you to have it."

"I know." Velma went over and picked up the envelope, then perched on the edge of the sofa and fanned out the bills. She seemed awed by them, as if she'd never seen that much cash together at one time.

"My Pick was a good boy," she kept saying as she tried to count the bills with trembling fingers. "Look what he send me. All this money. Lord, I can't hardly count that high, but I'll make it last. I can manage. You know I can manage."

"It should help with the kids. We don't want them getting sick again."

Velma stuffed the money back into the envelope and slipped it into the vest pocket of the suit coat, as if her son had just walked in the door bringing it home. "This is hard for them. They don't understand where their brother be."

"Will Minnie hate me forever?"

Velma looked up from the suit, her eyes softened. "Oh, Miss Hetty, you wouldn't do nothing to hurt my boy, I know that."

"You do?"

"Sure. You done so much for Pick. You was his savior."

"Pick, dear Pick. I never dreamed they'd kill him. I'm so sorry, Velma."

"I know you is."

"Will you forgive me then?"

"I don't keep room in my heart for hate. I just can't." She smoothed the lapels of the suit again and buttoned the coat. A whiff of Pick's scent rose into the air between them. "This grief is hard to bear. I can testify to that."

"It's horrible for me. I feel responsible."

"How come?"

Hetty gave her such a miserable look she reached out. They clutched each other's hands over the buttoned-up Sunday suit. Velma began crying. "It ain't we women who take life. We give it. The Good Book say you bring forth children in pain. It don't say nothing about watching what happens to 'em after. That's the real pain."

"I should have sent Pick home—I'm sorry."

"It ain't your cross to bear, Miss Hetty. I forgive you and Jesus forgives you."

"He does?"

"He say: 'Blessed are those who mourn, for they shall be comforted.' "

Velma's words released the choke up of shame Hetty had dammed in her heart, allowing a flood of relief. She wept tears of gratitude along with Velma's tears of grief. They held hands and cried together. Cora had been wise to send her here after all. The woman she thought would condemn her eternally was offering instead the blessed balm of forgiveness. Hetty felt like she'd been anointed, soothed in some deep place.

"Where is he?" Velma asked after a while, looking out at the truck in the street.

"The sheriff took his body. They wouldn't let me keep it."

"We'll remember him at church," Velma said, trying to compose herself. "That's what we'll do."

"You could have a memorial service."

"My Pick always sang in the choir."

"I know. You could sing all his favorite hymns." Hetty wiped at her eyes.

"That's how we'll remember my boy. My Henry Picktown Waller." Velma nodded, her tears dampened down for the moment.

After saying good-bye, Hetty sat in the truck and pulled out her passbook and her tortoiseshell fountain pen. Under the column marked *Balance,* she made a new entry. *Forgiveness,* it read.

Hetty spent a peaceful night with Pearl and drove back to San Antonio the next day. She found Cora and Pierce in the painting studio, looking at the tall windows through glass prisms. The smell of turpentine hung heavy in the air. Jars choked with brushes stood on a paint-caked table. Three paintings leaned on easels in various stages of completion.

"You were so right to send me to see Velma," Hetty said, joining them on the floor. "I feel so much better. She actually forgave me, *Tía*."

"Now you can forgive yourself."

"I know. I don't feel that noose around my neck anymore."

"I noticed it was gone the minute you walked in the room."

Hetty laughed. "What are you doing with these prisms?"

"I've been studying Goethe's experiments with color. I thought Pierce might find them fun."

"Don't you think he's a little young for optics?"

"I'm afraid you're right. He'd rather suck on them than look through them."

Pierce held a prism up, and Hetty took it from him. She looked through the sparkling glass at the windows and let a little gasp of breath escape when she saw the colors coating everything. "I see rainbows around the windows. Where did they come from?" she wondered, lowering the prism.

"They arise where the light and dark clash," Cora said. "That was Goethe's theory. He said something I find intriguing as an artist—color is the deeds and suffering of light."

Hetty looked again. She saw the usual rainbows, with their deep rivers of purple rising up into blue and green and falling back into streams of orange and red. But then Hetty spotted something else that made her eyes tingle with mystery.

"*Tía,* I can't believe this. I think I'm seeing *another* rainbow! Is that possible?"

"What good eyes your mother has," Cora said to Pierce. "Can you describe it?"

"It's like the butt end of the rainbow, where the purple and red overlap." Hetty studied this unfamiliar iridescence appearing around the dark strips that held the panes of glass in place. It gave birth to a radiant rose magenta framed by turquoise and gold. "Cézanne said we live in a rainbow of chaos. Is this it?"

"You're looking at one of the mysteries of the universe, my dear niece. Not chaos, but darkness. A rainbow of darkness. Out of it comes that indescribable shade of pink. I've been trying to capture it in paint."

"It's like a little glimpse of heaven." Hetty glanced at Cora. "But why did you call it one of the mysteries of the universe?"

"Look again. It's lighter than the two colors forming it."

Hetty lifted the prism to her eyes. Cora was right. The deep purple and red met and merged to form a prismatic pink many shades lighter. *I like this better than chaos,* Hetty thought. *Much better!* "I saw it once. In a sunset over the Galvez Hotel during my honeymoon. Garret and I were out on the sandbar. I won't tell you what we were doing."

"You do see magenta in the sky at times—if you're lucky. Goethe said it surpassed all other colors in beauty and splendor."

"He's right. It sure did that day." A pang gripped Hetty's heart when she remembered clinging to her husband in the ocean as a rainbow of darkness spread itself across the sky. She longed to feel his hands on her again. How could she let him leave without her?

Later, she heaved her baby off the floor and held him so he could see the paintings his great-aunt was working on. It looked to Hetty like Cora was driving her dreamscapes into the realm of nightmare. There were nuns with animal heads, melting boulders, monstrous beings part modern, part Mayan, and towns flooded by rivers. Everything was painted against a midnight blue sky blazing with stars.

"I put the stars on with gold leaf. They're all for a show at my gallery in October. I'm calling it *Quimeras*."

"They're fantastical, all right."

"Yes, but it's one of those Spanish words that has a delicious double meaning. It also means quarrels."

"Ah," Hetty said, noticing a half-finished canvas of nuns engaged in a bloody quarrel with knives. As she followed Cora out of the studio toward the kitchen, a painting stacked next to the door transfixed her. A large canvas, four foot by five, depicted the kind of sacrificial well where Mayans might have thrown their victims.

Hetty felt the air sucked out of her lungs as she stared into its depths. There were no gold leaf stars here. The well plummeted into blackness so complete, the vertigo one felt staring down into it was not physical, but spiritual. She hugged Pierce tight and stepped away.

As they threaded through the hallway, she stopped when she spotted another picture, this time the photo of the two sisters in sailor suits laughing and hugging their legs. Nella's girlhood face reminded Hetty of something. The painting that loomed over the living room, the one called *Sisters*. She went in and studied it. Under the black habits of nuns that lifted like the wings of fallen angels, a girl stood with outstretched arms trying to hold up ponderous volumes. And yes, it was the face in the photograph, the hair pulled up in a knot. *Nella went through some kind of crucifixion,* Hetty realized with a shock. *That's what Cora's trying to say in this painting.* There was something else that stood out. In the black building with high walls, only one window had a light on, struggling to stay lit in an overpowering darkness.

Over coffee the next morning, Hetty asked, "That girl in your painting? That's Nella, isn't it?"

Cora nodded, reaching for a pecan *galleta* off a plate of cookies on the coffee table. Hetty was grateful that Pierce was still asleep, so she could talk intimately with her aunt.

"Why have you painted her in the crucifix pose?"

Cora washed the cookie down with a gulp of black coffee. "Oh, my niece, my niece, my niece! You have to understand, when something very shameful happens to you, you bury it."

"Wait a minute," Hetty said, sitting up on the sofa. "Didn't you tell me you've been psychoanalyzed?"

Cora looked at her warily from the other end of the sofa.

"I thought the whole point of psychoanalysis was to dig things up."

"*Ay, m'ija.* You're too smart for me." Cora sighed deeply. "I did spend quite a bit of time on this—then I made that painting."

Hetty pulled out the black leather folder she carried with her everywhere, bearing the embossed gold letters *Citizen's Bank of South Texas*. "Ever since Kirby closed my bank account, I've been making my own entries into my passbook." She scanned the pages, then looked at her aunt. "I have one in here that reads: *Nella's knees*. Followed by question marks. A lot of question marks. Why won't anyone tell me about this? Lina said to ask you."

Cora gave her a baleful glance. "I guess I'm the lucky one."

Hetty felt a surge of relief until she saw what her aunt did next. Cora got up and went over to the decanter next to the antique birdcage. She poured some mescal into a snifter and lifted it to her mouth. Instead of sipping it slowly like she usually did, she swallowed two big slugs of it right down. Then she came back and settled into the sofa, kicking her shoes off. She turned to Hetty and bored into her with her eyes. *Jesus,* Hetty thought, *this is going to be good.*

"It all started with your mother's *quinceañera*."

"Fifteenth birthday?"

"*Sí.* Nella wouldn't have told you about this custom, but you have to remember that your grandmother, Liliana—"

"Mamá always called her Lili. Why didn't Granny Lili ever come to visit us?"

"You'll see! Her full name was Liliana Ardra y de la Herrera de Beckman. She was first generation out of Mexico, and there, when a girl turns fifteen, she is ripe for marriage. And Nella was—all rosy cheeks and high spirits in those days, a dazzling beauty always surrounded by a pack of boys. But the one boy she never flirted with was the one she intended to marry. The Folksinger."

"Who was the Folksinger?"

"We called him Tipo. He was at my level, two years older than Nella. Junior and senior high were in the same building. Tipo was one of the Mexicans—not the best-looking boy in school, but definitely the friendliest. We girls cheered wildly whenever they let him sing a solo at school assemblies. His voice made up for his face; it was so rich and melodious as he sang in Spanish and strummed his guitar.

" *'Ella te ama,'* I whispered to him one day at the back of the class.

"His reaction surprised me. 'But she is a *güera,*' he said. *Light-skinned.*

"It was true. Although we were both mestizas, Nella never looked it. Tipo couldn't believe that a *güera* girl could love a *moreno* man. Skin color was what controlled your life back then, of course, and determined your destiny. I was always aware that Nella was whiter than I was, not that I cared. But Tipo would never have dared approach such a light-skinned girl without some prodding.

"He began to notice Nella, the way she looked at him. Soon, they began to disappear into the mountain laurels lining the playground. I would find my sister back in there with her arms around his neck, gazing into his black eyes, lisping Spanish into his ear as he kissed her neck, daydreaming through her classes for the rest of the day."

"They must have really been in love," Hetty said.

"They were, *con delirio*. Once Lili decided that the young man was suitable, she approached Anton. Nothing prepared us for the storm that followed. He cursed at the Folksinger and locked Nella in the house."

"No! He can't!" Hetty said. "They must be together."

"He did. Nella was placed under house arrest for days and couldn't even go to school. Under no circumstance was she to marry a Mexican, he declared. He hadn't worked this hard so we could become Chili Queens like our mother. That's what your grandmother was, you recall, when he met her."

"Papi always said she was the prettiest of all the Chili Queens."

"She was, too. She had the reddest dress and the hottest chili on Military Plaza. Her stall was a favorite among the soldiers. They all wanted some of Lili's chili. It's because she wore a crown of peacock feathers in her black hair and pinned roses on their lapels."

"Granny Lili in peacock feathers! *¡Jejeje!* That must have been a sight."

"*Muy mona*—like a doll. Anton saw himself as her redeemer. He rescued her from that life by marrying her—quite an audacious thing for a German officer to do back in those days. I've always said Papá was seduced by chili con carne! But he wasn't about to let his daughters go back to that life. Within a month of finding out about Tipo—*¡vámonos!* He moved us into this house, far from the

Mexican Quarter." Cora looked about the living room, as if searching for ghosts in the shadows.

"You remembered quite a bit," Hetty said.

"It all came back during my analysis."

"So how did you feel about moving here?"

"Like I'd been ripped out by my roots. I just wilted."

For the first time, the dank shadows of the river house felt ominous to Hetty. She pulled her feet up onto the sofa. "How did Nella take it?"

"Defiantly. She continued flirting with Tipo behind the mountain laurels. But then the school year came to an end. Nella knew she wouldn't see her lover for three long months. She began meeting him *en secreto* that summer, took terrible risks—"

"Good for her!"

"Oh, but she got caught! Mid July."

"Uh-oh. What did Anton do?"

"He retaliated by sending us both to All Saints Academy for Girls in September. He made us board there—we weren't even allowed to come home at night, even though it wasn't that far from where we lived."

"I can't believe Mamá let herself be locked up!" Hetty said, reaching into her bag for a Lucky. Beside her on the sofa, her passbook sparked a memory. She checked an entry she'd made under *Balance:* "Tell me something—is All Saints on Dolorosa Street?"

"Yes, at the foot, on a hill overlooking the river."

"That's why Mother doesn't like driving down that street. See, I wrote it in my passbook the first time Garret and I came to visit you. It sounds pretty grim."

"It's all in my sketchbook. Let me see if I can find it."

While Cora was rummaging around in her studio, Hetty went in to check on Pierce. He had apparently just awakened and was lying in dappled sunlight reaching for the shadows, cooing. She picked him up, cooed back at him, and set him down on the bed to change his diaper. Back in the living room, she fed him a *galleta* and a glass of milk, then pulled out musical instruments for him to play with on the floor. Cora emerged with a sketchbook dated 1904. Hetty leafed through and saw how the images changed. Saints replaced the grapes and papayas of still lifes. Page after page was filled with the praying hands and uplifted eyes of the statues in the *nichos* along the hallways. The medium changed from pencil to India ink.

"Pencil wasn't dark enough," Cora said when Hetty asked. She described how gloomy the place was except for the floors that the sisters kept so highly polished. The girls weren't allowed to talk in the hallways, so they were always utterly silent except for the swishing of the nuns' habits, the nuns who emerged out of the shadows unexpectedly, starched and frowning. The brick walls rose all around, locking them in, the saints keeping watch from their *nichos*.

Hetty lit one of the Luckies and let its smoke rise in the air like incense to ward off evil.

"If we slipped into our secret sisters' language and spoke a word of Spanish, the nuns would rap our hands with a ruler. It really hurt."

"You couldn't speak Spanish!"

"The first thing they do is take your language away. We used to steal toilet paper and write notes to each other in Spanish late at night. Then we'd flush them in the morning."

"Oh, *Tía,* how sad." Hetty took a long drag off the cigarette.

"Sad but true. They'd rather minister to rich Anglos, not to us humble devotees of the *Virgen de Guadalupe*. We were sent to All Saints to have the dirty Mexican scrubbed out of us. All Saints was short for All Saints of Ireland Convent and Academy and the nuns were as Irish as you could get. They had us reading Shakespeare and Wordsworth and Yeats. Nella was used to the poetry the Folksinger sang. *'Como naranja la granada, cuan dulce las gardenias.'* How orange the pomegranates, how sweet the gardenias. Come to me, oh my love! *El amor,* that's what was on Nella's lips—the hot-blooded words, the sunlit words that rolled off her tongue so melodiously. But every relapse brought another stinging slap on the hand and a hiss from one of the sisters: 'Say it in English!' "

"It's like they cut out your tongue."

"*Exactamente.* And our eyes. We were taught to see things in a whole new light, a cold Northern, Puritan light."

Pierce held up a leather strap studded with bells, trying to get Hetty's attention. She waved her hand back and forth. He imitated her, making the bells ring and drawing a cat out from under the sideboard. Hetty knew she should be down on the floor playing with him, but was too absorbed in what her aunt was telling her. She turned to another drawing in the sketchbook, a schoolgirl floating in the sky above the black walls of the convent. One could see the river in the background with retama trees blooming along its bank. It didn't look like Nella. This girl was taller and more angular. "Is this you?"

"Yes. My analyst was very interested in that drawing. He saw it as an image of disassociation."

"I wondered how you coped."

"That's how. I think the disassociation saved me. I read a lot of books, went elsewhere in my mind." Cora sighed.

"But Mamá couldn't do that, could she?"

Cora shook her head, then rang the bells that Pierce had brought over to her. He began pulling the leather strap across the carpet, playing chase with two cats. Hetty turned back to the sketchbook, to the dark swirls of India ink. She could see the black place where Cora's story was headed and dreaded going there, but couldn't resist hearing more. She stubbed out her cigarette. "No floating for Nella?"

"She simply couldn't do that." Cora raised her hands into the air. "She lived too much in the moment. Heartsick with love, she withdrew and became sullen. Her personality changed. She rarely said anything in class, until the final block of lessons in the spring.

"Officially they were called 'political science,' but really it was just another way for the sisters to inoculate us with their particular strain of Texas history. We only had enough girls to make up a junior and senior group, and we were all together in this final session. The classes were taught by Sister Flanna, a third-generation San Antonian heavily invested in the virtues of the Texas Republic. I can still see her today. She had a flaming Irish temperament, her wimple barely concealing the fire of her red hair. In studying the formation of the Republic, we had to hear about the Battle of San Jacinto and the Fall of the Alamo.

"Sister Flanna laid the hyperbole on thick, how the little band of one hundred and fifty brave souls had held off an army of fifteen hundred until the bitter end—martyrs who had sacrificed their lives in the name of freedom and democracy. Indians and Mexicans were described as bloodthirsty savages."

"You're not serious!" Hetty said, nervously lighting another Lucky.

"Perfectly serious. Nella and I looked at each other amazed."

Hetty sniggered with smoke. "I guess you'd heard a different story from Liliana?"

"*¡Claro que sí!* In fact, when all us girls were taken on a field trip to the old mission, Nella became incensed. Sister Flanna was in her glory, of course, ushering us through the hallowed rooms and describing the events that had taken place on what she described as 'the saddest day of time.' We gathered under the north wall, where the attackers had made their first breach and 'poured in like sheep.' We stood in the dark sacristy, where even children had been murdered by the Mexicans, then gazed into the small room where Bowie had been slaughtered on his very sickbed as he fought for freedom with his last breath. Something in Nella snapped at all this. She couldn't sleep that night. The next day in class, she interrupted the lecture and proceeded to recite the Mexican version of the Fall of the Alamo.

" 'But, Sister Flanna,' she said, 'most of the men at the Alamo weren't even native Texans. My mother told me.'

"Sister Flanna tried to point out that there weren't any native Texans back then—that was the whole point, we had to fight for our independence.

" 'But the land belonged to Mexico,' Nella retorted. 'The Anglos were aliens living in a foreign country. Most of them were recent arrivals. And my mother said they broke every treaty they made with Mexico.' "

"Yes!" Hetty raised her cigarette in the Statue of Liberty pose.

"It was gutsy, all right. But that didn't stop Sister Flanna. A beatific smile dawned on her face. This was exactly the opportunity she'd been looking for to explain the doctrine of Manifest Destiny.

She pontificated for a full fifteen minutes, then ended with, 'It was God's will, you see.'

" 'The Mexicans didn't think so,' Nella said, and got a laugh from the whole class."

"I love my mamá!" Hetty said, lowering the Lucky and taking a furious drag.

"Patiently, Sister Flanna explained how the Mexicans were tyrants and that the Americans were fighting in the name of democracy. She raised her chin high and said, in a ringing voice, 'They were men of honor!'

" 'Oh, really? My mother told me they were the dregs of society. That Travis deserted a wife and two children, then committed homicide. Is that true?'

"Sister Flanna didn't quite know how to respond to this.

" 'And that Davy Crockett also deserted his family to go fortune hunting. And that Bowie was a pirate and slave-runner and had a terrible reputation as a brawler—'

"The sister tried to point out that he'd invented the Bowie knife, but Nella was not to be stopped now. She forged on: 'And that so many undesirable characters began to pour into Texas seeking quick riches that the Mexicans had to cut off any further immigration. Isn't that true?'

"The nun's face grew as red as her hair. What Nella was saying was blasphemy. It was bad enough she was speaking up in class without permission and being the unruly 'Mexican'—but on top of that she was disputing her teacher, striking at the very roots of Texas history and pride. A third-generation San Antonian couldn't allow this."

"What did she do to Mamá?"

"Put her in the crucifix pose."

"Oh," Hetty said, looking up at the painting.

"She made Nella stand holding heavy books in her outstretched arms while she recited ten Our Fathers. Most girls never made it, but Nella refused to give in. She finished the ten recitations even though her arms were shaking at the end. This was done in front of the class, of course."

Hetty couldn't imagine her mother enduring such trials. "How did she react?"

"Nella was quiet for the rest of the day. She sat at her desk, feeling shamed, hugging herself with her aching arms. I prayed it was over."

Pierce pulled himself up on the trunk, looking for a new toy. Hetty retrieved the xylophone and handed him the mallets. He started banging away on it.

"Unfortunately, it wasn't. Word got out to the other teachers. All the girls were talking about it. An epidemic of disobedience swept through the school like measles. The Mother Superior grew alarmed. She and another nun joined Sister Flanna in class the next morning and demanded that Nella recant what she'd said. When she refused, the Mother Superior insisted that Sister Flanna use a more severe form of discipline—the kneeling station."

Oh, the knees. Jarring notes from the xylophone scraped at Hetty's ears as she waited to hear what came next.

"It was a little shrine at the back of the classroom where you were sent to do penance. You were forced to raise your skirt, roll down your stockings, and kneel with bare knees on pebbles while you recited a rosary."

Hetty remembered the flash of a kimono closing and Nella hiding her knees in shame. *So this is where it started?* "But Mamá didn't cave in, did she?"

"Wait a minute, *sobrina*. You have to realize that a rosary takes about twenty minutes. Have you ever tried to kneel on rocks?"

"No."

"Well, it's very painful. These weren't smooth pebbles. They were little river rocks the sisters gathered out of Río San Antonio."

"Oh," was all Hetty could say, beginning to sense the gravity of the situation. *Still.*

"Usually, you only had to recite one or two rosaries, but Sister Flanna wasn't going to absolve Nella until she recanted. I sat frozen in my seat, horrified. I could hear her voice behind me droning away during lessons—all day long—'Hail Mary, full of grace, the Lord is with thee . . .' "

Cora paused and swallowed hard. *Bang! Bang!* Hetty wanted in the worst way to get up and go take the mallets away from her son. Each jangle hit her nerves with a jolt. But she could only sit there on the sofa appalled, trying to imagine how many days it would take to push someone over the edge. "So," she finally asked. "How long . . . ?"

When Cora finally turned to Hetty to speak, there were tears in her eyes. "She was there three days."

"Three days!" Hetty lost her breath for a moment. "That's torture."

Cora's voice thinned out with grief. "Poor thing. I was the one who had to dress her knees at night. They were all cut up. And then to have to kneel again the next day, when the old wounds would start bleeding again. I begged her to give in, but she refused. She simply couldn't refute what she knew to be the truth. Her very soul was at stake."

Hetty stood up impatiently, went over, and fished a hand puppet of a witch out of the chest. She knelt, tore the mallets out of Pierce's hands, and laid the puppet in his lap before he could protest. Hetty lunged back onto the sofa and turned to her aunt, frowning. "Go on."

"I offered to kneel for her, but Sister Flanna would have none of it. Nella had to atone for her sins. I tried to negotiate a truce. I implored my sister to relent. I offered to write a confession that she wouldn't even have to read, just sign. I petitioned the Mother Superior, but she only slapped my hand and scolded me for interfering. Each day, I felt I was losing Nella more and more."

"At least she didn't back down." Pierce dropped the puppet, stood at the edge of the coffee table, and reached for the mallets. Hetty shook her head no. She stuffed them into her purse. He whined.

"She held up pretty well until the other students joined in the shaming. Like any girls' school, All Saints had little cliques. There were lots of Anglo girls, of course, and an especially hateful group of Germans. Because Nella was being made an example, they started picking on her. They called her cunt in three languages. The German girls would walk to the pencil sharpener at the back of the class and whisper *'Dumme Fotze'* to Nella as they passed. The other

Hispanics started shouting *'Cara de chocha'* at her in the hallways and giggling. That was the one that stuck. *Chocha* became her nickname ever after."

"Cunt was her nickname?"

Cora nodded. "We would hear girls whispering outside our room at night, with a shouted *'Me cago en ti'* as they ran down the hall."

"I shit . . . over you?"

"This on top of the physical pain she was in. We actually found feces in her bed the second night."

Hetty could only stare at Cora with her mouth open.

"I know. It was dreadful for me. When I escorted her to the kneeling station the third day, I felt so desperate. There was blood on the rocks. By lunch, it was running down her calves. It just got worse and worse, and there was nothing I could do to stop it. That was the hard part"—Cora choked up—"I couldn't help her!"

The tears turned into weeping as Cora dredged up the old sorrows. Pierce crawled over to her and pulled himself up on her knees. Her sobs upset him, and he started crying, too. She pulled him up into her arms, and they wept together for a while. Hetty took the baby and rocked him until he stopped. "It wasn't your fault," she said. "They stole Nella away from you."

"No . . . it was like she fell into—a deep well."

"Oh," Hetty said. "The painting."

"Yes," Cora continued in a ragged voice. "I had to watch her sink into that blackness. I could hear her voice changing as she recited the rosaries. Her resolve crumbled, and the words became a crazed whisper. 'Holy Mary, Mother of God, pray for us sinners.' "

Hetty felt a kind of horror gripping her with a cold hand. The well's gravitational pull was strong. "Poor Nella. They broke her."

"Sí." Cora nodded. "The next morning, a totally humiliated child stood before the political science class at the All Saints Academy for Girls and read her recantation in a dull, lifeless voice. That was the end of it."

"What did she read?" Hetty asked. *I have to know!*

"It's there, in the sketchbook," Cora said, nodding. Hetty

picked it up off the coffee table and let Pierce help her turn the pages until she found a sheet of wrinkled notebook paper that had been pasted in. Words had been hastily scribbled across it. The ink here was not black like the India ink, but had faded to the color of dying flowers. Hetty read the words out loud:

> *I wish to withdraw my statements about the fall of the mission and fort they call the Alamo. I have been made to see that Santa Anna was a cruel oppressor and that it was the will of God that Texas become part of the American nation. My mother was wrong in making me believe that the fighters at the Alamo were disreputable men. I now know that these heroes, Travis and Bowie and Crockett and Bonham, were fighting in the name of Liberty and gave their lives nobly so that we Texans of today could live free of the dictatorship of the Old World. I apologize for misleading the history class at the All Saints Academy and ask my teacher, Sister Flanna, to forgive me in the name of God.*
>
> *Signed,*
> *Nella Beckman y de la Ardra*

"Her reading was followed by a heavy silence," Cora said. "Not one of the girls moved for the longest time. Only Sister Flanna. The layers of her starched black robes began to stir. Nella was dismissed with a mere nod. We all watched as she shuffled down the aisle of desks, her bandaged knees covered by her skirt. She didn't look at anyone, just stared straight ahead. Her eyes, which had been so sparkling before, were glazed with the dull passivity of defeat." Cora dried her tears on a tea towel.

"I can't believe she wrote those words!" Hetty shut the album and slammed it down on the coffee table. "Anton ruined his child, sending her there. Didn't you call home and tell them what was going on?"

"Father wouldn't have cared. It's what he wanted. He even kept her there after I graduated."

"Mother was left alone at All Saints?"

Cora nodded sadly. "She was there for another year. Miss Chocha."

"That must have killed her."

"Wait till you hear the rest."

"I can't take any more." Hetty rubbed her temples. A headache was banging its way into her forehead. "Now I'm the one who needs a drink."

"Good idea." Cora stood and started cleaning up the coffee table. "Mescal?"

"Yes! And I'll have mine straight up." Cora brought over the decanter and tipped some of the golden liquid into snifters. Hetty didn't wait for the toast, but let it blaze like a fuse all the way down her throat until it exploded in her stomach. "Ahhhh!" She gasped and held out her snifter.

"Easy." Cora laughed, tipping more in. "You must drink mescal for your tummy, not your head." She put the decanter away.

"Look who's talking!" As Hetty sipped at the second glass, the glimmering sunlight began to swim in her eyes and her rage relaxed. "I need some time, *Tía*."

"Take all the time you need. You've come to the right place to heal. San Antonio is built over many springs."

Hetty would have drowsed until noon if Pierce hadn't woken her midmorning. She carried him into the kitchen, where Cora was already at work brewing coffee. Together, they made *huevos rancheros* and toast. She sat her baby on her lap and fed him some of the toast before she ate herself. After Hetty unpacked the Wichita truck, they talked more about the family over cups of fragrant coffee. The sun began to trespass on the house and heat it up. Cora yanked the chain on the ceiling fan, and a cool breeze swirled between them. Pierce and the cats scampered about on the carpet.

"There's something else I wanted to ask you about, *Tía*."

Cora nestled back into some cushions and waited.

"I have dreams."

"About the future?"

"Yes! How did you know?"

Cora smiled. "You have the ancient eyes. It's in your blood. You're an Ardra."

"Do you have dreams like that, too?"

Cora snickered. "Not since I was psychoanalyzed. That hammers it right out of you."

"I'd like to get rid of them, too. I've decided they're evil." Hetty explained how she had come to view her gift as more of a curse than a blessing.

"Sobrina," Cora said, shaking her head. "You can't get out of it that easily. Such dreams arise from an old, untamed clairvoyance in the blood. Entirely amoral."

"So they're not inherently evil?"

"Would you call wild animals evil? They are what they are."

"Just pictures?"

"*Exactamente.* It's all in how you use them."

"I guess I used them for the wrong purposes." Hetty reflected on what her visions of the faucet had led to, and the two pines bent together. They had afforded her glimpses of goddesses—Santa Adiva and her own magical grandmother who could turn water into wine—yet she had focused solely on tapping the secrets to gain power and wealth. "Does Mamá have the dreams?"

"Not for a long time."

"Is that part of the story?"

Cora nodded sagely.

"I guess I have to hear the rest of it," Hetty said, scooting down to the floor to play with Pierce. "Whether I'm ready or not."

"Let's see. Where was I?"

"You had to leave Nella alone at All Saints. Another year in that place must have finished her off . . . dreams and all."

"Well, if that didn't, the next place did."

"She was sent to another school?"

"*Exactamente.* Nella's last year was spent at Miss Hockaday's Finishing School for Girls in Dallas." Cora slipped her shoes off and curled up with her feet underneath her on the couch. "I didn't recognize her when she came home. My little *hermana linda* had somehow shape-shifted into Miss Nella Beckman. She talked without a trace of a lisp, refused to speak Spanish, and corrected our table manners. She and Lili fought bitterly, Mamá cursing *en Español,* Nella ranting back at her in English: 'I'm not a dirty Mexican anymore, Mamá. I'm Anglo now. Talk to me in English.'

"So began my sister's assimilation into WASP society. Since we were known in San Antonio, Anton took her to Houston for her coming out. The name Ardra was never uttered. She was Nella Beckman, daughter of the mysterious lieutenant who had rented a house at the corner of McKinney and Fannin. She danced beautifully, conversed well, and had a dazzling smile and long lustrous black hair that she wore swept up into a Gibson Girl except for a few curls, which trailed tantalizingly over her pure white complexion. Kirby was smitten right off, and in only a few months, with permission from Anton, asked Nella to be his wife."

"When did he find out about *la familia?*"

"Not till you were born."

"Really? How?"

"Liliana appeared in Houston for the first time, bringing a Mexican midwife, a *partera,* with her. Liliana hoped that Kirby would be so filled with the glow of fatherhood that he would accept you and her graciously. But unfortunately, there was no hiding the secret when you were born. Kirb took one look at Liliana, then at the *partera,* then at you. His white skin turned even whiter as he backed out of the room.

"He wouldn't touch Nella for months after that, I heard, so angry was he at the way he'd been tricked. No one was allowed to see the baby or its grandmother. People were told you were ill. You were all kept locked away. Ask Lina. That was when they had to hire her—to take care of you."

Hetty caught her breath. "You mean—Nella . . . ?"

"Talk to Lina, *please*."

"All right . . . then. I will."

Cora pursed her lips and veiled her eyes. "I know this for sure—the only thing that saved you was your light skin. If you'd been the least bit brown, I fear Kirby would have divorced Nella and that would have been the end of it. There was no way an Old Houstonian, especially an Allen, could have a mestiza as a wife. They could remain married only under the following conditions: Liliana had to leave immediately, *en secreto* as she'd come, and never return to their home. That's why you never met her. She went back to Mexico. Not a word of this was to be spoken to anyone. Nella would have to join the Episcopal High Church and raise the child Esther as a Protestant and an Anglo, bereft of any Mexican heritage. Nella was allowed one secret room where she could keep the artifacts of her previous life. But no one was allowed to go in there. That was the choice she was given."

"But what other choice did she have?"

"Return to San Antonio in the hope that Tipo would take her back and adopt you."

"Do you think he would have?"

"Yes, I do. He waited for her for years. And he would have loved you like his own daughter. That's how Mexicans are. Any child brought into their family is raised like their own blood."

"She took the coward's way."

"Perhaps." Cora sank deeper into the cushions and sipped at her cold coffee for a few moments. "But somehow I can't condemn my sister. Not when I remind myself of what she went through." Cora looked down at Hetty. "And I was hoping it would help you understand things a little more."

Hetty sighed. "It does. Now I see why Kirby's always preferred Charlotte. He rejected me from the beginning."

"*¡Exactamente!* And why I wasn't invited to her wedding."

"That would have blown their cover completely. *Pobrecitas*—they don't even know what love is anymore, do they?"

"Love is a language unto itself. You have to practice it every day or you forget how to speak it."

One of the cats hissed at Pierce, making him cry. It was almost time for his nap. After lunch, Hetty put him in his stroller and bumped it down the terraces by the river. She rocked him until he fell asleep, then she sat down on a mossy stone bench and gazed into the glistening water. She wasn't sure how long she sat there, watching the San Antonio river flow by and thinking about their *familia*'s past. At one point, she shivered. Pierce woke up, but still she didn't move.

That night, she ignored the cradle and carried her baby straight into bed with her. She nestled him amid pillows and fell asleep snuggling close to Pierce's warmth. She dreamed in Spanish.

The next morning, Hetty sat staring at the black telephone beside the sofa. In the corner of her eye, Pierce reached into the wooden trunk and pulled out a gourd. The seeds inside swished as he dragged it across the floor. Cora had gone to the market down in the Quarter. Hetty took another swig of coffee and reached for the receiver, then withdrew her hand. She took a deep breath and forced her fingers to curl around the cold black enamel. She dialed the Warwick number.

Hetty could hear the phone jangle, calling the maid in from the kitchen. "Allen residence," Lina answered.

"It's Hetty."

"¿Donde está?" Lina's startled voice came lisping out of the receiver.

"I'm at Cora's," Hetty said. "Tell Mother not to worry. *Estoy bien*." Hetty couldn't talk for a moment. Silence stretched across miles and miles of telephone line, and seeds rattled in the gourd Pierce raised into the air. "Actually I'm not fine. Cora told me the story of my birth."

Lina whimpered at the other end of the line. "That was so long ago. *Ya no está importante.*"

"If it's not important, then why is everybody hiding it from me. What happened?"

"*M'ija*—ask your mother."

"You know she won't talk about it. Why did they hire you, Lina? You're the one who has to tell me."

"No, no."

"Do you love me?

"¡Por supuesto que sí! Siempre."

"Then you'll tell me."

There was no response. Hetty wondered if Lina had hung up. Then she began talking in a voice shaken with old shame. "I did what I could, *m'ija,* but I was not your *madre*. Mr. Allen, he wouldn't go near Mrs. Allen. Nobody spoke to nobody. The worst thing was, she wouldn't pick you up. When they brought me to that house, you were in a cradle yellow with jaundice, screaming, and she was sitting in a chair, rocking, rocking, just rocking. I tried to hand you to her, but she wouldn't take you. I wanted to place you on her breast, but she always wore these high-necked dresses with long sleeves. There was no way you could crawl your way through all those layers of fabric to find her breasts. The lace scratched your skin. I've never heard a child howl like that. I had to make bottles for you. And she had so much milk. She was sick with it. Her breasts grew hard as rocks."

"What did you do?"

"I had to call Doña Serafina back to nurse Mrs. Allen through the breast sickness. The *partera* gave her willow for the pain and sage tea to dry up her milk. She went into a fever and grew delirious. They packed her breasts with ice. All her love, *el amor de madre,* was frozen there. She wouldn't give it to you, her child, the one it belonged to. 'The baby is dead,' she would tell me when I took her temperature, even though she'd heard you crying. 'My baby died,' she kept saying."

"She wanted me dead. She always has."

"No, no. Mr. Allen wanted *her* dead. He made her crazy. He said she belonged in the kitchen with me, not in bed as his wife. He was so cold to her, poor thing, and she fell into *una depresión.*"

"But she had tricked him first—"

"*Sí.* She sold herself as a white girl in order to marry him."

"I know. Anton put her up to it. Cora told me."

"*¡Qué barbaridad!* Look what it led to. So much suffering. As we say in Mexico, *A la fuerza, ni los zapatos entran.*"

"You can't force . . . a shoe to fit?"

"*Sí.* There was nothing any of us could do to make it fit. I could only comfort the baby who cried, cried, cried. I tried to be a mother to you, *m'ija.*"

"You *were* my mother, Lina. The only one I ever had."

"No, no." Lina fretted into the phone for a moment, then said in a tight voice, "Mrs. Allen, she loves you, too. She says things about you when you're not here, good things."

"She just never says them to my face."

"Oh, *m'ija.* It's over now. You have your husband and your baby. Forget what happened."

"*Sí.* I have my baby . . . but not my husband. He left me, Lina."

"*¡Ay, no! ¿Por qué?*"

"I'm not sure. He said something about an anaconda."

"He'll be back. I know it."

Hetty hung up the phone but kept her hand on it. For the first time, she understood the emptiness in her arms. The coldness that coated her skin, like sleeping without a cover on at night. She pulled her hand back and curled up into a ball on the sofa to find some core of warmth. But none was there. No bright nursery nestled deep in her memory, only an inglenook where the fires had long gone out. Nella hadn't breastfed her, but neither had she held little Esther on her breast and let a baby's warmth wash balm over those old wounds on her knees. *Postigos* everywhere. Doors locking people out. Kirb locking Nella out. Nella locking Hetty out. Shutters and clicks, and a key long lost. Charlotte Baldwin enthroned on eyelet lace.

Hetty dragged a throw over her cold arms. The crackle of her anger collapsed into the embers of sorrow. She lay there for a long time, listening to the dry rattle of the gourd in her poor baby's hand. It reminded her of the stock ticker that used to sit on her father's desk, the one that was always tap-tap-tapping out messages in code. Now she understood what it was trying to tell her.

She pushed herself up and looked about the living room, not knowing where to go or what to do. She lit a cigarette, took a few drags, and then snubbed it out. Pierce called for her, and she ignored him. She spotted a pile of magazines on the coffee table and reached for the *Ladies' Home Journal.* She thumbed through, scanning the ads:

Save water with the new MERMADE WASHERETTE!
When there's only a little laundry

SILVER SHEEN SHAMPOO—414 of the 440 stars
on the silver screen use Silver Sheen!

HER BEST BIRTHDAY EVER!
A porcelain kitchen cabinet with swinging sugar jar!

She threw the magazine down and felt close to tears, the ads making her own life feel so empty by comparison. The journal fell to the floor, and Pierce crawled over and started tearing its pages out. Then the title of an article on the front page of the *San Antonio Express* snagged her eye: BROADWAY BOOTLEGGERS. She picked the newspaper up off the coffee table and scanned it. The piece said that the most successful new rumrunners in Manhattan were members of the fairer sex. No longer just covers to distract police, these enterprising ladies had risen to positions of power, riding about in chauffeured cars and almost never getting arrested. Hetty's eyes flew across the lines of type: They even had their own title, "ladyleggers." She said the name out loud, "Ladyleggers," and felt much better. With a smile, she tore the front page off, kissed it, and folded it into her purse. At last, she had a reason to use her alias, Kelly Bushings.

She withdrew to her room early that night, rocking Pierce to sleep in his cradle. She turned off all the lights and stood naked at the French doors listening to the lisp of a mimosa tree that quivered in the night wind.

The next morning, Hetty decided she'd better wear pants. She dug out one of her few pairs of trousers and pulled them on, followed by lace-up boots. Bending over Pierce's cradle, she kissed him good-bye as he slept and tried to memorize his baby smell. She needed to remember what it was like. She might never see him again.

While she was cleaning up the breakfast dishes, Hetty asked Cora if she'd be willing to look after Pierce for a couple of days.

"Where are you going?"

"Just some loose ends from our import/export business." Hetty kept her gaze sunk in the sink. "Irksome."

"Be careful, *m'ija*. A woman alone . . ."

"I will."

Hetty drove straight to the Mexican Quarter and parked on Haymarket Plaza. The minute she stepped up to the cooler in the ice house, Miguel ripped his apron off and came around with a hearty laugh. He kissed her hand, tipped his black bowler hat, and said, "*Señora,* I prayed you would come back to see Miguel."

"I wanted to thank you for the"—Hetty glanced around—"information you gave my husband and me. It was . . . mmm . . . helpful."

"*Bueno*. So you found *Las Ánimas?*"

Hetty nodded and rolled her eyes. "And how!" She told him about the success they'd had importing mescal until the Rangers had cracked down on bootlegging with the San Diego massacre. "Odell was put in jail. He's still there."

"*¡No me diga!*"

Hetty tried to find out if there was still trade going on down at the ranch. Miguel looked evasive and said he didn't go there anymore. *"Los federales,"* he whispered.

"Is Seca alive?"

"*¿Quién sabe?* Why?"

Hetty looked away.

"*Señora,* you cannot go there by yourself. Where is your husband?"

"I don't know," Hetty said, and realized how much she missed Garret.

Miguel must have seen the loneliness in her eyes because, when the noon bells rang at San Fernando, he insisted she come home with him for lunch. "*Mi casa* belongs to Cora's niece. *Ándele,*" he said, closing his shop and pulling her along by the hand he'd kissed and couldn't seem to let go of. As he led her down the street, he kept praising Cora, calling her *mi corazón* and saying that she was the *comadre* of his daughters. Hetty wondered why her aunt hadn't told her that she was godmother to Miguel's children, as that is such an important position in a Mexican family, a notch below grandmother. Hetty was beginning to realize that Miguel was something more than the source of Cora's mescal. *Why had she wanted me to meet him?*

When they entered the little wooden house off the plaza, Miguel raised the serape and said, *"Con permiso, pásele,"* and waved her through. Hetty found a sitting room that was simple but spotlessly clean. Light flashed across the wooden floor from two small windows crammed with zinnias planted in brightly painted tin cans.

Miguel called into the kitchen, and in a moment, his wife and two teenage daughters appeared, bowing and smiling. He doffed his bowler and placed it over his heart. *"Ella es Ester, la sobrina de Cora."*

Their faces lit up at the mention of her aunt's name, and the three women welcomed Hetty and bustled about to make her comfortable. She was told to sit on the sofa to the right of Miguel's wife, while the daughters brought her coffee and asked if she preferred milk and sugar.

"No es para tanto," Hetty said, but they made a fuss anyway, not content to rest until they felt she had everything she wanted. No one would sit down until Hetty sipped the coffee and smiled. Señora Delgado started inquiring into the health of Cora, then Cora's sister, then Cora's sister's husband, then Hetty's child, then Hetty's sister, and so on. She had her daughters bring out their embroideries, crisp white cottons decorated with red and orange flowers or turquoise birds. These items were displayed with beaming pride on the part of the parents. *My mother never showed off anything I'd done to friends. It didn't go with her decorating schemes.* Miguel went over and hugged his daughters, praising them, and the younger one wouldn't let go of him, her arms hanging around his neck as she grinned at Hetty.

Eventually, Señora Delgado began serving customers, hoisting a huge tray in both arms. The spice of chili haunted the room. Miguel would lift the serape for her. Once he forgot and she called out, "Tipo!" to remind him.

"Tipo?" Hetty asked.

He didn't say anything, just pulled out his guitar and launched into a Mexican folk song: *"Como naranja la granada, cuan dulce las gardenias."* How orange the pomegranates, how sweet the gardenias. *"Ven a mí, mi amor."* Come to me, oh my love!

Hetty's mind flashed with the story Cora had told her about the Folksinger. Her eyes stung from more than the vapors of chili con carne. Miguel was Tipo, the *moreno* her mother had fallen in love with so many years ago—as Cora said, "Not the best looking boy in school, but the friendliest."

Of course, now it all made sense.

That's why Cora had sent her to him two years ago and why he'd wanted her to come back to see him alone. She thought he'd made a pass at her, but no. He wanted to meet Nella's daughter. The girl he had hoped to adopt as his own. Hetty swooned as one golden note after another poured out of his mouth. They sifted into her soul like the pollen of cinnamon flowers.

When he finished, she said, "You knew my mother, didn't you?"

Miguel just smiled.

"You're the man she really wanted to marry. You're Tipo."

He touched his finger to his lips to signal *shhh* as the serape lifted to reveal bare brown feet.

"I'm sorry," Hetty whispered, just before Señora Delgado stepped back into the room.

"Nella's daughter is very beautiful." He kissed Hetty's hand. "You always have a home with Miguel. Come and stay with us." He stood and went over to his two girls, embracing them. They rested their heads on his shoulders shyly.

This could have been me, Hetty thought. *I could have had this gentle man for my father and hung on him like his daughters do. Kirb hardly ever hugs me, and when he does, it's very stiff. Token hugs. But here you could drown in the love and never come up for air.* Hetty ached to go over and join their embrace, to be part of the warmth and happiness. But she didn't want to be a gate-crasher; she wanted to be invited.

On the way out, the Madonna Morena caught her eye, the one she'd noticed before. A little shelf for votive candles was held up by a rawhide strap tied around nails. Miguel came up behind her. "I've never seen a Virgin with dark skin," Hetty said. "Who is she?"

Miguel snorted. "Nella never told you?"

"There's a lot Mamá never told me."

"¡Qué desgracia!" He gazed at Hetty in amazement. *"Ay, mi amiga,* you must know about Guadalupe. You will only find her in Mexico. She is ours—yours and mine. Sit—*aquí.*" He pulled out a bench. "Tipo will teach you."

He told her breathlessly how a simple peasant was walking on Tepeyac Hill outside Mexico City when he heard the tremulous sound of birdsong. He looked up the hill and at its summit she stood, the Virgin of Guadalupe, shining like the sun, standing on the moon and cloaked in the stars. He fell to his knees in ecstasy. The Virgin was appearing *here*—on Mexican soil—not to a Spanish nobleman but to *him,* Juan Diego, a common Indian. She commanded him to go to the bishop of Mexico and have him build her a temple on the site. Juan did so immediately, but the Spanish bishop doubted him and demanded proof. He returned to Tepeyac Hill and humbly asked the lady for a sign. Even though it was December, she filled his tilma—his rough maguey cloak—with roses of a heavenly fragrance that sparkled, not with dewdrops, but with pearls.

"When he dropped the corners of his tilma in front of the bishop," Miguel said, "the roses spilled out and there, on the cloak, appeared this"—he pointed at the tin painting—"*efigie.*"

"She's beautiful," Hetty said.

"As fresh today as four hundred years ago. Her message to all Mexicans is, 'Let not your heart be disturbed.' She brings us peace. And a mother's love."

Hetty noticed again the golden stars on her midnight blue mantle. "It's like she's clothed in the heavens."

"Sí." He crossed himself. "She performs miracles."

"She does? I could sure use one of those."

"Then you must visit the Chapel of Miracles on Ruiz." He told her all about it and gave her directions. "It is run by an old woman named Madame Candelaria. You will be welcome there."

She hung about in the doorway. There was something she had to have before she left, but it wasn't something she could ask for. Miguel would have to give it of his own free will or it would mean nothing. Hetty smiled sheepishly at him and waited. He smiled back at her, his deep black eyes swimming with sweet affection. Hetty could see why her mother would fall in love with this man. What woman wouldn't?

They gazed into each other's eyes for a few moments, then Miguel gave her what she'd been longing for. A long, long hug. He held her close to his body, her heart beating right next to his. Hetty let her arms slide around him and held on as tight as she could, murmuring in his ear, "How I wish you'd been *mi padre.*"

Hetty followed the directions Miguel had given her and parked on Ruiz Street at the corner of Medina. There sat the tiny adobe chapel she was seeking, the shrine of *El Señor de los Milagros*. The door was open so all could enter, just as Miguel said it would be. Hetty stepped into the dim interior, lit only by two tall candles burning on either side of the altar. Above them loomed the Lord of the Miracles himself, the life-sized Christ sculpted so long ago out of copper. Even now, in early afternoon, the chapel was stirring with worshippers. An old man crept forward on crutches. A blind woman dressed in elegant black silks was led away by a nurse after kneeling at the altar. A young couple, the woman looking like she could give birth any moment, added a bouquet of flowers to the heap on the altar. Hetty stood to one side, wondering if any of the old women shuffling about was Madame Candelaria.

Amid the wilting flowers, she could see various body parts crudely carved out of wood: hands, feet, and hearts, signaling the miraculous cures the faithful had experienced after praying here. Hetty wondered why Miguel had sent her here. It all struck her as the usual Catholic superstition. Then she turned and noticed another altar to the side. Every inch of wall space above it was covered with *retablos,* crude paintings on tin showing worshippers being saved from dire illness and death. In place of the *señor* stood the Madonna Morena in her inky blue cloak. The stars had been crudely painted with white dots, but she was clearly Our Lady of Guadalupe. Hetty walked over and strained to make out the details through the dim light. In one scene, a child was about to be run over by a train, but the Madonna stood in the tracks and stopped it. In another, a rattlesnake was poised to strike a field-worker, but the

Madonna caught its fangs in her cloak. In a third, a blindfolded man was about to be executed by a firing squad, but Our Lady of Guadalupe held up her hand and stopped the bullets in midair. In a vase on the altar, someone had left a single white lily with a love note tied to it. *Empress of the Americas,* it read. Hetty's heart lit like a votive candle.

While others knelt before the giant crucifix, Hetty went down on her knees before these images of the starry Virgin. No wonder the Mexicans revere her as their patron saint. No matter how flawed our own earthly mothers might be, here was one avatar of the Divine Mother who was perfect in her love: a gossamer, celestial goddess that all mestizas could adore. *I think I've finally found my lady,* Hetty thought. She prayed for her protection, visualized the blue cloak flowing around her like warm arms and staying with her no matter where she went.

Then she got into her truck and headed south on Route 281 toward San Diego, Texas, and the brush country.

Chapter 17

Hetty steered along the gravel road slowly, braking as the truck rattled through the ruts that flash floods had left in the spring. She followed it until the road dipped down and crossed the dry creek bed itself. Here she parked and got out, checking the ground before she put her foot down. She looked up and down the creek bed, but saw no sign of a pack train. Only furrow after furrow of hoofprints from heavily laden mules. Perhaps it wasn't dark enough for them to make their final approach to *Las Ánimas*. She backed the truck up onto the embankment and sat in the cab, waiting.

Friday used to be pickup day, but a lot could have changed in three years. It already had. When she'd arrived at the ranch, she'd learned that Jeremiah was in jail and that Seca's real name was Gus—Gustavo. He was bringing in the first pack train tonight, the man behind the table had told her—an impudent fellow sporting a bow tie and suspenders. But the man had also told her she had to register with the Duke of Duval, Archie Parr himself, and pay a hefty *mordida. A hundred and fifty dollars! That's half my money!* That's why she had broken the rule and driven out into the brush alone. If she could just talk to Seca, she knew everything would be all right.

She rolled down her windows and listened to the sounds of the brush as daylight began leaking away. Insects called in shuddering waves, and a lone coyote howled somewhere far off. *If I get lost,* she reminded herself, *I could always do what Mac did—follow a fence back to the road, down a* sendero, *a path cleared through the thorns.* Reassured, she took the teller's envelope out of her bag and slipped it into one of her boots, drawing the laces even tighter. Then she tucked her handbag under the driver's seat. A whiff of cumin teased her nose. She opened the fragrant paper bag on the seat beside her and ate a couple of the pork tamales she'd gotten in San Diego at the stand Odell had told her about. "They're the real thing," he'd said, "steamed for an hour inside corn shucks."

The sound of hooves thudded below. Not galloping, but loping along cautiously. She looked down into the creek bed, and he appeared, faint in the dusk light. *El explorador*—the scout they sent ahead to be sure the coast was clear. He spotted the truck immediately, of course. He did two things simultaneously: slid his 30-30 out of his saddle scabbard and formed his lips into the plaintive cry of the great horned owl. He was answered from a distance by several quick hoots. Then Hetty heard more hooves as two other armed *vaqueros* came riding in behind him. All three rust-colored faces glowered up at the truck. Hetty stashed the tamales on the floor, then got out slowly and kept her hands splayed to show that she carried no weapon. She tried not to let her fingers tremble too much. The other two drew their rifles.

"Buenas noches, señores," she said as she stood on the edge of the embankment. *"¿Se encuentra El Víbora Seca?"*

The scout sniggered that none of their snakes were dry and groped himself, bringing a bawdy laugh out of the other two. They began debating what they were going to do with her. The scout said that he was ready to bed *la gringa* right now in the back of her truck, but the bearded man on his right could see that she was *muy macha* and would require more than one man to quench her fire. He suggested they take *la puta* captive and keep the whore in their camp tonight. That way they could each have a turn enjoying her. He pulled a bottle out of his saddlebags and guzzled some, wiping his black goatee with the back of his hand. *El explorador* snarled at him, and they began exchanging insults, challenging each other's virility.

"¿Se encuentra El Víbora Seca?" she insisted again, lighting a cigarette and leaning on the fender. The scout shot her a menacing glance and swung a leg up to slide out of his saddle. *Uh-oh, this may have been a huge mistake.* Hetty turned to jump into the truck and back out of the culvert, but she was too late. He was already swaggering up the embankment. She braced herself against the fender.

"¿Quieres conocer al víbora?" he asked. He said that his snake was ready to spit some venom now and unzipped his pants. He pressed himself against her, kissing her roughly and scratching her skin with his stubble. She dropped her cigarette. He tried to squash her between his legs, unbuckle his pants, and hold on to his rifle at the same time, but couldn't quite manage all three. Hetty wiggled out and tore open the truck door. When he tried to follow her, his pants sagged around his ankles, giving her time to hop into the cab, click the lock, and roll up the window. He twirled his rifle around and swung the butt as hard as he could at the window. It shattered. Hetty flinched away from the flying glass and honked the brassy horn over and over. He undid the lock and came after her. She slid over to the other side and kicked the door open. She jumped out and came face-to-face with the Mexican in the black goatee. He stood leering at her in the dim light. When she tried to run by him, he caught her in the vise of his arms. His breath stank of mescal and cigarettes. "Seca! Seca!" she screamed over and over until her captor clamped his sweaty hand over her mouth and dragged her down into the creek. The scout trailed behind, hitching up his pants and dragging a roll of rawhide rope out of his saddlebag. He sliced some off and tied her hands behind her back. When she tried to kick him away, he backhanded her across the cheek and sent a sharp pain ricocheting through her head. He spit out words she was glad she didn't understand and kicked her in the legs and buttocks with the blunt toe of his cowboy boots.

"You're going to be *sorry!*" she screamed. "Seca's a friend of mine. Gustavo—Gus!" When she tried to scream again, they gagged her with a couple of kerchiefs tied together, then beat her some more.

Finally, the scout knotted a noose around her neck and tied it to the horn of his saddle, giving her several yards of slack. He mounted his horse, cursing at her, while one of the others made the *krrooo-oo* of the great horned owl. They rode forward, tugging Hetty behind them like a peasant arrested by the Rurales. She stumbled through the twilight as best she could, knowing she had to keep up or be dragged along on the ground.

Hetty laid her head on her knees in despair. She'd miscalculated, gambled one time too many, and lost. She cursed herself for being such a fool. The three Mexicans were going to turn her into just another lousy *chingada,* raped and undone. Did it matter anyway? Who would care as long as she paid back the money she owed and kept to herself? She had to give in, let herself be taken, and surrender, finally, to *nada*.

Nothing.

She reminded herself to breathe.

Hetty had no sooner taken several deep breaths to calm her nerves when the *krrooo-oo* of the great horned owl bleated in the darkness. It was the same ghostly sound that echoed down the creek bed before she'd been captured, and Hetty knew that mournful cry didn't rise out of the throat of an owl. Another *krrooo-oo* sounded in answer, then a light swept over the ground. She craned her neck to see what was happening. Someone emerged out of the ranch house dangling a farm lantern. He swung it slowly—sending black tree shadows seesawing across the dusty earth. That must have been a signal because as soon as he snuffed out the wick, Hetty was plunged into a tumult of terrifying sounds—thuds of many hooves, the clash of bottles being unloaded, mules braying with relief as the weight was lifted off their backs. She pulled her legs close for fear of being trampled.

The animals soon grew still and the wind rose again, bringing with it the smell of smoke. Before long she heard the crackle of twigs and saw an orange light flickering. She twisted her head around again. Through the lace of mesquite branches, a campfire lit up the clearing. She caught a whiff of roasting meat. She tried to count the number of copper-colored faces hovering over the flames—close to a dozen. Cigarettes dangled from their mouths, and the conversation reaching her through the smoke was anything but polite, with cries of *"pingas"*—"dicks"—and *"¡No me jodas!"*—"Don't fuck with me!"—growled more than once. She felt an increasing sense of dread imagining what was going to happen to her when they'd finished eating. She hid her face behind the tree again. Trembling, she tried to work the kerchiefs off her mouth so she could call to the ranchers for help, but they were tied on too tightly. Her cheek throbbed, and her legs felt sore and bruised from being beaten. The rawhide cut into her wrists.

After a while, she heard rustling and whispering. Her three captors stole through the brush and eyed her with relish, arguing over who would have the first turn. *El explorador* felt it was his privilege, as he was the one who'd subdued her. The bearded man disagreed, boasting that he'd been the one who'd caught her when she'd escaped from the truck. All three decided they would need a serape to spread on the ground. They set off in search of one.

Hetty's mind went adrift in the darkness as she cried quiet tears. She saw Garret reaching out his hand to her as he'd done so many nights ago. Why didn't she take it? Why did she let him walk away from her? She couldn't see any answers in this blackness. The night seemed endless, inside and out. It was a lonely place, filled with the distant howls of coyotes. Make that singular. One lone coyote, half starved, with a bad case of mange. That's all that lived in this wilderness. Nothing brave and bloodthirsty here. Just things that slunk and skulked, elusive eyes dry and cracked in the drought. That made her think of the fable her mother had once told her, about the fox and the coyote. Now she understood what it meant. The coyote had gotten cut to pieces trying to chase the image of the fox reflected in the mirrors of a hacienda. That was Hetty, cut by dark mirrors that reflected back her own image. There was nothing there after all, just broken glass. She was as stupid as that coyote and just as dead. She thought of all the tales her mother had told her and ached to hear her voice once more. Other faces flashed in the shards of mirror: Garret, Cora, and baby Pierce. Would she see any of them again?

Then something flickered in the darkness. Not a campfire but two candles. Burning on the altar at the Chapel of Miracles today. Miguel had sent her there for a reason. Hetty pictured the blue mantle with the stars on it, called it down out of the heavens to surround her, pictured the Virgin's hands coming together between her legs like a chastity belt, like a prayer—*Oh, Virgen de Guadalupe*—Empress of the Americas—*protégeme, protégeme.*

She held this image in her mind as she heard the three men come back and spread the serape on the ground, then free her from the trunk and untie her hands that were so cramped behind her. She could feel them stretching her arms out into the crucifix pose as in the painting by Cora, tying her wrists to two different trees so her body was completely open and vulnerable. She didn't even try to kick them as they unbuttoned her blouse and pulled her pants down to spread her legs. She still saw the hands of the Empress, clasped there in the shape of a V. Serenity settled over her like a misting of stardust, quelling her fear. She listened calmly to the sounds around her. The crackle of the fire. The sound of a belt being unbuckled. The breathing of a man aroused. The three Mexicans must have settled their argument because *el explorador* was the first to slouch between her legs and unbuckle his pants. They sagged at his feet. He sniggered with pleasure, yanking on his raw brown erection. It grew shockingly large and pointed right at her in the firelight.

In her state of calm, Hetty was able to distinguish a man's voice a little way off. It was a voice she recognized. He was giving commands over by the fire, and someone was answering him: *"Sí, mi jefe."* She knew it—Seca was here! She tried to glance that way, but then the scout was on top of her. She felt his fingers join those of the Empress at the crux of her legs. He began catching his breath and gyrating his hips. Then he made one mistake. He slipped the gag off her mouth roughly so he could kiss her. For a few moments, she pretended to kiss him back, letting his tongue into her mouth and pushing hers into his. Then she twisted her lips away long enough to scream *"Seca!"* as loud as she could. He clamped his hand over her mouth, but it was too late.

"¿Y éso qué es?" she heard the distant voice demand.

"Es la gringa," someone answered.

There was silence. The scout pushed himself into a standing position and buttoned up his pants. His cockiness collapsed into servility as footsteps approached. Hetty heard the creak of cowboy boots and felt a man straddling her. She couldn't make out who it was in the darkness but thought she recognized the bend of his beaten-up Stetson.

He turned her face into the firelight. Amazed, he asked, "Esther de las Ardras?"

Seca untied Hetty and carried her over to a rock near the fire. The Stetson shadowed his features as he wrapped her in a serape and examined her wounds. Then he knelt before her on one knee and removed his hat, asking if she were all right. Hetty nodded, her fears uncoiling when she saw his face. She was afraid he would look different from her memories of him, less dangerous, more ordinary. But the man kneeling before her was as rugged a *norteño* as ever, the warrior's gaunt cheekbones shaded by three days of stubble, a new scar stabbed across one cheek. The eyes gazing at her were definitely the same—those haunting black mesquite eyes flickering in the firelight with their glint of hidden power. After reassuring her, he stomped around the fire, forcing his men to fall back and let him through. Everyone could hear him spewing out wrathful Spanish at the three would-be rapists hiding in the trees.

Then he came back and apologized for the way his men had treated her. Out of his pack, he offered her some pinole, the parched corn—spiced and sweetened—that he said all his men carried on the trail. A few bites, along with swigs of water from his canteen, drove away Hetty's thirst. "*Gracias.* I'll never find my truck in the dark."

"The big light will come soon. *La luna.* Hold out your wrists." He poured silver tequila over her abrasions, causing her to gasp from the stinging. He splashed some on her cheek.

"¿Y aquí?" she asked, pointing at her lips. "I need a drink after

what I've been through." After a couple of shots, the trembling inside Hetty grew fainter and fainter, like the aftershocks of an earthquake. She wrapped up in the blanket and waited for her heart to stop racing. "I knew you were alive," she told him. "I always believed it."

"Coyotes are hard to catch."

"*Ay, sí.* But, you used to be a snake. A rather dry one."

"Nobody calls me that anymore."

"So I heard, Gus."

"Not Gus! Gustavo."

"You'll always be Seca to me, I'm afraid. It's funny. I was thinking I was like a coyote tonight, too. The one in the fable with the fox. *¿Lo sabes?*"

"*Claro que sí.* That coyote was stupid. *Oye, gringa,* why did you come here alone?"

"*¿Por qué no?* You always said I was *muy brava.*"

"*Y loca también.* Where are your partners?"

"Odell's in jail. Mac hasn't been back here since the San Diego massacre." She found herself talking a lot about Garret—how his prediction of the East Texas oil field surprised everyone, how his dedication at the drilling site surprised even her. "He worked sixteen hours a day to bring in the well. We'd be rich by now if the damned government hadn't stepped in."

"*¡Ay! ¡Los federales!* They are keeping us all poor."

"So, to answer your question. That's why I came back here alone. We made an agreement to pay back the interest owners on the well. I need to make some big money fast. I was hoping you'd help me."

Seca didn't say anything. He sprinkled some salty worm on the skin between his thumb and forefinger and tossed it into his mouth after a swig of tequila, then sucked on a slice of lime. He looked at her with glazed eyes as he chewed on the fruit. *"¿Cuánto necesitas?"*

Hetty held her breath, then mumbled, "Three thousand dollars."

"How much?"

She spoke up. "Three thousand."

"And you have . . . ?"

"Three hundred."

Seca spit the lime out. *"No, no. Es imposible."*

"¿Por qué?"

"How much you get for Mexican liquor in Houston?"

"Good silver tequila? We used to have clients who paid ten dollars a bottle for top grade."

"Then you will need three hundred bottles."

"It looked like a long pack train to me."

"*Oye, gringa,* each bottle of Jose Cuervo is now four pesos. Two American dollars."

"That's six hundred dollars. I only have three. You'll have to give me a discount."

Seca leaped off the rock. *"¡Ay! ¡Que mujer tan mala!"*

"Why? Why are you calling me a bad woman? I'm just trying to pay back a debt of honor."

"¡Carajo!" He paced as he cursed, circling her like a wild animal. "There will be no discount. Tequila is not a toy for gringas to play with. Tequila is the heart of Mexico, which is already crushed and roasted. And now you want to crush it again with your greed?"

"I only—"

"Only, only, only! *Ay, mujer*—do you have any idea what it takes to produce a bottle of tequila?"

"No, I guess I don't."

"The *jimadores* must work the fields their whole lives. They only have one holiday each year, the feast of the *Virgen*. All day, in the hot, hot sun, they cut out the hearts of the agave plants—the *piñas* weigh three hundred pounds!" He lifted his Stetson up with both hands. "These must be carried to the hacienda when they are baked and crushed before the juices can be fermented. The men have to turn the great stone themselves. It is backbreaking work." He slammed his hat down on the ground in front of her. "As if that's not enough, when the juices flow into pits, the men have to jump in naked to work the must. It is their sweat that gives tequila its flavor—*el sudor del hombre.*"

The passion in his voice rendered Hetty mute. She only sat there watching as he picked up his Stetson, blew the dust off, and slung it back onto his head.

"That is why you must never ask for a discount on tequila. *¡Nunca!*"

"*Perdóneme.* I guess I didn't realize what it's worth."

"I should give you back to my men as a toy. You value nothing, Esther de las Ardras, least of all yourself." He strode away from her in scorn.

As Hetty watched from the rock, the big light Seca had promised her, *la luna,* floated into the eastern sky only to get moored in a drift of mesquite trees. When it finally washed free, its icy light settled upon her like a mist. Even though there were lots of men nearby, she felt completely alone there in the lunar coldness. She'd been shunned by the one friend she thought she could count on here in the desolate brush. She tried to think of something to say, some way to rescue the night. She was good at that. But nothing came to mind that she thought would work. It was useless. She might as well give up and go home.

In the distance, the lone coyote began howling again.

Once away from the fire, the watery moonlight flooded in all around her. Hetty had never seen the brush country glazed with such a silvery sheen, the creek bed rippling with light and shadow as she followed its twists and turns. Such unearthly beauty should have lifted her out of despair, but she was sunk in way too deep. She walked along the cleft of the sandy bottom in the track that would brim with rain in the spring. Her heart felt every bit as dry as the stream. She had driven all the men in her life away. When she'd wrapped Pick up in her wedding shawl, it was as if she were saying, "*I've killed my marriage along with my friend. Both are dead to me now, and I must spend the rest of my life alone.*" She had to stop pretending that Garret would come looking for her. It was time to admit the truth. He was gone for good, and she would have to walk back to the truck all by herself through moonlight that was the color of loneliness.

She climbed the embankment, cranked open the door of the Wichita, and brushed shards off the seat. When she went to slide the key into the ignition, her hand emerged into moonlight. She remembered that the Empress stood upon the crescent moon, whispering, *"Let not your heart be disturbed!"* The black thoughts roosting in Hetty's mind rose like a colony of bats. The air cleared. Her senses sharpened. And there it was. The scent of cumin and chilies emanating from the bag on the floor. She'd forgotten about the tamales.

Hetty found Seca slouched on a straw mat by the fire. She knelt and spread the ten tamales in front of him, their husks yawning open teasingly in the flickering light. She knew what tamales meant to Mexican men, how they were always served at weddings and for festive holidays such as Cinco de Mayo. Opening the corn husk was a ritual, the moist pork stuffing that spilled out a treat no *tequilero* could resist after a long trip through the dry brush. She was right. He picked one up, parted the husk, and began nibbling on the corn masa. Wordlessly, he consumed four of them one after another with a swig of tequila in between. He licked his fingers and handed her the bottle.

"I'm sorry if I seemed greedy and thoughtless before," she said, "but there's something I haven't told you. My husband left me."

He raised his eyebrows. "Mac . . . ?"

"Sí." Hetty couldn't stop a few tears from trickling down her cheeks. "He's gone. I'm alone now. He left me owing a lot of money to a lot of people, including my parents. That's why I came to find you. I don't know who else to turn to. Isn't there anything you can do to help me? I'm begging you."

Seca thought for a moment, then nodded. "*Sí.* You could buy *botas.*"

"¿Botas?"

"Goatskins. Five gallons each. You bottle it yourself."

"I don't know how to do that."

"Your friend, Miguel—he will help you. He always bought *botas.*"

She took a gulp out of the bottle. "How much are they?"

"Forty pesos each. I can give you ten."

"Could I . . . possibly . . . have twenty, *por favor?*"

Seca snorted. "Why should I do that?"

"You owe me."

"Why I owe you?"

"Because I made you famous. You have a drink named after you—the Dry Snake. They're even serving Dry Snakes in Dallas now."

"¿De veras?"

"*Sí.* I was just there this spring and had one. Everyone in Texas knows about Seca. You're something of a folk hero, thanks to me. That's why you shouldn't change your name to Gus."

"Gustavo!"

"Besides, I'm going to be bringing you more business." Hetty ferreted a bent cigarette out of her pocket, lit it, and told Seca all about her plans to start a new business called the Kelly Bushings Bootleggers. "My ladyleggers will be coming here every week to pick up supplies."

"Women? You want me to do business with women? You are *muy mala.*"

Hetty fed him some more tequila, then tried to make him understand why women made better rumrunners than men because of their ability to elude arrest. She could feel her line of gab coming back in spades. "Take New York, for instance," she said, sending a plume of smoke into the night air, "did you know it's crawling with ladyleggers making pots of money? They're almost more popular than the men. I'm going to do the same thing right here in Texas! Houston first, then Dallas." She made it sound like she knew what she was talking about, even though every word she uttered was taken straight out of the article she'd torn off the front page of the *San Antonio Express* and still carried in her purse.

Seca admitted he found this strange. "In Mexico, we say a woman belongs at home . . . with a broken leg."

"Charming. I'll relocate immediately. Look, *amigo,* if you want to do business with Americans, you have to be up to date. Things are changing."

"More than you know, *gringuita.*" He looked at her mysteriously, then explained how his father—the *patron* of all Tamaulipas, the state that wormed its way along the Rio Grande just south of the brush country of Texas—was positioning himself to become a legitimate importer of mescal, as he saw sentiment turning against the Volstead Act and knew it would only be a matter of time before the law was repealed. His political connections confirmed this.

"So if you're going to become a—*¿qué dijiste?*—ladylegger," Seca told Hetty, "you'd better do it *pronto*."

"That means Odell will be getting out of jail soon," Hetty realized. "Wait'll I tell his wife!"

The tequila was working its alchemy in her blood, transmuting the world around her. She lay back on the mat and peered into the sky directly overhead. The moon looked to Hetty like a great glowing pearl whose surface had been scratched. It rose higher, radiantly full.

After midnight, Seca stretched out on his straw mat and invited Hetty to join him under a wool blanket.

"Don't you think I should have my own?"

"Gustavo only has one."

"That's convenient."

"Conveniente, no. Necesario, sí."

She climbed in without further comment, groaning as she stretched out her bruised legs. He did unstrap his bandoleer to sleep but kept his gun belt on. As she lay beside him in the moonlight, she caught his wild scent again, that savory mingling of leather and Latin musk. *El sudor del hombre,* what gives tequila its flavor. He had his back to her, his head resting on one arm. She edged a little closer and whispered, "Tell me about the town of Guerrero," but there was no response. He was fast asleep.

Hetty was startled awake by the blue light of dawn. The moon still swam in the west, reluctant to submerge itself for another day. When she rolled over, stiff and aching, Seca was lying on his side, watching her.

"You can have fifteen *botas,*" he said.

"Seventeen."

"You are very beautiful, *gringuita*."

"Then why didn't you touch me in the night?"

"Because you are still in love with him—that *Mac*."

"I am?"

"*Por supuesto que sí!* That is why you are here."

Hetty started to object, then fell silent. She knew he was right. Underneath it all, she was starving for her man, suffering through a famine of love's needs so deep she would have given herself to Seca last night without a thought. But it was Mac she hungered for, that particular smell of his, his silly cigarette breath, his pleading blue eyes—just some word of where he was and whether he missed her, too. He should have been along with her on this trip. It wasn't right for her to be here alone with so many unpredictable men. If only she could get the investors paid off, then maybe she could hunt her husband down and persuade him to come back to her.

She heard the other men stirring and pulled the blanket over her head. Seca ducked under with her, and they whispered together there in the pale light. "Tell me about the town of Guerrero."

"It is very old, and the houses are all built with great stones from the quarry."

"There's a quarry?"

"*Sí.* At Rio Salado. And a waterfall, too. There are citrus trees that make the whole town smell like orange blossoms in the spring. My father and I go hunting."

"For what? Coyotes?"

"No, no. In Tamaulipas, there are wildcats and jaguars, pumas and wolves. They eat the cattle."

"But what's the town like—describe it to me."

"There is a beautiful old church, Nuestra Señora del Refugio, whose bells you can hear all through the streets. There is the Hotel Flores and the Municipal Palace and great stone benches in the plaza where the old ones go to tell stories because there is nothing else to do."

"Tell me more about the houses."

"They stay cool in summer because of the thick stones. They have high ceilings held up by one long beam of wood. There are no addresses."

"How do you send a letter?"

"Every house has a stone over the entrance with a carving on it—a snail, a monkey, a sandal, different things. When you send a letter, you put the name of the person, then the Snail House, or the Jaguar House. Guess who made the carvings?"

"Giants!"

"No. Ardras."

"Oh, that's right! I forgot, we were stonecutters."

"They were artists, *gringa.* Makers of beauty. That is why you must not bring yourself so low. You are an Ardra."

"I'll remember that."

"Seca commands it. And I am *jefe.*"

"Sí, mi jefe. Gracias."

They smiled at each other, their faces close. He breathed the words "*De nada*" into her mouth just as he'd done three years ago. Only this time, he followed it with his lips, kissing her gently. "*Vete con Dios,* Esther de las Ardras. Never forget who you are."

She kissed him back eagerly, opening her mouth. It made her senses reel. "Take me back to Guerrero with you."

"No, no." Seca chuckled. "That is not your way. You must find your own *sendero.*"

And so he sent her off with seventeen goatskins gurgling about in the bed of her truck. They loaded them as dawn broke so she could elude the sheriff and his *mordida*. She watched the light creeping toward them on the ground and knew she had to rev up the windowless truck and retreat quickly, speeding up the risky road to San Diego, but she couldn't tear herself away from Seca. She kept hugging him and kissing his hands and muttering *"Muchas, muchas gracias"* over and over. She was radiant with gratitude in the clear morning light, not so much for the three extra *botas* he'd thrown in as a bonus, but because he'd reminded her that she was not only descended from the founders of cities but was also a daughter of the Ardras, makers of beauty and carvers of stone.

Hetty left a plume of dust behind her as she roared through the thickets of mesquite, expecting to encounter a roadblock at any moment. But luckily, there were none. She arrived back at the ice house before lunch. When Miguel saw her bruised face and the cargo she carried in the bed of her truck, he panicked and spit out, *"¡Híjole!"* ordering her to move it immediately to the back of his shop, where he quickly transferred the *botas* into his storeroom and covered them with burlap bags—lecturing her the whole time in Spanish about what a foolish coyote she was.

"But it worked," she protested. "Now I can pay off my debts."

"You are just like your *madre,*" he muttered. He put her to work, emptying the tequila into a basin, then ladling it into the dusty glass bottles he had stashed on his shelves. In the lull of the afternoon, he came back and helped her. By dinner, Hetty had three hundred and forty bottles of crystal clear tequila plata that she knew she'd be able to sell to connoisseurs back in Houston for ten dollars apiece. Miguel even had labels she could glue on the bottles. She would be able to pay off Cleveland and still have enough money to live for at least a year without worry. She parked the Wichita along the dark street at the back of the ice house, and Miguel helped her wrap and load her plunder between layers of burlap bags.

Hetty gave him a long, lingering hug and kissed his hand. "Will you accept my apology, Tipo?"

"No, but I love you, my little Tipa. *¡Ándele!"* He waved her into the truck.

She glowed with triumph and pride until she returned to Cora's for a late supper and saw the look on her aunt's face.

"You've been back into the brush, haven't you?"

"You knew about that?"

"Of course, Miguel told me."

Hetty blushed deeply, exposed in front of the person she probably loved more than anyone else. She sat on the sofa, too stunned to know what to say.

"How did you get the bruise?" Cora came and sat beside her.

Hetty blurted out the whole story of her kidnapping, her rescue by Seca, and the purchase of the seventeen *botas*. "I guess I didn't learn my lesson after all. I've put people in danger again."

"Yourself, most of all. You should have been honest with me, *m'ija.* I would have warned you. The trade has become bloodthirsty since the massacre. Even Miguel doesn't go there. I wouldn't honor those men with the name *tequileros* anymore. Now they're just *ratones*."

Rats. Hetty shuddered, remembering the faces of the men who'd captured her. "I'm sorry, Aunty. What I regret most of all is taking advantage of your kindness. Do you forgive me?"

"Of course I forgive you. I'm a Guadalupana."

"You are?" Hetty looked around, surprised. "But you don't have her *efigie* anywhere."

"Look closer."

Hetty wandered through the rooms searching for some trace of the Madonna Morena, but no tins glinted on the walls. She rifled through drawers and opened cupboards. Nothing, not even a rosary. The last room she entered was the studio, and there, finally, she saw what her aunt was talking about. *How could I have missed it?* Every painting Cora had created for her new show *Quimeras* was composed in front of a deep blue sky blazing with stars. "I put the stars on with gold leaf," Hetty remembered Cora saying. She was creating a whole suite of paintings shimmering with the radiance of the Madonna's veil.

Cora came in behind her. "They've been making scientific studies of the tilma since 1751. Astronomers tell us that the stars on the mantle match exactly the constellations that would have been visible in the sky over Mexico City on the day Diego had his vision, December 12, 1531. I've taken it upon myself to conceal one of these constellations in each of my new paintings. There's Libra," she said, pointing to the painting of the flooded town, "Scorpio behind the nuns with the animal heads, and Hydra over the melting boulders—all the southern constellations. Then, from the left side of the mantle, the northern constellations in these works"—she waved toward a group of canvases stacked against a wall—"the great bear, the hunting dogs, an entire map of the cosmos on that historic night—the only appearance of the Virgin in the Western Hemisphere."

Hetty's eyes grew wider as she looked from one painting to another. "You're too clever for me, *Tía*. You've hidden these clues right in plain sight across the background of your new work."

"Many of the Madonna's secrets are hidden right in plain sight. For instance—" Cora reached into a drawer of her painting cabinet and handed Hetty an actual photograph of the image on the tilma. "What body part does this remind you of?"

Hetty studied the oval aura around the Virgin, the rippling folds of her mantle. She caught her breath. "Oh my God, it's a vulva."

"Exactly. She's our yoni—both sacred and profane." Cora let Hetty contemplate this for a moment. "I hope I haven't spoiled it for you."

"No!" Hetty handed the photograph back. "It makes me adore her all the more. Does the tilma still exist?"

"They say it's remained in pristine condition for four hundred years even though the fibers of the maguey should have rotted after thirty. You can view it at the temple in Mexico City. Which, by the way, sits at the exact geographic center of the Americas."

"I find all this unbelievable," Hetty said, as they returned to the living room and sat on the sofa. "Everything about Guadalupe is so magical."

"Listen to this!" Cora spread her hands in the air for emphasis. "If you enlarge a photograph of her eyes twenty-five hundred times, you find a tableau of all the people present when the tilma was unfolded, reflected on her cornea. As an artist, I know how impossible that would be to paint."

"¡Sí! ¡Fantástico!" Hetty said, trying to picture it. "I think I'm becoming a—what did you call it?—Guadalupana? I've been looking for a goddess."

"She's the only one we've got, really."

The quiet of the evening settled around them as stars started glimmering unseen in the sky above. "Where's Pierce?"

"I put him to bed long ago."

"Thanks, *Tía.*" Hetty sighed. "You make me ashamed of myself. You're so good and kind and loving and . . . regal. A true consort of the Empress."

Cora shook her head and smiled. "I'm only her handmaiden, trying to learn to serve her."

"That's what I want to become," Hetty said, pulling out her

Luckies and lighting one. "But I don't even know where to start. What advice do you think Guadalupe would have for me?"

"Just this. Stop starving yourself."

"Me? Starving myself?" Hetty's cigarette froze midway to her mouth. "You're saying this about me, of all people? I'm the one who—"

"Think about it, *m'ija.* When have you ever really allowed yourself to stop and feast upon life?"

Hetty felt the familiar coldness in her arms and saw the empty hallways that haunted her mind. "Never," she said sadly.

Chapter 18

Hetty wanted to get up the very next day and head back to Houston to sell the tequila plata, but Cora made her sit down on the sofa and not move for the entire morning.

"In fact, lie down," her aunt commanded.

Hetty found this hard to do. Her feet curled around each other, bare and restless, ready to move—her blood surged with Cora's dark, rich coffee. She tossed about like one of the cats turning and turning until it found a comfortable spot to lie in. In her mind, she saw road signs flashing by on the Sequin highway, while she rehearsed what she would say to Garret's old clients. Her aunt was right. She simply couldn't relax and let herself be. Some hidden place in her soul ticked away like a clock wound too tightly. Everything felt balanced on a hairspring. It took her a long time to find a comfortable position to rest in. She sank into it and took a deep breath. Thoughts swirled inside her. She remembered the message Miguel had shared from the Virgin: "Let not your heart be disturbed." She took comfort in that. As the morning stretched on, the mechanisms of her mind began to wind down. She could feel the second hand moving slower and slower until it stopped. And she was just *there,* in her aunt's river house, listening to the birds singing, feeling the ceiling fan brush cool morning air on her arms, catching whiffs of chocolate mole sauce bubbling in a pot on the stove. *It's all right to lie here,* Hetty told herself. *Aunty gave me permission.*

She watched the way Cora frolicked with Pierce on the carpet. She was down at his level, mirroring his moves, holding his eyes with hers, and weaving game after game out of the noisemakers in the old *baúl*. Hetty noticed for the first time how her aunt turned play into serious business: She merged her being with the baby's, partnering him—two hands in a dance that redefined space. It was a pleasure to watch them move about the room. Pierce could only go on so long without toddling over to his toy telephone and pumping the receiver to make it chime, then listening to what it said to him.

"I've never gotten down on the floor and played with Pierce like that," Hetty said.

Cora glanced up, brushing her long pigtail aside. "Have you ever listened to what his toy telephone says?"

With chagrin, Hetty admitted she hadn't.

"You should sometime," Cora said as she stood and wandered into the kitchen to prepare lunch. Hetty rolled herself off the sofa onto the floor. Pierce paid her no mind, engrossed in shaking a dried calabash gourd. Hetty tried recreating her aunt's choreography across the carpet, picking up a Bolivian flute and blowing into it, then waving the flute at Pierce. She had to do this several times before he crawled over to try it himself. Then she had to show him how to blow into it before he managed to elicit a faint sound. She clapped when it happened. Slowly, she drew her son to her, forsaking that mother's way she had of distracting him with a toy while she preoccupied herself with adult matters. She focused entirely on him and maintained a lot of eye contact. This new intimacy felt unfamiliar to Hetty. She was even surprised at how different the room looked from a child's point of view. You noticed other things down here—the legs of chairs, the bells that had rolled under the sofa, the green eyes of cats watching from the shadows of the hallway. When she lay down and looked up, she saw sky out of windows; the dark sideboard loomed overhead, and the ceiling seemed vast.

But most of all, she began to see Pierce in a different way. He became more than a mouth to be fed, a diaper to be changed. He started following her every move, sitting in her lap, crawling all over her, giggling and smelling of sour milk and talcum, showing her the games he'd learned from his great-aunt. As much as her child seemed a part of her, as often as she'd looked at him, Hetty was amazed to realize that she'd never *seen* him. And here he was now, using the sofa to pull himself up, standing in front of her in his seersucker overalls, one bare arm dancing in the air, the other holding on to the sofa, eyes as blue as his father's, watching her to see what she'd do next. She couldn't stop looking at him, as if a nimbus surrounded his entire body. He was the perfect mixture of them all: the MacBride brawniness, her mestiza spice, Kirb's clear English complexion. Pierce blazed with baby glamour, and Hetty found herself entranced. She kept waiting for him to go over and pick up his toy telephone. But as long as she played with him, he ignored it. Finally, she couldn't stand it any longer. She scooted over and picked up the phone herself, pumped the receiver, then held it up to her ear to see what he'd been listening to for months. At first it rang, then the diaphragm inside bleated with a reedy little voice. It said, "Mama."

The next morning Hetty stood holding her baby on the porch, looking out at the walkway that wound its way to the street under the giant pecan. When they left today, they would walk under the pink blossoms of the mimosa tree, through the overgrown garden, and past the sign that read, THE COSMOS: WE'RE OUT OF THIS WORLD. Sunbeams alighted here and there in the branches like birds. You could feel the day's heat dipping into the deep shade, haunted by the blue vapors of river water rising and making the wind chimes ring.

Cora stepped out, a hoop of cats skirting her.

"Gato," Hetty said, pointing at Cassandra. It was a new game she'd been playing with Pierce all morning: Tell Me What the Mexicans Call It. She hoped his first word would be Spanish. She used to resent it when he clung to her like this, but now she couldn't get enough of him.

Hetty saw Cora watching them with an aunt's sense of pride. "Thanks for showing me my son."

She smiled sagely. "Now you can throw his telephone away."

"Pues, sí." There was so much that could be said, but Hetty didn't know how to phrase it in either language. "I guess it's time for *adiós*."

"Not before a Pierce sandwich!" Cora threw her arms around them both, engulfing mother and child in her earthy aromas.

"Do I have your blessing to leave?"

"Sí, sobrina," Cora said, drawing back. "I'm ready to let you go. You'll be all right now."

"Seca said I had to find my own *sendero*."

"He's right. The way will open."

"Pretty smart for an old smuggler, eh?"

"Ah, but look at what he smuggles."

"Mescal. Another thing you introduced me to. I owe you so much, *Tía*. How can I ever thank you?"

"*De nada*. That's what aunts are for—don't you know that? Our job is to knock some sense into our nieces and get them drunk."

"Then you succeeded brilliantly. As long as I drink mescal for my tummy, not my head, right?"

Cora nodded. "Approach it tenderly. It is the heart of Mexico."

"Speaking of heart—how can I find my husband? Any advice about that?"

"Call him to you."

"Is it really that simple?"

"It's really that natural. The universe is run by intention, not chance."

"I hope you're right," Hetty said, stepping down onto the walkway—her lips already silently forming into the words, *Come find me, Mac. I miss you. And hurry up, dammit.*

That weekend, Hetty had her first experience of being a ladylegger. She drove to Houston and, using Pearl's telephone to call clients, spent most of Saturday and Sunday making her deliveries. She certainly looked the part, in her lace-up boots and pants, a purple bruise on her cheek, a Lucky hanging out of one corner of her mouth. *Just call me Kelly Bushings, men.* By noon Monday, she had sold her entire stock and stopped by Cleveland's office to pay off the balance. She retrieved the wads of cash bulging in her trouser pockets, the kind of limp, wrinkled bills bartenders always pulled out of their cash registers. There were a lot of ones and fives, so it took Cleve a good twenty minutes to thumb through two thousand dollars.

"Is it all there?" she asked.

He stashed the funds in the top drawer of his massive desk. "D'y'all rob a bank?"

Hetty smiled. "Let's just say I gambled everything and won."

When she got back to the boardinghouse, she found out that Pearl had taken a job cleaning up the lunch dishes for a part-time wage of fifty cents a day. While her friend was downstairs working, Hetty decided it was time to balance *all* her accounts. She took out her passbook and opened to the entries she'd made. She crossed off Dolorosa Street and scribbled her initials there like the tellers used to do: *HMB*. She drew a line through Miguel's name and replaced the question marks with a heart. She struck out "Lamar's love" and wrote "Account closed" with the date and *HMB*. That left the other three she'd made under *Withdrawals: My father's love; My place in society; Nella's knees*. How could she balance those out? She began by writing a letter:

Dearest Pearl,

I know you didn't want to accept this cash, so that's why I've hidden it here with your undies. I was hoping to restore all the money you lost on your house, but perhaps this will be enough for a down payment on a new one. I also have a piece of incredibly good news that I've saved to share with you in the letter. Seca told me that his father has it on good authority that Prohibition will soon be repealed. And you know what that means—Odell will be released! I've always felt bad that your husband was arrested and mine wasn't. It just seems so unfair—that's the luck of the Irish, I guess. So please, please, please accept the enclosed—it's a way

> *to give back to you and Odell all that you've given Garret and me. It's only $333.33, not the riches I wanted to rain down upon you, but the best I can do. I owe you so much more than this—please know, along with the money, this envelope is bulging with gratitude. I thank you from the bottom of my broken heart. I wish you roses, roses from now on. You've had your share of thorns.*
>
> *All my love,*
> *Your friend,*
> *Hetty MacBride*

She folded the letter up and slid it inside one of the bank envelopes she'd been saving, then tucked the envelope in the top drawer of Pearl's dresser, the one that fit crookedly on its track. When Pierce woke up from his afternoon nap, she dressed him in a sailor suit and headed south on Main Street to the Warwick.

Hetty parked the Wichita in the circular driveway of the hotel and carried Pierce into the solarium. As she walked down the long stretch of the lobby, the black walnut pillars gleamed as darkly as ever but, when she reached the elevator lobby at the back, only one of the three lifts was working. After a long wait, she finally arrived on the eighth floor and knocked on the family suite. Lina answered the door, throwing her hands up and exclaiming, "*¡Mi chiquito!* Come to your Lina. *Que grande estás, m'ijo.*" She gathered Pierce into her arms and said, "I'm going to give you *besos!*" She kissed him several times, then carried him into the drawing room. "Look who's here—your grandson."

Hetty followed her, catching the scent of Darjeeling tea in the air. *Damn, I forgot, it's Mah-jongg Monday. That means Lockett will be here.*

"Ah-ha! Aren't you the natty little boy," Nella said, reaching for the child and balancing him on her lap so Lockett could see him in his sailor suit. Nella was dressed in one of her mah-jongg–themed outfits, a lampshade tunic and turban designed by Paul Poiret.

"Oh, my," Lockett said from her armchair, "he does look like his father."

"You're a sailor boy. Yes, you are!" Nella rocked him on her knee for a few minutes, making him laugh. Lina withdrew to the kitchen. "Don't rock the boat. Don't rock the boat." She held his little hands and beamed with a pride that rarely irradiated her cool and detached manner.

"La barca," Hetty said, making a boat with her hands.

Lockett watched her wide-eyed.

"Come ride in a boat with grandmamá!" Nella swayed with the child.

"La abuela," Hetty said, pointing at Nella, who frowned up at her.

"Why is she speaking Spanish to that child?" Lockett said with indignation.

"I want him to grow up bilingual, Lockett. How are you?"

"I didn't even know you spoke Spanish—"

"Oh, yes, we always—"

"And is that a bruise on your cheek—"

"La contusión," Hetty said, pointing at her face.

Nella looked alarmed and quickly bundled the child up. "Guess what granny has for you? Strawberry ice cream. Let's see if Lina will feed you some."

As Nella carried the confused child through the swinging door into the kitchen, Hetty waved and said, *"Disfruta de tu nieve, mi carino. Mamá está aquí."*

"Be quiet!" Lockett shrieked. "Y'all sound like the maids."

"Maybe that's 'cause I was raised by one." Lockett looked at her, speechless.

"How about some *English* tea, dear?" Nella cut in with a reproving glance at her daughter as she strode back through the swinging door.

"Por favor," Hetty answered, returning the dirty look. She retreated to her favorite sofa, the one always smothered in silk cushions. When Nella brought the tea service over, she scowled down at Hetty and placed a finger on her lips.

"Thanks, Mamá." Hetty nodded. "How's life in the old bankrupt hotel? I notice only one elevator is working."

"It's becoming intolerable," Nella said, sitting back down wearily. "Everything takes an eternity."

"Next thing," Lockett said, "we'll be walking up the stairs." She had obviously decked herself out for the mah-jongg tournament, too, as her pink crepe de chine actually ended in ruffles. "And you don't dare go out after dark."

"The electric company has turned off the streetlamps," Nella said.

"And have you heard *this?*" Lockett turned to Hetty and paused dramatically.

"What, Lockett?"

"They're canceling No-Tsu-Oh next spring. Indefinitely!"

"The cotton carnival? How can they?"

"First time in over thirty years! Jessie Carter's on the committee. She told me personally."

Nella sighed. "It's the end of an era. I guess we can assume that the *siècle* is definitely *fin.*"

"But, y'all! You can't put on a masquerade in this economy. It's not going to wash." Lockett pulled her ruffles down over her knees. "Let's look on the bright side—at least we get our bridge tables free now in the women's lounge."

Hetty started spooning sugar into her tea. "Well, never fear, Mamá. I paid Cleveland off this morning, so you'll be getting all your money back."

"I knew Lamar would help. He's such a wonderful son-in-law. He'll always look out for us, all of us—and that includes you too, Esther. Not like that lousy Irishman of yours. Has he shown up yet?"

"No, he hasn't." She added three more spoonfuls of sugar.

"What did I tell you?" Lockett cooed to Nella.

"He's gone for good," Nella said. "You might as well accept it."

"That poooooor child," Lockett drawled sadly.

"Indeed. But at least Lamar came through."

"As a matter of fact, he didn't. I sold the Ada Hillyer to someone else."

"Why?" Nella demanded. "Out of spite?"

Hetty cradled her teacup in both hands. Its heat scalded her fingertips.

"Couldn't you let your sister benefit from it?" Nella asked.

"Lamar and Char have thirty wells of their own. I, now, have none."

Nella sputtered with exasperation. "But—but—did you talk to him at all?"

Hetty sipped at her tea calmly. "Oh, yes, Mamá. I humiliated myself just like you wanted me to. I drove over to the Goss farm and found him in the Splendora field. I offered the well to him for five thousand dollars."

The two women watched her. "So . . ." Lockett moved to the edge of her chair, pink ruffles spilling about her knees. "What did he say?"

"I don't think I should repeat it."

"May I remind you—I was your biggest investor," Nella said. "I think I deserve an explanation."

A gleam came into Lockett's eyes. *Gossip.* "She's right, Esther. You mustn't hold out on your mother."

"Let's drop this, please, or I'll have to speak the truth. And you won't like it."

"We're all adults here," Nella said.

"All right, if you insist." Hetty sank deeper into the silver cushions. "He wouldn't buy it unless I spent the night with him."

Lockett gasped, but Nella didn't skip a beat. "I don't believe you," she said. "You must have misunderstood."

"It's true. He offered to divorce Char and marry me."

"Did he actually say he'd divorce your sister?"

"Well . . . no . . . but—"

"Then you misread him. Lamar will never leave Char."

"My, we do have our illusions, don't we?" Lockett said with a tsk.

"I'm afraid it's true. He wanted to sleep with me another time, too, *after* he became engaged to Char."

Nella ground her teeth, then snapped, "Shame on you for slandering your poor brother-in-law like this. Just because *your* husband failed . . ."

"My poor brother-in-law was stealing my oil right from under my feet."

"I think you're being paranoid. Splendora has a right to drill wherever they like."

"But not in our offset location. One well can drain forty acres, you know."

Lockett's eyebrows shot up, but Nella appeared unruffled. "Why would he need to steal your oil? Like you said yourself, he has thirty wells of his own."

"Because he couldn't stand to see Garret successful. He had to squash him. And he did. Lamar is a snake—don't you see that?"

Both women crooned *"Nooooo!"* together. "How can you say such horrid things in my drawing room?" Nella asked.

"Because they're the truth. You can't shut me up any longer, Mamá."

"You're just bitter because you chose the wrong man and can't stand to see your sister happy."

"That's right," chimed in Lockett. "You made a mistake. Admit it."

"Oh no." Hetty sat up straight and faced them both. "I chose the right man. I know that now."

"You might change your mind when you hear what I have to say!" Lockett nearly jumped out of her chair.

"Exactly!" added Nella.

"Not the 'scandal' again?" Hetty said, making quote marks with her fingers. *How can I avoid hearing this?*

"For your own good," Lockett snorted, "you need to know what I found out about Garret's father."

Hetty sighed. *Maybe I should listen. Maybe it will explain why Garret left.* "All right, Lockett. I'm ready to hear what you have to say. But just stick to the facts, please. I don't need a lot of judgments."

"Well, the facts speak for themselves."

"So this was back in Butte?"

"Back in that pit!"

"No judgments. You promised."

"All right, then."

"So we're back in the mining town of Butte?"

"Actually, we're in the nation's capital. You remember I told you that Garret's father didn't finish out his term in the Senate . . ."

"Yes, Termite MacBride."

"Well, it's worse than I imagined. This is what I've been trying to tell you for over a year! He *lost* his seat!"

"Lost it? Garret never told me that."

"He wouldn't, of course. But Congressman Welch uncovered the whole sordid affair. In order to get elected, Termite had offered bribes. D.C. was overrun with terrified Montanans who had to testify in front of a Senate committee. He denied everything, of course."

"What did he say in his defense?"

"That he never bribed anyone. That he didn't have to. Termite was a hero among the workers apparently. They loved him because he was one of the few miners ever to take on the huge copper company that's always held Butte in its grip."

"Really? What company was that?"

"Oh, my dear, I thought everyone had heard of Anaconda."

Hetty caught her breath, remembering the ghostly look in her husband's eyes and his enigmatic statement: *"We'd better leave before we get swallowed by an anaconda."*

"The upshot was, Senator MacBride resigned in disgrace before they could vote him out. I just thought you should know."

"Yes, thank you, Lockett. I think I understand perfectly well."

Lockett looked at Hetty, puzzled, obviously disappointed in her rather blasé reaction. "Well, at least I've gotten that off my chest. I'll leave the rest up to you, of course. But I wouldn't expect to see that Irishman back, if I were you."

"Oh, I don't know, Lockett. He's a man of many surprises."

Taking one last sip of her tea, Lockett stood. "Very well, then, it seems I'm no longer needed here, so I'll just trip back across the hall. The congressman will be getting up from his nap. This heat does him in. I don't know *why* we didn't stay in Virginia. Give Pierce a kiss for me," she said, lifting her ruffled skirt with one hand. As she followed Nella out into the hotel hallway, she chattered on, scattering snippets of comment in her wake: *"You can bet on it—poor Irish orphan—I can't imagine—and why Spanish?—it's what the maids speak."*

Nella slammed the door when she came back. She walked straight over to the sofa. "May I remind you not to speak Spanish in front of Lockett. *¿Qué te pasa? ¿Estás loca?*"

Hetty stood. "No, I'm not crazy. I simply won't have my child hidden away in the kitchen with the help."

"Then be a little more discreet."

"Forget it. I'm not denying my heritage any longer, Mamá. Cora lives openly as a mestiza, so why can't I?"

"You can do that in San Antonio, but not here. Think of your poor sister."

"I just want to be what I am."

"Oh, God! Cora's gotten her clutches into you." Nella paced in front of the great Diana screen. "Just remember your aunt has trouble facing reality. She's an artist."

"That's funny. I'm rather fond of her reality."

"But she has no idea what living in Houston is like. We're farther from the border here. Mexicans just don't mingle with quality. Houstonians are gracious, but we're not *that* gracious."

"I find that cruel and narrow. It's time people got over those attitudes."

"You're living in a dreamworld just like your aunt. Nobody's telling Southerners what to think. I've found that out the hard way"—Nella collapsed into her black enamel armchair—"recently."

"How?"

"Well . . . for one thing, the Forum of Civics was voted down because of zoning. After all our work!"

"So you're not going to be able to turn Houston into the Paris of the South?"

"Hardly. I shudder to think what this city will be like in fifty years with no planning."

"It's a shame. The Allen brothers had such visions for the place."

"What's wrong with Houstonians? Zoning! Will Hogg is crushed." Nella gabbed on about boulevards and parklands, obviously relieved to have changed the subject.

Finally, Hetty stepped forth and said, "Mamá, I know what happened to your knees. Cora told me."

Nella leaned back and gave her an icy stare. "The first thing you have to realize about your aunt, dear, is that she clings to the past. I've long ago forgotten my school days."

"But I read your recantation. She has it in her scrapbook. Now I know why you keep the *postigos* locked. Why you hide my son away in the kitchen."

Hetty had struck flint. Nella's eyes flared up. "Don't try to psychoanalyze me, Esther! Cora's been doing it for years. Her and her Freudian theories! You can't explain everything by toilet training, believe you me."

"Still, I forgive you, Mamá." Hetty sat back down on the sofa.

"*You* forgive me? For what?"

"For not picking me up as a baby."

"Why would I want your forgiveness?"

"Because it releases you. Someone forgave me recently, and it felt so good. Pure balm. Don't you feel bad about what happened?"

Nella's eyes narrowed. "How do you know about that?"

"Lina told me."

Nella muttered something toward the kitchen.

"It wasn't her fault. I made her tell me. I have a right to know. Why have you kept all this from me?"

"What good would it have done to tell you?"

"Because I've been starving myself all my life as a result. These things have an effect. Cora helped me see that."

"You would have to go and visit your damn aunt. I'm warning you, Esther, Cora is dangerous. Why do you think I've kept you away from her all these years?"

"Because you're afraid of the truth, maybe?"

"The truth? Ha!" Nella stood and circled the sharp-edged armchair. "Truth is a very relative thing, believe me. Do you think we'd be welcome in No-Tsu-Oh if they knew the truth? That your sister would have been chosen Cotton Queen? That we'd have memberships in the Cupola Club? Would your girlfriends still talk to you if they knew your grandmother was a dirty Mexican who sold chili on the plaza?"

"I don't want friends like that. I don't want to be part of No-Tsu-Oh if that's the price I have to pay." Hetty stood up and took a deep breath. "Your life has been a lie since the day I was born. Even before that. Since you pawned yourself off as an Anglo to Dad."

"I *am* an Anglo." Nella turned the full blaze of her enraged eyes on her daughter. Hetty started to feel weak in the knees as she always did in the presence of Nella's incandescent power but, this time, she was able to stand firm and stare her down.

"Only half, Mother. Half. Mestiza means the black *and* the white—don't you remember? You've been showing your whiteness alone to the world, which is cowardly. Your black you've hidden until it's become something smutty and dark, toxic as tar. It's poisoned this whole family—can't you see that?"

"You're the one who's poisoned the family with your lies about Lamar."

"They're not lies. It's all true. I wish you'd take him off the pedestal you've put him on and see him for the vicious predator he is."

"I'm not listening to any more of this," Nella said in a furious tone as she fled down the hall, dodging behind the *postigos*.

Hetty followed right after her, flinging the heavy wooden door aside so hard it crashed against the wall. "You know, Mamá," she shouted. "You think of yourself as this madcap bohemian, but under those turbans your brain is 100 percent bourgeoisie." Hetty barged into the room painted the color of chili peppers. "If you really want to know what Lamar is like, bring him in here. Show him what his wife's grandmother looked like. See if he still loves her after that. Garret did."

"You may want to ruin your sister's life, but I don't."

"Maybe it will *save* her life. Tear down these creaky doors, Mamá. Stop hiding out back here. Let the world know who you are, for God's sake."

"It's too late for that," Nella spewed in an exasperated tone.

"No, it's not. Go get Lockett right now. Bring her back here. See if she remains your best friend."

"Why would you ask me to do that?"

"So you can see your grandson again."

For the first time ever, her mother looked genuinely stunned. Hetty had finally found a way in. Nella staggered back into one of the quarter-moon chairs. "You won't really keep Pierce from us, will you?" A piteous look passed across Nella's eyes. "It would break your father's heart, *pobrecito*."

"I won't withhold him intentionally. But I insist you honor him as the mestizo he is."

"What does that mean?"

"Don't hide his heritage from him. Speak Spanish to him in the drawing room as well as the kitchen. Be as proud of his Mexican and Irish blood as you are of his Anglo. And tell Dad he has to do the same."

"You're asking him to choose between you and No-Tsu-Oh. He would be shunned."

"Then he'll have to choose me. I won't be pushed off to the borders. And neither will my children."

"It's all he's ever known. You're asking us to give up the Old Houston."

"The Old Houston? Jesus Christ, Mamá, there's more to modernism than a couple of armchairs. Look in your art books."

"Books? I don't need books, Esther. I've been to Paris. To the salons."

"But did you understand what they were whispering to each other in French? Art is a wrecking ball. Swinging on a chain. The Old Houston, and all it stood for, is demolished. We're living in a Depression, in case you hadn't noticed. We can't afford these pretensions anymore."

Nella looked around the room, a little lost. "But what would people think?"

"They might admire you. Show them what it really means to be gracious. Show them what a real Southern gentlewoman is like, a woman whose heart is kindled by kindness and compassion. A woman who loves her grandchildren no matter what they're like."

Nella stood and turned her back to her daughter, stepping onto the dais to sit at the *bureau de dame.* "I don't know if I can do what you're asking, Esther." She removed her turban and placed it gingerly on a wire hatstand. She brushed her hair and gazed off into the great round mirror with eyes vacant and wounded. "What a terrible bargain my daughter drives. I don't know if I can give up my place in society. I've worked so hard to earn it. No one knows what I've suffered."

"I think I do. *Conocí a Tipo.*" Hetty sat at the foot of the dais and watched her mother's face change in the mirror. She'd intentionally used Miguel's nickname as if to say, "I know everything about your youthful *mal de amor.*"

Nella gazed off into the melancholic light of the mirror. "How dare you dig into my past. It's none of your business."

"Yes, it is. He could have been *mi padre.*"

Nella snickered as if this was the most ridiculous thing she'd ever heard. "You know nothing. *Nada.* You heard a story, that's all." Nella smeared cold cream on her face and began removing makeup. "You think you can blame me for everything that's wrong with your life? I did what I had to do. You were provided for. You always had Lina. Anyone can change a diaper and spoon food into a mouth. I was protecting you. That's what I was doing. I shielded you girls from my despair because that would have been much worse." She wiped her eye shadow off and dragged rouge off her cheeks. She looked older without her makeup. Dark rings emerged under her eyes. Lifting her lustrous hair off her face, Nella snared it with the teeth of a Spanish comb. She brushed at her spit curls mindlessly. "So don't try to make me feel guilty, Esther. What if I *had* sacrificed myself to you? How do you think I would feel now? After the way you've treated me? Bitter, that's what I would be. Bitter as wormwood. And now you're threatening to take my only grandchild away from me. You know how that makes me feel, *m'ija?*"

"How?"

"Glad that I made the choices I made. There were places I wanted to go, great ships that docked at the Port of Houston that could take me as far from Texas as I could get. I knew how to hunt all right. I sought beauty and brought it home. Art from Paris. Glass from Venice. Silver from England. The good stuff. I don't regret a thing. Not one. Not even Tipo."

"I do."

"What's that?"

"I regret we weren't closer. I love you, Mamá, in spite of it all."

"If you love me, you won't take my grandchild away from me."

"Have you heard anything I've said today?"

Nella slapped the hairbrush down. "I don't know what you want of me, *m'ija*."

"Mamá, just look at me. *See* me."

Nella glanced at her for the first time in the mirror. "All I see is a poor woman whose husband has left her and is now saddled with a child she'll have to raise alone."

"That's all you see? That's all you want for me?"

"Be fair, my child. You could have been living like a princess. That's what I wanted for you."

"I don't want to be that kind of princess. I'd rather be . . . a handmaiden . . . to the Empress."

Nella shot her a puzzled look in the mirror.

"La Madonna Morena."

Nella threw back her head and chortled. "That old *madre*'s tale? I didn't realize you were so naive."

"Cora says she's the only real goddess we have in America. Not an import like Diana."

"Oh, please. Mary miraculously appears to a humble Indian just when the Spanish were trying to convert millions of Aztecs? How convenient."

"But the tilma?"

"That relic? It was painted by an artist named Marcus. Didn't Cora tell you?"

"Then why has it lasted four hundred years?"

Nella sprayed perfume into the air. "Now *that* I would like to know. My Chanel suits rot in the closet." She set the bottle down and swayed her head back and forth in the fragrant mist. She caught Hetty's eye. "I'll never kneel to the Virgin again. And I can't imagine why you would."

Hetty thought for a moment, then said softly, "I want to learn how to love people."

"Why? So they can break your heart?"

She and Pierce left by the back hall. Lina gave her a long hug on her way out, confident Garret would turn up soon. "I'm more determined than ever to find him," Hetty said, "to prove my mother wrong."

"You will. Don't give up, *m'ija.* As we say in Mexico, *'Donde menos se piensa, salta la liebre.' "*

When you least expect it, the rabbit will jump.

Hetty drove through downtown on her way to the Heights. When she pulled up to the intersection at Main and Texas Avenue, the sign spelling out **MAJESTIC THEATER** in electric lights was still strung across the street, but many of the bulbs had burned out, leaving the message JEST EATER. When the signal turned green, Hetty edged forward, checking out the sale signs in the stores. She pulled up in front of Foley Brothers and sat idling at the curb. She had lots of cash with her. She could go in and buy herself a new dress. But when she looked at the fashions in the windows, she lost her enthusiasm. Everything for fall had a threadbare look to it: simple black dresses, boring wool coats, and hems that skirted the ankle. Silk was out; cotton was in. "Washable" was blazoned across almost every sign. *Is this what it's come to?* she wondered. *Streetlights turned off and fashion gone dark?*

Hetty turned left onto Preston Street to head over the bridge. Above the truck, high up in the humid air, Houston rose into a crimson sky. The sun smoldered in the west like a fire that refuses to go out. Down Travis, she glimpsed the cupola of the Esperson Building floating over the town like a temple in the clouds. She couldn't believe such a magnificent edifice was up for auction. She thought for a moment about stopping by the bank and giving Kirby one last visit with his grandson but remembered that the bank was closed. Even if her father were still there, she would be locked out. She gassed the truck onto the bridge.

Hetty lugged Pierce up the worn carpet on the stairs of the old

Victorian mansion that had been parceled off into rooms. She always knew what the boarders would be served for supper—the smells collected up here in the stairwell outside Pearl's room. Tonight the table would be spread with meat loaf, cabbage, and—Hetty sniffed again at the mouthwatering aroma of piecrust baking—probably cherry pie. Pushing open the door to Pearl's room, Hetty found her scrunched up on the bed pulling thread through the hem of a faded housedress.

"Come on in, y'all, I'm trying to get some mending done here."

The room was dim, curtains still barricaded against a barrage of afternoon sun. A circulating fan droned on the dresser, but still, the room was stifling. Hetty sat on the rumpled davenport and cuddled Pierce in spite of the heat.

"I found the envelope," Pearl said.

"You weren't supposed to find it till we left."

"I was looking for my sewing kit."

"I hope you'll keep it this time."

"Only 'cause of the other thing you said."

"About Odell?"

"I won't let myself believe it's true." Pearl talked through pinched lips, holding straight pins. "Is he really coming back to me?"

"Looks like it. Save the money for a down payment on the house you two will need."

Pearl took the pins out of her mouth. "All right. You know best, hon. How did you find out?"

"There's so much I haven't had a chance to tell you." Hetty caught Pearl up on her trip into the brush, the meeting with her mother, and Cora's advice about finding Garret. " 'Call him to you,' she said. 'The universe is run by intention, not chance.' "

"Have you tried that?"

"Yes. I keep whispering under my breath, *'Come find me, Garret.'* Has he called here?"

"No, hon, I'm afraid not."

"He'd know to call here or at Ada's." Hetty glanced at the black telephone beside the bed, its silence falling into her heart like a chill. "I guess it's not working. Cora must be wrong."

"Now hold on. You ain't done what she said."

"Yes, I have. I called to him."

"No, I mean the second part. The universe is run by—what did she call it?"

"Intention."

"There you be. Intention. Don't sit around waiting for him to call. Go find him."

"But where?"

"Well, I don't rightly know." Pearl thought for a moment. "I reckon you got to guess *his* intention."

"You mean why he left me and where he would go?"

"Exactly."

"Well, let's see. He'd be thinking about the future, about what he was going to do next. Maybe he'd go back to Electra or Desdemona."

"Old girlfriends?"

"Oil boom towns. Or maybe he's just off somewhere, drinking himself into a stupor."

Ouch! Pearl sucked on her finger. She had pricked herself on the needle. "My God," she spoke out of the corner of her mouth, "I know where he is."

"You do?"

"When you said drinking, that reminded me." Pearl took the finger out of her mouth and examined it for bleeding. "He used to go off for a week at a time. Said he had to do some thinking—I figured that was an Irish expression for a binge."

"Where would he go?"

"To The Hammocks."

"Oh . . . your place on West Beach."

"Would disappear there for days. He still has a key."

Hetty felt a surge of hope. "Can you show me how to get there?"

"No. But I can tell you. I think you should go there alone. You and Pierce. Take Garret's son to him."

Hetty wanted to leave right away. She longed to escape Pearl's stifling room and drive south until the Gulf breeze streamed in gusts through the shattered window of the Wichita. But Pearl talked her out of it.

"You'll never find The Hammocks in the dark."

"I can't bear to spend another night away from him." Hetty felt the blood blossoming in her cheeks.

"You must be coming into season." Pearl laughed. "Go take a cold shower. Y'all got plenty of time to paint the front porch."

Once it had cooled down and Pierce had fallen asleep on the davenport, Hetty finished reading the letters from Garret's mother. Pearl continued her mending on the bed. In a letter dated February 14, 1929, Hetty found the reason he'd been hiding the correspondence from her.

> *In receipt of your money order for $500 sent January 23. No doubt you have worried about me, having heard of the great blizzard in mid-December. For us it was a thrilling spectacle, but a bit of a trial for my poor old boiler, which started dripping water in the cellar. Your generosity afforded me a new Hercules that was just installed last week. I have also put in enough coal to last until summer. You have saved your mother from a dire fate, I fear, as it is still forty degrees below zero today. Please know that in Senator MacBride's house all is now warm and bright!*

And in a second letter dated April 25, she read:

> *You cannot imagine how elegant my parlor is now. The new French wallpaper I awaited so anxiously arrived, after five long weeks, in late March. It is a delicate shell pink with gold stars twinkling over it. The Aubusson carpet is cream with roses. My new davenport and wing chairs are upholstered in gold damask. Thanks to your last money order of $400, I finally have a suitable sitting room for guests. My*

> *mahogany whatnot displays your photograph and the handsome likeness of Senator MacBride, as well as the shells and butterflies from long-ago days by the sea.*

Other letters acknowledged receipt of additional money orders from those spring months of 1929, totaling over two thousand dollars. Hetty crumpled the pile into her handbag and lit a fag. "Pearl," she said.

"Yes'm."

"I'm just heartsick."

"Bad news in them letters?"

"I've misjudged my husband."

"I told you Mac was good as gold. I always said that."

"I thought he gambled away thousands of our mescal money. I was wrong. The whole time he was sending it to his mother, Arleen."

Pearl chuckled out of the corner of her mouth. She removed the pins. "That's an Irishman for you. More loyal to his mother than his wife."

"I don't care. This makes me want to see him all the more."

Hetty could hardly wait to get off the next morning. She spoon-fed cereal to Pierce while she ate breakfast with the other hand, then slapped on a diaper and dressed him in his sailor suit again. "We're going to the sea," she said. She loaded all her possessions on the truck with Pearl's help and gave her friend a warm hug, patting her spectral arms. "Thanks for telling me where my man is."

"You brung mine back to me, too."

"No more thorns, okay?"

"Don't worry about me." Pearl pushed her into the truck. "Go on now. You know what I always say—you got to live it up to live it down." As Hetty drove away, Pearl was there in the rearview mirror, waving all the way down the block.

Hetty was on the causeway by ten a.m. As she left the mainland, the haze of morning evaporated into a sky turning a deep tropical blue. The bay waters under her lapped with loneliness. She rolled out onto Galveston Island, where rows of palms had been planted to welcome tourists to the Playground of the South. Their fronds billowed like women lifting their skirts. Here in the subtropics, everything simmered with yearning and heat.

Then she noticed something she'd never seen before. On West Bay, canvas tents had been pitched along the shore. A few makeshift houses had been cobbled together out of cardboard boxes. She stopped for gas at a Texaco pump on 61st Street and asked the attendant who was living in them.

"Unemployed," he said. "Migratin' here for winter."

"Like birds," Hetty said, pulling out two dollars. She paid for the gas and bought a few apples from a basket on the counter. As she set out to West Beach, more tents appeared on the roadside. The nomads camped wherever they could along the inlets. Each ramshackle camp looked like the debris left by a tidal wave. And perhaps it was. A great swell had rolled across the country, sweeping everyone up in a surge of glittering success that had left them unprepared for its inevitable crash. Here were the homeless it had left in its path. She wondered how long they would be forced to live like this and how people would ever begin to patch their lives back together.

As far as her own life went, all she could do was keep driving westward, following Pearl's directions, past the Catholic cemetery and the white arches of the Hollywood Dinner Club. As she rumbled by Greens Bayou, teeming with cattails and crocodiles, she found her mind swimming with questions. *Had Termite really accepted bribes? Was he just another corrupt politician? Did that explain Mac's connection to the Maceos? Is that what brought him to Texas?* The only way to find out was to keep going—past the crooked oaks forever bent in the direction of the winds, out to where the pavement gave way to a dirt road that wound its way through the dunes. On her right, sea grapes twisted through patches of sedge grass, while on her left, laughing gulls soared as the water opened up, steel blue and calm, all the way to Yucatán. The Gulf of Mexico. She'd come to the very edge of America, to its rippling fringe where the sky fell into a different hemisphere. She wasn't even sure if she'd find her husband out here on this final finger of land or if he'd want her back when she did.

Then she spotted it. Like a tangle of driftwood thrown up on the shore. Pearl's family beach house, worn to a nub by the salt air. This was squatter's land that Pearl had said her uncles had fenced off and claimed as their own "against the entire world." No one else seemed to want to live on this desolate stretch of the island. It was the only house for miles. Hetty could see the hammocks slung like shaggy hair across the brow of the front porch and the wooden storm windows lifted like half-opened eyes. The old place huddled there on its spindly legs, drowsing in the September sun, lifted up on stilts. She half expected it to rouse and scuttle into the surf as she approached. Her heart lifted with the laughing gulls when she spotted the Auburn parked in the shade under the rafters. *He was here.*

She pulled next to it and set the brake. She carried Pierce out from under the house, showing him the snails that slid up the stilts. She walked around to the front porch and knocked on the battered screen door. There was no answer. It was unlocked, so she opened it and went in. Someone had been sleeping in one of the hammocks. Its ropes were covered by a rumpled sheet and two pillows. The house looked like a monk's cell, everything sandblasted to a gray simplicity. An open can of beans yawned on the stove; a bottle of milk and an iron pot of fish stew lurked in the icebox. Garret's luggage was there, open and overflowing with clothes, but no sign of him. She picked up one of his shirts and smelled it.

Hetty took Pierce out to the beach to look for his father. Sand crabs shuddered away to avoid being crushed underfoot. A tattered beach chair sat crookedly in the sand, a white beach towel tossed close to the surf. Off to the side, boulders jutted out into the water. She walked over. A lot of brown liquor bottles had been smashed on the rocks. She could still catch a faint whiff of whiskey. Some of the shards had been picked up by the tides and were being washed out to sea. She imagined that they would end up on another shore as sparkling pieces of sea glass, worn smooth by the waves.

Her eyes followed them oceanward . . . and saw him. A tiny head bobbing in the water, out by the sandbars where he liked to swim. He was cutting through the water freestyle, kicking up spray.

Closer in, fish were jumping: little flashes of silver in the waves. Walking back, she stripped her son naked and sat him in front of her on the wet sand like an offering.

After a while, Garret rode the waves in and waded toward them, salt water streaming off his black tank top. His hair was slicked back, his cheeks rosy from his run in the ocean. He picked Pierce up and held him high in the sun with both hands. He nestled the child in the crook of his elbow, little white buttocks spilling over his bronzed forearm. Hetty thought she'd never seen anything so beautiful in her life, her husband and her naked baby standing in the sea in front of her. *And this is what I gave up so carelessly!*

Garret set his son down on the sand and picked up the towel to dry himself off. White surf came bubbling around them. Hetty waited with her head bowed, blushing deeply, unable to speak. She didn't know what she could possibly say to make Garret forgive her, to ask him to take her back. Words would sound shallow at a moment like this. She might as well write *Forgive Me* in the sand and let the waves wash it away. Her presence would have to speak for her. She had solved her aunt's enigma of intention. She had made the effort to hunt him down. She had brought Garret his son. The rest was up to him.

The sea breeze cooled her cheeks. She overcame her shame and lifted her eyes. He had finished drying off and stood there with the towel draped over his shoulders, like a priest in a white robe. He was watching her, studying her face for clues. She tried to let her eyes say what her lips couldn't. *I'm sorry, I'm sorry, I'm sorry.* Finally, without a word, he opened the towel and invited her to step inside. She stood up and moved forward. His skin was cool to the touch; his hair smelled of salt water. When he kissed her, Pierce hugged their legs, looking up and babbling.

Then he said one word clearly in his baby talk: *"Beso."*

Hetty drew back. "Your son just said his first word—in Spanish!"

"What does it mean?"

"Kiss."

They lifted him up and planted so many *besos* on his bare belly that he squealed with delight.

* * *

Pearl had been right. Garret seemed completely charmed by the presence of his son. He had rarely fed him in the past, leaving such chores to Hetty. But when noon came, he insisted on holding Pierce in his lap and spooning fish stew into his mouth at the rickety table in the kitchen. Hetty sat opposite them, sopping up her portion with stale white bread and feeling awkward. She longed to speak but didn't know how to break through the heaviness of the salt air.

Garret sat Pierce on the floor and watched him play with seashells. The only sound, other than a constant plashing of surf, was the hiss of matches being struck. They smoked in silence until Garret asked, "How did you find me?"

"Pearl figured it out. I thought I'd have to sober you up."

"I did get ossified the first few days, till I spent a whole night vomiting. The next day I smashed all the bottles that were left around here."

"What have you been living on?"

"I dig clams. And buy trout from the fishermen. Mostly I just sit in the beach chair and watch the sea, thinking." He looked at her across the table for the first time. "What have you been up to?"

"Oh, I've kept busy. I sold the well, Mac."

"Why?"

"I realized you were right." That's all she could bring herself to say at the moment. She explained the details of the contract and reminded him who Mr. Kozak was.

"Did you pay off the interest owners?"

"Yes. The money's all been returned."

"Good." He nodded. "That's what I wanted us to do." Garret hoisted Pierce up and took him outside to play in the surf for a while. Hetty watched them through the screens of the porch, her heart sodden with all she had to say. That urge was coming back, the need to tell the whole story again to release the pressure dammed up inside her. When it was time for the baby's afternoon nap, she asked Garret to lay him in one of the iron beds at the back of the house. While he was gone, she stripped all her clothes off and stretched out on the hammock with the sheet thrown across it.

He looked surprised when he came back out.

"Mac, do you remember how we used to get naked when we had a confession to make?"

"So that's what this is about. I was hoping you were trying to seduce me."

"This is no time for joking. I have some bad news to tell you. Something happened to Pick."

"Oh, God, not Pick." The earnest tone in Garret's voice brought tears rushing to Hetty's eyes. "What?"

"He's dead, Mac." Hetty watched as a look of stunned grief gripped her husband's face. That cut her to the bone, fearing that Garret would blame her for their friend's death. She tried to explain what happened but could hardly talk for the sobs that came with the words. She finally got the whole story out but cried so hard, he crawled in beside her and took her up in his arms.

"I'm sorry I wasn't there," Garret said, holding her and letting the hammock rock her guilt away.

Hetty shuddered. "Now I understand why you left Kilgore. You were right, Mac. I should have gone with you. I hope you'll forgive me."

"It's all right," he said, stroking her. "It's not really your fault. Poke obviously decided to make an example of Pick because he was colored. And by the way, that's not why I left Kilgore."

"It wasn't?" she asked tearfully.

"I guess it's my turn to get naked."

"Okay."

He stood and peeled off his still-damp one-piece bathing suit. She relished a brief glimpse of his body before he rolled back in and pressed up against her. "Remember when I said we had to leave before we got swallowed up by an anaconda?"

"I finally found out what that means. Lockett told me. It's the name of a mining company! But what does it have to do with your father? I thought he had his own mine."

"I think it's time you heard the whole story."

"It might help me understand you better."

"First, you need to understand my dad. He was a man who worked in the mines all his life. He had a natural nose for ore. No one knew the business better—how to blast through rock, build tunnels in the deep. He was always down there burrowing, my dad, which is why they called him Termite. He was an earnest man, hardworking. He wanted me to have a better life than he did. He wanted to send me to college. He kept on learning more about the business. He even picked up enough surveying skills to make the discovery that turned him from a miner to a mine owner. This was where all his problems started."

Garret sat up in the hammock and steadied it with his foot while he tried to explain the technicalities of the mining business. There was a small triangle of land that remained unclaimed at the heart of the Anaconda holdings where Termite worked. It wasn't very big, less than an acre, Garret said, but a rich vein of copper apexed within the boundaries, giving his father the right by law to mine the vein. He filed patent upon it and began digging out his fortune. But his ex-boss, Marcus Daly, the owner of Anaconda, wasn't about to let him get away with such audacity. He filed a lawsuit to stop Termite from mining the claim, meanwhile sending crews underground to steal the ore right out from under his feet.

"Daly took almost a million dollars' worth of copper ore from the MacBride mine. That's money that should have come to my family," Garret said.

"No wonder you were upset when you found out that Lamar was stealing our oil. Talk about déjà vu."

"It brought it all back. I knew we couldn't win because my dad hadn't. They found a way to rob him of his Senate seat. They broke him in court. They would have done the same to us. They always do. That's why I gave up. That's the only reason. I probably shouldn't have left you, but I just couldn't stay."

"So your dad never took bribes?"

"He didn't have to. He made his own money. The miners loved him."

"Speaking of money . . ." Hetty showed him the wad of cash in her purse and described where it came from. She explained how she got the bruise rouging her cheek. Garret kissed it and acknowledged the risk she had taken to pay off their debts.

"Now I feel bad that I left you. But I had to clear out of there in a hurry. I was really afraid I'd end up like my dad." Garret lay back down on the pillows.

"What happened to Termite?"

"When they took his Senate seat away and people stopped believing in him, it just crushed him. He ended up drinking himself to death."

Hetty lay on her side and watched him as he talked, studying every nuance of regret on his face. His long eyelashes were at half-mast, his crystal-blue eyes darkened. His lips didn't smile, and he had a scruffy growth of beard. But still, she found his uncertainty irresistible, something broken she could mend with her love. The first night she met him, she hadn't been able to get a good look at his face, and now she wondered if she'd ever really seen him clearly. She'd fallen in love with his fearlessness, his courtship of chaos. Now she needed to embrace the faint heart that also quivered in his breast when he was afraid.

"Was that when you had to leave the university?"

"Yes, after my sophomore year."

"Were you disappointed?"

"The worst part was giving up my Olympic dreams."

"That must have been devastating."

"It's what sent me to Texas. I was hoping to make back the money we lost. I didn't want my mother to suffer."

"It doesn't matter now. We have each other."

Garret's beard scratched her lips when he kissed her, but she didn't care. She loved him just as he was, unshaven, unheroic, and barefoot.

"You're worth more to me than all the money," he said, in between kisses.

"Then why didn't you call me? You knew where I was."

"I was waiting to see if you'd come looking for me."

"Why?"

"Don't you know?"

She shook her head.

"I thought you were going to go back to Lamar."

"You did?" Hetty sat up, making the hammock swing. "Oh, Mac, you poor thing!"

"Well . . . you seemed awfully interested in fighting with him."

"I was stupid. I don't know what got into me. But it's not because I'm in love with Lamar!"

"It's not?"

Hetty looked out through the rusty screens in frustration. "No, honey. I don't want Lamar. I don't know how many times I have to tell you."

"It's really been eating away at me."

Hetty looked back at the man lying in the hammock. What she saw caused her to put her foot on the floor and stop it from swinging. Tears welled in Garret's blue eyes. His face was that of a boy's: guileless, hurt, his pain unprotected. "I left you before you could leave me."

She reached for him. "You're the one, Mac. You were always the one."

She'd never seen him weep like this. She held him close while a riptide of emotions broke loose, all the doubt and the disappointment and loss of the last few months flooding out. She could feel everything crashing around their heads: Pick and the Ada Hillyer, Cleveland and the interest owners, Splendora and Anaconda and a thousand oil wells sitting idle. Garret needed her to hold him while he tore through his anguish and told her how sorry he was. She consoled him, her breasts wet with tears.

Soon, Pierce woke up and started crying for her from the iron bed. Hetty and Garret dressed and took him out to the beach. Garret played with his son for a long time in the sand. When they grew hungry, she cut up the apples she'd bought and found some cheddar cheese to slice out of the icebox. Swaying in the hammock, they talked through the dusk, until the salty air put Pierce to sleep early on his blanket. Hetty nestled him in the old iron bed where he'd taken his nap. Then she swung back into the hammock and wrapped her arms and legs around Garret, swimming in his heavy scent. She rocked him for a while, feeling close but not erotic, blending her breath with his. The sound of the surf rose and fell like the voices of lovers murmuring at midnight. She nuzzled her mouth close to his ear and whispered, "Now I'm rich," but he had fallen asleep. Mac was finally at peace.

* * *

Hetty woke in the night and found Garret unbuttoning her blouse. An old moon had crept out of the ocean and built a nest of pale light in the clouds. She couldn't see her husband's face, but she could make out his naked body stretched out on the hammock, aroused and smelling like wetlands musky with heat. She let him undress her and suck at her nipples until they ached with pleasure. She wanted him so much she was delirious with it, still half asleep and reddening in the face. As he lifted above her, she spread her legs all the way, causing the hammock to fan out to its fullest berth. There were no more barriers in their way; she was dripping with fertility and ready to yield everything to his need. He lay on top of her and penetrated her slowly, taking his time. They were so ripe with love they couldn't have stopped if they'd wanted to. His arms came around her, her legs entwined him, and they cleaved to one another breathlessly as the hammock rocked and pitched through the night.

Hetty rises through the ceiling and stands on the cedar shingles of the porch. Music washes in from the Gulf. A yacht is passing by, the Rusk yacht, all one hundred and three feet of it lit up for a party as it glides through the water. On the back deck, Nella and Charlotte and Lamar sit in deck chairs talking. Hetty's friends Belinda and Wini lean over the railing. Diana Dorrance is flirting with the captain. No one is paying any attention to Hetty except for Cora, who smiles at her as the yacht flows by. She looks as beautiful as Hetty has ever seen her, lounging in a silk rebozo, *gesturing to the east. Hetty follows to where her finger is pointing: Dawn is splintering the darkness. Out of the blue fog, the spires of the Galvez Hotel rise into the morning light.*

"That's where we spent our honeymoon," she says to the partygoers, but they have drifted away.

Children appear in the clouds, refugees from a baroque ceiling. They sit there enormous, translucent, as if made of glass, gazing at her with ancient eyes. A boy and a girl. The boy is naked except for the paintbrush in his hands. He is painting the dawn by dipping bristles into the sun. He doesn't streak the sky with the usual russet and orange, but blends his palette from the dark side of the spectrum, mixing a radiant magenta out of red and purple, crowning it with golden light and resting it on the turquoise of the sea. He circles the girl with his rainbow of darkness and draws it across the sky like a comet's tail, a Roman candle. Hetty watches it arch and dive. Then it enters her womb.

The blue light of dawn drew Hetty out of a blissful slumber. She thought she heard voices in the tide. Rolling out of the hammock, she picked the striped beach towel off the floor and wrapped it around her shoulders. She opened the screen door soundlessly, descending the wooden steps to the sand. The old moon was setting, pale and evanescent in the growing light. She followed it along, wading in the surf, curious to see what the ocean had spawned in the night. A brine of cockleshells and twisted whelks littered the beach, along with braids of seaweed and broken sand dollars. The pink inside a seashell reminded her of the dark rainbow she'd seen in her dream last night. A dream that was not of the earth, born of the sea. She remembered how Cora had described what happens when the two darkest sides of the spectrum meet: something unexpected and rare, a shimmering pink lighter than the purple and red that give it birth—a cosmic color that must be what flows in the arteries of angels in place of blood. *That's what happened to Mac and me last night,* Hetty mused. *Our darkest colors touched and gave birth to something radiant and new. A light and joyful magenta. Love made visible.*

She looked across the gleam of the water at the ghost of a moon sinking below the horizon. It was speaking to her in its silent language, the language understood by every woman and by women only. She let the towel gape open in the morning breeze. Her breasts lolled out, full and promising. She cradled her abdomen with her hands. She remembered how the dream ends.

Please turn the page
for a very special Q&A
with Duncan Alderson!

What inspired you to write *Magnolia City*?

I grew up seeing photographs of my mother, Dottie May, as a flapper from a remote, more romantic time in Texas history. The exotic woman in the pictures wore furs and long strands of pearls, staring into the camera with a kind of flaming defiance missing in the practical housewife who was raising me. I had to write a book to explain who that other woman was. She sparked my imagination in so many ways as I tried to picture her on a honeymoon in Galveston, sneaking into the Balinese Room for one of the fashionable new bootleg cocktails. "Dottie" shape-shifted into "Hetty" and sprang to vivid life in my mind. Henry James said that every writer must find his donnée (what's given to him by life). I found the thread of my donnée in those old faded photographs of my mother. When I yanked on it, a whole book unspooled.

Why did you choose the title *Magnolia City* for a book about Houston, Texas? That brings to mind the Deep South.

As I delved into the history of my hometown, I discovered many surprises. The biggest one was that Houston's historic nickname was "the Magnolia City." This may seem odd until you realize that during the period my novel is set, the 1920s, Houston was still a gracious bayou town, steaming at the edge of the Old South but awash in the new money of Spindletop oil. The city didn't get varnished with the Western Myth until the Houston Livestock Show and Rodeo kicked off in 1932. Before that, there were no cowboys and Indians in Houston's history. But there was a Lost Eden. During Edwardian days, Houstonians took the trolley out to Magnolia Park along Buffalo Bayou, an earthly paradise that rivaled Central Park and was planted with 3,750 Southern magnolia trees. It was wiped out by urban sprawl in the 1920s but it lingered in the collective memory of Old Houstonians like the lost scent of the lovely white flowers that gave the city its name.

Hetty's mother, Nella, is a complex, fascinating character, one who can be both magical and infuriating. Is she based on a real person?

Nella is a fictional collage that I glued together from many different scraps of real life: an elegant grandmother who lived in a hotel; a witty aunt who wrote letters in calligraphy; a mystical Mexican woman who worked in an herb shop and entranced me with her glittering eye. I took an earring here, a pair of lips there, a gesture, a tone of voice, a memory, an innuendo, then cut and pasted them all together in my imagination, fitting the pieces like a puzzle. People who accuse writers of identity theft don't understand how the creative process works. Characters stolen wholesale from real life often come across as flat in fiction. There's an alchemical process that must happen, just as in making a collage. Suddenly all the clippings coalesce, and a new face is staring out at you.

Why did you choose to write from a woman's point of view?

I didn't choose it, it chose me. I was trying to write a novel about a male protagonist in the 1960s who was loosely based on myself. At one point in the story, his mother returns home and drifts off into a long reverie about her youth in the 1920s. I was studying at the Humber School for Writers at the time and my writing coach, the Canadian novelist Sarah Sheard, said, "You know, the best part of this manuscript is the flashback. Why don't you let the mother tell her story?" It turned out to be a good suggestion. As soon as I allowed my imagination to dance, Hetty MacBride was born. That one chapter mushroomed into a whole book, and suddenly, I discovered I had this strong female voice living inside of me. I was as surprised as everybody else.

Larry McMurtry pioneered a spare prose style for his novels about Texas, a lyricism as "clean as a bleached bone." Why have you chosen to write in a more descriptive style?

Most of McMurtry's books are set in the Panhandle Plains or the Big Bend Country of West Texas. *Magnolia City* unfolds along the Gulf Coast, in the moist subtropical part of Southeast Texas. In place of the wide-open sky of the West, Houston has moss-hung bayous and lush azalea gardens flickering in the shade of twisting post oak trees. It's a different geological zone and a different culture. In order to capture the intricacies of Old Houston, with its elaborate social customs and Art Deco skyscrapers, I needed a language as rich and heady as one of those big, fragrant Magnolia grandiflora blossoms.

A READING GROUP GUIDE

MAGNOLIA CITY

Duncan W. Alderson

ABOUT THIS GUIDE

The suggested questions are included to enhance your group's reading of Duncan W. Alderson's ***Magnolia City***.

DISCUSSION QUESTIONS

1. Hetty dates two charismatic men, Lamar and Garret. She has trouble choosing between them and, even up to the last moment, isn't sure she's made the right decision. She feels that the human heart, after all, has four chambers. Do you think a woman can love more than one man? Does Hetty make a good decision . . . or a foolish one?

2. Is Hetty's impulse to work at the Dowling Street Medical Clinic a pure one, or simply rebellion against her parents? She likes shocking her contemporaries by riding in the front seat with Pick and consorting with his family. Is this true philanthropy on her part? If she really cares about Pick, would she ask him to pump hot oil under cover of night? Houstonians are famous for their generosity, but is there such a thing as pure philanthropy—or is there usually a hidden agenda?

3. Why does Nella keep her heritage a secret? Why does Hetty insist on taking Garret into her mother's secret room? Why does she expect him to reject her when he sees what's on the walls? What does this reveal to us about society in Houston in the 1920s? Have things changed much since then?

4. Why does Hetty have precognitive dreams? What part do they play in the unfolding of the story and what do they tell us about her heritage? How does she use the knowledge that's revealed to her? Do you think dreams are caused by indigestion or are they a conduit to a deeper part of ourselves? What responsibility do we have in interpreting them?

5. Many sisters feel affection for each other. Why don't Hetty and Charlotte get along? What does their relationship re-

veal about family dynamics in the Allen household? Why is Charlotte compared to a Stegodyphus spider? Do you have a harmonious relationship with your own relatives today? Or do you still feel "trickles of irritation" like Hetty?

6. Does Hetty cross a line when she starts helping her husband break the law? Do you think she's justified in what she does, or is Pearl correct when she says "the wages of sin is death"? We have similar laws today forbidding recreational drugs like marijuana. Do you think drugs should be legalized or not? What lessons can be learned from Prohibition?

7. At one point, Nella quotes the Hopis: "When you dig treasure out of the earth, you invite disaster." What disaster does Hetty witness in the Splendora oil field? How is this environmental blight a metaphor for her relationship with Lamar? And what do more recent spills tell us about the dangers and ethics of the oil industry?

8. Do you think Nella should have stayed at the Kneeling Station for three days? Why didn't she recant her story of the Alamo sooner? What was at stake for her? Do you think we should teach our children both sides of the conflict? It's been said that "History is written by the victors." Do we need to rewrite Texas history for a new generation that includes a larger Hispanic populace?

9. Why does Hetty kneel before the Virgin of Guadalupe in the Chapel of Miracles? Wouldn't a modern young woman like her view the Madonna as Catholic superstition? How does this relate to her heritage and her relationship with Nella? Is it sacrilege for Cora to compare the sacred image to a vulva? Does this help or hinder Hetty's growing sense of womanhood? Do you think America needs a goddess of its own?

10. Why does Cora insist that Hetty confront Pick's mother, Velma? Can you deal with guilt alone, or do you need forgiveness in order to loosen its hold? Is Hetty responsible for what happens to Pick? Can she forgive herself or, like the Ancient Mariner, does she have to continuously retell her story, first to Cora, then to Garret, in order to break its hold over her?